I0691298

# THE SEA GLASS

# NECKLACE

# THE SEA GLASS NECKLACE

Georgia Hill

www.blkdogpublishing.com

To all friends, both doggie and human met on Roman Field, and to the spirits that linger; I hope you find peace.

*Also by Georgia Hill*

## On A Falling Tide

Two women. Connected by heartbreak, separated in time. Can Charity save the man she loves, or will Lydia's vengeful spirit prove too strong?

Two haunting love stories and a hundred and fifty-year-old curse... When the beloved grandfather who brought her up dies, Charity is left struggling to cope. Alone and rootless, she's drawn to the sleepy fishing village of Beaumouth near Lyme Regis and begins to re-search her family tree.

A chance encounter with attractive boat-builder Matt sparks a chain of mysterious and unsettling events and leads Charity to uncover the story of a young girl who lived in the village over a hundred years before.

In 1863 all Lydia Pavey wants to do is follow in Mary Anning's footsteps and become a 'fossilist.' Instead, she is being forced into marriage to a man she barely knows.

Charity's obsession with Lydia becomes all-consuming and she risks losing everything. With a longed-for family tantalisingly in reach, will Charity find the happy ever after she's yearned for and, most importantly, can she save the man she loves?

# Acknowledgements

Had I known just how much I needed to know for this book, I'm not sure I would have written it. Just as well I love the research.

It began as, sitting on a bench in my local dog walking field, I asked a fellow walker about the strange bumps and hollows. Turns out it's the site of a major Roman villa estate which occasionally gets excavated. Coupled with finding out a horde of Roman coins were found nearby, I had the first glimmerings of an idea.

The Seaton Down Horde is now in the Royal Albert Memorial Museum (RAMM) in Exeter and is well worth a look. How it was found is a fascinating story and yes, the metal detectorist really did camp out over several nights to guard it. I had much help with the Roman Britain research. Bill Horner, Devon's County Archaeologist was incredibly helpful on soil types, preservation of human bones, archaeological dig procedures and so much more.

My thanks also go to Lucy Shipley, the Finds Liaison Officer based at RAMM. Please visit the museum, it's free entry, a treasure trove of local history and has an ace café and shop. I'm indebted to the lovely Caroline K. Mackenzie and her book Culture and Society at Lullingstone Roman Villa (I enjoyed our conversations about impluviums, Caroline!). I must thank Roman expert Alison Morton for her early reading of the book, and to Carol Trow, a brilliant editor who was a joy. Robbie Guillory generously pointed me in the direction of curse tablets which brought the two parts of the book together.

My sincere thanks go to all these wonderful people. All mistakes are very much my own. I must also thank writers Rachel Barnett and Tracy Baines for their kind support and putting up with me when I was feeling low. And finally, HUGE thanks to Nicky and the fab team at BLKDog for giving this book a chance.

Dear Readers, I hope you love it!

# PROLOGUE

*The hills above Moridunum, 370 CE*

They laid the woman in the oak grove, at the base of the most ancient tree and covered her in hawthorn. Tears washed clean the blood from her face. Placing the golden torc around her neck, they slid the intricately carved armlet onto her wrist; she would need grave goods in her afterlife. The last gift was a coin, tenderly placed in her mouth, to pay the ferryman.

The other body they left sprawled grotesquely, frozen in his death agony. The wolves could have him. It was far more than he deserved.

Georgia Hill

# CHAPTER 1

*F*lete, *East Devon, 2023.*

'You found it then? Roman Field?'

Juno sat in Diana's comfortable kitchen, drinking her excellent coffee. She regarded her neighbour fondly. She was the first person she'd spoken to since moving to Flete.

'I did, thank you. I enjoyed the fabulous sea views and Joops loved the new scents. We'll definitely try it again.'

'Joops? I thought your springer was called Jupiter?'

'He is. Jupiter is his pedigree name, and a bit posh when he's covered in mud.' Juno grimaced.

'Ah. I see.' Diana smiled, understanding. 'It's a super walk,' she went on. 'I used to like watching the changing seasons and my little Bonnie loved a run around up there.' She eased her hip and grimaced. 'But Bonnie and my dog walking days are long gone. Bloomin' arthritis. Supposed to be the site of a Roman villa and a bathhouse too. Every now and again we get a team from the university popping by. They have a little dig, take lots of photos and off they go again.'

'Oh, I didn't know that.' Juno took a chocolate biscuit from the plate Diana offered.

'There's a theory Flete was a major Roman harbour back then. Sorry, my dear.'

'What for?'

'Even though I've been retired years now, I still can't resist teaching.'

'It's interesting. It's good to find out about the place you live in.'

'I completely agree. Have you been to our museum yet?'

'I haven't, but I will.'

'Old Bill who runs it is a bit eccentric but interesting. Friend of mine, as a matter of fact. The museum's tiny but packed full of stuff and well-supported by the volunteers. Can I top you up, my lovely?'

Juno held out her mug. She couldn't resist. 'I really ought to get back to work.'

'And how are you settling in?'

'Just about unpacked. One or two boxes still to go but I haven't missed what's in them so they can't be that important.'

'It's such a thrill having a writer move in. Although we're mostly a community of doddery, old, retired folk. I'm not sure how exciting you'll find it.'

Juno thought back to Paul and how his face flamed red when he was angry. She suppressed a shiver. 'Oh, I've had enough excitement for the time being,' she said and concentrated on her coffee.

'Well, it gets a little livelier when the tourist season starts. Things open. We even have a new bar starting up on the front. Cocktails and burgers type of place.' Diana shuddered delicately. 'Can't say it's exactly my sort of thing but anything's better than the sticky-carpeted pub that used to be there. It'll be lovely on a warm summer's evening.'

'It's a date, then. A mojito and a dirty burger each.'

'You don't want an old thing like me cramping your style. We need to find you a man.'

Juno grimaced. 'I'm off men at the moment. The only one I've time for is Joops.' Before Diana could enquire why, she peered out at the drizzle and changed the subject. 'Is it ever going to stop raining?'

'Come February, it'll be lovely. I've even been known to risk a t-shirt on the beach.'

'I'll hold you to that.' With a reluctant glance round Diana's delightfully cluttered and cosy kitchen, Juno slid off the stool. 'And now, I really must get back to work. No, it's okay, Diana, no need to see me out.'

The older woman demurred, limping and saying, 'It'll do me good to move. Little and often, the doc says and I'm not one to argue. Come again, Juno, any time. It's been a pleasure to talk to you.'

Juno slung her Barbour around her shoulders with the hood up like a cloak, splashed down the path and along the pavement to her own front door. Joops greeted her rapturously and she followed him along the narrow passage to the sitting room, jettisoning her coat as she went.

She sank onto the lumpy sofa and the dog jumped up beside her. As she fondled his long feathery ears, she looked around. The layout mirrored Diana's next door and probably the others in the short row of seven identical three-story cottages, their small-paned windows and local stone facings marking them as early Victorian. Diana's was immaculate, her own less so. Juno wryly observed the nineteen-seventies floral wallpaper and not quite matching carpet. A table with a scarred top and two ladder-backed chairs had been placed against a window which looked out onto an uninspiring square of lawn. With the dull weather it looked even more depressing and, not for the first time, she wondered how she had ended up here.

It was the name that had decided her. Begin-Again Cottage was irresistible, especially as she'd been in desperate need of one. The house had been in the family for years, left to them by a great-aunt and tenanted ever since. When the last had moved on, Juno's mother debated, at length, what to do with it. She wanted to sell but to get the best price, it needed work; the house was unacquainted with even so much as a radiator. While she dithered, Juno's father pointed out it wasn't doing the old house any favours standing empty.

It had been a dreary November night, the London Christmas lights blurring in the rain and her tears, when Paul had thrown Juno out. She'd sofa-surfed for a few weeks, too traumatised to know what to do next before her best friend Mabyn had driven her, semi-comatose, to her parents. After a fraught family Christmas in Winchester, Juno had piled her stuff into the Freelander borrowed from her father and driven to East Devon. As her mother unhelpfully pointed out, she didn't have any ties now she was rid of that awful man and, unlike her brothers, could work anywhere. The unspoken being, *also unlike her brothers, she didn't have a proper job. And after all, it wasn't even as if she wrote literature.*

It had taken her most of the first week to warm up. Each room had its own wall heater, but they did little to dispel the chill and the faint whiff of damp. The weather hadn't helped. Ever since she'd been in Devon, it had rained constantly. Or so it had seemed.

Despite all this, Juno was becoming fond of Begin-Again Cottage. Her mother's family came from this part of Devon, and it felt good to reconnect with some of her heritage. Damp and dodgy décor aside, she was clinging to the solitude and security the cottage offered. She was beginning to feel safe. One day she might even tell her parents the full story of what had happened with Paul.

'And you love it too, don't you, Joopsy? What with the beach and now Roman Field, you're spoilt for choice for walkies.' Too late she forgot to spell out the word. Joops leaped off the sofa and chased his tail, barking furiously. She laughed. 'You'll have to console yourself with a run around the back garden. It's not time to go out again yet.' Going through to the kitchen, she opened the back door and tried not to feel too envious of Diana's garden room extension in full view next door. 'Go on, out you go and then you'll have to sleep while I work. My hero and heroine won't get their meet-cute without me writing it.'

Pouring a glass of water, she sipped as she watched Joops gallop around, stopping to sniff every now and again, finally remembering to do what he'd been let out for. His long pink tongue lolled from his grinning springer mouth, and he looked happy and settled.

'Let's hope I can feel the same soon, Joopsy boy,' she murmured into her glass. 'Although I might draw the line at peeing on the lawn.'

Easing her shoulders, thinking thank goodness the bruises on her back had gone. The scars no one saw would take longer to heal. Shivering in January's cold, she called the dog in from the garden and slammed shut the kitchen door, checking three times to make sure it was locked.

Georgia Hill

# CHAPTER 2

*T*he *Villa Estate of Flavius Honoratus Secundinus,*
*Moridunum 370 CE*
'Mistress!'

'Vulcan's fire!' Flavia's hand flew to the sea glass necklace around her neck. 'You startled me, Ursa!'

'I came looking for you. I did not expect to find you in the garden. Where have you been? Why are you out here in the cold?'

Flavia flopped onto the stone seat and stared into the pool. The water was a sluggish green, the fountains dedicated to Sulis Minerva dry, the box hedging ragged and her mother's prized flower garden lay barren. There was little to attract and it was much too cold to sit outside. Janus's month was a hard one. What excuse could she conjure? Chill crept through even her heavy cloak so she sprang up again. 'I craved fresh air. Why should I not enjoy my parents' *hortus?*' She attempted nonchalance but shivered so wrapped her hands against the winter gloom and hoped her pinkened face did not betray her scramble down the hill and the battle with the lock in the back gate. Shifting her cloak over her mud-stained boots, she put one foot over the other defensively.

'You have not been in the gardens. I searched them thoroughly.' Ursa raised one sceptical brow. 'None of the garden slaves have seen you and your mother has not seen you since she came from prayer.'

'I do not have to answer to my slave.' Flavia's chin lifted defiantly.

'You do not. But you have to answer to your father. If Flavius Honoratus suspects you have been outside the villa walls again, to keep you in check he'll marry you off to the first boorish oaf who asks and afterwards will have my head.'

Distraught, as she knew the truth behind Ursa's words, Flavia took the woman's hands in hers and dragged her back to the bench. Darting a glance behind them she huddled against her slave for warmth. She may own Ursa, but she revered her far more than her actual mother who, since discovering her new Christian god, had little time for her errant daughter. 'I only went to the top of the hill,' she protested. 'I wanted to feel the wind on my face.'

'You can do that in the front courtyard,' Ursa retorted.

Flavia scowled. 'I can, but with the wind comes the stench of pony from the garrison next door.' She screwed up her face in disgust.

'Well, you may not suffer for too much longer. Rumour has it the legion is to leave. Trouble in Germania, they say.'

'There's always trouble in Germania. The legion will never leave Moridunum.'

'Don't be so complacent.'

'Where do you hear such gossip?'

Ursa shrugged. 'In the forum when I go to market.'

Flavia gave an enormous sigh. 'I *so* wish to go to the market.' Her voice was pleading. It was an old argument between them.

'And that will never happen,' Ursa replied, firmly.

'But why? I understand why I cannot visit the harbour. I know it to be full of soldiers and harlots and hostels full of drunks but surely the market would be safe?'

Ursa gave her charge an amused look. 'You know all this, do you, child? Pray how?'

'You're not the only one to listen to gossip. Before he left, my brother would often go to the brothel houses at the port.' She scuffed her boots together, rubbing off the worst of the mud. 'He told me all about it.'

'Then your brother should have kept his mouth shut. And, Flavia, look at the state of your boots!'

'I'm sorry. I promise to clean them myself. If you show me how.' She leaned against the older woman's bulk. It was comforting now she was no longer cross. 'I miss Marcus. It's no fun here without him. In truth, I'm bored.'

'So you may be. But that's no excuse to go adventuring beyond the villa walls.' Ursa's tone changed from hectoring to concerned. 'My chick, anything could have happened.' She took Flavia's hands and chafed them into warmth.

'I was perfectly safe. I didn't go far. Besides, if you say all the soldiers have left, there's no one left to cause me harm.'

'No. No one at all.' Ursa's voice dripped sarcasm.

'The hilltribe people are harmless. Their Druids are peaceful.'

Ursa shivered. 'Believe that if it gives you comfort. I fear, with the legion leaving, another uprising may come. There was trouble in Durnovaria at Saturnalia last.'

'But that is far in the east,' Flavia said scornfully. 'The tribes around us are peaceable trading folk.'

'Until they choose not to be.' Ursa turned to the girl and stared her straight in the eye. 'Flavia, it is dangerous out there. Danger from beast if not man. Why do you insist on doing it?'

'I don't know.' The girl's bottom lip jutted out. 'I feel so trapped here, Ursa,' she added wildly. 'I help mother run the household, I spin acceptably well, I make due offerings to Minerva and Juno. I do all that is expected of me. And yet I feel my destiny is elsewhere. Not to be married off as a convenience as Marcus was, not to breed a pack of children.'

She screwed up her face. 'And no, I do not intend to enter the temple either. A life of pious prayer is not for me.'

'Then what *do* you want, child?'

Flavia remained silent.

Ursa sighed. 'You are not going to promise me you won't go out again, are you?'

The girl looked down. 'No,' she said quietly.

'And I cannot forbid you. I can only warn you. There will be consequences, Flavia Honorata. Consequences of a kind you cannot imagine. Will you promise me one thing?'

'What?'

'That you take Balbus with you. As a guard.'

Flavia shuddered violently. 'No. Not Balbus. I will take anyone but him.'

'But he is the best of your father's guards. He would fight off even a wolf if needed.'

'I will not have him following me, spewing his foul sulphuric breath over me. He would be worse than any wolf or bear. Or Druid, come to that.'

Ursa sighed exasperated. 'Then at least take one of the dogs. They are fond of you. Take the biggest. He will at least keep you safe from most danger.'

Flavia remained mulishly silent.

'Promise me you will take the dog,' Ursa warned, her voice hardening, 'or I will tell your father, risk to my neck or no.'

'I will take the dog,' Flavia conceded.

'And go no further than the top of the hill, not beyond the drover's route?'

'You drive a hard bargain.'

Ursa put her arm around the girl's thin shoulders. 'I do. To keep you from harm. No further than the holloway, you hear?'

'I hear.' *But I don't promise.* Flavia sent a swift prayer up to the goddess Juno in apology.

'And is that my cloak?'

Flavia shifted guiltily. 'It is. I borrowed it. You don't mind, do you?'

'I mind very much. You have caked it in mud all along the hem, child!'

'I'll buy you a new one.'

'You better had.' Ursa elbowed the girl. 'Payment for my silence?'

Flavia smiled at her, sudden tears in her eyes. She didn't know what she'd do without her slave, her friend. 'Payment for your kindness and loyalty.' She threw her arms around her. 'Thank you, Ursa. Thank you.'

'Jove's bones, get off me,' Ursa said gruffly, tears of her own starting. 'And look at how low the sun is. Come along, let's get you bathed and dressed. Your father hates latecomers to dinner. If I don't get you there in time, it'll be two heads rolling, not just mine.' She stood up, stiff from the cold. 'We both need a cup of warming *calda* after sitting out here for so long.' Holding her hand out, she added, 'What's keeping you, girl?'

Flavia gave a tremulous sigh, took Ursa's hand and let her pull her up. Taking one last longing glance at the hills rising beyond the villa and which represented freedom, she followed her into the house.

Georgia Hill

# CHAPTER 3

*023*

For Juno, on that damp January morning, the dog walk on the Roman Field had represented a freedom she hadn't tasted for two years. It had been an interesting experience but not for the reasons she had given Diana. Since Paul she had been extra cautious when going out. Watchful and ever aware of the confidence he had robbed from her, she had stuck to the beach and the riverside where there were always others around. It had taken all her courage to try somewhere new.

She'd parked in the lane and slipped in the mud as she got out of the car. It had rained in the night and the trees were dripping sullenly. She was discovering Devon winters could be depressingly wet. She looked to her left and right, the sense something was watching was etched deep. An old, ingrained habit. The spaniel scrabbled at the window, impatient for his walk.

'It's alright Joops, I'll let you out in a minute but I'm not sure this is the right place.'

Diana had insisted there was a good dog walking field somewhere here and had given precise directions. *Turn left at the top of the hill, park under the chestnut trees and walk to the end of the lane where there's a kissing gate.* Juno peered towards where the lane ended in a thick bustle of evergreens. Was there a gate there? In the pink early morning light, it was difficult to see. Low cloud drizzled through the trees and, even though she was barely out of town, it felt remote and very rural. If she were still in London, she would have turned around and found somewhere with people. A second sense warned her a solitary walk in a lonely spot wasn't the wisest of ideas. Feeling in her pocket for the reassuring weight of her mobile she hesitated.

'Maybe it's another walk on the beach, Joops boy?'

At her voice, the dog cocked its head, his hot breath misting on the back window of the Freelander. He whined in protest.

The lack of confidence, which clung to her like the sea mist, had little to do with being alone. 'Thanks a bunch, Paul,' she muttered under her breath. 'Another of your legacies.' Resenting how he was still making her feel, she stamped her foot in frustration. Was she ever going to be able to move on? 'Oh, this is ridiculous. We wanted to try a new walk, didn't we Joops? And Diana said this was a good one. We live in sleepy Flete. Paul doesn't have a clue where I am, what do I think is going to happen?' An icy drip from the trees above her, which speared its way right down the back of her jacket, spurred her into action. 'Come on,' she said, suddenly decisive. 'Let's go Joopsy. Walkies!'

The dog needed no further encouragement and pulled her up the lane, around a corner and through the promised gate which had been hidden from view by an ancient yew. The field which opened out before her was enormous and stretched upwards out of sight beyond a ridge on the hill.

Spotting the dog waste bin, she unclipped the spaniel's lead. 'Must be the right place, after all, Joops.'

The springer shot off to investigate rabbits in the undergrowth and she followed at a more leisurely pace, finding a bench which faced out over the bay. The sun spread long fingers of gold along the horizon, skimming over a milky sea. The field nudged the edges of town and the sprawl of white-painted bungalows leading to the sea front, but it felt a different world up here. Juno let go some of her tension.

Diana had been right; it *was* the perfect dog walk. Joops bounded up to her, a bald tennis ball in his grinning mouth. He could scent a lost ball at fifty paces. She threw it for him and, watching him hurtle over the grass, idly wondered why the field hadn't been built on. So close to town and with such enviable sea views, it was prime development land. Perhaps the Roman remains had stopped it.

Habit made a prickle of unease squirm down her back. Turning quickly, she looked uphill. Perhaps she wasn't alone after all? Now she'd relaxed a little, having the quiet morning and the view all to herself was a luxury she didn't want to share. Even if Paul was hundreds of miles away, there might be another man around. And, in her experience, men were bad news. Nerves on fire, she screwed up her eyes to see someone in the far distance; tall and dressed in something long and pale. Not the most practical of clothing for a muddy dog walk. She shot a glance to the bottom of the field calculating how long it would take her to run back to the safety of the car. And resented doing so. Joops was staring at the figure too, all excitement over finding the tennis ball gone. His hackles were up, his stance rigid. More astonishingly, as he treated every stranger as a potential friend, his teeth were bared and a low growl rumbled.

'Jupiter, here!' she said sharply.

The dog ignored her and galloped towards the figure, barking aggressively. Swearing, she had no choice but to run after him. It was a fair distance and all uphill. Cursing that she'd allowed herself to get so unfit, by the time she scrabbled over the ridge, it was to find the dog running in manic circles, nose to the ground. Getting her breath back, hands on hips and panting, she looked around. It was quite different up here; a vast flat space, interspersed with odd-looking ruts and bumps. Bounded by trees and a Devon bank to one side, the dips and hollows were filled with rank water. Joops ran towards a pool and she whistled him back. Low cloud, turned pink by the sunrise, hung in the trees. For a second Juno thought she glimpsed the other walker and blinked hard, but it was only an eddy of mist. She shivered, feeling the chill of the January day for the first time. The field was completely empty.

The dog whined at her side, eager to get going again. Repeating her safety mantra and satisfied whoever it was had disappeared out of another hidden gate somewhere, Juno was determined to carry on.

'I will not let Paul defeat me,' she'd muttered, scowling and shaken. Gulping in the salty-fresh sea air, she'd thrown the ball again and continued the walk.

# CHAPTER 4

*T*he hills above Moridunum
The dog whined and flopped at her side. Flavia clutched him to her for warmth as there was little in the watery late January sunshine. Seated against the old oak tree she had a fine view of the town, the great port's harbour walls reaching out into a sea sparkling a frigid blue. Far below her was her home, the vast villa estate walls ribboning the countryside, puffs of smoke rising sluggishly into the still heavy air, small figures in the distant fields tending the animals. Behind her, beyond the line of yew and ash and an ancient pathway, and far away up a steep incline lay the nearest hillfort. So far she had kept her promise to Ursa and had never ventured nearer to it than this. Even in her borrowed dull brown cloak she wouldn't dare. It would be too easy to fall victim to a ransom. Or worse. She put a hand on Trajan's head for comfort, she also did not want the dog stolen. It would cause too many questions and, besides, she was becoming fond of the beast. Turning her attention to the sun she watched as the long line of soldiers snaked westwards along the road towards the great city of Isca Dumnoniorum. The cavalry followed, the light sparking off armour and the horses' gleaming flanks. Mules pulling loaded wagons were at the back, the wheels occasionally skittering off the road to get stuck in the churned-up mud. It had been a long, wet winter. Sounds drifted up the valley on

the sea breeze: men shouting, horses snorting, the clink of armour and the deadly rhythmic march of the foot soldiers.

It felt like the beginning of the end. Moridunum had never been without its legion. The rumours had been correct. Almost immediately after her conversation with Ursa, the garrison became a frenzy of activity. Her morose and preoccupied father had become even more terse and unapproachable. As magistrate and the town's civilian leader, she was sure he feared an outbreak of disobedience.

Flavia had sneaked out again, on the first fine day, unable to resist the lush green hills and the freedom they offered. This time she had done as Ursa had bidden and taken one of the guard dogs with her. She'd chosen her favourite, the enormous hound she had named Trajan. Solidly built, he stood to her waist and was fiercely protective; she doubted anyone would get near her while he was around. There could be anyone roaming the hills now the soldiers had left. A cohort remained at the garrison – raw young boys and old men on the cusp of retirement. Flavia chewed her lip. How was the town to defend itself? Although nothing like the uprisings in the north and east, the local tribes occasionally caused skirmishes. They were brutally put down and retribution was swift. Many were taken as slaves, many executed. It served as a lesson: defy mighty Rome at your peril. But without the presence of an army what was to stop anarchy breaking out? Selfishly, Flavia wondered how much longer her escapes from stultifying life at the villa might be considered safe. Ursa had never thought they were. Now Flavia wondered the same. The thought depressed her. It was only up in the hills she felt able to breathe.

She watched the long line of soldiers for a long time, a growing sympathy for the wives and children left behind. The legion was headed to Gaul and then on to Germania. How many would survive the fighting and return? As the last mule wagon disappeared from view, she stretched out her cold stiffened limbs and then froze. Out of the corner of her eye she had glimpsed a flash of white. Her hand strayed immediately to Trajan's neck, but he seemed unperturbed. An owl perhaps? Minerva's sacred symbol but it unlucky to see it in daytime; it was a portent of death. She prayed quickly and hard to Silvanus, the god of the woods and followed it up with one to Juno for good measure, asking for her protection. Had it been a Druid? She'd heard tell of their ability to transmute into other beings, to slip in and out of sight silently and with ease. Her father kept an uneasy truce with their leader, no Roman politician underestimated their influence. With the departure of the legion, their ascendant might well rise again.

She huddled close to the dog, willing herself invisible, hardly daring to breathe and then laughed. If the Druids had the powers they were rumoured to have, one would seek out a girl hiding against an oak tree with ease. She recalled the old story of a Druid striding into the midst of battle and stopping it with a single command. If one could do that, she would prove no obstacle. Relaxing she began to get up and then heard the unmistakable sound of twigs snapping underneath feet. Ducking down again, she wrapped her arms around Trajan's comfortingly well-muscled neck. This time she felt a growl in his throat and shushed him.

The sound came again. Another twig broken. Definitely feet. Walking confidently. Someone unafraid of being seen. Someone not stalking silently to ambush. The sun slid out from behind a scudding cloud and caught on a tall man striding along the path directly below her. He was coming from the direction of the town, walking uphill and making good progress on a pair of firm thighs. His hood had fallen off revealing burnished red-gold hair and a long beard.

Flavia stiffened and held her breath but Trajan growled again. The man stopped immediately, his hand clasping his sword hilt at his side. Flavia screwed her eyes tight shut, like an animal gone to ground. Stupidly she pretended if she could not see him, he would not see her. Ursa had been right; this was too dangerous an enterprise. Anything could happen! Opening one eye she dared to glance down. The man was looking about him, on the alert, his eyes wide and observant. Even from this distance she could see his regular features and that he was handsome. Stifling a gasp, she watched, frozen, as he unsheathed his sword and began to make his way towards her. She was saved by a blackbird shooting a warning from the oak tree behind her. It cackled and flew low over the man's head. To her utter relief, he stopped, shook his head, put his weapon away and carried on along the path.

She waited until he was well out of sight and then for some time longer. On stiff legs she got to her feet. Trajan, frustrated at being confined for so long, jumped up and pawed at her. One of his claws caught at her necklace of blue-green sea glass and it broke, sending the beads spilling into the grass and leaves. Some bounced into the stream bubbling through the moss and were lost completely. Cursing, as it was one of her favourites and one her mother had given her when a child, she floundered around collecting as many beads as she could find, gathering them into a corner of her cloak. Then, seeing the sun was drifting down into a purple sea in the west and there was not much more day to be had, she held up her skirts and ran.

# CHAPTER 5

*2* *023*
After several hours of furious typing on her laptop, Joops pawing at her jeans finally broke her concentration. Juno rolled the kinks out of her neck, grabbed her coat and clipped an excited dog onto his lead for his second walk of the day. It was nearly dark but had thankfully stopped raining. A stroll along the sea front, giving the dog a quick run off lead on the beach would be perfect. She glanced at the clock; it had just gone five. *Not too late, bound to be other people around.*

As she walked, her progress towards the sea front hampered by Joops's insistence on stopping to sniff every few minutes, her thoughts strayed to the work in progress. She wrote light romances, they sold well but her choice of career disappointed her mother.

'Juno, you have a good class of degree in English Literature from an excellent university. Why do you insist on throwing it away by writing these trashy books?' Amanda often asked and that was when she was feeling charitable. It didn't help that Phillip and Crispin, Juno's brothers, were both in academia and wrote great tomes on sociology and Roman history respectively. Phillip, much older and remote, didn't often peer out from his ivory tower to acknowledge her existence but she got on well with Cris who was closer in age.

Phillip, her mother and maybe even Cris, would definitely not approve of this latest book. After a long chat with her agent, she'd agreed to sex things up a bit. The bonk-buster was making a come-back apparently. Her mother would blow a gasket; claiming she'd never be able to show her face at the tennis club again, especially as Juno's pseudonym, Eden Loveday, wasn't far enough removed from the family name. *Maybe I should think up another pen name? That would be fun.* The temptation to re-invent herself was strong.

She reached the promenade but, despite her optimism, there was no one around. Letting the dog off the lead he immediately headed on to the beach, so she followed. The hiss and sigh of the sea on the shifting pebbles soothed her and she stood for a second looking out onto an inky-purple sea, light still hanging in the sky to the west. It was cold but fresh and invigorating and she could feel the air clearing her brain of its preoccupation with her family.

Joops hurtled back to her and dropped his nose whining. Crouching to see what had caught his attention, she saw something gleaming in the light given out by the streetlamps on the promenade. Picking it up, she turned her back on the dark sea and sky and pointed it at the lights to see better. It was spherical and an enchanting blue-green in colour, about the size of her thumbnail. Sea glass probably. Putting it in her pocket she was distracted by a labrador ambling up to them, its golden coat watered down to a pale ochre in the gloom. Habit made her tense up, Joops had gone through a reactive phase, especially after Paul had been looking after him for a few days. She often wondered if the man had played the same mind tricks on the dog as he had on her. A wave of fury washed over her. Why hadn't she got herself and her dog out of harm's way sooner? She watched carefully, ready to call him back and then relaxed as the two dogs began to play. In London there had been too many aggressive dogs which had reacted to Joops's insecure barking. Maybe, now he was away from Paul, he'd revert to the gentle dog she knew he was? She searched for the Lab's owner but couldn't see anyone so contented herself with watching them bounce around.

Flete's sea front was long and flat, stretching out to a small harbour at the east end and some towering cliffs at the other. Diana had warned her about going too near the cliffs as rockfalls were common, so Juno trudged over the uneven pebbles towards the harbour. The Lab tagged along, padding happily at her heels but Joops galloped away, his spaniel nose drawn to the stench of seaweed. He tugged at some and threw it up in the air and then splashed at the edge of the waves, barking with glee. The noise caught the attention of a middle-aged couple, walking gingerly on the beach, the woman carrying a dog lead. The Lab's head reared up and she raced over to them, to their obvious relief. Juno followed, stumbling over the pebbles.

'Where have you been Maisie?' the woman scolded. 'We've been looking all over for you!' She went to attach the dog's lead but the lab escaped at the last minute and ran off to join Joops in the sea. 'Little bugger,' she said, putting her hands on her hips and addressing Juno. 'Never believe what people say, that labradors are born half-trained.'

Juno started. She was out of the habit of striking up conversations with fellow dog walkers. Paul had always told her not to do it, warning her of the odd people there were about. Besides, when she was out with him, he insisted on having all her attention to himself. 'I'll go and get my dog.' She gestured to the sea.

The woman looked to where the springer and Maisie were still cavorting in the froth of the sea as it hurled itself against the shore. In the gloom all that could be seen were their glossily wet seal-like heads. 'Great. That's a stinky wet dog car all the way home.' She glanced at Juno's face. 'Don't worry, my lovely, it doesn't shelve very deeply here. It's safe. Can't say the same for the harbour, though. Have to watch the currents there, especially at this time of year. Best avoided.' She reached out a hand. 'I'm Annie, by the way. This is my husband, Dean.'

Juno murmured hello.

'You new to the area or visiting?'

'Just moved here.' Juno recollected her manners. 'I'm Juno.' She nodded to the dogs. 'And the out-of-control springer is Jupiter, or Joops when he's behaving.'

Annie laughed. 'Ah, an out-of-control springer. Goes with the territory. Never met one that isn't but they're so loving.' She turned to her husband. 'Remember the one Gran used to have? Completely nuts. Mad as a box of frogs, it was.'

'Certainly had some energy, that one,' Dean added. 'Oh, here they come. Repel all borders.'

As the Lab bounded up to them, shook off water and then jumped all over Annie, Juno appreciated his comment. She laughed as Joops did much the same to her. They staggered up to the promenade, enjoying a doggie conversation of how difficult recall training could be, comparing breeds, agreeing on how lovely natured both were before clipping leads back on.

'Well, welcome to Flete,' Annie said. 'I hope you're very happy here. It's a friendly town and everyone tends to know one another, or at least they do outside of the tourist season. We'll look forward to seeing you and Joops again.' Peering down at her dog, she added, 'I think our Maisie's in love with your Joops so we might not have a choice in the matter. If you fancy a coffee any time, come and find me in the museum. I help run it. I'm in there most days but check the website for winter opening times.' A stiff breeze sliced over the pebbles, off the sea. She shivered violently. 'Time to go and rustle up some grub, I think. And if I don't get out of these wet trousers, there'll be nobody left alive to ping that microwave.'

As they said their goodbyes Juno felt strangely buoyed. A casual conversation, maybe the beginnings of a new friendship. That and the invigorating salty air had been the tonic she'd needed after bending hunch-backed over her computer and a knotty plot problem all afternoon.

Invigorating was one word for the sea breeze. Freezing was a better one. Pulling her collar up around her neck, she turned to go but, before she did, she paused to watch Dean and Annie stroll away. Dean put his arm around Annie's shoulders, pulling her in for a kiss and the couple laughed. Juno suppressed the wave of longing. Something in her wanted that easy closeness. But she didn't need a man. After Paul she'd decided she *wouldn't* need a man. *Just because I write about romance doesn't mean I have to be in one, does it?*

The wind at her back had her hurrying along Church Lane and to a lukewarm cottage. Seeing Diana's front door open, she was about to wave hello when she saw a man emerge, his longish blond hair catching the light from the streetlamp. Shutting the door behind him, he pulled on a beanie and loped off.

'Ooh, Joops,' she whispered to the dog. 'Do you think Diana has a toy-boy? Atta girl. No wonder she's always so happy.' Juno giggled and let herself in, dropping the lead so she could wrangle keys and the pint of milk she'd bought on the way back. 'Okay boy. Chappie for you and pasta for me. And maybe a glass of the old vino. Let's hope I don't get the two meals mixed up. I'm sure you'd eat my pasta but I'm not touching that stinky Chappie. And I may live alone, tragic and man-less, but there's a lot to be said for an M&S spaghetti carbonara and sole control of the TV remote.'

Georgia Hill

# CHAPTER 6

*The Secundinus Villa Moridunum*

'Flavia, please sit still.' Ursa took hold of the fidgeting girl's shoulders and straightened them, forcing her to gaze into the polished silver mirror where her reflection reflected dully. She folded in another twist of hair and fixed a finely carved bone comb in place. 'There, you will have all eyes upon you this evening.' They were in Flavia's chamber and she was trying to ready the girl for dinner. It had been a battle. The other slaves dismissed, it was just the two of them.

'I do not want all eyes on me tonight.' Flavia hitched up the shoulder of her gauzy tunic and pouted. 'Oh Ursa, do not look at me that way!'

'Do you not want to find yourself a husband? A girl of your age and unmarried. It brings disgrace to your family.'

'I may be accused of many things but bringing disgrace on my family is hardly one. I have proved to be a good daughter. I am dutiful and devout.'

'Devout to which gods?' Ursa's lips twitched in amusement.

Flavia poked the leg of the dressing table with a moody toe. 'I care not for Mother's Christian god, you know I remain loyal to Juno and Minerva.'

Ursa kissed the top of her mistress's head. 'And so it should be.' She sighed. 'Thank the gods Moridunum only pays lip service to this Christos. I cannot fathom this new zeal of your mother's.'

'Nor can I. You know she has ordered a new house shrine and a room to put it in? It is to be built in an underground cavern beneath the current one to Sulis Minerva. Father is wild at the cost.' Flavia turned and clasped her slave's hands. 'But it keeps her busy and stops her eternal nagging of me.' She rolled her eyes and said, in an uncannily accurate impersonation, '"Daughter, when are you going to agree to a suitor? You're gone nineteen. You bring shame upon this household by not marrying."'

Ursa laughed. 'Child, you will need to marry at some point. Do you not wish for a home and children of your own? A husband to boss? And your mother is quite right. Pah nineteen! You are nearing twenty summers.' She clucked her gently under the chin. 'An old maid!'

'I do wish to marry.' She met Ursa's eyes. 'But I want to marry for love.'

'And have any of the young men brought here met that desire?'

Flavia sighed. 'None.'

'Not even Septimus Severus?'

'Not even he.'

'He would make a good match. I hear he's ambitious to secure an imperial post. Would you not like that?'

'How would I know, I've never been to the capital. I know Father raves to go. He sees it as a return to the homeland. But that's ridiculous. He was born here, as was I and so was Marcus. It would seem so alien. Surely this is our home?' Flavia sighed again. 'I miss Marcus so much, Ursa.'

'I know you do, chick.' The slave lifted Flavia's face to apply colour to her cheeks.

'It's so dull here now he's gone to Mediolanum.' She poked a finger at Ursa. 'And my brother's marriage was most definitely not a love match.'

'No, but it was a good one. His wife has connections. Some say he is even destined to serve the great man

Theodosius.' Ursa paused and a cunning look overcame her plain features. 'If you were to marry Septimus and go to Rome, you would be near your brother.'

'And Julia.' Flavia kicked the painted leg of the dressing table and some red chipped off.

'Stop it. If you destroy the furniture your father will be most displeased. Why do you dislike Julia Plautina so much? Because she took your brother away?'

'Because she's a cold-hearted sow.'

Ursa chuckled. 'Your brother did not think so.'

'My brother saw a good thing when it was offered. But isn't that just like a man? How could he bed a woman who has ankles that thick?' Flavia's voice was full of horror.

Ursa laughed again. 'Men will take most things to their bed if it suits.'

'But I cannot be like that, Ursa.' Flavia snatched at her slave's hands again. 'I cannot do as my brother did. A political match is not for me.'

'You may not have the luxury of choice, my chick. Septimus is not so bad. Why not talk to him tonight, get to know him a little? You may not find him so terrible. Marriage has a way of breeding love. And then, when you have your babies you will no longer have the time to hate your husband.'

'He has a crooked nose. And his eyes are too close together.'

Ursa wiped her hands on a linen scrap and knelt on the floor. The heat rising up through it felt good on her aching knees. 'He is a kind man, a little old to be sure, but you could do a great deal worse. Your father grows impatient, Flavia. He has exhausted the supply of eligible men here. If you continue to reject the ones who are not so bad, he may force on you someone who is cruel and heartless just because it is the last option.'

Flavia saw tears spring into Ursa's eyes. The woman cared for her, for all her nagging. Everyone nagged at her. She tried so hard to be a good daughter, but her father was dismissive, with some crisis with one of the tribes, or a problem in town always occupying his time. Even when he did have time for her, he was cross and impatient. And while her mother slathered compliments upon her saying she was more beautiful than any other, she spent too long worshipping at the church of this new idol who was taking the fashionable elite by storm. At least Ursa was with her day and night, and she was inordinately fond of the woman. After her recent excitement at nearly being discovered, she had not ventured out of the villa again. She had tried to be demure and dutiful, to heed her weaving, to help her parents in any way they commanded but she chafed at the confinement. Watching Ursa as the woman put away the perfumes and scented hair oils, she promised she would reward her in some way. Her heart softened. As well as a new cloak, a new woollen tunic perhaps? Nothing too showy. It would not do to make Ursa stand out; her parents might ask questions and the other household slaves were a quarrelsome and jealous lot. She cared too much for Ursa to make her life any more difficult than it was. Idly, she wondered what there would be to eat tonight. It was the lean time of year when, despite the best efforts of the kitchen, their winter stores were becoming dismal. She hoped the new supplies of *garum* had arrived at the harbour. Food was bland without the condiment and winter storms had sent the trading ships elsewhere until better weather came. Perhaps there would be suckling pig? Her father's farmers kept good pigs and they made tasty meat. Oh, but she did not want to go and pick at braised salad all evening, listening to the men talk business and the women talk children. She had interest in neither. She would rather dive under the furs on her bed and dream. Trying not to trip over her gown, she flounced over and flung herself on it. 'Tell me a story,' she demanded. 'Tell me one of the Greek gods, one of the old tales.'

Ursa smiled with a mixture of fondness and exasperation. 'We do not have the time. You are needed at dinner.'

'Tell me the story of Perseus and Andromeda,' she begged.

'Again?'

'It is my favourite and it has the advantage of being short.' Flavia picked at her skirts. Her gown was of fine wool, a soft violet in colour. She knew it brought out the gloss in her dark hair and had been bought especially for today. It was not only the piglet which was being sacrificed for this evening's pleasure. Ursa's words held true. She would have to decide which of her father's offerings would suit or she would end up with some gnarly old stoat and shipped off to the heathen north. A shudder ran through her. 'The story soothes me.' She lifted her chin defiantly. 'And then I will go into supper and be a good daughter and simper and smile at Septimus Severus while all the time dreaming of my saviour Perseus swooping from the sky, releasing my chains on the cliff face and saving me from the sea monster.' Closing her eyes she shivered delicately and, as Ursa told the age-old story, in her mind the hero Perseus took the shape of the man she had spied on, with his penetrating eyes and hair with its glints of red.

Georgia Hill

# Chapter 7

*023*
Juno woke with a start. Staring at Joops, lying fast asleep in his usual position at the foot of the bed, she tried putting together the fragments of the dream. There had been a man, tall with reddish-blond hair and robustly built. He'd been wearing some kind of loose tunic, with a sword hanging off the belt at his hips. There had been sunshine too, thin and watery but with the promise of spring warmth to come.

Shaking wakefulness into her head, she nudged the dog who stretched and yawned. It had all been so vivid. Going to the window, she threw open the curtains, shivering as the cold air hit. Her glance landed on the little blue-green piece of sea-glass she'd found amongst the pebbles. She'd arranged it on the windowsill along with some cockle shells. Picking it up, she examined it closely for the first time. As well as being entrancingly pretty, it had a hole through it. Maybe some sea creature had burrowed through? She remembered Cris mentioning once that stones with holes were thought to have special properties. From behind her, she heard Joops patter to the door. She blinked, the image of the man bouncing violently back, so vivid he could almost be in the room. The sea-glass burned against her palm. Dropping it back onto the windowsill with a clatter, she stared down at it in horror. *What was going on?* The dog whined and scratched at the door. He wanted to go out. Rubbing her hands on her pyjamas, she opened the door and followed him downstairs and out into the garden, concentrating on the mundane task. Hard as she tried, she couldn't shake the man from her mind.

She'd found comfort in a routine of sorts and walked Joops in the Roman Field regularly. She didn't spot the strange figure in white again but often encountered the mist wreathing through the trees. It was odd; she expected any fog or sea mist to be trapped lower down in the estuary valley. Once or twice, she felt goosebumps rise and Joops had stopped, hackles risen, staring straight at the far northern part of the field. Blaming the prickle of unease on her lack of confidence, a legacy from Paul, she took to walking later, when there was a sprinkling of other dog walkers. Strangely, none of them ever wore a white coat. It meant delaying starting her writing day, but it was more relaxing. Besides, it gave Joops an opportunity to chase around with a few dogs, which he loved. It also gave her a chance to talk to other humans. If she didn't ring friends or family, she could go days without speaking to a soul. Once this book was written, she promised to make more of an effort and get to know people. She needed to find the outgoing sociable Juno that Paul had stolen. Deciding a start would be to take Annie up on her offer of a coffee, she hoped, once the tourist season struck, things would open up. It was dead at the moment, with most of the shops only opening for a couple of hours a day.

She didn't have to wait long before finding out who Diana's mysterious man was. A week after their cosy chat over coffee, she was invited to dinner.

'It'll be nothing fancy, just a kitchen supper,' Diana explained, 'but my son's here and I thought it would be nice for you to meet him. Bring Joops, too. I can get him a bone from the butcher's. Tom loves dogs.'

Ridiculously, Juno found herself fretting over what to wear. She normally stayed in her dog walking kit all day. Consisting of trackie bottoms and over-sized sweaters, the sleeves were useful to pull over her frozen hands when working. Surveying her wardrobe, she knew it was far too scruffy, she didn't want to insult her host by not making an effort. Her smarter clothes, saved for the occasional trip to London, were also wrong; they looked too obviously work outfits. She had one or two glitzy party dresses, but they'd be over the top for a kitchen supper. If it were Mabyn, or one of her other London friends asking her over, she'd wear jeans and take a bottle of tequila, but Diana was older and she doubted it would be the sort of evening which would descend into slammer-induced drunken hysterics while lolling on bean bags. Regret caught at her; it had been years since she'd done anything like that. Paul had a lot to answer for.

In the end, she decided on a neutral pair of black trousers teamed with a scoop-necked matching sweater made of wool with a glittery silver thread running through. It was subtle and not too dressy. It was only as Joops barrelled up to her she understood her mistake. He left a generous smear of white dog hair across the knees of her black trousers and when she went to pick them off, the wide neck of the top fell off one shoulder, exposing her black bra strap and copious amounts of bosom. Hauling it back in place, she grimaced; no time to change now. Throwing her Barbour around her shoulders and clipping the dog's lead on, she ran around to Diana's. It was raining again. Of course.

Diana met her at the door. 'Come in, come in. What a dreadful night. Cold too. Oh, don't worry about wiping off the dog's paws, he can't make much mess on the wooden flooring.'

As Juno handed over her coat, Joops's lead escaped from her hand and he shot off in the direction of the kitchen. She heard a masculine voice greet him.

'I'm so sorry, Diana. He has no manners.'

'Not a problem. He can probably smell the bone I've got for him. Oh, is that for me? How lovely. I do like a drop of Shiraz. And flowers too. Oh Juno, you shouldn't have gone to all this trouble. Come on in, we're in the garden room. You look lovely by the way, my dear.'

Diana led her along the narrow hall, through the kitchen and into the extension. Joops was jumping all over the person sitting on one of the rattan sofas.

'I'm so sorry,' Juno repeated, hauling the dog off while simultaneously dragging at her jumper. She wished she'd left him at home. 'This is Jupiter, otherwise known as Joops. He's a bit excitable.'

The man stood up and held out a hand. It was the same guy she'd spotted leaving Diana's house the other night. Average height, a shock of unruly straw-coloured hair and an unseasonal suntan. 'No problem. I like dogs, especially springers. I'm Tom.'

They shook hands. 'Juno.'

'Mum's new neighbour. Good to meet you.'

'And Joops,' Diana put in, eyeing the dog with humour. 'I'll get that bone; it'll help him settle.'

Once they'd all sat down, drinks in hand with the springer now ensconced on a blanket happily gnawing, Juno risked a closer look at Tom. So, this was Diana's son, not some toy boy. *Makes more sense.* Suppressing a nervous giggle, she compared him to her ex; she couldn't help herself, it was a bad habit. She didn't think him particularly good-looking, certainly not a patch on Paul. Large nose, a full upper lip, giving him a default sulky expression unless he was talking and smiling. And, whereas Paul was solidly built from spending hours in the gym, Tom was wiry with an underlying tight sort of nervous energy. He sat, with a foot crossed on one knee, jiggling it a little, as if the last place he wanted to be was in his mother's conservatory making small talk. If Juno were to cast him as the romantic lead in one of her books, the tawny-brown stubble would have to go, as would the tatty jumper; she spied a hole in one elbow. With his Stuart tartan scarf knotted around his neck, he gave every impression of not wanting to stay long.

'Have you warmed up yet?' Diana asked him. 'Tom's just back from Turkey so he's feeling the cold,' she added to Juno as explanation. 'Let me top up your glass. None of us have to worry about driving so we might as well enjoy ourselves.'

Juno held out her glass. It might explain the scarf, it certainly explained the suntan. 'Have you been on holiday?'

'No, I returned briefly after being here during lockdown.'

'Tom's an archaeologist,' his mother said, proudly. 'He was working at Ephesus.'

'Oh.' Juno didn't know a great deal about archaeology, she knew even less about Turkey and had never heard of Ephesus. Or had she? She wrinkled her nose, recalling a vague conversation she'd once had with Cris.

Tom's mouth quirked. 'I can see you're impressed.'

'It's not so much that, I just don't know much history.'

He shrugged. 'No reason you should. Ephesus was a major ancient Greek city. I was leading a team uncovering some Roman remains.'

Juno wasn't much wiser.

'Tom spends most winters abroad where it's nice and warm. He's only in Devon every now and again. More wine, Tom?'

'Thanks.' He held out his glass. 'What do you do, Juno?' His eyes flickered, he had very long dark brown lashes.

'Juno's a writer,' Diana answered before Juno could open her mouth. They all laughed and Juno felt the mood relax.

'Let her answer for herself,' her son protested. He met her look from sapphire blue eyes. 'What do you write? Not history, obviously.'

'Not history. I write fiction.'

'And, as you know I love a good read, that's why I was so excited when I heard Juno was a writer,' Diana interrupted. 'My favourite at the moment is Eden Loveday. I can't get enough of her books. Can't wait until the next one comes out.'

'It'll be October hopefully,' Juno said. 'If I ever get it finished.'

Diana's mouth fell open. 'Are you ... you can't be Eden Loveday?'

'The very same. That's my pseudonym. I used my surname, Eden, as my first name and pinched my great-aunt Betty Loveday's to use as a last name.' Juno pulled a face. 'My family don't approve; they think it's too easily traced back to them.'

'Well, I never.' Diana got up swiftly, causing Joops to raise his nose from the bone. 'I can't believe it.'

'Where are you going, mum?'

'Off to get my books so Juno, I mean Eden, can sign them. How exciting is this? Oh, you coming too, Joops?' she added as the dog followed her. 'Come on then.'

Tom and Juno smiled tentatively at each other in the wake of Diana's disappearance.

'You say your family don't approve?' he asked. 'What exactly do you write?'

Juno met his look. Used to defending her choice of genre, she straightened her shoulders feeling her stupid jumper slip again. 'Romance. I write women's romance.' She waited for the usual comments. *Are you ever going to write a proper book?* and, *don't they give a sense of false hope?* along with, *aren't they predictable?* being in the top ten of what was often said to her.

They didn't come. Instead, Tom frowned and leaned forward. 'There's a Crispin Eden. Roman history professor.'

'That's my older brother, Cris. And my oldest brother, Phillip, is Emeritus professor in Sociology at Durham. Cris lectures at South Western in Exeter. So, you can see I haven't exactly upheld the family's academic standards.'

'But you write books, which sell presumably.'

Juno nodded. 'They sell.'

Diana bustled back into the garden room and the conversation. 'Of course, they sell. Eden is often in the top ten of the *Sunday Times* best seller charts, aren't you, dear?'

Juno hid her blushes in her wine. Joops jumped up next to her on the sofa and cuddled in with a happy sigh. She began to push him off.

'Oh, leave him,' Diana said. 'He looks so contented there. And it's lovely to have a dog about the house again, isn't it, Tom?'

'It is.'

'You've mentioned Bonnie before. What was she?' Juno asked, imagining some kind of terrier or Shih-Tzu.

'She was an Irish Wolfhound,' Tom answered. 'Huge but gentle.'

'Came up to my waist. And so loving,' his mother added. She sighed. 'I do miss her.'

'Maybe you could have another dog? Maybe something smaller this time?'

Diana shook her head. 'Nothing could replace my Bonnie,' she said, firmly. She eyed the springer. 'Although, I'm getting very fond of this little man. If you ever need a dog-sitter, I'd be happy to oblige.' Casting an oblique look at her son, she added, 'It's a bit like having grandchildren. All the fun and then you can hand them back when you've had enough.'

'I am *not* rising to the bait,' Tom said.

'No chance of you even settling down. I ask you, Juno, thirty-eight and no sign of even so much as a girlfriend. I reckon, even if she came covered in dust and shaped like an amphora, he still wouldn't be interested.'

Juno looked from mother to son. It was obviously a well-honed argument. She had had similar conversations with her own mother and rescued him. 'Well, if you want to babysit Joops and remind yourself just how much trouble dogs can be, please do. Actually, it would be marvellous knowing I had someone to leave him with if needed. I have to go up to London occasionally.'

'You can count on me,' Diana said, firmly. 'I suppose you have to attend parties and things?' Her voice was wistful.

'Sometimes. A writer's life can have its glamorous moments, but I hate to disillusion you, I mostly spend my time hunched over a laptop, drinking cold coffee and staring into space for inspiration.'

'Speaking of things going cold, we'd better eat.' Diana rose decisively. 'It's salmon en croute, with homemade potato and leek soup to start and my special trifle to finish. Does that suit?'

Juno got up too. 'Diana, speaking as a woman who has been living on ready meals for one, it sounds like heaven.'

# CHAPTER 8

The food was good and the company, when several more glasses of wine had been downed, was much more relaxed.

Diana relayed several funny stories of when she was a primary school teacher and Tom explained more about his peripatetic lifestyle.

'I go wherever there's a dig,' he said over coffee as they sat back in the garden room. 'I'm a specialist in ancient Greek and Roman remains.'

'Which means spending lots of time in the Mediterranean sun,' his mother put in.

'After the winter we've had, it doesn't sound too bad a deal,' Juno said, on a laugh. 'Apart from walking Joops, I've barely stuck my nose out of the door.'

'It can get like that here in the winter,' Diana said, sympathetically. 'But you soon forget by the time spring arrives.'

'It's also why I look for jobs abroad. Usually.' He shuddered. 'I managed a dig on Hadrian's Wall once and it was thick fog for weeks. And that was in August!'

'It's about time you got yourself a proper job and settled down,' Diana said, with asperity. 'Bought a house, found a wife.'

Tom drank his coffee in one gulp and poured himself another. 'Change the record, Ma. I'm fine as I am.'

Diana took the coffee pot off him and refilled Juno's cup. 'I bet Juno here has a boyfriend and she's probably years younger. How old are you, Juno?'

'I'm thirty-two,' Juno answered faintly. Diana, on a bottle of wine, was quite something.

'And I expect you have a steady boyfriend.'

'Erm. Yes. Or rather I did.'

'Stop haranguing our guest,' Tom put in. 'I hear you've discovered Roman Field, Juno?'

Thankful for the change of subject, Juno found herself gabbling enthusiastically. 'I have! I go up most days now. At about ten there's quite a crowd of us who gather. Joops likes to play with Stella the cocker and Rudi the red setter. I've met their owners too. It's great having someone to talk to, especially as my working day is a solitary one. The first time I went I was up there about eight in the morning and I found it a bit lonely.' Recalling the strange figure dressed in white who disappeared into the mist, she shivered. 'I didn't feel safe somehow, which is weird as I'm a city girl. I'm used to looking after myself,' she added, lying.

Diana nodded. 'Best to be up there when there's one or two others about. Even in Flete, there are some peculiar folk around.' She tapped the side of her nose. 'And people have seen things up there.'

'Mum!'

'What? I'm only repeating what folk have said.'

'Well don't. You'll scare Juno.'

'What sort of things have they seen? Take no notice of your son, Diana, I'm interested. Have they seen ghosts?'

'As a matter of fact, yes.'

Tom groaned.

'Don't you believe in ghosts, Tom?' Juno asked. 'I would have expected in your line of work, you might have come across one or two.'

He gave a quick shrug. 'Things have happened which don't have a logical explanation, but I can say, hand on heart, I've never seen a ghost.'

'Well, that's not what Marjorie Sneddon said,' Diana said. 'She was up on the field one evening in the summer, just as the light was going. Out with her rottie, Mabel, she was. She was on the top bit and a mist came down. She thought it was odd, it had been a lovely sunny day and was a clear evening. All of a sudden she was surrounded by a fog. Thick and dense and cold.'

'What did she see?' Juno asked, realising she was holding her breath. She could see why Diana had made such a good teacher of small children; she told a tale well.

'A figure. Tall and dressed in white. Mabel went for it and –' Diana left a dramatic pause, 'and it only went and disappeared into thin air!'

'Oh!' Juno exhaled. It sounded exactly like what she'd seen – or thought she'd seen.

Diana, gratified by the response, continued. 'And some people have heard singing on the wind and a whistling when there's not a living soul there.'

'Well, it's the site of a considerably large villa estate,' Tom said, bringing them all down to earth with a jolt. 'There's bound to be some kind of atmosphere there. An imprint of the past, if you will.'

'Is that what you think ghosts are?' Juno asked him, deciding to keep her own experience to herself.

'It's as good an explanation as any. A sort of remnant of the past that's embedded itself into the ground, or the walls of a house. It's a fairly commonly-held theory.'

She thought of the old house next door. It must be early Victorian at least but she'd never felt anything but happiness emanate from its walls. That and a bit of benign neglect. 'Was Flete a big Roman settlement?' she asked Tom, wondering what was beneath the foundations of Begin-Again Cottage.

'It's thought to be what was then considered a major provincial town, with an important harbour, roughly where the harbour is today. There was at least one vast villa estate up on the fields where you walk, with another heading over to the Sidmouth Hill. The villas were much more than simply houses. They were farmsteads, with buildings for animals and slaves, which would be largely taken from local British tribes, a huge house for the Romano British family, bathhouses, stabling. Possibly a garrison. You get the picture.'

'I do. I'm surprised you haven't excavated the field. Or do the ghosts put you off?'

'Touché.' He gave a short laugh. 'It's cropped up once or twice, but ghosts aren't the issue. Funding is. If I could prove Flete was the site of Moridunum which was thought to be the last major Roman settlement before Exeter, I might be in with a chance. Some argue Carmarthen in Wales is Moridunum but my money's on Flete.' He shrugged again. 'Until I can prove my theory Flete's secrets will remain hidden.'

'What a shame,' Juno exclaimed. 'It would be such an exciting thing for the town. It would bring in tourists, wouldn't it?'

'Thought you weren't interested in history?'

'I'm not particularly.' Juno repressed a shudder. She tried very hard not to think about history, especially her personal one. And she didn't know what the future held so that meant concentrating on the present. Which she did with a ferocity. 'But growing up with my dad who's a medievalist –'

'Professor Wilfred Eden?' Tom interrupted.

'Yup.'

'You really do come from academic stock, don't you?'

Juno couldn't decide if he was being admiring or poking fun. 'I suppose some of it rubbed off,' she acceded.

'Hence Jupiter?'

'Jupiter?' She frowned, puzzled. 'Oh, you mean the dog? No, he's not named after a god or anything. I usually only call him Jupiter when he's naughty. It's part of his pedigree name. You know how involved they can be.'

'Not really.'

Juno couldn't decide if Tom had taken a dislike to her or was generally grumpy and antisocial, but she was getting fed up of fending off his spikiness. *Bloody men. I've had enough of them.* She turned her attention to Diana and smiled at her. 'It would be lovely to see a few more tourists here.'

'I can see you're getting fond of our little town,' Diana said, patting Juno's hand. 'But even though we're considered a bit of a Cinderella compared to Sidmouth and Lyme Regis, we don't do too badly. Wait until the Easter weekend, the place will be heaving, especially if we get good weather.'

'And then you'll do nothing but moan about not being able to park,' Tom put in.

'Absolutely!' Unabashed, Diana rose. 'I'd better clear the table. Has everyone had enough to eat?' she asked anxiously.

Juno groaned. 'More than enough. I'm trying to move in order to help you with the plates but I'm not sure I can.'

'Wouldn't dream of you helping. You're our guest! Tom, shift yourself. Make yourself useful for once.' Diana winked at Juno. 'Got to get the use out of him while I can. He'll be off somewhere exotic again as soon as it's possible.'

Juno used the time to sign the books Diana had brought down. Stacking them neatly on the coffee table, her attention was caught by a copy of Greek Myths. Leafing through it, she settled on the tale of Perseus and Andromeda, vaguely remembering it from an old film she'd once watched on the TV. She was so absorbed she didn't notice Tom's return. He stood at the entrance to the garden room, an odd expression on his face.

'You can borrow it if you want.'

'Are you sure?'

He shrugged. 'It's an old copy from my childhood. I know where you are if I want it back.'

'Yes.'

There was an awkward pause.

The dog got up and began to circle, rescuing them. Juno recognised the signs. 'Well, if you're sure I can't help with clearing up, I'd better take Joops for his last-minute constitutional. Don't want him disgracing himself when he's been pretty well behaved.'

'He's been perfect,' Diana appeared, standing next to her son, a tea towel in her hands. She beamed impishly. 'See Juno to the door, will you Tom?'

Juno didn't miss the scowl he gave as response.

'Please forgive my mother. She's hardly subtle,' Tom said, as he handed Juno her coat.

'She's adorable,' Juno defended. 'I love having her as my neighbour. She's the first friend I've made in Flete.'

Tom, his hand on the front door, paused. 'It's just that I can't stand it when she gets on her high horse about me finding a girlfriend. Six years happily divorced and not looking.'

Juno pulled her coat around her with a sharp tug. 'Just as well I have absolutely no intention of – what's the old-fashioned phrase – setting my cap at you, then. Last boyfriend left me for another woman and I can assure you I'm most definitely not looking either. Just to make it clear,' she bit out, crisply. 'Besides, don't flatter yourself. You're *so* not my type.' She didn't know why she'd added the last part. He wasn't her type it was true but even she could see he was attractive in his own way. It made her sound silly.

'Well, we've cleared that up then.'

'Certainly have. Night.' She turned to go but he stayed her arm.

'Wait a sec, Juno. It's good for me to know there's someone reliable next door. A friendly face. I mean, she's hardly in her dotage yet but I'm away such a lot and I worry.' He bit his lip. 'It would be good if I thought she had someone to turn to if necessary.'

Juno hesitated. She liked Diana and, she too, liked having her next door. 'I'm happy to be a contact, if that's what you're asking. But I don't know how long I'm going to be in Flete. Living here is temporary until I get myself sorted.' She fished in her coat pocket for her phone. 'But I'm happy to help if needed while I'm here. Have my mobile number for her and give me yours in case I need to get in touch with you.'

They exchanged numbers and Tom opened the door for her. 'Thanks. I appreciate it. See you, Juno,' he said softly.

'See you.'

As Juno pulled up her collar and turned into the wind, she strode out her irritation with Tom Lyndsay in the short walk to her front door. But it was a shame he wasn't going to be around more. And not just for his mother's sake. *Now why am I thinking that?*

Turning the key in her front door, she let Joops run in. Closing the door behind her, she leaned against it. It had been a good evening but it was even better to be home.

Georgia Hill

# CHAPTER 9

*M*oridunum

'Flavia, we should return home. If your father finds you have come to town, he will fly into one of his rages. He'll send you off to a husband in Rome.' Ursa clutched her cloak to her against the wind. They had left the litter before the streets became narrow and crowded and the watery spring sunshine did not compensate for the strong breeze. 'If not Hibernia!'

Flavia tutted. 'He's always moaning on about returning to Rome. It means nothing, his job is here, in this godforsaken province.' She knew she was being harsh with Ursa but she couldn't help it. After so long, the freedom was giddying. The only other trips into town had been to the amphitheatre, an entertainment her father loved. Flavia had little taste for gladiatorial combat; the bloodshed made her nauseous. 'And what concern is it of yours? I decide what I do. Where I go and when I leave. And I have a yearning to visit the market today.' The words were out and she immediately regretted them for their cruelty.

'The market?' Ursa said, appalled. 'Oh no, we should not venture there, not without Balbus as our escort. It's a dangerous place, my lady.'

'Nonsense. It's where the stalls are. I need material for a new cloak. I want some wool and the tribespeople weave the best there is.' Flavia shivered. 'It's always so cold and damp in this place I need something to keep me warm. The

51

wind today is keen. Besides, it's such joy to go about without that vile lout Balbus breathing down my neck.'

'Then send me to the market. I know the best stalls and the best prices. If they see you, they will push up the cost. They will recognise you as the daughter of Flavius Honoratus. Flavia, listen to me. Go back to the litter and I will seek out your cloth.'

Flavia raised an imperious eyebrow and strode off, ducking down a narrow alley.

Ursa gave chase. 'Flavia. Stop. Listen. If we get into trouble, it will be me who pays. It's the slave who is disposed of due to a misdemeanour of their master or mistress,' she added bitterly. 'May I remind you,' she called out to Flavia's rapidly disappearing back, 'my only brother ended up shackled in a ditch and left for dead when a statuette of Vesta went missing in the house to which he belonged. He wasn't guilty but no one would take the word of an enslaved man against a free-born citizen of the mightiest empire in the world. Flavia, come back now!'

Flavia disappeared behind a bread seller who was holding his board up high to better display his goods.

Ursa, cursing her under her breath, had no choice but follow. 'I have been loyal in your service these past twelve years,' she muttered to herself, puffing, 'and have long witnessed your capriciousness but, by all the gods, you are testing me. I am truly fond of you but today I could cheerfully wring your scrawny little neck. This impulsive venture into town has been more than foolhardy,' she yelled, narrowly avoiding a dung pile. 'The sooner you are married and have less time for such follies the better.' Running to catch her up, dodging the street hawkers and a heap of clay pots piled up outside the wine merchant, Ursa prayed to all the gods in Rome her mistress would come to no harm. Charging around the corner she almost ran into her as the girl had come to an abrupt halt in the market.

'Oh,' Flavia cried, as she absorbed the bustle and noise in the forum. 'It's magical!' A beaming smile split her face as she surveyed the rows of stalls with their goods heaped up, the pottery ware stacked on the floor, the barrels of oysters, olives and beer. Over the racket of sellers calling out their wares, she clapped her hands together and added, 'It's enchanting. Look at the spices over there and,' she paused, 'what is that delicious smell?'

'Sausages from the *popina* over there,' Ursa put in sourly. 'Full of sawdust and most likely rotten.'

Flavia ignored her. 'Take me to the best cloth stall. I want to choose something myself. For once I want to feel it between my own fingers, run it against my skin before buying. Have you money ready?' She did a childish and very unseemly skip. 'Oh, and I want to try some of those sausages.'

'I have some money. It may not be enough for everything you desire today. And you'll not be going near the *popina*. Place is full of ruffians.'

'Oh, stop grumbling, Ursa. This is fun! The sun is shining, quite possibly with warmth for the first time this year, and we're out in the world.'

'Then the sooner we get it over and done with and get you back to your father's house, the better.' She edged them through the throng to the nearest cloth seller. 'At least it's more open here in the forum and we can keep a better eye out. I nearly lost you back there in the streets. They were so busy I could hardly keep sight of you.'

Flavia strained to peer at a stall heaped with cloth in the furthermost corner of the forum. 'Look at that heavenly blue. That's the stuff for me.' As she began to move off, she collided with a man coming in the opposite direction.

'Have a care, sir,' Ursa yelled and gathered Flavia to her. 'I might have known there would be trouble.' Keeping one arm around Flavia's waist and one hand on the money bag strapped around her own, she braced herself for a confrontation. 'I told you we should have Balbus with us. He might be brainless but he's as big as a bear and good in a fight.'

Flavia stared up at the man she had run into. It was the man she'd seen in the hills! He was tall. Much taller than any in her father's household, even bigger than Balbus. His long, plaited hair and deep blue plaid cloak marked him out as a tribesman, possibly one from the nearby hillfort.

He bowed. 'My apologies, my lady. I hope you are not hurt. But I do believe it was you who walked into me.'

'Such impertinence! Is that how you would speak to me? Do you not know who I am?'

Ursa groaned. She began to pull Flavia away, but the girl stood rigid.

'How do you know our language?' Flavia asked.

The man's bright blue eyes twinkled. He didn't seem put out at her question. 'We are not all barbarians. I speak it in order to trade.' He gestured with his chin, making his beard flick. 'Here, in the market. Do you know *our* language?'

'Of course not,' Flavia answered scornfully. 'What need would I have?' She pushed the cloak off her head a little to get a better look at him. She peered up at him, the sun making her squint. Beyond all the blond hair, he had a nice face, a strong nose and a wide mouth which was currently grinning with an impudent smile.

Ursa tucked the cloak back over Flavia's head. 'Mistress,' she whispered, 'this could get out of hand at any moment. It would not be countenanced to be recognised.' The girl flicked it back impatiently and the hood fell off completely, to lie on her shoulders, revealing glossy dark hair and her beautiful, oval face. The slave looked around in panic. 'Come away,' she urged. 'At this rate we'll be lucky to get out of town with our virtue intact, let alone our lives.' She tugged on Flavia's arm.

Flavia was intrigued by this Briton, once spied from a distance and now to be examined at close quarters. 'What, pray, do you trade?'

'Wool.' Again, he gestured with his chin, the beads woven through his beard clicking as he moved.

Flavia stared, fascinated. All the men she knew were shaven, their hair closely cropped in the accepted style, but this man had hair everywhere it seemed. She felt herself blush. She even glimpsed coppery hair at the neck of his tunic. Collecting her brains, she said, 'Wool? Then show me the best you have. We were on our way to buy some. I want blue, perhaps like the blue in your plaid.'

'Of course.' The man held out a hand to show them the way. 'Come, then, I'll make sure you get the best price and the finest weave.' He took them to a stall which had its goods laid out on a wooden trestle. He said something in his own tongue to the stall holder who jumped to his command and picked up a roll of material from a basket underneath the table.

'We save our best for our most loyal customers,' the man smiled. Taking it from the stall holder, he rolled out a length and spread it on the trestle. 'Feel. It's the best we have. The finest weave and the softest wool. We are experts and are recognised as such, even by our conquering masters.'

Flavia ignored the jibe; she was well aware some tribesmen despised their so-called shackles. Even in this quiet backwater in the southwest of the province, where the Britons and citizens had inter-married for centuries and peaceful trading was the norm, there was still the occasional attempt at overthrowing their rulers. Her father did not hold back his scorn; she knew he saw the hillfort tribes as enemies of Rome.

Put on the spot over purchasing the plaid, she hadn't a clue what to do. She'd never bought anything herself in her life. Glancing tentatively from the man to a nervous-looking Ursa, she reached out a finger and stroked the cloth. 'It's so soft,' she cried. Emboldened, she took the material between her fingers and rubbed gently.

'Will it do, my lady?' he asked. The words were deferential, but his tone was most certainly not.

'It will.'

'Thank the gods,' Ursa muttered at her side.

'Oh, how much do I need?' Flavia flapped a hand at the slave. 'Take over, will you? You know what to do. Oh, and buy a length of the drab. I wish you to have a new tunic and cloak.' She moved away as Ursa negotiated the transaction.

'It will suit you well,' the man said.

'More impertinence. I think you underestimate to whom you are talking. Do you not realise my father is Flavius Honoratus Secundinus?'

The man nodded. 'I know your father. How could I not? I pay my taxes to him, after all.'

'As is right.'

The man gave a sardonic smile. 'On that we must disagree.'

Flavia gasped. 'You talk treason!'

'It is a differing opinion. That's all.'

'Barbarian!' The word was meant as an insult but came out almost as a compliment.

He turned to go but changed his mind. 'You may find there are barbarians of another kind hammering at the great gates of Rome soon.'

'What do you mean?'

'Just that Rome cannot keep its enemies at bay for much longer.'

'What nonsense you utter. The might of Rome will never be defeated.'

'Aye. You keep to that thought, daughter of Flavius Honoratus. It might give you comfort.'

Again, he went to leave but Flavia put a hand on his arm. It was strong and rigidly muscled and thrilled her. 'If you are prone to give out such portents, then you owe me your name. What is it?'

'It is Padrig.' He bowed. 'Padrig of the Durotriges.' He raised his brows as he gazed at her hand, looking tiny on his broad forearm. 'And now may I go?'

'You may.' She stood watching as he strode away. 'And mine is Flavia,' she called but the sounds were twisted away by the wind.

Warmth engulfed her. A heat that had nothing to do with the thin February sunshine.

Georgia Hill

# CHAPTER 10

*2023*

January slipped into February and with it came softer, gentler weather. There was even some heat in the sun if you kept sheltered from the wind. Juno worked on her book, walked Joops and desperately tried to keep the house warm.

She phoned her brother in Exeter and they made vague plans to meet up. Mabyn, rang several times and promised to visit. Juno put her off until the weather truly warmed up and the new bar on the seafront opened. She'd walked past it often with her dog in tow. The scaffolding was down now and it looked close to opening.

Standing outside it reading the menu early one morning, she thought it looked okay. A good range of burgers and cocktails. Named Colosseum, amusingly they'd decided on a Roman theme, with a Julius Cheeser Burger, a Claudius Pasty and a Caesar Salad amongst the offerings. Not very sophisticated but it might make for a fun night out should Mabyn decide to stay. They'd definitely have to try the Fiddle While Rome Burns Snack Plate.

Grinning and anticipating Mabyn's reaction, she walked away and almost bumped into the woman coming in the opposite direction. 'Sorry. sun's in my eyes.' Shading her face she saw it was the woman she'd met on the beach with the yellow Labrador. *Ellen? Alison?* 'Annie! Hello again.'

'Hi there. It's Juno, isn't it? Hard name to forget.'

'It is.'

Annie bent to fuss Joops. 'And I remember you, young fella. And you have to watch that low sun in the mornings, especially if you're driving. My Dean has to go into Bridport every day and he says it's hell at this time of year. Shines right in his eyes. Then he gets it on the way home too! He works at Waitrose. Keep on at him to transfer to Sidmouth as it's nearer but he doesn't listen. Says he likes the crowd he works with.'

Juno wasn't sure what to say. She'd never had a job where you had to commute. She shrugged. 'In London, commuters disappear into a hole in the ground. No sun there!'

Annie eyed her keenly. 'Is that where you're from then? London? Went once. Don't think I'll bother again. Far too busy, like.'

Juno smiled. 'It can seem very busy, but you get used to it.' Had she got used to it? It had seemed very different to Winchester where she'd grown up and where her parents still lived but Paul had been there, guiding her, protecting her. She suppressed a hard laugh. Sometimes he had a funny idea of what protection meant. She shivered.

'Look, don't stand there getting cold, let's grab a coffee. It'll have to be a takeaway.' Annie held up a bag out of the springer's reach. He'd been nosing at it with interest while they'd been talking. 'Taking Gran her lunch. She forgot it, so I'll pick her up a coffee on the way. And then do you fancy having a look-see at our little museum?'

Annie took her arm and marched her back in the direction of the town. The promenade glowed pink with the early morning light and it softened the look of the hard concrete.

'Not the prettiest seafront, is it?' Annie said, reading her mind. 'Not a patch on Lyme or Sidmouth but I like it. Good honest folk here in Flete. Don't get many of them for a penny in Lyme Regis and don't get me started on the rude old folk in Sidmouth!'

Juno giggled. Annie was good fun. Relaxing, she let her lead her, first to a café on the corner where they bought coffee and then up the gentle incline of a pedestrianised street quaintly named Narrow Sheep Walk.

They stopped at an unappealing-looking door next to the butchers. 'It's not officially open for the year yet,' Annie explained. 'Gran's getting it sorted for the new season. Spent the winter setting up a website. It's ever so good, although I suppose I'm biased.' She knocked on the door, listening intently. 'She's probably in the back room and can't hear.' She knocked again.

'Won't she mind Joops?'

'Oh, no. Bring him in out of the cold. Gran loves dogs. She and Grandad used to have a springer. Rebel he was called. Bonkers.' She shifted the carrier bag with difficulty. 'Here, can you take the coffees? I'll have to ferret out my key.'

Just as she did so, the door opened and an elderly woman peered out. She was tiny, with a long white plait reaching to her waist and round metal-framed glasses through which she blinked owlishly. Despite her stature, she radiated an indomitable strength.

'In a hurry, our Annie?'

'Hi, Bill.' Annie reached down and kissed her cheek. 'Can we come in? It's brass monkeys out here.'

'Come on in, then. Wind's got up, I reckon. Tide's turning. And who's this?'

Was this the Old Bill Diana mentioned? Her friend who ran the museum. Juno had assumed it would be a man.

'Juno and Jupiter,' Annie explained.

Her gran burst out laughing. 'Never expected to be visited by the gods on this good Monday morning. Which one's which?'

Juno had to admit it was funny. 'I'm Juno and the spaniel is Jupiter, although he's called Joops most of the time.'

'Hello there, fella.' She tickled the delighted dog. 'I'm Bill, although most folk call me Old Bill and me only just turned eighty.' She pulled an indignant face. 'They like their jokes in this town. Christened Wilhelmina for my sins.' She shook her head and tutted. 'Don't know what my folks were thinking of. Always hated it. Always called myself Bill until it stuck.' She ushered them in, shut the door behind them, locked it and led them along a narrow corridor through a room packed with photographs and artefacts and into another which obviously served as an office-cum-kitchen. Taking the bag off her granddaughter she lobbed it onto a cupboard next to the sink. 'Sit yourselves down.'

Annie lifted a pile of papers off an ancient kitchen chair for Juno to sit on and Bill collapsed onto a shabby armchair.

Annie perched on the arm. 'How far have you got, then?'

'Dusted the whole place down. Don't know why this place gets so dusty when it's closed up all winter, but it does.' Bill saluted Juno with her coffee and sipped while simultaneously scratching the springer's ears.

The dog gazed up adoringly and Juno was relieved Bill had turned out to be a woman. Ever since Paul, Joops had been wary of men although, strangely, he'd taken to Tom. 'What's the museum all about?'

'The town. The story of it through the centuries. Once you've finished your coffee we'll take a look around shall we?' She winked. 'Then Annie can tell me off for missing bits.'

'As if!'

They beamed at one another and Juno had the impression of a close bond. A pang of envy shot through her. She'd never known her own grandparents. Hers wasn't a close family. 'I'd like to have a look if I may. When do you open properly?'

'I'll try to get it shipshape before half term. We don't get too many coming in that early in the year but always pays to be prepared.'

'Who runs it?'

'Me! Labour of love this place. My Dad set it up and I took over when I retired.'

'How's it funded, then?' Juno was curious. The museum was barely more than two rooms, but it must still cost money to keep going.

'Oh, don't get her started on money.' Annie rolled her eyes. 'Let's just say we get by on a wing and a prayer.'

'Be nice to have some of that funding Lyme always gets,' Bill grumbled. 'Never gets this side of the border.'

'Border?' Juno said confused. 'Oh, you mean the Dorset Devon border.'

'Yup. We're too far west for the folk in Dorchester and too far east for Exeter. Pig in the middle.'

'Or a rose between two thorns, Bill!' her granddaughter teased.

'Always think this part of the world is like neither Dorset nor Devon. Has a feel all of its own. Should be its own county.'

'Oh, not that old chestnut again,' Annie groaned.

'Well, I do,' Bill huffed.

'I agree, actually,' Juno put in. 'From the little I've seen, it's not like Dorset, or Devon proper.'

'So you come to Flete to research your roots, then, girl?' Bill asked.

'I'm not really interested in all that.' It was a lie. Juno felt a strong, if inexplicable, pull to the town.

'Shame. Pays dividends to know where you come from. What's the family name?'

'Loveday.' Juno answered without thinking. Sometimes her writer's name seemed more her own.

Bill sniffed hard. 'There was a Betty Loveday who lived in one of them cottages on Church Lane.'

'Yes, that was my great-aunt. On my mother's side. I'm living there now.'

'Ar, I knew her. Wise woman was Betty. With your dark hair and eyes, you've got the look of her when she was young. Always been Lovedays in town. You'll have to pop by the soap shop in Clappers Lane. Beth Loveday runs it. Must be a relative.'

'She's away now, don't you remember, Gran?' Annie put in. 'Gone to the States for a holiday.'

'Oh yes, so she has. Still, worth a look see along Clappers Lane. Cobbled it is, half-timbered buildings. Only nice bit of town we got.'

'I promise to investigate.'

Bill narrowed her eyes at Juno. 'Your aunt didn't have any kiddies, did she? Reckon she was the last. Young Beth comes from over Exeter way.'

Juno shook her head. 'She never married. I'm pretty certain she didn't have children.'

'Sad when a line runs out like that.'

'I've still got a family,' Juno protested, wondering where this conversation was going. She wanted to tell her that, as she'd adopted Loveday as her writing name, there was one back in the town now, but she didn't.

Bill looked at her. 'But that's your dad's family, isn't it? Where's he from?'

'I don't know,' Juno protested, feeling put on the spot. 'I've never given it much thought. As I said, I'm not really interested. I was brought up in Winchester, so I've always assumed he came from there.'

'Leave over, Bill,' Annie said. 'Folk don't pay attention to that sort of stuff. We live in a global world. People move around all over the place these days.'

Her grandmother snorted. 'I happen to think where you come from is important. Your ancestors, no matter how far back, mould you, leave their stamp. But you young ones don't pay no heed.' She finished her coffee in one and seemed deep in thought for a moment. Then said suddenly, 'Come on then, you lazy pair, let's have a look round.'

Juno followed them into a large room, low-ceilinged and smelling of damp.

'This is our modern history room,' Bill announced. 'Anything post-1800 goes in here, although we've got more stuff from the nineteenth and twentieth centuries as you'd expect.' She sucked her teeth. 'Lots of war stuff.'

Juno looked around. The room was crammed with cases displaying everything from an old naval uniform to World War Two gas masks and ration books. It was haphazard and chaotic and musty. She stopped by a hideous-looking object consisting of an over-sized helmet with a visor and some kind of tubing attached to it. 'What's this?' she asked, repelled.

Bill came to her side. 'Baby's gas mask. From the last war. See the pump there? Mum had to keep pumping the air in otherwise the little one would suffocate.'

Juno shuddered. 'That's awful.'

'It is. If anything happened to Mum, the baby copped it too. But they were awful times. Folk thought we were going to get gassed, see.' She flicked her long plait over her shoulder. 'You know what, Annie, we ought to get a doll to put in this. It would show how it was used.'

'Good idea. I'll have a scout around in the attic. Bound to be one of Rowie's lying in a box somewhere. She won't mind. My daughter. Twenty and at university now,' Annie added as explanation to Juno.

'What's she studying?'

'History. It's a bit of a family tradition.'

Juno smiled. 'Will she take over here at some point?'

'She's too busy going out clubbing every night at the moment,' Annie replied with a grimace. 'But maybe, once she's got all that out of her system.'

There were lots of photograph albums heaped up on a table. 'I gets photies donated all the time,' Bill said. 'Can't think what to do with them so I put them here for people to look through.'

'Annie said you were building a website. Maybe you could scan them in and put them on there?' Juno suggested. She eyed the pile of albums. 'Although it might take a while.'

'Well, that's my job for next winter sorted, then.'

Juno was about to offer her help but faltered. She didn't know how long she was going to be around. Begin-Again Cottage and Flete were strictly temporary. She didn't want to put down roots here. Or did she?

'Come on, next room,' Bill ordered.

Annie rolled her eyes. 'What my gran isn't telling you is it's the *only* other room.'

'At the moment, our Annie. At the moment.' Bill tapped her nose. 'I've got plans for the place. Come on, Juno, come in to our ancient history room. It's where things get really interesting.'

# CHAPTER 11

Juno followed them. This room was smaller, with white-washed walls and a tiny window looking out onto an equally tiny yard. In the middle was a table with a magnificent model.

'Come and take a look-see,' Bill invited. 'My father's pride and joy. He spent most of his life making it.'

Juno ventured nearer and read the description plate: *A model of the Roman villa which lay on Roman Field.* 'Oh,' she cried, gazing up at Bill with shining eyes. 'Is this what it looked like?'

She shrugged. 'It's what my dear old dad thought it looked like. There's not been much digging done up there but what has been done suggests it was a large house. Would have had stabling and outhouses with the farms beyond, maybe even a garden an' all. The wealthy Romans liked a garden.'

Juno bent over. The model was exquisite, it even had tiny figures.

'Main entrance there at the front,' Bill went on. 'Leading into the atrium and beyond into an inner courtyard where the impluvium was. That's the pool where the rainwater was collected. It ran off the roof, through a hole and was piped into a tank.'

'They had a hole in the roof? In the British weather?'

Bill's lips twisted. 'Bit of guesswork on my dad's part. I reckons it's more likely there was a well instead. If you look at the reconstruction of the villa down at old Lullingstone in Kent, the house had its own bathhouse system with a well to service it and probably a closed roof. But,' she shrugged, 'the Romans imported their lifestyle into the province, that's us by the way, poor ignorant provincials. We were a province of mighty Rome, so built their houses in the style from home sweet home. Same way the British tea planters did in the highlands of India or Ceylon. So you never know.'

'Must have been cold.'

'Oh, they had heating.' Bill nodded to the back of the model where the basement of the villa was exposed. 'See. *Hypocaust.* They lit fires in grates in between the pillars, looky-here, and the hot air rose up through ducts in the wall.'

'How clever,' Juno said, impressed.

'Didn't you do the Romans at school?' Annie asked amused. 'I thought everyone knew about their central heating system.'

'Yes, but I think I've blanked it all out. When you come from a long line of academics like I do it's one way of rebelling.' Juno screwed up her face. 'Some of it's coming back, though. Didn't they eat roast dormice or something?'

Bill laughed. 'Think it was on the menu, along with beef, pork and a whole load of birds. Pheasants and the like. They probably got their fill of fish and seafood here on the coast and gull's eggs were popular. Scallops, cuttlefish, sea urchins, lobsters. The whole ruddy lot. Mind, if my theory is right and Flete was a port, a lot of things would get imported too. They liked a type of fish sauce called *garum* or as it was sometimes known, *liquamen.* Made from fermented fish entrails, it was. Sprinkled it on their food to make it tasty.'

Juno pulled a face. 'Sounds like the fish sauce I've put in some Thai recipes.'

'Maybe not so different I suppose,' Annie put in. 'Although I'll stick to a bit of vinegar on my chips.'

'So will I,' Juno answered on a laugh. She pointed to a room in the model full of clay pots and tables where the tiny figures were preparing food. 'The kitchen?'

Bill nodded. 'And next to it the dining room, or *triclinium.* Bedrooms and offices beyond. Sometimes villas had an upstairs but, as far as we know, it wasn't common. Mosaics on the floor, frescoes painted on the walls, lots of slaves to cook and clean. It wasn't a bad old life if you were wealthy. And the owners of the villa up on Roman Field must have had money. Lots of money around here, I reckon. More evidence to back up my claim Flete was once upon a time Moridunum. An important port.'

Juno wondered if Tom had talked to Bill. 'It's remarkably like our way of life, isn't it? I mean, without the slaves, although my mum has a daily who goes in.'

'Lucky her,' Annie said with asperity. 'Wish I could afford one.'

Juno, realising her middle-class roots were showing, rushed on to explain. 'Mum's just been appointed as a magistrate and hasn't much free time. The poor woman has to dust millions of my father's books, so it's not much fun for her. Mum goes through cleaners like I do hot water.'

'You're right, though,' Bill said, rescuing her. 'It isn't a million miles away from how we live now. They paid taxes, had to fight through a right old nightmare of bureaucracy, most folk lived in towns and cities. Although I don't know about you, but I don't have a shrine to my chosen god in my house.'

'Oh yes you do,' Annie said warmly. 'It's called the seventy-inch screen you've just bought to watch Sky Films.'

They laughed.

'Come and have a look at this, Juno.' Bill took her arm and led her to the back wall where there was a huge painting in a frame. 'Now this *would* seem peculiar to us.'

'What is it?'

'This is how we think the hill tribes lived. Lots of hillforts round here, you know. Local tribe would be the

Durotriges. Bolshy lot, they were. Always causing trouble for their masters.'

Juno studied the meticulously detailed illustration. A series of earthworks led up to a camp high on a hill. Surrounding each rampart were fences made from what looked to be tree trunks with pointed ends, a tall gate at the main entrance. Round huts, with their thatched conical roofs reaching almost to the ground lay sheltered behind the defences, with animal enclosures dotted in between. It was very different to the Roman villa.

'And next to it is a drawing of what the inside might have looked like,' Bill added.

The interior, with its dirt floor and shields hanging on the walls looked cramped.

'See the quern stones for grinding the wheat and the weaving frame? Open fire in the middle and beds against the wall. Cooking, working, sleeping all in the same space.' Bill laughed. 'Thatch lets the smoke out, but it must have been pretty ripe in there.'

'It's two completely different lifestyles,' Juno marvelled. The history was beginning to lick at her, but it was the stories it suggested that fascinated her more. Who were these people who lived cheek by jowl and yet in very different ways?

'It was that.'

'And did they have anything to do with one another, the hilltribes and the Romans?'

'The Romans were here over four hundred years so yes, by the end there was a lot of mixing. The Dumnonii tribes down west Devon and Cornwall way traded a lot and were less bother, but the Durotriges were more warlike. A bit more like Boudicca's lot in the east in the early days. There was probably trouble rumbling away at most times. But the Roman army was fearsomely well-organised. Ruled by the sword and it was a militarised economy.' Bill laughed. 'Think the Britons had to pick their arguments or face being wiped out or enslaved. They weren't savages though, never think that, although the Romans thought they were. Some of the jewellery and weaving was skilled. We'd buy it now, I reckon. I know I would. With all the inter-marrying, by the time they left, there were a lot of Romano British families. They took on the Roman life proper, had houses like the one in the model. No round hut and everyone living, eating and sleeping in one space malarkey for them! Our friends who lived in the villa on Roman Field had the luxurious Roman life.'

'The Romans left? I suppose they did.'

Bill nodded. 'Had enemies to fight elsewhere, didn't they? Left the Britons to their fate and the invasions from the Saxon tribes in the east.'

'And what happened then?'

'The so-called Dark Ages.'

Annie laughed. 'Don't get Gran started on her favourite hobbyhorse or we'll be here all day. She's got a whole theory about how the Dark Ages have been misunderstood.'

Bill glanced at her granddaughter. 'I have as well, but that'll keep for another day. Once the Romans had gone, Juno, so did the need for all the bureaucracy and the administration. The towns began to crumble and folk began to go back to the old way of life, back to the safety of the hillforts.' She pulled a face. 'They soon needed protection against a new enemy; the Barbarian hordes who were invading from Denmark and Germany. The Romans had gone but so had their armies. Told the Britons as they'd always wanted them gone, now they'd got what they'd been asking for. Off they buggered, leaving the province of Britannia undefended.'

'Charming!'

Bill tapped her nose in a gesture Juno was beginning to know well. 'But the Dark Ages, well, the Dark Ages are being re-examined. Wasn't such an uncivilised time as everyone thought.'

'It's astonishing. And this all happened when?'

'Fifteen hundred years ago, give or take.' Bill paused and stared at her intently. 'You say you come from a family of academics? Historians?'

'Yes. My brother and father. My other brother is a sociologist. I'm beginning to see what Dad and Cris have been banging on about, but you've made it all far more enthralling in an hour than they have in my entire lifetime.'

Bill laughed. 'I'm flattered. And now, my lovely, seeing as you're getting all interested, come and have a look at this. As well as a model maker, my dear old dad was a bit of a painter.' She led Juno to the wall nearest the door and pointed out a large painting.

Juno gasped.

'Good, isn't it?'

It was, but that wasn't why Juno had exclaimed. It was a painting of a man. Tall, with long blond plaits and beads in his beard. He wore a thick patterned tunic and boots with ties criss-crossed around his shins. It couldn't be. Juno stared, blinked hard several times and then stared again. It was the man from her dream.

'My dad's romantic notion of a Durotriges tribesman,' Bill continued. 'See the cloak pin and the finely worked armlet on the upper arm? Probably the best Welsh gold. And get a load of those leather breeches. And to think the Romans thought they were barbarians.' She huffed. 'They were just different, that's all.'

Juno tried to take in the details but her brain was fizzing. 'Would you mind?' she asked, holding up her phone.

'Not at all. Taken your fancy, has he?'

'You could say that.' Juno took several photos. She'd try to make sense of this later. 'Thank you. It's all been so interesting,' she croaked. 'Really fascinating.' Bill looked at her through narrowed eyes. Juno was sure the old woman knew what was going on in her head, although how when she couldn't make sense of it was a mystery. Maybe Great-Aunt Betty Loveday wasn't the only 'wise woman' around.

Bill seemed amused. 'Well, make sure you come back and take another look-see. We've lots here. I don't puts all of it out at the same time, although the model villa is always on show. Too big to shift and it's what most people want to see, what with the Roman Field and everything. On top of that, we've a Roman Road, Roman Lane and a Roman Way in town. It gets interest piqued, especially with the kids when they've done it at school.'

'I expect it does.' Juno had a sudden desire to escape. The dog whined at her side and nudged his cold wet nose into her hand. It put an end to any more discussion. 'Sounds like Joops has had enough history for one day and needs a break,' she said on a shaky laugh. 'But thank you Annie and Bill, it's been fascinating,' she repeated. 'It really has. I'll definitely come back.' She clipped the lead back on and followed them to the front door. After saying good-bye, she meandered back to the cottage, deep in thought. As she and Joops stopped to cross the main road to get into Church Lane, she noticed it was called Roman Way.

The Romano British life really hadn't seemed a million years away from her own, although she envied them their *hypocaust*. She could do with some efficient central heating in Begin-Again Cottage. And they paid taxes too! That reminded her; she needed to get onto her accountant. Her own tax return was due. As she made her way along Church Lane, the picture of the Durotriges tribesman muddled itself with pound signs and refused to leave her mind. *What was that all about?*

# CHAPTER 12

*The Secundinus Villa*

Flavia loitered behind a pillar under the *peristyle* bordering the outer courtyard. Standing not far from the table where her father's stewards sat and collected taxes, she watched fascinated as one counted the amount and then checked it off, handing the coins to another who poured them into a sack. There must hundreds of *nummi* as it weighed heavy as it was lifted and taken inside. It was one of the few days outsiders were allowed into this courtyard and even then they were closely guarded by those in her father's pay. Trajan loped up and shoved his enormous muzzle into her hand. Fierce when needed, the dog was now her loyal friend; she often smuggled out titbits from the kitchens to him and his two companions. She'd kept to her promise and had taken him out with her. It made sneaking out of the back gate all the easier if the trio of dogs didn't bark to announce her escape. Emboldened by her visit to the market, she had taken to roaming the hills again but had been extra cautious and had stayed within striking distance of the villa.

A spring breeze whipped across the courtyard and snatched at her cloak. The season had ducked back into chilliness. Flavia looked around to see what could spike her interest. In truth, she was so bored her teeth ached. On behalf of her mother, she'd overseen the menu for tonight's meal, had checked on the quality of fresh goods brought in, approved the last jar of pickled plums to be taken out of store and tasted the new wine – a lee of red imported from Campania. Her final chore had been to castigate one of the serving slaves for breaking a brand new Samian bowl only just unpacked in the latest consignment from Gaul. And now the rest of the day stretched ahead, empty and lacking in anything remotely exciting. The stench of warm pony drifted over on the wind from the barracks next door along with shouts from the few soldiers left. Her nose twitched. They'd recently had word her brother had, indeed, been successful in securing an important position. He was to support Theodosius, hero of the recent northern skirmishes and a man said to be headed for further greatness. She envied Marcus. He was at the very heart of the empire in Mediolanum itself and his ambition matched a purpose in life.

She rested a cheek against a cool marble pillar. Beyond the walls she could see the tantalising green hills rolling into one another. They represented freedom and adventure. In one of those secretive hills lay the fort of her father's enemy. The Durotriges had lately been causing low level trouble; stealing livestock, raiding the more vulnerable outlying villas. It was one cause of her father's many tempers. She had heard tell the tribespeople lived in squat round huts with straw roofs with no heating except the fire they cooked upon and was intrigued. It seemed exotically outlandish.

Sighing, she kicked at a gobbet of soil. She had nothing to do and too much energy to spare. Maybe she should accept Septimus Severus after all and set up her own household? At least it would give her something to do. He'd been pleasant company at the dinner. Dull but inoffensive and at least he didn't get drunk and coarse like the other men there. But every time she imagined married life with Septimus, another man's image rose; one who was tall, with reddish-blond hair and piercing blue eyes.

Closing her mind to thoughts which disturbed her in ways she didn't understand, she wondered if her new cloak was ready, the one she was having made with the cloth bought from the market. She'd had new clothes made for Ursa too, although the slave had been quarrelsome and peevish for days after the visit to the forum. It made life uncomfortable with her slave cross at her. The harbour beckoned but was too distant and far too dangerous – venturing into the market had been precarious enough. The port was full of felons and vagabonds and no place for anyone highborn, even she wouldn't risk it. Her father, a senior decurion of the ordo, had made some unpopular decisions concerning governance of the town. He was disliked and, if she was recognised, vengeance would be swift and brutal. Unless she took Balbus with her on her adventures, she could guarantee no one's safety. She shivered but not from cold. If she took Balbus, there would be no fun to be had; he would loom over her, polluting her space with his foul man stink and watch her with his avaricious eyes. She took great care not to be anywhere alone with Balbus. The man was a lecherous monster.

The queue to pay shifted forwards and her eye was caught by a tall figure at the back dressed in sumptuous plaid. Padrig of the Durotriges. The hard spring sun made his hair and beard spark gold and as he reached forward to pay, it glinted on a finely worked armlet he wore decorating his bicep. Barbarian he may be, but he was obviously high status.

Waiting until he'd paid and the tax collectors were busy, she sauntered past, Trajan at her heel. A mischievous impulse overtook her; Ursa always said her impulses would get her into a cartload of trouble one day. 'Meet me at the back gate,' she whispered, before thinking it through. Her words were tugged by the wind and she was immediately part thrilled, part aghast at her impetuosity.

He did well to control his surprise, but she saw the swiftest of nods.

Flavia glanced around. Apart from the dog no one was paying her the slightest attention. Thanking the gods she'd thrown on her oldest and least flamboyant cloak she pulled it over her head, suppressed her giggles and ran to the back gate, Trajan shadowing her. It was quiet at this side of the villa. Although it was always termed the back gate to differentiate it from the main one at the front, it was, in fact, situated on the side wall next to the well system which provided water to the bathhouse and through the gardens. It suffered from neglect from the estate's lazy and mulish garden slaves and, often deserted, security relied on the trio of guard dogs usually roaming nearby. Flavia chained up Trajan's two companions, promising a feast of scraps later and then slipped to the gate. Unlocking it with the usual difficulty, as it was rusty through lack of use, she lifted the latch. Slipping out, she gasped. She was free!

Leaning on the wall, her legs trembling too much to move away, she scanned the woods left and right. There was no sign of him. The adrenaline leaked away; he hadn't come. And she was outside the villa and alone having asked her father's enemy to meet her. She kept a hand on Trajan's neck, but he seemed relaxed and unworried. There was no one here. Turning to go back in, the anti-climax and relief flooded her.

A low call sounded. 'My lady.'

Trajan stiffened, his coat rough and springy under her fingers, but did not growl or bark.

Her head whipped around. She could see no one. The voice had been thin and almost not there at all. 'Who calls out?' she hissed. 'Show yourself.' For the first time she was aware of the danger she'd put herself in. This was sheer folly! It could be anyone out there. 'Show yourself or I'll set my dog on you.'

Keeping Trajan close to her, with one hand clutching the stone behind her so fiercely the cement splintered her nails, she edged closer to the gate, ready to flee back to safety.

'Do not be afeard.' A figure detached itself from one of the ash trees. 'It is I. Padrig of the Durotriges. I am here at your request.'

He stood in the clearing between trees and villa walls. Where had he come from? Where had he been hiding? Her father's words, that the tribesmen were fierce warriors with mystical ways, came back to her. Had he magicked himself out of the woods?

He bowed. 'I mean you no harm.' Standing erect, he spread his arms so she could see he was weaponless. A brave and foolish thing to be in these uncertain times. Taking a step nearer he stopped as she put out her hands. 'Forgive me, my lady. 'Twas *you* who summoned *me.*' Humour lit his voice. 'And here I am.'

Trajan tensed, watching, waiting for his mistress's command.

Flavia didn't know what to do. A multitude of confused emotions and thoughts assailed her. She knew she should run back through the gate to the safety of the villa and lock it behind her. She knew it had been a stupid and reckless thing to ask him to meet her. Boredom had much to answer for! She took a step sideways to the gate and then stopped. He hadn't moved again. He was waiting patiently. She'd seen her father's stable manager do the same with a feral pony. She'd seen Ursa, a country-born woman, tickle a trout in the stream back in the safer times years ago when they could travel about the countryside with impunity. Gentle watchfulness. But with a purpose, an end result in mind. She wondered what Padrig wanted of her.

'Truthfully, I mean you no harm,' he repeated.

Trajan whined. He did not seem to detect any threat. Trusting his instincts, Flavia let him go to Padrig. He trotted up to the man and sniffed around his feet. Padrig stood, legs apart and braced, letting the dog get used to him.

Moistening her dry lips, she said, 'I wanted to talk to you.'

He smiled. 'Then you have me at your disposal. What did you want to talk to me about?'

Good question. What *did* she want to talk to him about? 'I – I am not sure.' Clutching at straws she gabbled out, 'I am curious. I want to know of your village, of your way of life. It is very different to ours, I believe.'

His smile widened. 'In some ways it is very different. In many ways it's the same.'

'How so?'

'My lady, would it be better to sit? This wind is cold. It would be better to take shelter by the oak over there.'

'I –' Flavia was paralysed.

'I mean you no harm, truly,' he said again. His brows rose. 'I dare not imagine what fate would befall me should any injury occur to you and I was found to be to blame. And I am sure this beast of a dog would prove an effective assailant should he think I were harming you, although he seems biddable at the moment.'

Trajan seemed entranced by the man, he was snuffling at him and shoving his mouth into his hand. Padrig's grin deepened a groove in his cheek. 'I am not stupid. I will endeavour to protect you, should any danger come our way. Come, let us walk.'

Flavia sent up a swift prayer to Silvanus and followed him up hill to the clearing in the woods where there was a view of the sea glistening in the distance.

Georgia Hill

# CHAPTER 13

*2* *023*
Juno viewed Roman Field with a new perspective after her chat with Bill. Sitting on the bench early one morning and enjoying the view over to the town and the sea she tried, without much success, to picture the Roman port. She really should have paid more attention to history when at school. Too busy staring out of the window, chewing a pencil and daydreaming stories.

Her family had despaired at her. Expectations to follow her brothers' academic path were high. Horror at her refusal to do so equally so. Her parents compromised on the subject she'd chosen to study only on the promise she'd go to a good university. Her father scratched his head and quietly wondered why his only daughter hadn't gone into teaching with an English degree and, when she hadn't, mostly ignored her. She suspected he'd give her more attention if she was leather bound and contained pages of medieval history. Phillip got away with sociology because he was professor at a Russell Group university. Cris was the favourite. Roman scholar and history lecturer – he fulfilled their parental expectations doubly.

She'd never got on with her mother. Not really that well. Again, the boys took precedence. Juno sometimes wondered if her parents had ever really wanted her, or that she'd been a late life accident, having come along five years after Cris. Her mother had been planning a return to teaching when she'd found out she was pregnant and decided two little boys and a baby, plus an absent-minded husband was too much to deal with on top of working out of the home. Was that behind her mother's odd attitude? Had she wanted Juno to follow in her footsteps as a history teacher and felt rejected when her daughter had done a series of badly paid part-time bar jobs until the writing took off? Juno sighed. Who knew? And, with her mother's preoccupation with being a newly appointed magistrate, it wasn't a conversation she was going to have any time soon.

Taking out her phone she once again studied the photo of the Durotriges man from the museum. It must be some kind of coincidence. Or maybe she'd come across a print of the painting in one of Cris's books, or online? Yes, that must be it. There were billions of images online. She must have seen it somewhere, forgotten all about it and then it had invaded her dream. Then it was pure coincidence she'd been shown the original. Blowing out a deep breath, she decided that was the most logical explanation and put it to the back of her mind.

She concentrated on the view instead. With its gentle slope and wide-open views along the river valley to the sea and the towering cliffs, in Roman Britain it must have been not only a great defensive spot but also a pleasant place to live. Sea views were a premium for coastal property. People prized them and she could see why. Maybe it was the same back then? But where did the town stop and the villa estate begin? And what did it consist of? From what Bill had said about the rowdy hilltribes, she assumed there would be some kind of barracks or military presence too. Was this the garrison Tom had mentioned? And where were these hillforts? Craning her neck, she peered uphill as if to magic one up. Cris was coming over for a visit next week so maybe she'd ask him more then. That's if she could bear the inevitable ribbing she'd get that she was finally taking an interest in anything historical. The image of the Durotriges man flashed into her vision again. He was so clear, striding across the field, the light glinting on his blond hair, that for a moment she thought he really was here, walking amongst the dog walkers. It was busy today and she felt reassured by their presence, the usual knot of anxiety loosened, the crawl of fear between her shoulder blades less.

'Phew. That climb up gets steeper. Hi, Juno!' Annie flung herself down onto the bench.

Juno chased away thoughts of a plaid-wearing bearded man and smiled at her. The woman used a flinger to throw a ball for Maisie, which made Joops bark and dash after it too.

They watched as the dogs hunted for it in the long grass, with Joops and his superior springer nose succeeding.

'Lovely morning.' Annie held up her face to the sun. 'Feels like spring's on its way.' She unzipped her fleece and flapped it to cool down.

'I don't usually see you up here,' Juno said.

'No,' she grimaced, slapping her thighs. 'Too much like hard work but I'm trying to get fitter. When the beach is busy, I sometimes walk Maisie on the flat bit up yonder, in the other field.' She jerked her head uphill.

'I didn't know there was another one.'

'Oh yes.' Annie nodded vigorously, her long earrings flying. 'Walk up to the top of this field, through the kissing gate into the holloway and you'll see it. Easy to spot. If you want, you can park in the layby off Roman Lane, that's the main road into town. It's flatter there before it rises up the hill and Maisie loves the little stream. Not as sociable as here, though, and there's no bin or even a bench but, to be honest, with my hours in the museum it's sometimes all I can manage.'

'I'd be happy to walk Maisie if you're running short on time.'

'Oh, that's ever so kind, Juno. I might take you up on that. And right back at you if you ever need a dog walker.'

The women swapped numbers.

'I've always thought it would be a good idea to have a few dog walkers' numbers anyhow,' Annie said. 'It's easy to turn your ankle in one of these dips. Then you'd be stuck up here. It's alright for you, your Joops would do summat useful like get help. My Maisie would just disappear after rabbits.'

Juno laughed. 'Well, you've got my number now, so any problems you can call me.'

Joops galloped up, ball in mouth, fending off Maisie who ambled round half-heartedly barking.

Annie sighed. 'See what I mean? Totally useless.'

Juno wrestled the ball off Joops, who was very reluctant to give it up and handed it back.

Annie glanced at her watch and stood up. 'That's probably me done for today. You walking back down to the gate?'

Juno made a rapid decision. 'No, I think I'll head up and take a look at this other field. It's a nice day, I'm going to make the most of it.'

'Probably wise. I've heard it'll snow next week. Nice seeing you. Ta-ra!'

'Bye, Annie. Take care.'

The woman didn't look round, she was concentrating on walking over the rough ground but put up her hand in farewell.

Juno whistled to Joops and headed uphill. She traversed the strange bumpy part where she thought she'd seen the weird figure in white and where the mist usually hung in the trees. Today, the sun blazed down from an impossibly blue sky and a robin danced from branch to branch, eyeing her curiously. Spring was making an early appearance. Making her way to the very top of the field she navigated the kissing gate and stood motionless in delight.

'This must be the holloway, Joops.' Juno gazed about her entranced. The holloway was exactly that – a hollow way cut into the ground. The banks on either side soared skywards, crowned with trees, the branches of which met overhead. Leafless now, when they had foliage, it would be a living green tunnel. Exposed tree roots twisted and entwined through the red clay earth and Juno moved closer to run her finger along the patterns and words carved into the bank. Along with graffiti, were hearts, crosses, pentagrams and one or two ominous looking faces. It felt magical and more than a little unnerving. Juno shivered a little. It also felt very ancient.

Joops stiffened and Juno saw the white flash of some bird taking flight through the bare, meandering branches. Clicking her tongue at the dog to follow, she went through the gate into the new field. Now she was alone, the sense of being watched overcame her again but she shrugged it off as paranoia. She'd been in Flete for over two months and was beginning to regain some semblance of confidence. Nothing except positive things had happened to her since she'd been here. And there had been no evidence of Paul sniffing around. It was something she'd been terrified of; that he'd somehow get hold of her new address and follow. Flete had welcomed her, she was making reasonable progress with her book and life was beginning to feel pretty good. Patting her jacket pocket, she reassured herself; at least she had Annie's phone number in case of emergencies.

'Although,' she said to the dog panting at her side, 'I doubt if Annie could come running up that hill fast enough to rescue me.'

It was wet and muddy in the corner of the field by the gate but once she'd made her way through, she was back in a blessedly open field and sunshine again. This field had a very different feel to the other. Where she'd sat on the bench and chatted to Annie was often too crowded with dogs and their owners to be anything but a pleasant place to walk dogs and socialise. The bumpy part at the top, with its trees gnarled like old men and its atmosphere of watchfulness still made fear shiver down the back of her neck. Here, though, it felt peaceful, almost soporific. An out of season bumble bee flitted by and she could hear the babble of running water somewhere.

'Well, this is pretty gorgeous, isn't it, and I think we've got it to ourselves.' She unclipped his lead. 'Off you go, Joops, have a good sniff around, but no rabbit chasing, please.'

The going was rough and uneven and, after the initial flat part, continued uphill so Juno kept her eyes to the ground, giggling slightly thinking that Annie and her twisted ankle rescue mission might be needed sooner than she thought. When she paused to get her breath, she looked up to find Joops nowhere in sight.

'Damn dog. Where are you?' Putting up a hand to shield her eyes from the sun, she spotted movement in the far hedgerow and walked towards it, calling him. His answering bark was a relief. He ran halfway towards her and then doubled back to the man who was standing there. With his bright hair gleaming in the hot sun, it could only be one person.

# CHAPTER 14

'Tom, hi.' Juno hid her displeasure. She'd hoped to have the field to herself having exhausted her store of small talk in the other. Besides, she still wasn't comfortable being on her own with a man. Any man.

'Hello, Juno.' He sounded equally guarded. He was wearing headphones which he slid off and an embarrassed expression which remained.

Juno stared at the tool he held in his hand - *surely not* - 'Are you a metal detector?'

'This is the metal detector.' Tom waggled it. 'I'm a metal detectorist.' He held a long stick-like thing with a circular disc on the end, some kind of monitor on the other and a support which went around his elbow.

Juno couldn't believe it. While Tom may have been offhand and arrogant enough to assume she was interested in him, he hadn't seemed nerdy - and that's what metal detectors were, weren't they? She had a vague picture in her head of a weedy bloke with a huge beard wearing a parka. Tom, with his straw-coloured hair blowing in the breeze and strong sun-tanned face was anything but.

He gave what her mother would call an old-fashioned look as if reading her mind. 'Go on then. Hit me with the jokes.'

She nearly began teasing him about how it came across as a hobby for sad old blokes who had no friends and then remembered how much stick she got as a romance writer, and that Tom hadn't made a single cheap jibe. 'It's just not what I expected you to do, that's all,' she settled for lamely.

'Don't see why not.' He was still gruff. 'Gets you out in the fresh air. Good exercise.'

'I'm sorry. I don't know anything about it apart from the general image.'

'Which is?'

Juno thought hard. There was a TV series her mum was obsessed with a while ago and which Juno had watched to see what all the fuss was about and she remembered someone popping up on the news saying he'd found a load of gold in the Midlands somewhere but that was the extent of her knowledge. She blushed, aware she was being horribly judgmental. Maybe it was all to do with her summary rejection of her family's obsession with all things historical? She had the impression Tom was watching her carefully and felt her face heat more. 'I don't really know.'

'I'm about to break for a coffee. Want to join me?'

Juno looked about, nervous again. There was no one else around but this was Tom, son of her friend and neighbour, so surely it would be okay. 'Where?'

He nodded further up the field. 'There's a raised part up there. In the sun. Good spot. You can share my flask.' He flicked a glance over her. 'That is, unless you don't want to sit on the ground.'

It was a challenge. She shrugged. 'I'm in my dog walking gear, so it's not a problem.'

'Good.' He sounded more cheerful. 'The sun will have dried the dew by now. Follow me.'

They walked for some time and the last stretch was so steep that Juno was happy to sit down, lean on her elbows and catch her breath.

Tom, obviously fitter, sat by her side untroubled by the climb. He reached into his rucksack, brought out a battered flask and unscrewed the top. Filling a cup, he handed it over. 'Just with milk I'm afraid.'

Juno sat up and took it. 'No problem. I don't take sugar.' The springer nosed around a little and then collapsed next to them, panting in the heat. He was perfectly content in Tom's company so that was good enough for her, she trusted the dog's instincts.

They sat in silence, sipping coffee and gazing at the sea which spread vast and tranquilly blue before them, and listening to the birds gearing up for spring. The robin had followed them and hopped about, perhaps in the hope of crumbs. Tom was refreshing company, a man of few words. She began to relax. 'What an amazing place. It feels incredibly peaceful.'

'It is and it does.'

'This lumpy bit we're sitting on, it feels significant somehow.' Juno looked around at the dips and ridges in the ground. 'There's a pattern to the furrows.'

Tom gave a short laugh. 'This lumpy bit is believed to be the lower ramparts of an Iron Age hill fort.'

'Okay.' *So is this where my Durotriges man roamed?*

'It's where the ancient native tribes lived. And still lived even though there was a Roman town down in the valley. And it's where they retreated to after the Romans left. It's probably been a settlement for well over three thousand years.'

Juno was desperate to share her experience of seeing the tribesman's portrait and it being identical to the man in her dream but thought she'd sound mad. 'I've seen a drawing of a hill fort in the museum. It had a fence around it made from tree trunks. They looked like sharpened pencils.'

Tom laughed again but this time it was warmer. 'For defence. They've found hordes of pebbles carted up here from the beach. Great ammo when fired down at an enemy out of breath from running uphill.'

Juno looked about her, trying to picture the round huts with their conical roofs, smoke seeping through the thatch. She remembered something Bill had said. 'Are we talking the Dark Ages?'

'It was settled before then, and even long before the Romans invaded, and afterwards too during the so-called Dark Ages. Historians have been rethinking that period. Some suggest it was a highly organised society rich in culture.'

'But under attack.'

Tom looked surprised. 'Yes. When the Romans went, it left Britannia defenceless to attacks from the Anglo-Saxons. The Romans spent some considerable time shoring up the coastal defences in the southeast. Probably not so much here, although as it was an important port, they may have done. They certainly built a series of outward-looking defence systems in Kent and Essex. There's a theory there was some kind of lookout tower not far from here, but no one's found any evidence of a military presence yet. If the villa ever gets a proper dig, it would be interesting to find out if it had defensive walls. Not all did.' He lay back on his elbows. 'Why are you laughing?'

'I just told myself you didn't say much and then you suddenly get all chatty.'

He picked a stalk of grass and chewed it thoughtfully. 'It's my subject, I suppose.' He fell silent for a minute, then added, 'So you went into the museum and met Old Bill?'

'I did. It was fascinating.'

'Thought you weren't into history?'

Juno pulled a face. 'I didn't think I was. I bumped into Annie, and she invited me to meet her grandmother. They showed me around the museum.'

'Bill's quite a character, isn't she?'

'She is.' Juno finished her coffee, tipped the cup up to shake out the dregs and handed it back. 'Thank you. I'm sorry you had to drink straight out of the flask.'

Tom shrugged. 'I've slummed it worse than that.'

'So tell me about all this.' She nodded to the metal detector. 'When did you start metal detecting?'

'I used to come up here with my dad when I was a little kid. It was his hobby really and I sort of tagged along. Never really got the bug but I'm at a bit of a loose end at the moment so thought it might kill a few hours.'

'Have you found anything today?'

'Yes, as a matter of fact.' He sat up and reached into his breast pocket. 'I found this.' He passed over a coin. 'Late Roman *nummus*. Copper alloy. If you look closely, you can see the image of Constantine I. Makes it mid fourth century.'

Juno examined it. The size of her thumbnail, it was thinner and lighter than its modern equivalent. It was heavily tarnished and green but she could just about make out a winged figure. 'Not from the Iron Age, then?'

He grinned, his face creasing into well-worn grooves. 'Never found anything that old but a Roman coin or two is always exciting.'

Juno thought of its journey through many hands until it had ended up buried in a field in east Devon. *So many stories in one tiny coin.* 'Is it valuable?' She handed it back.

'For its history, yes. I'll donate it to the town museum when I've cleaned it up.'

'I'll have a look next time I'm in.'

'Do that. It's the only thing I've found lately but I've got a feeling there's more up here. If only I can track it down.'

'Is your spidey-sense tingling?'

'Something like that.' He shot her a teasing look. 'In my head I chant, "Spirits of yesteryear take me where the coins appear."'

'You don't!'

'I don't,' he admitted. 'I just wave my metal detector around in the hope of getting a good signal. There *is* an element of instinct about it all, though.'

'And there's me thinking you were a cold-hearted scientist.'

'Well, maybe I am.'

There was an odd frisson to the exchange which Juno couldn't place, but he was certainly proving better company than the other night at his mother's dinner party. 'Has any metal detector I mean, metal detectorist, found anything valuable?'

Tom narrowed his eyes and looked at her from under dark lashes. 'I take it you've never heard of the Staffordshire Hoard then?'

'Might have,' Juno said vaguely. 'But fill me in with the deets.'

'A bloke back in 2009 found some gold items with his metal detector in a field in Staffordshire. Turned out, when the excavation team dug further, to be a hoard of over three thousand gold pieces. It was eventually valued at over three million pounds.'

Juno's jaw dropped. 'Three million. Wow!'

'Exactly.'

'What was it? Jewellery?'

'Some jewels but no jewellery. Bits of a helmet, sword-hilts, a couple of crosses. All Anglo-Saxon. It's in the museum in Birmingham if you want to have a look. "Spirits of yesteryear take me where the coins appear," indeed.'

'How did it get there? *Why* did it get there?' She wasn't really interested in the historical aspect, or even the monetary value; Juno's writing antennae was prickling. It was the story she was interested in.

'Ah, that's the big question. Could be the spoils of battle buried to retrieve later, no one really knows. We can examine the artefacts but that's only half, no, probably a quarter of the truth.'

Juno blew out a breath. 'That's so frustrating.'

Tom laughed again. 'Tell me about it. If you ask me, most of it is about educated guesswork and academic egos desperate to prove their own personal theories.'

She eyed him curiously. It was a loaded remark. 'So, is this what you do? Metal detecting for archaeological digs?'

'No.' He stretched and gave a yawn. 'Although there are professional detectorists who work with archaeologists. I head up archaeological teams.' He lay back and rested a hand over his eyes. 'Mostly worked around the Med. I don't do much actual digging any more, to my chagrin. More likely to be stuck behind a screen wrangling bureaucracy. Not that there's much work around. I've been putting out feelers but nothing's come up.'

The comment didn't ring true. Things were back to normal after the lockdowns and Juno didn't understand why he wasn't heading off abroad again. Maybe he just wanted a few months in Devon.

He yawned again.

'Early start?' she asked, amused. The earlier prickliness between them had vanished. She felt surprisingly relaxed being around him, even if they were alone in the field.

'Mmm. Been up here since six.'

She lay back too. The sun had real warmth now and it was making her drowsy. Peculiarly, although making every effort to avoid men and especially being alone with one, she didn't fear Tom. Thinking about it, she hadn't before. He had annoyed her, aggravated and irritated her with his arrogance but she'd felt safe. It took some getting used to – being safe in the presence of a man. It hadn't happened for a long time. Joops shifted so he lay with his back along her side and she put a lazy hand on his neck. If anything were to happen, he'd guard her. Jupiter, king of the gods and king of dogs. Her special boy. 'What's a holloway?'

'A what?' His words were slurred, on the edge of sleep.

'The lane I had to cross to get here.'

'Oh. It's an ancient routeway. A drover's track.'

His voice was deep and soothing, with a slight gravelly quality. He'd probably be a baritone if he sang. Maybe he did? Juno turned her head so she could watch him. He'd pulled a hat, a scruffy cotton affair, over his eyes. She could only see his well-chiselled cheekbones, his thin face, and his mouth. His skin had that weather-beaten look which spoke of days spent in a hot climate and from which the tan never really fades. 'It felt magical, almost mystical.'

Tom's lips curved into a smile. He had a very full top lip that was decidedly sexy and the beginnings of golden stubble which glistened in the sun. 'Maybe. There's one over Chideock way called Hell Lane. It was a smugglers' route. Over the centuries, the footfall and the wagon wheels wear the ground away so the banks on either side build up or grow up and create a tree canopy. Old native trees. Holloways do feel magical. They're extremely ancient so perhaps it's down to imprinted memories. Or maybe it's just because they're some of the few places we've left undisturbed, unchanged. Left to the ferns and the bluebells, the ash, the oak and the rowan.'

Juno smiled too. It was like being told a bedtime story. A bee buzzed somewhere, and the robin sang in a tree nearby. It was very, very peaceful. Her eyelids drooped, heavy. She closed her eyes and slept; her dreams patterned with vivid green oaks, leaves shifting in the breeze.

# CHAPTER 15

*T*he hills above Moridunum

Having prayed to Silvanus, god of the woods, Flavia agreed to sit at the base of a spreading oak tree. Not yet in leaf, its bulky trunk nevertheless provided shelter from the breeze. It was also within easy sprinting distance of the gate and sanctuary. A robin hopped down, cocked a curious eye and flew off. Flavia took comfort in the fact. Ursa always told her they were a good omen.

'Are you cold, my lady?' Padrig took off his thick plaid cloak and spread it on the ground so she could sit on it.

'Thank you. That is kind.' With Trajan at her side, his enormous body emanating warmth and protection, she felt safe.

Padrig settled against the tree trunk, one leg bent up, the other stretched out long. 'So, what did you want to ask?'

She relaxed her guard. If the man had any intention to hurt her, he'd had ample opportunity to do so already. She looked down, suddenly shy and unable to meet his eyes. She pleated the wool of her cloak into wrinkles. 'I don't know,' she began lamely. 'You have a family?'

'Yes, I have a family.'

She had the impression he was desperately reining in his laughter.

'I have an older brother and two younger sisters.'

'I too, have an older brother. I am lonely now he is gone.'

'I am sorry for that.'

'I have Ursa, my slave.' Flavia tipped her chin up in defiance. She would not have him pity her. 'She is my constant companion.'

'But not today.'

'No. Not today.' Flavia pulled a face. 'If she discovers I have ventured out on my own again, she will be angry.'

A sardonic brow rose. 'You allow your slave to be angry with you?'

'Well, I suppose she is a friend, too.'

'But one you own?'

Flavia tossed her head. 'Is that not how it is?'

'In your world maybe.'

'Ursa is good and loyal. She will come to no harm in my employ. I take it there are no slaves in your community?'

Padrig gave a short, harsh laugh. 'Only the ones who have been seized by our conquerors. Some families of the Durotriges over in the east I believe, take slaves but no, it's not done in my village.'

Flavia pictured her life without slaves to cook for her, to attend her in the bathhouse, to prepare her hair and face oils – and failed. 'So what tasks do you have? Do you weave?'

'Aye. And make pots and weapons and dye cloth. Knead bread, make pottage, tend to our livestock, our horses. Live.'

'How do you cook?'

'How do *you* cook?' The amusement was back.

'I oversee those in the kitchen, of course. Liaise with our cooks.' She plucked a handful of grass and regretted it, as her fingers stained green. That would take explaining. She held out her hand and observed her ruined nails from where they had bitten into the wall and sighed.

'Those are not hands which pluck feathers or chop onions,' Padrig observed.

'They are not. Even so, I shall have to soak them in rosewater and almond oil when I return.' She glanced at his, the fingers of which were long and strong. 'Do you pluck feathers and chop onions?' she asked, half tongue in cheek.

'I do not. That is woman's work.'

'Are you too grand for such menial tasks?'

'But we do not consider it menial work. It is important to feed bellies, is it not? My people, unlike your society, consider women equal but different. They have equivalent status within the tribe. In fact, many of our leaders have been women. Unlike your Caesars. But yes, the cooking is done by the women and yes, as the second son of the chieftain, it is not expected of me.'

So she was right. He was high-born. Or as high-born as a tribesman could be. 'What do you do with your time, then?'

He eased his shoulders back against the tree trunk and gave a great sigh. 'Mostly my time is taken up with politics.' Flicking a leaf off his knee, he added, 'I am a peacekeeper. A go-between. I listen to my father and brother and take their concerns to your people. I take back your people's demands and report them to my village. It is tedious in the extreme.'

'Would you prefer war?'

Padrig hesitated. 'Perhaps some in my village would.' He rubbed away the crease between his brows with a weary hand. 'No man prefers war but if it comes then a war it will have to be.'

Flavia was mystified. 'But our people have lived alongside one another, married one another for centuries. My own family can trace its roots back to a Briton; a woman who my great-grandfather married when he retired from the Legion. We have many of your people living in town, some of whom have learned to live like us.'

'And many have no choice, as you have enslaved them,' he bit back.

'This is true. But, with a good master or mistress, the life is not so bad. Work, food, a roof over their heads.'

'But not their freedom.'

'No.' Flavia went quiet. She vowed to ask how Ursa felt about her status. She'd taken the woman for granted. Now, she doubted her loyalty. It was a paid for luxury. 'I had not considered it so. Do you not think we live alongside well, though?'

'Perhaps. Mostly. But Rome's demands grow ever more unreasonable. The taxes ever higher. My people will take only so much.'

'You have no power against the Roman army.'

'I believe Boudicca had some success.'

Flavia laughed scornfully. She knew the old tale. A one-off and centuries ago. 'And look at what happened. Her daughters defiled, Boudicca herself took poison to escape our wrath.'

'The story I was told, at my grandfather's knee, was that she did not die,' Padrig said carefully. 'That she is lying, still breathing, all these centuries later and will return to lead us again.'

'I do not believe in such magic,' Flavia answered scornfully. There was a pause and the light teasing banter of their earlier conversation disappeared. 'You say there are barbarian hordes at the gate of Rome? You told me so at the market.'

'You remember that?' He sat up and hugged his knees. He pulled thoughtfully at one of his boot ties. 'There are some who say Rome is tired of governing this northern province so far distant. There are some who say they are unwilling to defend us against the enemy which comes at us from the east.' He met her eyes. 'There are some who say Rome will return to Rome.'

Flavia shivered under his gaze. She had heard her father speak of such things. It was another cause of his anxiety and bad temper. Another reason behind his febrile preoccupation to find a way back to Rome. He termed it going home but *this* was their home. Her father had been born here, as had his father. But still he called Rome his home. And still it wrenched at him. 'I should like to go to Mediolanum.' It was only a half lie. 'I should like to see my brother again.'

'And you may have your wish.'

She tugged her clothes around her; the damp from the ground, despite the protection of Padrig's thick cloak, had chilled her through. 'I must go.'

'Perhaps we will meet again? To talk? I have enjoyed it.'

She was surprised. 'Have you? I thought we argued.'

'I like to argue.' He said it mildly. He stood up and reached down a hand. 'Let me help you.'

His touch was like Jupiter's bolt, like lightning from the sky. As she stood the breath left her body. She inched nearer, he smelled of the trees and the earth and leather.

He lowered his mouth and for one heady moment she thought he might kiss her – the impudence of the man – but instead his eyes dropped to her necklace. She had made a clumsy attempt at re-threading the rescued sea glass beads onto a rough leather thong.

Looping his little finger around it, thrillingly grazing her breastbone, he lifted it gazing intently. 'Not the jewels I expect the daughter of a powerful man to wear.'

She felt herself blush furiously, remembering when she had nearly been caught spying on him. 'I broke the original. I was careless and the beads scattered to the winds and the water. I mended it as best I could.'

'My sister can do better work. May I?'

She nodded, mute from an emotion which flooded through her but which she did not understand.

Gently, he lifted the necklace over her head, taking care not to disturb her hair.

Flavia couldn't control her breathing; it came shallow and fast. She was aware of her body in a way she never had before. His touch was nectar and she wanted to drink deep.

Her breasts rose and fell, and she longed for him to reach out and cup them, to bury his mouth between. Inching her mouth to his, their lips were but a gossamer thread apart.

'May we meet again.' A wry smile twitched at the corner of his mouth.

He had a very full bottom lip and she longed her mouth to meet his. 'I wish it so.'

He trickled the beads through his fingers. 'And now we must for I have to return your necklace.'

Their eyes held for a second and something powerful passed between them. It shocked Flavia with its urgency. Desperate to get away to the peace of her room and analyse all that had happened between her and this strange, intoxicatingly different man, she murmured, 'I must go.' Backing off, not understanding herself and the need which hammered at her body, she called on Juno for protection. 'I really must go.'

He, too, was breathing heavily. Frowning, his voice guttural, he said, 'So you keep saying. Let me see you to the gate and the safety of your home.'

'There's no need.' How could she tell him she was possibly safer out here in the bosky woods and with him, than confined in the villa with Balbus lurking, festering sweatily at every corner.

Padrig looked around. 'There's every need, my lady.' He stepped away, with seeming reluctance. 'Come. Let me see you home.'

Followed by the faithful Trajan, they walked back towards the villa's walls, the scented damp of the salt-laden sea whipped up the valley by the breeze. It misted around them and clung to their clothes, tiny beadlets of moisture standing proud on the wool.

# CHAPTER 16

*2023*

*2* 'Aww, babe, I mean it's not north Devon but it's pretty good here.' Mabyn whirled around, stumbling on the pebbles. She spread her arms wide and sucked in a deep breath. 'So good to smell the sea again.' The sea breeze whipped her curly red hair across her face. 'Even if the damp air makes my hair frizzy.'

Juno laughed. She'd picked up her friend from the London train. Mabyn, Devon born and bred, worked in a lowly position at the Victoria and Albert. They'd met at a yoga class, had hit it off and had been thrown out for giggling too much when the male instructor's leggings had revealed rather more than they wanted to see. Although they'd never returned to yoga, a firm friendship had grown. Mabyn had seen her through the worst of the situation with Paul, even through the times when he had actively discouraged Juno from seeing any 'unapproved' friends.

They'd brought Joops straight down to the beach for a walk as Mabyn had proclaimed, after months of stuffy London, she was desperate for the sea again. Picking up on her excitement, the springer barked and shot off towards the water, plunging in with glee. The women shrieked and ran after him.

Juno clipped him back on his lead. 'That's ruled out a café lunch then. We'll have to take him back and dry him off. Stinky wet dog smell isn't generally tolerated.'

'Oh, I don't mind, honeybun. As long as there's decent coffee and a chance for a natter, I'm good.' She looked directly into Juno's eyes. 'Been too long.'

Juno swallowed with emotion. 'It has. It's so good to see you again, Mabs.'

Her friend took her arm, and they began to walk back to the car. 'I can't wait to see this house of yours.'

'I wouldn't get your hopes up. As estate agents say, "it's an ideal renovation project."'

Mabyn winced. 'A money pit in other words. Lots of period features though?'

Juno unlocked the car. 'Yeah, if you count wall-to-wall pebbledash and damp.'

Her friend got in, giggling. 'You're really selling it.'

'Well, you weren't wrong in saying it needs a bit of work,' Mabyn said, once she'd been given the tour round. 'I mean, it only needs a new bathroom, kitchen, complete redecoration ...'

'New windows and central heating and I suspect the roof needs looking at, too,' Juno finished. 'Sorry about the size of your bedroom by the way.'

'It's alright. I only need a bed and I'm all out of cats to swing anyway.' Mabyn picked up a smooth grey pebble from the growing collection on the kitchen windowsill. 'I see you're adding your own touches though. Something irresistible about beachcombing, isn't there?'

Juno thought about the blue sea glass on her bedroom windowsill. 'I come back with pocketfuls of shells too. I don't get near any driftwood though, Joops gets to it first.'

It was warm enough to sit outside so they took their coffee and sandwiches and perched on two rickety kitchen stools.

'I need to invest in some garden furniture I suppose.' Juno stared across the scrappy patch of grass; there was barely enough to mow. It could be lovely though, with a bit of care and attention. It faced south-west and was a real suntrap. A rose scrambling over the fence, maybe, or a honeysuckle or jasmine? Or even some container grown vegetables? They didn't take up much room. A half smile crept over her face. She didn't have much of an idea about plants. *Maybe start by investing in a couple of chairs and a table?* At least she could take those with her when she left. *If* she left, she amended. A robin flew down and landed on the fence. Her mother always said they were a sign of a loved one thinking of you. He cocked his eye hopefully and then flew off disappointed. Perhaps she could get some bird seed and a feeder too? She loved watching garden birds, and robins were her favourite. Always so cheery. Wondering how the ever-present gulls fitted into the cosy scenario she was creating, she frowned.

Mabyn looked across. 'You planning on staying?'

'That's the problem. I don't know what Mum and Dad have in mind for the house. The original plan was to sell it.'

'Could you buy it off them? Could you be happy here, do you think?'

Juno thought over the two and half months she'd been here. 'Bit too early to tell.' There was no denying she liked living here and was getting nesty, despite the damp. She'd seen from Diana's house how it could look, with some money spent on it. A garden room like hers would be fabulous addition. 'In theory it's a good place to write being so quiet but I've been struggling to get the words down lately.'

'Why?'

Juno frowned. 'I've got a bit distracted.' She went on to explain about the visit to the museum and her new interest in Flete as a Roman town.

'Doesn't sound like you to be into history. Didn't think it was your bag at all.'

'I didn't either. I'm confused why I'm finding it all so fascinating.'

'Of course, the past is fascinating. You're talking to a historian here.'

'Duly noted. It's just that I've always taken pains to avoid anything even vaguely historical. Had enough shoved at me at home. Speaking of which, do you fancy trying the new bar that's opened up? Big bro is coming over from Exeter for the evening and I thought we'd hit the town.'

'Ooh,' Mabyn made a face. 'A new bar! Get you.'

'Alright. Alright. It's not anything like you've got but it's the talk of Flete.' Juno shrugged. 'Seeing as not a lot happens in Flete, this counts as news with a capital N.'

Mabyn pointed her sandwich. A slice of cheese fell out which Joops caught before it hit the ground. 'Sounds good to me. And I may have loads of stuff in the big metropolis, but I haven't any money to spend there. Getting wicked expensive in the city, girlfriend. I can see somewhere like here has an appeal but maybe see through a summer season before you make the decision.'

'You mean to see what it's like when things start opening up again?'

'Get off Joops, the rest of this sarnie is mine.' Mabyn shooed the dog away and shook her head, sending her red curls flying. 'I mean, see how it is with the tourists.'

'Ah. I can't see it getting all that busy here.'

'You'd be surprised. The Parents reported the last few years, before folk could go abroad again, Woolacombe was rammed.'

'How are they?'

'They're good. Send their love.'

'You going to see them?'

'Yeah. I'll go on from here for a couple of days.' She stretched and held her face up to the sun. 'It's good to get out of London. So, you've really got that man out of your system?'

For a second, Juno wondered how she knew about Tom. Her thoughts meandered back to the field and lying in the sunshine. After sleeping next to one another for an hour or so, they'd woken, had a mumbled embarrassed conversation and parted ways. It had been strange how relaxed she'd felt with him. And heartening. There was a time when she thought she'd never be able to trust another man ever again.

'Juno?'

'Who? Oh, you mean Paul.'

Mabyn turned. 'Intriguing. Don't tell me you've got a hot guy in tow down here already?'

Juno could feel herself blush. She let her hair fall over her face. 'Mabs, you can be the soul of tactlessness sometimes.'

'Sorry, honeybun. Didn't think. But you never had any problems attracting the men, did you? I was always the ugly bestie who tagged along.'

'That is so not true, and you know it. And there is no new guy, I can assure you. It's the last thing I want. I'm more than happy with this little man here, even if he is a food thief.' Joops trotted up, grinning expectantly. She gave him the crust off her sandwich which had gone dry in the hot sun.

'So, what really happened between you and Paul? I could never figure out that relationship.'

'You weren't alone.' Juno took in a deep breath, flaring her nostrils. 'He was,' she gulped, it was hard to admit, 'your average classic abuser. Love bombed me to begin with, showered me with affection and expensive stuff, weekends in Barcelona, that sort of thing.'

'Yeah, I remember that phase. You were off all over the place.' Joops nudged Mabyn's hand. 'What did you do with this chap here?' She tugged his ears gently.

'Dog sitter. Joops hated it but I was so besotted by that point I didn't notice. Still feel guilty. Paul tried to get me to rehome him, but it was about the only thing I stood my ground on.'

'Well, he's not the ideal breed for London.'

'That's what Paul said. Looking back, I think he was jealous of how much of my time Joops took up.' She shook her head slowly. 'I can't believe I was so stupid. So blind not to see what he was like.'

'He didn't hurt him, though, right?' Mabyn said, horrified. She tickled under the dog's chin. 'I mean, how could anyone hurt this fella. Look at those eyes!'

Juno gave a short laugh. 'He's on the scrounge for more cheese. To answer your question,' she said slowly, 'I don't know. Something happened. I was on a book signing tour and Paul promised me he'd look after him. When I got back, Joops was all subdued. I put it down to him pining for me while I'd been away but now I'm not so sure.'

'God, that's awful Ju. Bastard. Anyone who hurts animals comes high up my hit list.' She took the springer's face between her hands. 'How could anyone hurt you, little man?' Releasing him whereupon he licked clean her abandoned plate, she added, 'Oh, gross!' Turning her full attention on her friend, she said, 'What exactly happened between you two, then? I mean, what *really* happened?' Mabyn put out a hand. 'I was so worried about you, you know. But it was impossible to get past Paul. You know he even told me, when I rang you once, that you didn't want to have anything to do with me anymore. Think his phrase was, "She's moved on to more grown-up things." I knew you hadn't said anything of the sort. I knew it wasn't you. I mean, we all accepted when you and he were in the loved-up phase no one else existed, that's what couples are like, isn't it, but then we hit lockdown and I thought at least we'd have a catch up Zoom or something but nothing.'

Juno was silent for a moment. Everything Mabyn had said was true. When she and Paul had first got together, they'd shut the rest of the world out. It had been exciting being in that bubble of love and attention he'd surrounded her with. No one else had ever taken that much notice of her before. In her family she was the third wheel, the girl child, the one who was determined to be as anti-academic as the others were pro. At university she'd not been the star pupil but hadn't struggled either and muddled along to get her 2:1. She'd crashed on a couch in London, disappearing into the murky world of short-term contracts and zero hours in bars and restaurants until getting her first success with a book. Even then, she hid behind a pseudonym. When Paul had hit on her in the bar she was working in, she'd rebuffed him as yet another posh bloke in a suit. He'd come back every night for a fortnight until she agreed to go out with him, bringing her daft little presents; a bunch of wildflowers, a tiny mug with her name on it, a sparkly blue collar when he found out she had a dog. The cutting out of her friends had been so gradual, she hadn't noticed until near the end. Lockdown had made things so much worse. She'd moved into his flat by then, the lure of somewhere quietly luxurious had been too much to ignore. And then it had begun. The mind games, the gas-lighting, escalating to physical violence. And still she stayed. He'd convinced her she had nowhere to go, no one else who would love her the way he did. It wasn't until he'd decided to end things and announced she had to move out as someone called Madeleine was moving in, that she began to wake up from the stupor.

'I can't tell you how grateful I was that you took me and Joops in.'

'No biggie. Girl, you were traumatised. I could see that. Your parents never liked him, did they? To be honest, neither did I.'

'You could've told me I was screwing over my life.'

'Only five years of it, honeybun, and would you have listened?'

'Probably not.'

'Did you love him?'

'Love?' Juno screwed up her face as she analysed it. 'I'm not sure it was love. Lust certainly. But I was more mesmerised by him. In thrall. It was as if he'd convinced me I couldn't exist without him, without his permission.' She shuddered. 'Never known anything like it.'

'Even when he was hitting you?'

Juno started. 'How did you know?'

'Didn't take much working out. You'd lost about two stone, had this hunted look and shadows under your eyes an

FBI agent could hide in. Besides, remember, my sis is a social worker. She's told me enough tales; I recognised the signs.'

'And I still didn't leave him.'

'That's what men like him do. Play with your mind until you can't think straight. And I bet after he hit you, he'd love bomb you some more.'

Juno nodded. She covered her face with her hands. 'I'm so ashamed. I'm so embarrassed,' she whimpered.

Mabyn got up and pulled her friend to her in a hard hug. 'You have nothing to be ashamed or embarrassed about, my friend. *He's* the one who should be that. But he won't be. He doesn't think there's anything wrong in what he does. I bet he told you it was you making him do those things?'

Juno nodded against her.

'Thought so. I hope there's a very special, extremely, violently hot place in hell for him.'

Juno had never heard her friend sound so vitriolic. She tried to soak up all the strength and confidence that Mabyn had. If she could be half the person Mabs was, she'd be something.

'I'm just glad I was there for you, and I could get you to your parents. You were in no fit state to sort yourself out. You were barely making any sense.'

'I remember.' Vaguely. Juno sniffed. Packing up her things, grabbing the dog and getting a cab to Mabyn's had been a blur. The one clear memory was of Paul holding her by the throat as he said, 'It's been good, kiddo. But all good things come to an end.' Then he'd shoved her up against the door jamb and kissed her. She'd had the bruises on her shoulder blades for days afterwards. The scars inside were still there. 'I just wanted to be somewhere safe,' she said with a trembling voice. 'I just wanted to lie down somewhere safe knowing I could sleep. The exhaustion was –' she let the sentence trail.

'Well, I'm just glad I've got my bestie back.' Mabyn released her, fished out a tissue and handed it over. 'And now you've got this place. Begin-Again Cottage. It could be amazing, refurbishment project or not. It's a fresh start, honeybun. A new you. Now you've got somewhere of your own to feel safe.'

Juno clutched her friend's hand. 'I have,' she replied. 'I have.'

Georgia Hill

# CHAPTER 17

They decided to try out the new bar that evening. Sea spray gusted at them as they turned the corner onto the sea front, so they resigned themselves to eating inside rather than on the terrace. Scurrying past the stacked-up chairs and the umbrellas tightly furled against the fierce wind beating off the sea, they stood in the entrance, shaking off the slick of seawater. The place was packed.

'I hope we can find somewhere to sit,' Juno said, looking around the crowded bar, at the fake white columns and the marble-topped tables. 'Cris said he might come over tonight.'

'Your brother?' Mabyn yelled, over the racket. 'It would be good to meet him.'

Juno tried to catch the eye of a busy waiter and failed. 'Yes. He said he'd make it if he could. I haven't seen him since I moved here which is daft as he's only in Exeter.'

'Juno! Over here. Come and share our table.' It was Diana Lyndsay. She was sitting at a table by the window, Tom at her side.

They squeezed their way through the crush. It was protected from the worst of the noise here. 'Do you mind?' Juno asked. 'We don't want to spoil your evening.'

'Of course you won't spoil our evening,' Diana replied. 'If I'm honest, you'll make it.' She waggled her brows. 'Only so much metal detecting talk a mother can take.'

After they'd settled and made their introductions, Tom ordered them all drinks on his phone. 'Quicker this way,' he explained. 'When I went to the bar, it was three deep.'

'I hadn't expected it to be so busy,' Juno said. 'I suppose, with it being new, everyone wants to check it out. I didn't think it was your sort of place, Diana?'

The woman leaned forward. 'To tell you the truth it isn't. Although, after my first Pineapple Nero, I'm warming to it.'

'Pineapple Nero?'

'I gather it's a Roman take on a Pina Colada.'

'Oh,' Juno said. 'Bit of a stretch of the concept. What makes it Roman?'

Tom's lips twitched. 'This.'

A girl in a white toga came to their table, holding a tray aloft. She had a coronet of gold leaves slightly askew on her piled up hair. 'A Pineapple Nero, two glasses of white and a pint?' she asked breathlessly, looking harassed. 'Ooh, hello, Mrs Lyndsay.'

'Hello Amelia-Mae.'

'It's rammed in here tonight and they haven't put on enough staff. I'm doing the owner a favour, like.' She slid the tray onto the table, spilling some of Tom's beer. 'I'm ever so sorry if it's not right.'

'You're doing fine, Amelia,' Diana said reassuringly. 'And we've hardly had to wait at all. How's your little brother?'

Amelia put out the drinks and flicked beer off the tray, narrowly missing Mabyn. 'He's good, ta. Just joined the navy.'

'Oh, my goodness. Time flies. Give him my love when you see him, won't you?'

'I will. He always said you were the only teacher he could stand.'

Diana laughed. 'Well, I can't say he was the easiest of pupils, but he was one of the most rewarding.'

'He always remembers your impersonations of the queen.' Amelia giggled.

'It was the only way I could get him out of one of his rages. I used to talk him down using a posh, high-pitched voice.'

'Yeah, he's still got a temper.' She glanced towards the bar. 'Talking of tempers, I'm getting the rage from the boss.' She hitched up the shoulder of her toga. 'Gawd, I'm cursing whoever decided wearing these things would be a good idea. Enjoy your drinks. Give me a shout if you want anything to eat, I'll get it shoved to the top of the kitchen list.'

'That's very kind. Have a good evening and don't work too hard.' After she'd gone, Diana pulled her cocktail towards her and sipped through the straw. 'What?' she asked as she saw Tom staring in amusement.

'One day it'll be possible to go out in Flete and not bump into one of your previous pupils.' Tom pulled a comical face at Juno. 'Happens every time.'

'One of the disadvantages of living in a small community?' She grinned back.

'I think it's nice,' Mabyn put in, flicking a knowing look at Juno. *'He's lush,'* she mouthed, hiding behind her glass of wine. Addressing the group, she added, cheerily, 'I love going home to Woolacombe and bumping into all my old mates.'

'Room for another?' A tall man, smelling of cold and damp, squeezed through the crowds to their table.

'Cris!' Juno cried. 'You made it. This is my brother, everyone. Cris, this is Diana Lyndsay my neighbour, her son Tom and my pal from London, Mabyn. You'll have heard me mention her.'

He squeezed his length onto a chair in between Juno and Tom. 'Good to meet you all.' Taking off his glasses, he polished them with the edge of his shirt. 'Rough night out there, but I'm glad I made the effort.' He gazed about him, laughing boyishly. 'This place is quite something. Very worth the bother of coming out.'

'And I'm glad you did. I haven't seen you since Christmas. Beer? You can sofa slum if you want to have a drink.'

'After the week of meetings I've had, that sounds like an excellent plan.'

'Get off, you love your job like a man possessed.'

'I do. I cannot lie.'

He began to get up, but Tom stopped him. 'Nah mate. I'll order you one from here, it's quicker.' They had a brief exchange about what craft beers were on offer and then Tom ordered, asking, 'Shall I get another round in while I'm at it?'

'Not for me,' Diana answered. 'I've hardly touched this one.'

'Juno, Mabyn? Cocktail?'

Juno eyed up Diana's drink. It was a vicious yellow with chunks of oranges and pineapple decorating the rim and maraschino cherries bobbing about. 'Why not? If we don't get served food, I can eat the fruit to stave off starvation.'

Amelia-Mae repeated the ritual a few minutes later.

Cris watched in slack-jawed amazement. When she had once again returned to the bar, he asked, 'Is she *really* wearing a toga?'

'It's a Roman-themed bar, Cris,' Juno pointed out.

'But hardly authentic. Only men who were citizens of Rome were entitled to wear togas and even then only in official ceremonies.'

'That's just what I said!' Tom exclaimed in triumph.

'Oh, don't start him off,' Diana giggled. 'I had all that for the first ten minutes we were sat down.'

'It's a bar, Cris,' Juno said, 'not a museum.'

'Even so, they ought to –'

'Get it right,' Tom finished.

Diana groaned.

'Maybe we'd better not tell our lovely waitress that togas were also worn by prostitutes to denote they were fallen women!' Cris grinned.

'I don't think that would go down at all well with Amelia-Mae so I'd rather you didn't,' Diana reproved, in best teacher fashion and they all laughed.

'Of course!' Tom tapped the side of his head. 'Juno's brother. You're Crispin Eden.' He held out a hand for Cris to shake. 'Tom Lyndsay.'

'The Ephesus dig man?'

'That's me.'

Cris took his hand and shook it vigorously. 'Good to meet you.'

'Honoured to meet you. Your reputation goes before you.' The men clinked pint glasses.

This time it was Juno's turn to groan. 'I sense kindred spirits. No history talk, please.'

Cris ruffled her hair. 'Nice to see you haven't changed, little sis. Still a denier of history.'

Ducking out of the way, she replied airily, 'You'd be surprised. I'm getting interested, I've even visited the town museum. It's just I could do with a night out not centred around discussing the finer points of fashion in ancient Rome.'

Mabyn and Diana had begun a spirited conversation about teaching so Juno shifted her attention to Tom. 'Been out metal detecting again? Tom's a metal detector,' she explained to her brother, expecting him to laugh.

Instead, he raised a brow. 'Metal detectorist, don't you mean?'

Juno felt wrong-footed. The cocktail must have gone to her head. She didn't usually make cheap shots.

'Found anything lately?' Cris asked Tom.

Tom rummaged in his jacket pocket. 'As a matter of fact, yes.' He held up a polythene sandwich bag containing a coin. It was muckier than the one he'd shown her in the field, a gloomy greenish-brown. 'This is the second I've found recently. The other is Constantine.'

Cris took it from him and peered at it with interest. He held it up to the light. 'Fascinating. This one might be earlier.'

'Yup. I think so too. I'll know more when I've cleaned it up.'

'Where are you finding them?'

Tom glanced at Juno. 'In the field beyond the holloway, off Roman Lane.'

Cris nodded. 'I know it. Let me know if you find anything else, will you? Might be a chance to get some of the students out on an exercise. Who owns the land?'

'Roman Field, where the villa is supposed to be, is owned by the Calder Estate but the field on the other side of the holloway is council owned. I've permission to detect on both sides so I've got contacts who would help if you wanted to dig.'

Cris gave the bag back and Tom put it away. 'So, you headed back to Turkey?'

Tom took a deep swallow of beer before he answered. 'Things are slow in getting started up again. Word on the street is that Turkey is choosing to front digs with their own people at the moment.'

'Makes sense. Plenty of work in this country if you're interested. I'd be happy to ask around if you like? You'd have to do a few commercial contracts, though. There's a big housing development planned for over Exeter way and the land needs surveying and checked out first.' Cris shrugged. 'I mean it's a bit below what you're used to, but it would pay the bills until you get something else.'

Juno thought Tom looked unhappy but he nodded and said thank you. 'So, do you use metal detectorists in your digs, Cris?' she asked her brother.

'Yeah, of course. They're really useful. They often bring sites to our attention and we employ them to help with the initial survey and the geo-phys.'

'Oh.'

Tom grinned. 'Not so nerdy after all, then?'

'Depends on your point of view,' she replied with asperity.

Cris sighed dramatically. 'Oh, you'll never convince my little sis of the merits of studying the past. She's too busy with her made up people. Did you know she wanders around with voices in her head?'

Juno remained silent, concentrating on her drink. It was a well-worn family joke. *She* was a well-worn family joke.

'I did,' Tom said mildly. 'And, according to my mother, does very well out of them. You've had several best-sellers haven't you Juno?'

She was so surprised at his support she spluttered into her straw.

Cris slapped her on her back. 'Don't be so shocked, sis. Several of my students admit to reading you. I'm almost ready to confess we're related.'

'Thanks,' she mumbled.

'Are you three discussing Juno's books?' Diana asked, butting in. 'I can't tell you how much I loved the last one. You have such a talent, dear girl.'

'Of course she has,' Mabyn added, loyally.

'I now have a complete set of signed copies so I can swank to all my friends,' Diana said. 'I'm going to put them in pride of place on the sitting room shelf.'

Cris's brows shot up. He looked around at them all. After a pause, and looking surprised, he raised his glass. 'Then cheers and congratulations to Juno.'

'Cheers,' Diana echoed. 'And congratulations to Eden Loveday too!'

Georgia Hill

# CHAPTER 18

Several hours later the group stumbled, slightly drunkenly, along Church Lane back to the cottages. Diana peeled off saying she was calling it a night, so Juno invited Tom to join them for coffee.

After an excited Joops had rapturously greeted them all and had bounced off some energy in the back garden, they settled in the tiny lounge, with Tom seated at the table, Mabyn and Cris on the sofa and Juno on the floor. She leaned against the wall, a devoted springer half sitting in her lap.

'You spoil that dog,' Cris said.

Juno tugged gently on one softly feathered ear. 'He deserves to be spoiled. For a long time, he was my only friend.'

'We would've done more to help, sis, had we known.'

'I know. I think I had to be ready to accept help. And thanks to Mabyn here, I got out.' Turning to Tom, she added, 'I've just emerged from an abusive relationship.' *Goodness, the alcohol has loosened my tongue!*

'Ah.' He peered at the table and followed a groove worn into the wood with his finger.

Juno couldn't work out if he was feeling awkward or being tactful. He was a very difficult man to read sometimes. He'd caught the sun, it must be all the days spent metal detecting and it had burnished his blond hair lighter. As he bent his head, she could see the tan line from the neck of his t-shirt. *He's a good-looking man.* The thought came unbidden. Shame she wasn't in the right place in her head to go looking for a man. Observing his strong hands gripping his mug, it occurred to her that as well as being good-looking, he was also intelligent and exciting. Downright sexy in fact. She thought back to how she'd happily fallen asleep beside him in the field. Somehow, she'd trusted him in a way that was unexpected and touching. But it was definitely too soon to think about a relationship. Besides, hadn't he warned her off?

'What?' He met her stare with his startlingly blue and direct gaze.

She felt the heat rise in her face. She mustn't fall for him. He had complication written all over him. 'Nothing.' Hiding her face in her mug, she tuned in to the conversation Cris and Mabyn were having. Cris was explaining how his week had consisted of endless meetings and how frustrating he found departmental politics. They seemed to be getting on well. She watched them curiously. To her knowledge, Cris hadn't had a serious relationship since his student days. He was in danger of developing into an old fogey. She smiled at the sight of him, in his horn-rimmed specs and tweed jacket that actually had leather patches on its elbows. No wonder her parents despaired of either of them ever settling down. At least Cris had a career they understood. Just as well their older brother was providing the obligatory happily married life and grandchildren. *Thank God I didn't get pregnant with Paul!* The thought came suddenly and was unwelcome. It horrified her so much her breath choked in her throat. For a second his face loomed in front of her, so vivid he could almost be in the room. A baby would have trapped her even more. And what sort of father would Paul have been? The idea of him harming her child had her gasping and clutching her middle in panic.

'You alright, Juno?' It was Tom, his voice warm with concern.

'Fine,' she stuttered out. 'I'm fine.' To change the subject and make the ghost of Paul disappear, she added, 'Show me this latest coin then.'

For the second time that evening, he reached into his pocket and pulled out the plastic bag. Handing it over, he said in dry tones, 'I didn't think you were interested.'

'Maybe I'm not. Not in dates and wars and things but this is something a person gripped in their hand. It has all sorts of stories attached.' She held it up to the light of the standard lamp. 'Someone used this to buy stuff. What sort of things?' She turned it to get a better look. It was hard to see any marks but it was recognisably a coin.

'Who knows? The usual. The sort of things we buy now. Wine, olives, dates, cloth. Coins were used to pay soldiers too. If Flete was the important harbour we think it was, goods – and people – from all over the Empire would have landed here. It would have been a vibrant, multi-cultural sort of place. Or maybe this one had been used to pay the ferryman.'

Juno looked at him. 'The ferryman?'

He tutted but with humour and not unkindly. 'Your classical education is sadly lacking. In ancient Greece, when someone died, you had to pay the ferryman. In mythology, Charon must be paid to take you across the river Styx to Hades. A coin was put under the tongue or over the eyes.'

'And in Roman mythology?'

'It's much the same. The Romans took on the Greek myths as their own, simply changing names. The king of the gods, Zeus, became Jupiter. Aphrodite became Venus, Athena Minerva and so on, but the stories remained the same. I take it you haven't got far through the book on Greek myths that you borrowed.'

'I haven't, but I will. As you pointed out, my classical knowledge is woeful.'

Tom laughed. 'I didn't mean to insult. It's a surprisingly good read. I always think of Greek myths as a bit like an ongoing drama or soap opera. Everyone connected and squabbling. My favourite is the myth of Perseus and Andromeda.'

'Ah, I read that one! Yes, that was good. Andromeda chained up on the rocks as fodder for the sea serpent until Perseus swooped in and saved her.' She gave him a keen look. 'You like a damsel in distress, then?'

He shifted uncomfortably but remained silent.

Taking pity, she rescued him. 'I promise I'll definitely read them all, I love a good story.' Juno stared at the coin. 'So your spidey-sense was bang on. There was something else to be found up there.' She shivered lightly. 'There's a whole story here. I might be the first person to touch it for – how long?'

'Two thousand years. Although I think this one's early fourth century. So maybe only sixteen hundred or so.'

A smile curved her lip. 'Ah. Only sixteen hundred years.'

'And technically you're the third person to touch it in all that time, after me and your brother over there.'

'Trust him to get there before me. He did when we were kids too.'

'You seem close.'

'I suppose. I'm far fonder of him than of my older brother. We're closer in age. Some days I can even forgive Cris for being the family favourite, following Dad into history lecturing. Dad's a medievalist though.'

Tom winced. 'The modern stuff.'

'Yes. Suppose.' She laughed and handed the coin back to him. 'What happens to it now?'

'Now I've found two, I'll report the finds to the FLO.'

'Flo? Who's she?'

'He. Guy called Max. He's our Finds Liaison Officer. Works out of the museum in Exeter. FLOs work under the Portable Antiquities Scheme and record finds. Strictly speaking I don't have to report such a small find, but

I think Max will be interested, especially seeing where I found it.'

'Is he another backing the theory that Flete was a major Roman settlement?'

Tom looked surprised.

'I got chatting to Bill in the museum.'

'Ah. Old Bill. Great character. And yes, Max also thinks Flete was once Moridunum. It's just that none of us have a lot of evidence to back up his claim.'

Juno nodded to the coin Tom was still holding. 'Well, you've got two Roman coins now.'

He looked rueful. 'They're not all that unusual. Lots found in fields right across England although rarer in the far southwest. You're more likely to find them around Gloucestershire or Somerset. That was the wealthy part of the country back then.'

'I quite like the idea that Flete was important once.'

'Why?'

Juno screwed up her face as she analysed. 'I haven't lived here very long but it seems to get overlooked a lot.'

'Up against the glamour that is Lyme Regis you mean?'

'Yes. It's a shame. I think Flete has a lot to offer.'

Tom shrugged. 'The new bar for one,' he said drily.

Juno giggled. 'It was an experience, wasn't it? I've got to go back and try the Melted Mars Bar Tart.'

'As long as it comes without the comedy toga.'

'Oh, don't go on about them being historically inaccurate again.'

'No. I was simply worried about it dangling in my beer.' He smacked his lips together. 'That pint of Neptune's Trident had a distinct tang about it that wasn't purely hops and malt.'

Juno laughed again. It caught the attention of her brother who looked across. At that moment the landline rang.

'Shall I?' Cris offered. 'As I'm nearest.'

Juno nodded. 'Weird. I wasn't sure it was even connected. Everyone I know calls me on my mobile.' The retro phone, with its old-fashioned dumbbell handset had sat on the corner table unused ever since she'd moved in. She hadn't even been sure if it was a working phone and not just some antique collected by her aunt.

Cris picked up the receiver, listened intently for a few seconds, shrugged and replaced it. 'No one there, or wrong number maybe. Hey, Ju,' he said, changing the subject, 'Mabyn has been telling me all about her childhood in Woolacombe. Did you know we're supposed to have rellies there?'

'I never knew that.' Juno pulled a face. 'Although I can't say I've given it much thought. I always thought we were an east Devon family?'

'Mum's side is but Dad's got north Devon ancestors. Don't you remember us all going to Woolacombe for a holiday once?'

'Not really.'

'Well, you were very little. Dad spent all his time asking the locals if there was anyone with the surname Eden who had ever lived there. Drove Mum mad. She just wanted to get on the beach.'

'Can't believe you might have family in my hometown,' Mabyn put in. 'We could be cousins!'

Cris laughed. 'I'd just like to point out that Dad never found any evidence of an Eden branch of the family.'

'Why did he think we were from north Devon?' Juno asked.

'Something an aged member of the family said years ago. Dad got fixated on it for a while.'

'Maybe it was an ancestor fleeing the Saxon hordes?' Tom suggested. 'Lots went west when the Anglo-Saxons invaded and there are a number of hillforts on the north Devon coast, one in Woolacombe itself.'

Cris started. 'Funnily enough, that's about the gist of it. Dad claimed he'd been told there was an old story in the family, passed down the generations, of people having to head west.'

'Oh, come on Cris,' Juno put in. 'That's a hell of a reach. I mean, I like a story but we're talking thousands of years ago. I can't believe something like that would be passed down so many generations.' She turned to Tom. 'It's not possible, is it?'

He put his empty mug on the table. 'Maybe it's not all that far-fetched. After all, stories were told at the fireside and passed from one storyteller to another. Think of Beowulf. First written down in the tenth century but almost certainly dating from earlier.'

'But, if that were the case, why couldn't Dad find any Edens in Woolacombe?'

'People migrate for work, they have daughters and the name dies out.'

'Hey, Ju – I reckon we're related. Deffo,' Mabyn said. 'I should teach you some of the local words. Dimpsy for one. It means dusk. Grockle, that's another. That means tourist.'

Cris scoffed. 'Juno has enough of a problem with the English language, let alone learning a Devon dialect.'

He was given swift retribution in the shape of a flung cushion. Juno laughed and then stopped suddenly as she felt her mobile vibrate. *Who was ringing at this hour?* All casual enjoyment in the evening fled. The old feeling of being trapped returned.

Georgia Hill

# CHAPTER 19

*T*he Secundinus Villa

Flavia was feeling ever more trapped. Fear clutched around her like the retiarius's weighted net. She still hadn't given Septimus Severus and, more importantly, her father, her decision on whether she would accept marriage to Septimus or anyone.

On her return from talking to Padrig, she had slipped into the house, skirted past the storerooms and narrowly missed Balbus as he stood in the entrance to the hortus. He was haranguing a kitchen slave. It was a quiet part of the house, one usually frequented by the house slaves and she'd thought it safe. Hiding behind a pillar she watched, sickened, as he thrust a filthy hand under the girl's tunic and grabbed her between the legs. As she squealed in pain and shock, he dragged her across the floor and backed her against the very same column Flavia was hiding behind. With eyes too glazed with lust he failed to notice and she'd screwed her own tight shut, hardly daring to breathe. When he'd finished his filthy business, he'd kicked the sack of flour the slave had dropped, ordering her to sweep it up.

Flavia had waited, clinging limply to the column, until he'd strode away into the gardens, a self-satisfied sweat gleaming on his broad brow. With her hand across her mouth, fearing she would vomit, she ran for the sanctuary of her chambers.

There, she had collapsed on the bed shivering and retching, clutching the furs in white-knuckled hands. How had the day so many disparate parts? The ennui of the early morning, the excitement and turmoil of feelings when talking to Padrig. The horror of what she had just witnessed. She incanted a prayer calling upon the goddess Juno for protection and tried to rid her mind of Balbus's disgusting grunts. It had been no act of love that she'd witnessed, beasts in the yard had more dignity. Even worse was the kitchen slave's stifled sobs as she had attempted to save the flour, the waste of which would earn her a beating once she returned to her place of work.

If her father ever found out his favourite slave was abusing another, he would have Balbus killed. Not on account of the girl's honour, slaves were routinely used in such a way, but *never* by other slaves. That privilege belonged to their owner. But what proof could she offer? She had trespassed in a part of the house that would have everyone questioning her presence. Besides, her father was blind to Balbus's ways; he was besotted by the lout and let him get away with far more liberties than any other. Rumour had it that he was even considering granting Balbus freedman status. Flavia squeezed her eyes shut and prayed again.

By the time Ursa arrived to attend to her, she had hurriedly soaked the grime from her nails and begun to recover her composure. Ursa dressed her for dinner and put up her hair in an elaborate concoction of plaits, curls and silver pins. Flavia remained white-faced and silent throughout. Ursa, worried, had prepared a tincture to stave off a nervous headache.

And then Flavia had gone into the triclinium knowing that Balbus would be standing in his corner behind her father's couch and watching her, licking his lips. Marriage to Septimus would at least be an escape. Of a sort.

Now it was April. The days were long and warm. The day of her birth had been and gone; she was twenty summers old and beyond being considered an old maid. Her father continually pressed for an answer. And she was about to go into yet another meal where Septimus had been invited. She knew her father was being kind in his way. He did not want to marry her off to someone she did not know or like and so kept inviting Septimus to encourage her. But, no matter how hard she tried, she couldn't see herself married to the dull, slightly lumpen man her father was so keen on for her. Would Septimus do to her what she'd seen Balbus do to the kitchen slave? How would she bear it?

Part of her fantasised about escaping, to seek the protection of her brother and his fat-ankled wife. But, even if she took Ursa, two women without means wouldn't get very far. And Balbus would no doubt be sent after them in any case. As a picture of Padrig's kind and handsome face rose in her vision, she wondered if she would ever see him again. As Ursa dressed her hair, she caressed her neck, unadorned without her sea glass necklace. She remembered Padrig's soft touch and how his gentle fingertips had danced over her skin.

'You should wear the topaz collar this evening,' Ursa said as she arranged her hair around a sparkling headdress. 'The one your brother gave you before he left. It is one of your favourite jewels.'

Flavia bit down on her irritation. She'd had enough of being prodded and primped, the headdress was heavy and made her eyes ache. 'Perhaps. I care little what I wear.'

'Then perhaps you should.' When Flavia didn't answer, not even to reprimand her slave for impertinence, she added, 'You're playing a dangerous game, my lady.'

'How so?'

'The man from the Durotriges.'

'I don't know who you mean.'

Ursa sighed. 'You were seen running back from the gardens. You'd been meeting him, hadn't you?'

Flavia remained silent.

'And it's the same man we met in the forum?'

'I don't see that it's any of your concern.'

Ursa slammed the bone comb onto the dressing table and crouched down. She took her mistress's hand. 'It is my business because I care about you.'

Flavia turned to her, feeling her eyes fill with tears. 'Then you should know I am unhappy.'

'I know you're unhappy, mistress. I see it every day.'

'Then you should also know I cannot bear for this life to continue.' A tear spilled over and ran down, tracking a passage through the just-applied rouge.

'But what life is this that is so difficult to bear? A caring father, a loving mother.' Ursa gestured to the ruby-red painted bedchamber. 'A beautiful home. Good food. All the trinkets in the empire to buy.'

'I should sacrifice everything for my freedom. I do not want to marry Septimus. I do not want to marry anyone!'

'Mistress, I urge you to accept him.' Ursa hesitated and then rushed on. 'There is gossip in the house. Your father has been overheard making plans to free Balbus.'

Flavia jerked in horror. 'The rumours are true, then?'

'It would seem so. If you hasten and marry Septimus Severus, then you will have protection from –' Ursa let the sentence trail but her face was eloquent.

'You don't mean?' Flavia shook her head vigorously. 'He wouldn't. He couldn't marry me off to an ex-slave, to *Balbus?*'

'Who else is there? You have rejected all others, my chick. Besides, Flavius Honoratus trusts Balbus with his life. He has some hold over your father, I believe. Who better to husband a wayward child than his right-hand man? Your father cannot bear the disgrace an unmarried daughter brings upon the household. Why not marry Septimus and have the safety and protection of your own home?'

'I will have safety and protection, but I will not have love.'

'Love will come. Septimus Severus is not an unkind man.'

Padrig's red-blonde hair and penetrating blue eyes rose in her vision. She felt again the warmth of his flesh upon hers, the sound of the beads in his beard clicking together, the scent of his skin ... Had she so quickly and easily given her heart to man who was her father's sworn enemy and a stranger? 'He is boring and I do not love him,' Flavia repeated stubbornly.

'And what is a boring man if he were to protect you against Balbus?' Ursa shook Flavia's hands in attempt to shake some sense into the girl. 'You need to listen, my chick. This is serious. There is talk amongst the house slaves that he has developed a great passion for you. If you were to be offered to him, he would not hesitate and I doubt he would be as kind to you as Septimus. Better the bore than the monster.'

Flavia wiped away the tear and straightened her shoulders. Adjusting her jewelled headpiece, she said, 'Very well. I shall consider it.'

Ursa ducked her head in relief. 'Thank the gods. I shall pray to Minerva tonight to speed you well.'

'I need a favour from you first.' Flavia's voice was suddenly determined.

'What is that? You know I would serve you most gladly.'

'You have little choice. I own you.' Too late, Flavia saw the hurt in her servant's eyes. 'I'm sorry Ursa. That was unkind. You are a kind and faithful servant and friend too.'

The slave got up and began to fold away Flavia's day robes. 'What is your command, mistress?'

Flavia heard the sullen resentment and regretted causing upset. Going to Ursa, she took the woollen gown away, throwing it on the bed. She clasped her hands. 'I am unhappy and I take my temper out on those nearest – and dearest. And seeing as my father is Flavius Honoratus, *summus magistratus* and busy, and my mother spends her time in devotion to her Christos in an underground temple, it is you who takes the brunt. Forgive me,' she added wildly.

Pulling the woman to her, she repeated, 'Forgive me, Ursa. You are kind and thoughtful and look after me so well. I wouldn't know what I would do without you.'

'Hands off me, child, you will muss up your hair which I've just spent the past hour dressing. And how would that look when you go to dinner, eh? A crumpled tunic and hair hanging down all over the place. Do you want me flogged, for it would be I who would take the blame.'

Flavia stepped back. 'No, indeed. I could not bear life here without you. You must know that.'

Ursa straightened her own simple woollen tunic. It was in direct contrast with Flavia's plum-pink silk. 'Then what do you request of me?'

'Take a message to Padrig.'

'The man from the Durotriges?' Ursa was horrified.

'Yes. I need to ask him to meet me.' Flavia again caressed where her beads usually lay.

'Where is your sea glass necklace?' Ursa asked sharply.

'He took it.' Flavia's voice took on a dreamy note. 'My re-stringing of it was poorly done. He took it so that his sister Steren may mend it.'

Ursa looked startled. 'Steren? I have heard of her. She is a chief's daughter. The house slaves gossip about her family. This Padrig, he is high-born then?'

Flavia nodded. 'A second son. Please take him a message. Please, Ursa. It's so very important to me,' she pleaded. 'I can authorise a mule from the stables and you can take Trajan too. It should not be difficult to find the way to the hillfort and there are not so many of the legion around to spy now they have gone to fight in Germania.' When she saw Ursa hesitate, she added in a wily tone, 'Please. It may not only be Balbus who will enjoy his freedom.'

Ursa's eyes widened. 'You would do that?'

Flavia hated the deception, but she was desperate. She doubted her father would allow her to free a slave who had consequence only for his daughter. Nodding, she said,

'Yes.' Reaching for the woman's hands again, she added, 'But I would like to think, even if you are made a citizen, you would stay and still be my friend.'

Ursa gave a cynical laugh. 'And here's me thinking Flavius Honoratus has all the cunning and politics. He has taught his daughter well.'

Flavia clapped her hands together. 'Then you will do it?'

'Only if you go into dinner now! Off. Go.' The slave blew out a great breath. 'You'll be the death of me, child. We can discuss the details later but if you don't get your missish behind into the *triclinium* now, we shall all be in trouble!'

Flavia closed her eyes in relief. She needed to see Padrig so desperately it hurt. Shaking the creases from her silks, she again touched her neck. Without her necklace, she felt strangely unprotected.

Georgia Hill

# CHAPTER 20

*023*

Juno stood at her bedroom window staring down at the blue stone she'd found on the beach. Picking it up she examined it carefully. She'd forgotten to show it to Cris, just as she'd forgotten to ask him about the painting of the Durotriges hillfort man. Looking at the stone now she no longer thought it was something a creature had burrowed a hole through. It was a bead, she was sure of it, possibly made of polished sea glass. Holding it up to the strong April sunshine she turned it so that it caught the light and shimmered. She wondered if it had come from a necklace of similar beads. If so, it must have been an exquisite piece of jewellery. A static charge sent a snap of energy running from the bead through her fingers and she dropped it hurriedly, rubbing her hand down her jeans.

At the same time, in the room below, the landline rang out. Juno felt her breathing hitch. It was the third time it had rung today and it had rung in the night too, jolting her awake horribly. She'd answered it only to find, as when Cris had answered, that there was no one there. Screwing her eyes shut she tried to ignore the shrill sound. What was it about a ringing phone that impelled you to answer? It must be a faulty connection, or another wrong number. The alternative was too horrible to contemplate. Surely it couldn't be Paul? He didn't know where she was. And besides, why would he want to ring her? He'd made it abundantly clear he wanted nothing more to do with her when he'd moved Madeleine in. The phone stopped and she began to breathe again. Stupidly, her legs were trembling so she perched on the edge of the bed, tensed, half expecting the ringing to start again.

With Cris and Mabyn gone, the house seemed, even for a tiny cottage, empty and echoing. As the days lengthened with April and the weather grew warmer, the town of Flete became busier. Juno had walked Joops early, showered and planned to write all day. But she felt restless and edgy and not in the mood. The fact that she was behind with her deadline didn't help. She chafed against it, feeling trapped. Realising there was nothing for it but to get down to some work, she stomped bad temperedly down the stairs.

It was almost a relief when, two hours later, her mobile rang. She'd lolled on the sofa, the computer on her lap and had written one chapter only to delete most it. Half fearing she'd see Paul's number flash up she answered Tom's call far more cheerfully than she'd intended. 'Hey Tom.'

'Juno? I need your help,' he barked out.

'Okaaaay.'

'Can you go round to Mum's?'

Juno sat up straight. 'What's wrong? Is Diana all right?'

'She's fine. I need you to go and get my bag. She'll know what I mean. Bring it up to the holloway and drive the Freelander through the gate into the field. I'll have it open for you. I'll meet you there and explain.' His voice had an urgency undercut with a febrile excitement.

'Tom, what's all this about?'

'I have to go. I'll explain it all when I see you.'

The line went dead. Juno looked at the phone in shock. 'Arrogant tosser,' she said to Joops. Looking at the mess on her laptop, she saved what she'd written and clicked the lid down. 'Still, it's a choice between re-writing that lot or a weird errand on behalf of our ill-mannered neighbour. What a choice, eh, Joopsy?' Getting up, she stretched. 'Fancy another walk?'

As she shut her front door and turned the key, she heard her landline ring out yet again and shuddered.

Diana was disappointingly unsurprised at the request. 'Hold on a mo,'' she said, when she answered her door. 'I'll go and fetch it.'

Juno stood at the bottom of the stairs hearing Diana clump about overhead. The scent of a casserole wafted along the hall and her stomach rumbled. She hadn't bothered with lunch.

Her neighbour returned, passed a large bag to her and said, 'Hang on a moment longer. I'll make up some food.'

Juno followed her into the kitchen. 'Diana, what's this all about? Is Tom in trouble?'

'Oh, no, my lovely. He's fine. It just means he might have found something and he doesn't want to leave it.'

'Found what? And why's he worried about leaving it? Who for?'

Diana flicked on the kettle and then began to decant chicken casserole into a Tupperware container. 'He'll explain it all when he sees you, no doubt.'

Joops, nostrils flaring at the enticing aromas, pulled hard on his lead and jumped up.

'Best take him into the garden room my dear,' Diana said. 'Then I can get this done in two ticks straight.'

Questions burning, Juno kept Joops on a very short lead as Diana made sandwiches smoothly and efficiently and, with the kettle boiled, filled a flask with coffee. She put it all into another bag. 'You staying up there with him?' Without waiting for an answer, she reached into a Tesco carrier bag and brought out a couple of toothbrushes and a tube of paste. 'Just as well I've just come back from the supermarket shop. Car outside on the street? Come on then, I'll help you carry this lot outside. Come on, Juno, tick tock. Time is of the essence.'

Bemused, Juno drove the short distance to the lane at the top of the field, turned left and edged the Freelander cautiously along the holloway. As promised, Tom stood at the open gate and waved her through. Pulling the handbrake on while he closed the gate behind her, she buzzed down the window.

'Follow the line of the river and park up where you see my spade marking the spot.' As she went to ask questions, he cut her off. 'I'd be grateful if you could get there as soon as possible. I don't like leaving it.'

'This is getting seriously weird,' Juno muttered to Joops who was watching with keen interest from the back seat, tongue lolling. 'And it's just as well you're strapped in, it's going to be a bumpy drive. I know this is supposed to be an off-roader but I don't think it's ever even seen a field.'

Tom jumped in and half mile or so further along pointed to where he wanted her to park. Luckily, it was on the level lower part of the field. Juno had doubts she'd get the car up the steep incline she and Tom had climbed a few weeks ago. Nosing the Freelander around a beach in the curve of the river, where it flowed shallow over a bed of pebbles, she parked up behind a copse of ash and willows. His spade was stuck in the ground a short distance away.

Clambering down, she released Joops from the back seat. He shot off into the shallows from where the distant quacking of alarmed ducks was heard. At Tom's look of concern, she said, 'Don't worry, he's never caught anything in his life, despite coming from good working stock.'

'It's not that I'm worried about. I don't want anything drawing attention to us.'

Juno put her hands on her hips. She'd had enough. 'What *is* this about? I couldn't get any sense out of your mother and now you're being all 007. What's going on?'

'This way.' He led her to his spade and the shallow hole he'd dug. Kneeling down he reached into the hole and drew something out.

'You were right then, there were more coins to be found.'

He looked up at her, eyes shining, his whole being rigid with excitement. 'I got a signal on the detector and began to dig. I found these.' He opened his palm to reveal a clutch of coins the same tarnished greeny-brown as the last he'd found.

'Wow,' Juno said, impressed. 'There must be at least ten there.'

'Oh, yes, I've got twelve here. Then I began to dig a little more.' He shot a glance around him and beckoned her closer. 'Then, the more I dug, the more I found. Look!'

She knelt down at the side of the hole and peered in. About a foot below the surface she could see an enormous mass of coins fused together. The mound was about two feet wide. She gasped. 'There must be hundreds there!'

'Reckon so. I stopped trying to get any more out in case I damaged them. And then, well then, I found this.' Reaching into his pocket he brought out something small and glinting in the sunshine.

'Wow!' Juno took it from him, her mouth dropping open. 'Is it gold?'

Tom nodded. 'A gold *solidus*. It's unusual to find Roman coins in Devon. I thought I was lucky finding those two others but all *this* and then to find a gold coin.' He shook his head, bewildered. 'It's beyond anything I could have hoped.'

Going with the moment, she flung her arm around him. 'This is so exciting.' As she pressed herself against him, she could feel his heart racing. He smelled of earth and damp grass. Not totally unpleasant. Sitting back on her knees, she grinned. 'What happens now? Do you excavate further?'

Tom took the coin back from her, staring at it in wonder. 'You never get over the fact this was buried in the ground and it emerges two thousand years later perfectly untarnished. Exquisite.' He held it up where it caught the bright sunlight. 'Gold. The most prized, the most beautiful metal. You can see why.'

A robin, high in one of the ash trees, began to sing, lacing the moment with magic.

Dragging his attention back to her with obvious difficulty, Tom returned to the question. 'I can't do anything just yet. I have to declare it, so I've rung Max the FLO and he's going to contact the council who is the land owner, plus the university and the coroner.'

'The coroner?' Juno asked, alarmed.

'The coroner has to decide if this, plus whatever's still in the ground, is to be declared treasure. If it is, it can be acquired by a museum although the little one in Flete will likely lose out.'

'Cris will be amazed.'

'He's not alone.' Tom grinned broadly, his face wreathed in smile lines. 'I can't believe I found it.' With one last adoring look at the gold coin, he slipped it into a plastic bag and put it in the breast pocket of his shirt.

'Oh, Tom, it's brilliant!' Juno hugged him to her again and this time his arms came round her, moulding her body to his. An electricity passed through them, heating their skin.

Backing off slightly Tom stared into her eyes. He was about to say something when twenty kilos of wet hairy springer spaniel leaped at them.

'Joops!' Juno cried. 'Get off.' She pushed the dog down. As he continued to dance around in a frenzy of excitement, she grabbed at his collar. 'He hasn't damaged anything has he?'

'No, but that reminds me I need to cover it all back up. Hang onto him, will you, while I put the divot back.'

Juno wrapped her arms around the wet dog and watched as Tom carefully replaced the circle of turf he'd cut. 'You can hardly see where it is,' she admired.

'That's the idea. I'll pitch the tent over it and no one will be the wiser.'

'Good. I'll give you a lift home then.'

He looked at her amused. 'I'm staying here. I'll sleep in the tent.'

Juno let go of Joops now it was safe and frowned at Tom. 'Why on earth would you want to stay overnight?'

'It's not a question of wanting to, it's more having to.' He stood up and dusted himself down. Holding a hand down to her, he pulled her up. 'Max won't be able to get a team organised all that quickly. I'll have to stay here until we've got the dig sorted and everything's out.'

Understanding was dawning. 'Your bag!'

'Yup. It's got everything I need should something like this arise. Plus a power bank. I'm running out of battery.'

'That's why you were so short on the phone.'

'One reason.' He grinned again. 'The other being I can only get a signal at the far end of the field by the gate. I didn't want to risk leaving the find for too long.'

He was a different man. Gone was the reticence which could easily be mistaken for sullenness. He'd come alive. 'But what's the risk?'

'Night Hawks.'

'Night what?'

'Night Hawks. If they get wind of a find, they swoop down, rob the site, sell the stuff on the black market.'

'You're joking.'

'Oh, I'm in deadly earnest.' He nodded to the filled in hole. 'There could be a small fortune in there. They operate without permissions and make a fortune off the hard work of others. Plus, no museum or academic ever gets to study what's found, so the knowledge is lost too.'

'Permissions?' Juno's nose wrinkled. It was a whole new world to her.

'I have written permission to metal detect on this land. I'll profit from the sale of whatever I find, along with the landowner.'

'And these Night Hawkers, I mean Night Hawks, come along and nick all your hard work?'

He nodded.

'That's awful. It's almost like plagiarism.'

'You could say.'

'So, you're going to camp out up here until the dig gets going?'

'Yup. It shouldn't take too long to get the stuff out of the ground, but the university can't organise a dig in two seconds flat.'

Juno raised a brow. 'You'd be surprised. If it's Cris who's involved, he'll be in like Flynn.'

Tom laughed. He spread his hands. 'Well, until then, this is my home. I'd better get the tent up.'

They unloaded the car and Juno, feeling redundant, watched as Tom began to put up a small two-man tent.

'You could do me a favour and find some kindling,' he asked. 'Plus a few medium-sized stones.' At her blank look, he added, 'for a fire pit.'

Joops shadowed her, his nose to the ground, as she collected rocks from the beach. Every now and again, the robin hopped down, staring at them curiously from avidly black eyes. It occurred to her this was an activity done for millennia. The image of the Durotriges tribesman from the museum flashed into her consciousness. He may have walked these very fields doing exactly the same thing.

She looked about her, half expecting him to appear. 'Probably more wooded back then though, eh, Joops?' she said to the dog, to ward off the sensation she was being watched. 'And I bet he didn't need a portable phone charger either.' Joops snuffled, distracted by a new scent trail.

By the time she returned with her third armful of twigs, Tom had the tent erected and had made a fire pit with the rocks she'd collected. It was already lit. He looked thoroughly at home, far more so than when she'd first met him in his mother's garden room. Something primeval stirred within her as she watched the dark blonde hairs on his sturdy forearms glisten in the low sunshine. There was something very elemental in such basic activities as collecting firewood and creating a shelter. Stifling a giggle, she wondered where the old city girl had gone.

'You're really going to camp up here overnight?'

'Longer, if needs be.' He threw a log on the fire and, after sparking, it settled into a warming glow.

Juno sat in front of it, cross legged and held out her hands to the flames. 'I like what you've done to the place.'

Tom grinned and emptied the casserole into a metal tray. Putting it on a trivet to heat up, he tossed over a tin plate and a fork. 'I can't promise you cordon bleu, but my mother's chicken casserole tastes good anywhere.'

It did. As did the coffee from the flask.

'I might be converted to this camping lark,' Juno said, as she fished out a scrap of chicken and fed it to Joops. 'How long do you think you'll have to stay up here?'

He settled on his side, leaning on his elbow, legs stretched out. The flickering light from the fire warmed his suntanned face. 'Max said a team might be here by the day after tomorrow. So probably two nights. At least the weather's warm and dry and the nights are short. It would help if I had a guard dog,' he added, staring at Joops speculatively.

Juno put an arm around the dog. 'Joops doesn't go anywhere without me.'

'Then maybe you could stay, too? Keep an old archaeologist company?' He shot her a challenging look, blue glinting humorously through dark lashes.

'I'm not sleeping in that thing!' Juno said in horror, indicating the tent.

Tom laughed. 'I wasn't going to suggest it. I think your car might be more comfortable and a good deal warmer. I've a single malt in my survival bag and Mum's put in some lemon drizzle cake if that sways you.'

Juno remembered the toothbrush and paste Diana had added. She looked around at the field. The river burbled past behind the willows, the evening bird chorus was revving into action and the sky was darkening to a jewelled sapphire. There were worse places to spend an evening. She thought about the shrilling of the landline piercing through what had once been her sanctuary of a home. She didn't relish returning to an empty house and facing that. Contemplating Tom, she chewed her lip, trying to decide. She'd disliked him at first, he'd irritated her, and she still thought he was arrogant, but she'd always trusted him. If she locked herself in the car, what harm could come to her? It might even be an adventure.

'Well, as you pointed out,' she began, gabbling a bit. 'You're not attracted to me so I'll be perfectly safe. I mean, we don't even have that sort of relationship, do we? I'm not sure we're even friends.'

He paused for a second, staring intently into the fire. 'No, we don't have that sort of relationship,' he answered eventually. 'But I'd hoped we'd become friends by now.' He sat up suddenly. 'Scrap the idea. I was stupid to suggest it. Of course you'd rather go back and sleep in your own bed. Who wouldn't?'

'Don't get all huffy. I'd be happy to stay. It'll be fun. Or it will be once I've had a wee. Don't suppose you've a portaloo in your survival kit?' His expression told her all she needed to know. She returned from an uncomfortable crouch and an encounter with nettles, hindered by Joops who thought it was all a great adventure, to find Tom had rigged up a light and banked up the fire.

'Whisky?' He passed over a tumbler.

'Are we saving the lemon drizzle for breakfast?'

He laughed. 'We can although there are sausages and eggs in the kit.'

'No way.'

'Mum knows the score.'

'Have you done this often, then?' She sat down on the groundsheet he'd so thoughtfully supplied and sipped her whisky.

'Not often. And never in Devon. As I said, it's rare to find Roman coins around here. Even rarer, anywhere, to find what might be a hoard. Mum and I had discussed what would need to happen should I have to do this. There was no way she'd get her little Mini along the holloway let alone across the field so your 4X4 was a godsend.'

This time it was Juno who laughed. 'Don't ever tell my dad. It's on loan from him. Think it's only glimpsed off-road from the safety of the country lanes of Hampshire.'

'But you lived in London, is that right?'

'Yup. For a while. It's where I met Mabyn.'

In the distance something hooted softly.

'Was that an owl?' Juno's eyes went huge.

'It was. Good hunting time.'

The vastness of the field seemed even more empty now it was growing darker. Shadows hung in the trees and small snufflings and scurryings could be heard. At the far end, a squeak was cut short. The owl must have found its target. She shivered.

'Are you cold? Come this side of the fire, the tent blocks out the worst of the breeze.'

As she stood up her attention was caught by the glimmer of headlights and the rumble of a car on the distant side of the hedge. 'Is that the road? I hadn't realised it was so close.' Reassured they were so near civilisation, she spread the groundsheet nearer Tom and flopped down, her back resting against the tent pole. Joops followed and with him settled on one side and Tom on the other she felt warmer and more secure.

'Is this man, the one you had the abusive relationship with, in London?' Tom asked, topping up their glasses.

'Did I tell you about Paul?'

'You mentioned something on the night we came back to your house after the night in Colosseum.'

Juno leaned forward and wrapped her arms around her knees. 'Oh yes.' A half full moon was rising above the trees and her eyes were gradually adjusting to the light. She watched, amused, as several rabbits hopped about at the edge of the field, white bob-tails advertising their presence. She kept a tight hold on Joops's collar. 'Paul? Yes. He was a bastard. An out and out bastard.'

# CHAPTER 21

*The Secundinus Villa*

'Bastard!' Flavia muttered the insult at Balbus's back. He lumbered off through the atrium towards her father's office. Every bunched muscle hinted at his evil.

Ursa fluttered to her side. 'What is it mistress? Has he harmed you?'

'He didn't lay a finger on me.'

'Then what?' Ursa put a hand on her arm. 'My chick, you're shaking! What did he do?'

'He did nothing. He had no need. It was all in his words and the evil in his face.' Turning on her heel, Flavia ran to the hortus. Standing in the gardens with her fists clenched, she raised her eyes to the cloudless April sky and sucked in deep breaths until she was calm enough to talk. Collapsing onto a stone bench, she felt a wet nose press enquiringly into her hand. It was Trajan. Throwing her arms around his neck she wept her fury and frustration into his fur.

Ursa sat beside her, waiting for the storm to pass. Eventually she offered a corner of her palla and the girl dried her face. 'What happened?'

Flavia fixed her eyes on the dog. She scratched behind his ears and he snickered in ecstasy.

'What did he say, mistress?'

Flavia heaved an enormous sigh. 'He told me, in exacting detail, what he plans to do to me on the occasion of our marriage.'

'What?' Ursa gasped in shock. 'What did he say?'

'I do not wish to give his words any more power by repeating them.' She bit her lip and shuddered. 'Suffice to say it was not ... pleasant.'

'The bastard!'

Flavia managed a laugh and met Ursa's eyes. 'Indeed.'

'But he cannot be allowed to get away with this. You must tell your mother. Your father. This is an outrage. He is a slave like me. It should not be allowed for him to abuse you such as this.'

Flavia put her hand over Ursa's. 'Your indignation does you credit, and I love you for it.' She shrugged. 'He said,' she paused, on the verge of tears again. 'He said he was promised to be a free man very soon and that my father, if he had not married me off before, would match him with me. And then I would be his for,' she paused again, 'I think the phrase he used was, "his delectation."'

Ursa took in a quick breath of rage. 'I knew it to be rumoured but to hear it stated so bluntly and defiantly is truly shocking. Do you think it true? Flavia, you *must* tell your parents.'

'My mother cares for little beyond her Christian god and Balbus made it very apparent he has my father's ear. Neither see his true character. He is cunning like that, maybe he is cleverer than we think? They simply would not believe me.' She shrugged hopelessly. 'They would see it as an excuse against yet another man I did not want to marry.'

The women sat in silence staring at the pool, now no longer brackish. The fountain of Sulis Minerva played a soft accompaniment to their thoughts, the water drops turning to iridescence in the sunshine. A robin hopped down, eyed them beadily and drank.

'Have you no word from Padrig?' Flavia asked.

Ursa shook her head.

'And you made sure to take the message to his tribe?'

'I told it to the gatekeeper. He assured me it would get to him.'

'You didn't see Padrig himself?'

'Mistress, they would let me no further than the outer gate. If truth be told, I fear I could have gone no further. It is a steep climb.'

'Perhaps, then, he has not received it?' Flavia picked miserably at her robes.

'I could do no more, trust me. Shall I try a message via one of the kitchen slaves? They know the family and talk of them often.'

'Would they betray me? I do not wish to give Balbus any more ammunition than necessary.'

'They fear Balbus, but they do not trust him. I'll ask around. See who is willing and who has contacts. There are many slaves from the Durotriges in the kitchens.'

'Then I shouldn't think they have much love for me.'

'But they have less for Balbus. What would you have me say?'

Flavia pondered. 'Nothing too incriminatory. Something short that has meaning only to me and Padrig but is inconsequential to anyone who intercepts it.' She thought for a moment and then clapped her hands. 'I know. What about, "Sea glass bead needs help!"'

'Sea glass bead needs help.' Ursa nodded. 'Even the most thick-headed kitchen serf should be able to remember that. Good. Leave it with me.'

Flavia sighed again, her lips trembling. Tears were not far away again.

Ursa put an arm around her. 'Courage, my chick. We will find a way.'

'But it might take too long!' Flavia thumped the stone bench in frustration. 'Balbus has a noose around my neck and it is tightening by the day. If he is freed before I have word from Padrig, then I am lost.'

'Can you not entertain the thought of Septimus Severus as a possible suitor? It might keep your father happy if he feels you are coming round.'

'And it might enrage Balbus even more and make him more determined to have me. Besides, Septimus has brains. He'd be astonished at my change in attitude towards him. I think he'd see through the plan in an instant.'

The robin flew off, settled on the villa wall and began to sing in the sunshine.

Ursa gazed at it thoughtfully. 'Might be worth a try. Anything's worth a try. Just to hold off Balbus until you have word from Padrig. See the robin there? A good omen. Perhaps we can put something else into action while we wait?'

Flavia swivelled round. 'What? I will consider anything.'

'What would you like to say to Balbus? What is in your deepest heart?'

Flavia laughed, this time with a hard mirth. 'What would you have me say?'

'Your worst thoughts for him. Your worst desires for him.'

Flavia laughed again. 'Oh Ursa. Where shall I begin?'

*

While she waited for Ursa's return, Flavia wandered aimlessly around the villa, expertly ducking her father and mother's attentions should they see her idle and find her some meaningless chore. She prayed at each of the house shrines, sending up swift messages to Minerva for Ursa's safe return and for her own deliverance against Balbus. Praying that Padrig would receive the message and act upon it, she questioned whether Minerva's protection would extend to a non-believer. As extra insurance, she made sacrifice to Juno, protector of women. She plucked at her weaving but got everything into a knot as she couldn't concentrate, so, as the day was fair, she wandered out into the front courtyard and watched as the tax collectors counted their day's haul. Her interest quickened as she spied a small leather sack of coins leaning against the pillar outside the offices. The men left it unattended while they chatted before heaving the bigger sacks of coins inside. A half-formed plan edged into her consciousness. Restless, she returned to the garden and sat on the stone bench asking Disciplina to will her patience and mulling over what she had just witnessed. There had been a moment, the briefest moment, when the smaller sack had been unguarded. Even though the coins would be humble *nummi,* there would be hundreds of them and useful. Could she be so bold and daring? Trajan found her again and he was a comfort. She was sitting there tickling his ears when Ursa returned.

'Ah, good, you have found a secluded spot to sit in,' the slave said and collapsed beside her, huffing. 'I am too old for the town these days. It is too busy and there are too many vagabonds.'

'I am sorry to put you to so much trouble, old woman.' Flavia put a soft had on the woman's shoulder. 'But I will make sure you get your favourite supper.'

Ursa sighed. 'Eggs and saltfish? You spoil me, my mistress.' She wiped her sweaty brow. 'It is hot today but,' she stole a glance around her, 'I have what is required.' From under her cloak, she produced a small grey cylinder.

Flavia took it curiously. 'I have never seen a curse tablet before. What do I do with it?'

'Unroll it carefully first. See if it meets your approval.'

Flavia picked at the edge of the lead with a fingernail. Unbending it with difficulty, it was eventually straightened and readable. Her mouth twitched as she began to read the letters scratched into the metal surface:

"On this day, I, Flavia call upon you, Minerva and you Juno, to curse the slave Balbus. May he be accursed in his blood and eyes and every limb and even have all his intestines quite eaten away if he in any way abuses Flavia again. In Sulis Minerva's name, Flavia curses the slave Balbus and his life and mind and memory and liver and lungs so that he may never know peace in this life or the next."

'Vulcan's fire, do you think it too much, Ursa?' Flavia flicked her a worried glance.

'Do you?'

She saw again the evil glint in Balbus's eyes and the drool at the side of his mouth. Her lips thinned. 'No,' she said defiantly. 'I do not.' She handed it back and Ursa carefully rolled it back into shape. 'What do I do with it now?'

'We must find somewhere to cast it adrift. Somewhere we can leave it undisturbed and not found by Balbus. We chant a prayer and send the curse out into the world to do its will.'

Flavia shivered. 'There is a place sacred to the Druids. There is a kind of beach under the ash trees where a stream feeds into the river. Do you remember it?'

Ursa nodded. 'It was where we fished. I remember. A peaceful place or it was when we had a legion to *keep* any peace.'

'There is an old oak tree there too. The tribespeople hang offerings on it for their own prayers. I walked past one day.' Flavia blushed guiltily. 'It was on one of my escapes.'

Ursa's nostrils flared in annoyance at the confession. There was a pause and then she added, 'Sounds like it would suit. Maybe the Druids will add their gods to the mix? Evil is as evil is, recognised by all.'

'When shall we do it?'

'As soon as possible. We don't want this curse tablet falling into the wrong hands.'

'Then this evening? It is light so late at this time of year and it isn't far. We can be out and back before anyone misses us.' Flavia's hand strayed to the dog's neck. 'And we can take Trajan with us.'

'We may be in need of him,' Ursa said sourly. 'But I agree. Tonight is the time to do it. There is a good moon too. May Juno protect and guard us.'

*

The women crept out of the villa the usual way. Flavia noticed, with a wry smile, how the key turned much more easily in the lock now it was being used so often. Ursa had dressed her in an old cloak and, with both anonymously clad, their movements drew little curiosity. Her father was entertaining fellow members of the ordo and her mother was at prayer again so with Fortuna's good grace they would not be missed.

They had chosen their moment well. The day's light lingered and a bright half-moon rose low amongst the trees. It would be easy to see their way.

Once they reached the clearing by the stream they paused and looked around. Trajan trotted contentedly at their side, his head low to take in the enticing evening scents. He seemed unbothered so Flavia let out sigh of relief; they were alone. She glanced at the venerable oak as they walked past. Its branches were hung with an odd assortment of scraps, pretty stones tied on with leather thongs, she even glimpsed the glint of metal catching the moonlight. At its base were strewn pots and remnants of bones from ritual sacrifice. It must be considered a very holy place. She hoped the ancient Druidic gods would combine with the Roman ones and rid her of Balbus forever.

They stumbled over the beach, the rough stones digging into their soft-soled boots until they reached water's edge. The stream, swollen into a river by the winter rains burbled and bubbled as if it were a live creature. The water silvered and shadowed in the moon's light was entrancingly beautiful. Flavia could see why the Druids had chosen a place such as this for their prayer and ritual.

An owl hooted nearby and the creature, as white as a spirit, flew silently over their heads. It was so low that Flavia felt the brush of air from its wings.

'Minerva is with us. A good omen,' Ursa whispered. 'Now is the time to do it and then we must make haste before

we are missed and before it's too dark to see our way back.'
She handed Flavia the curse tablet.

'What do I say?'

'Say what is in your heart, mistress. Speak your most innermost desire.'

Flavia, feeling foolishly self-conscious, lifted the curse tablet high above her head. 'I call upon,' she stopped, her voice sounded overloud in the quiet.

'Go on,' Ursa encouraged.

Flavia cleared her throat and began again. 'I call upon all those in this holy and sacred place to witness that I, Flavia Honorata, with all that is in me, curse most violently the slave Balbus. I call upon the goddess Sulis Minerva, may she serve law and justice; the god of the forests and woods Silvanus, that he may keep us safe this night; and the mighty goddess and protector of women Juno. I also ask that those ancient spirits and gods of the old religion who dwell amongst us here tonight to take on my cause and keep me and those I love safe from the evil that is Balbus the slave!'

The owl flew over again, screeched and then silence dropped. The breeze stilled. Even the very water fell quiet. The air around them charged. Had Jove sent a thunder bolt, Flavia would not have been surprised. She tensed. The ground seemed to shift and rumble beneath their feet. A great wind sprang up, stiff and scented with the sea. It whistled past their ears and hummed through the branches of the ash trees and the ancient oak making the leaves shiver. A tremendous wave rose in the river making the water hurl itself at the bank, overflowing onto the rocky beach, soaking their feet and the hem of their gowns. Unearthly mutterings and groanings whipped about them and Trajan lifted his head and howled at a moon which glowed and bulged, illuminating all with a cold metallic light.

Flavia paused, the tablet clutched in her frozen hands and then, filled with an energy she did not know she possessed, threw it as far as she could. It ducked along a running current, became stuck for a moment against a boulder, then the water tugged at it and it rose up, gleamed in the moonlight as if a thing alive and then sank from view.

The women stood in silence and contemplation, their cloaks shifting around them in the wind, their hair plucked from its fastenings. A now subdued Trajan sat close to Flavia trembling a little. Eventually the wind dropped, the trees ceased their whisperings. The owl flew once more over their heads, an eerie being, it screeched once and disappeared. The moon shrouded with a cloud and darkness descended. It broke the moment.

Ursa took Flavia's hand to find it frozen. 'Come mistress, it is done. We must return.'

They turned and stumbled their way back, eyes gradually adjusting to the blackness, using the dog as a guide. Ursa put her arms around her mistress and half carried her; she was weak and trembling.

As they staggered back through the woods, now dark, gloomy and closely threatening, Flavia whispered in an exhausted voice, 'I wish it to work, Ursa. Oh, I wish it with all my heart. I want to be rid of that man forever.'

Georgia Hill

# CHAPTER 22

*The hills above Flete*

'There was a time when I wanted to be rid of that man,' Juno declared, violently poking a stick into the fire. 'Forever. Trust me. If I'd known how to do it, I would've stuck pins in an effigy and cursed it.'

The silver half-moon had risen high in the sky now. It glinted off the abandoned metal food trays and illuminated her car, the windscreen gazing back blankly. With the camping light Tom had set up and the glow from the fire, she was very glad they were surrounded by a welcome circle of light.

'I'm not surprised,' he said. There was something so calm about his voice it encouraged her to confess more.

'In the end, and to my shame, it ended when he wanted it to. He'd moved on to another woman and wanted me out.' A branch broke in half in the fire and collapsed, sending shards of sparks out. 'I didn't even have the courage to get myself out of there,' Juno said bitterly. 'I had to be forced out. It was so humiliating.'

'But not unusual. You've heard of coercive control and the effects on self-esteem? Stockholm Syndrome?'

'I've read up on it.'

Tom finished his whisky. 'The human mind is a powerful tool. For good and for evil. If Paul followed the pattern, he probably love-bombed you, then began manipulating you, telling you what was wrong about you, eating away at your confidence.'

'Sounds familiar.' Juno sighed wearily. 'Were you a fly on the wall?'

He shrugged. 'I had a friend at university who it happened to. We all watched on the side-lines but were incapable of helping her until she realised for herself what the guy was truly like.'

'At least she did that. I didn't.'

'Thing is, it's careful grooming. You lose all sense of who you are, you continuously doubt yourself and the one constant you can rely on is the very person who is making you feel that way. It's all about unequal power and maintaining a position of control over someone else.'

Juno shuddered. 'Makes sense. But why couldn't I see that at the time?'

'Because you were in the middle of it and at your most vulnerable. Paul may have even done you a favour by finding someone else.' Tom flicked a quick glance her way. 'Was it getting physical? The abuse?'

She nodded, shrinking into herself and putting an arm around Joops's comforting neck.

'I'm so sorry.' He threw more wood on the fire and swore viciously under his breath.

'Thing is, I'd always thought of myself as self-confident, self-reliant. A savvy woman about town. I never thought I'd fall for the bullshit.'

'As I said, the human mind is a powerful thing. And you'll be that again, you'll get back to who you were.'

'I hope so, although it seems an uphill struggle sometimes. He robbed me of myself and I'm still coming to terms with that.' She bit her lip willing the sudden tears away.

'Juno, it's early days yet. When did you split up?'

'November. Mabyn was a star. She drove me to my parents' house in Winchester and I stayed there for a bit.'

'Do you get on with your parents?'

Juno shrugged and fed another twig into the fire, staring into the flames. Burning something felt cathartic. 'I suppose I do. Dad's a bit removed from real life. If I was a fragment of ancient medieval manuscript, he'd probably be more interested. I've never worked out how Mum feels about me. With three children and my father, she had her hands full running the home and didn't go back into teaching. And, out of all of us, she's easily the one with the sharpest brain. She's quite hard on me and my life choices. Maybe she had ambitions for me to have what she hadn't?' Juno sipped her whisky thoughtfully. 'And I've gone my own sweet way and not in the direction she wanted. I suspect she resents me for scuppering her life plans and for not fulfilling her own ambitions.' She blew out a sigh. 'But, hey, she's my Mum and she loves me in her way. It just gets spiky between us sometimes. And, after all, they took me in and looked after me when I could barely string a sentence together, Dad loaned me the car and they're letting me live in the cottage here.'

'Sounds like they love you very much.'

Juno gave a short laugh. 'Yeah. It's just that we have that English middle-class horror of expressing any emotion.'

'Instead, they've demonstrated their love in eminently practical ways by lending you the car and the house.'

'That's very true, now you point it out. I shouldn't be such an ungrateful brat.'

'I've never met anyone less like an ungrateful brat. Are you having counselling? For what happened with Paul, I mean? It might be an idea.'

'I hadn't thought. Suppose it might be an idea. I wouldn't have the first idea of where to look for some, though.'

'I'll ask Mum. She'll have contacts from her teaching days. Don't worry, I won't tell her more than she needs to know.'

'I don't mind Diana knowing. I like her a lot. She's great.'

Tom grinned, the light from the fire sliding across his cheekbones, emphasising his face's dips and hollows. 'She is.'

'But why would she know about counselling?'

'She was big on the pastoral front when teaching. She always said teaching was as much social work as anything.'

'I'd imagine that's true. She must miss it.'

'I think she does, but she still volunteers to hear readers at the school she taught at.' He laughed. 'They can't get rid of her. She's a school governor too.'

'I should think she's a real asset,' Juno said warmly. 'My mother's just been appointed as a magistrate. I think she's coming into her own now she has more free time. She'll be brilliant at it.'

'From what you've said, I'm sure she will. Mine's looking forward to cruising again, she stopped going with the pandemic obviously. She likes travelling solo. Very self-sufficient is my mum. She's had to be. It's only been her and me for years.'

'What happened to your dad, if you don't mind me asking?'

'He died when I was eight. I don't remember much about him.'

'Oh my God, Tom, I'm so sorry. What happened?'

'He got knocked off his motorbike. Apparently, the driver wasn't going all that fast, but dad hit his head at an awkward angle.'

'That's terrible. I'm really sorry.'

He pushed a hand through his hair making it stick up. 'Don't be. It's a long time ago and we had friends around us. Flete is a tightly knit community. We did okay.'

Juno reached out and put a hand on his arm. 'You did more than okay.'

He turned to her and smiled. 'Thanks.'

They stared into one another's eyes for a long moment. The only sound was their hitched breathing and the crackling of the fire. The thought that Juno could easily reach forward and kiss him came as a shock. His unexpected insights into her relationship with Paul and now this sudden vulnerability over his father made him very attractive. But she'd sworn off men, hadn't she? She had to admit, though, his eyes looked dark and deep enough to dive into. Gabbling slightly, she said the first thing which came into her head. 'And I agree Flete is tightly knit. I'm thinking I might stay a while longer.'

Tom looked down and cleared his throat, appearing awkward. 'That's great. Mum for one will be very happy. She's delighted to have you as a neighbour. The previous tenants didn't stay around long enough for her to get to know them.'

He turned his attention back to the fire. Juno wondered if he'd be happy to have her as a neighbour too? He was impossible to read. He'd been full of compassion and understanding, warm and sympathetic when listening to her sorry tale about her and Paul, but now he'd retreated into himself again. She shifted uncomfortably on the hard ground, feeling the chill penetrating. 'Will you be going back to Turkey?'

'Possibly. Possibly not. Depends where the work is.'

'Why did you leave in the first place?'

Tom shrugged. His face had closed down. 'With the pandemic the situation was very uncertain. I was concerned for Mum. I suppose, with everything that was going on, I felt the need to come home.'

'But aren't things opening up again? I mean, I know the disease is still around, but the world has been getting back to normal for a while now.'

'Maybe I've done with Turkey.'

Juno observed his hunched shoulders, certain he wasn't telling her everything. Cris had been curious over why Tom hadn't gone back to Ephesus. She, too, wondered why he wasn't returning. Maybe it had something to do with his divorce? Her memory flickered back to the awkward conversation they'd had in Diana's hall when he'd warned her off. It had killed the mood. As if she'd go for him. As if she'd go for any man right now! He was frowning, his moody upper lip pronounced, a pulse beating on his jaw. Whatever had happened must have hurt him tremendously. He'd been incredibly perceptive about her situation with Paul; she wondered if the same had happened to him? Women were as capable of coercive behaviour and Tom was coming across as defensive and as damaged as she. For the first time she looked upon him with sympathy. Perhaps the arrogance was covering up an awful lot of insecurity. A physical attraction, swift and compelling as it was, was overlaid with compassion and a strong desire to get to know him better. She suspected Tom Lyndsay might be worth the effort. But not tonight.

Faking an enormous yawn, she said, 'Think I'll turn in. Doubt if I'll get much sleep.'

'Good idea. I expect we'll be woken by the dawn chorus in a few hours.' A glimmer of humour returned to his voice. 'Here, take this.' He opened the holdall and drew out a thick plaid blanket.

'What else have you got in there? Just how big is that bag?'

'Just call me Mary Poppins. Should keep the worst of the chill off. Do you want the torch?'

'What for?'

'So you can see to clean your teeth in the river.'

Juno glanced nervously towards the dark trees and the water beyond which was glistening silver and magical in the moonlight. She shivered. 'I'll pass if you don't mind. Don't think my dentist will be bothered about me missing a flossing session just this once.'

'You can go home, you know. I'll be fine here on my own.'

'I know you will. Just thought I'd keep you company, that's all.' She pulled a face. 'I've probably drunk too much whisky to legally drive anyway.'

'Then let me see you to your luxury accommodation.'

They hovered at the Freelander trying to decide if she would be more comfortable in a reclining front seat or in the back.

'Back, I think,' Juno decided. 'I can use the dog blanket as a pillow. Luckily, I've just washed it.' She clambered in and cracked open a window for ventilation. Making a wedge with the dog blanket she lay down. Her legs were curled up but it wasn't too uncomfortable. Joops jumped in after her.

Tom put the plaid blanket over her, tucking it round. 'Don't forget to lock yourself in.'

'Why?' she asked cheekily, the whisky talking. She'd loved the feel of his hands on her. 'Thinking of having your wicked way with me?'

He gave a dry chuckle. 'Night, Juno.' Then he slammed the door.

She pressed the internal lock and heard the system give a satisfying clunk. Joops jumped onto the back seat and, after endless circling, settled in the space created by her curved body. He gave off a wall of heat and she cuddled him to her. She lay listening to the sounds of the night: an owl hooting in the distance, the wind rustling through the trees, the babble of the nearby stream. With Tom's lantern and light from the fire it wasn't completely dark but she could still see stars twinkling. The same stars had shone on her Durotriges man. It was absurdly comforting. She heard Tom moving about the makeshift camp, possibly washing up their food trays or going off to have a pee. And then she heard a zip. It must be the tent flap closing. She wriggled a little as she felt Joops drift into sleep and breathe heavily. 'I bet I don't sleep a wink,' she protested. He began to snore. Five minutes later she was fast asleep too.

\* \* \*

A robin singing his heart out woke her up, along with a cloudless sky and a sun eager to get the day started. She revisited the spot where she'd had a wee the night before and returned to camp to hunt through the holdall for the toothbrush and paste.

Washing in the icy cold water of the shallows simultaneously woke her up and chilled her to the bone. She sat on the little beach for a while, face upturned to the sun, soaking up its warmth. It was intensely peaceful, with the birdsong and the water tumbling past. She watched as Joops wandered into the river, taking great noisy gulps of water. He must be starving. One small piece of chicken wasn't going to sustain him. She was almost regretful at the idea of returning home. Even though so close to the town and a main road, it felt very cut off here. Timeless. They had water, food, a fire. All basic needs met. And it was certainly freeing being removed from the pressure of social media and the phone.

'Morning.'

'Morning, Tom.' She turned to see him hobble gingerly over the rocky beach barefoot and wearing nothing but a pair of snug fitting boxers. He flung a towel at her. Of course he'd have a towel in that Mary Poppins bag. She wished she'd thought to ask and hadn't endured the chilly drip drying. 'I'll go shall I, if you're going in for a wash?'

He ran the last few feet to the water's edge, waded in to his knees and yelped as the cold hit. 'No, don't bother. I'll not be staying in all that long.' He began to jump about. 'It's freezing!' Joops got excited and splashed in deeper to join him. Man and dog were soon soaked.

Juno began to giggle and laughed even more as Joops jumped at Tom sending them both underwater. Holding onto his towel, she tip-toed around the most jagged of rocks to the edge of the beach, where the shallows lapped contentedly. As Tom stood up, she admired how the water streaming down his body emphasised his lean muscles. He was brown all over but darker where his t-shirt ended at neck and arm and he had a finely toned pair of tanned legs, with dark golden hair glistening in the wet. He had very sexy knees. She gulped and looked away, staring downstream. A flurry of rocks and pebbles had been dislodged by the activity and something cylindrical bobbed to the surface and floated away. Idly, she wondered what it was. Then she was interrupted by Joops, floundering back to shore and choosing to shake himself right next to her. It had her shrieking and running off.

Half an hour later Tom had sausages sizzling in the pan over the fire and they'd downed their first mug of tea. Black but hot and much needed.

Juno was sitting opposite the tent which was open. She could see right inside. Apart from the groundsheet there was nothing else in there. 'Did you sleep well?' she asked him.

Tom pulled the collar of his rugby shirt up around his neck. His hair, still wet, was in golden spikes. 'Not bad,' he said carefully.

'Where's the other blanket?'

'There isn't one.'

'You gave me the blanket? And I was in the car with Joops belting out heat?'

He shrugged and concentrated on turning the sausages over.

'And they say chivalry's dead.'

He gave her a rueful grin. 'Not so much that as the earful my mum would give me if she found out I'd nicked the only blanket.'

'Quite right too.' She smiled. 'Well, you can have it tonight as I've really got to go home.' Did she imagine it or had his face fallen slightly?

'Of course.' He shifted the cooked sausages to one side and broke a couple of eggs into the pan.

'I've a deadline to meet and Joops needs feeding.'

'He can have a sausage.'

'And he'd love one but that's not going to keep him going. It's either that or him hunting down a duck and that won't be pretty.'

'Thought you said he was no good as a hunter?'

'He isn't. In the past he's got hold of tail feathers at the most but I can't vouch for when he's half-starved. Besides, I need a proper shower.' She shuddered. 'I'm not going near that river again.'

He pulled a face. 'I take your point.'

'You'll be okay, won't you?'

He dished out a plate of egg and sausages and handed it to her. 'I'll be absolutely fine.'

'I can bring you up more food if you like,' she said, fending Joops off.

'That would be excellent.'

Juno put an entire sausage onto her fork and held it up. She was ravenous. Biting off an end, she added, 'So what exactly happened between you and your wife? You mentioned you were divorced.' She watched him hesitate, cut into his egg with his fork and eat slowly.

'Nothing like getting half frozen to give you an appetite.' When she didn't answer, he added, 'It's the usual story. Got married. Probably too young. Thought it was for life. Drifted apart.' He paused. 'Then she had an affair with a younger man.'

'Oh.' Juno was surprised. Who would have an affair when you had Tom?

'She's Turkish so it's kind of put me off going back there for a while.'

'I see.' Juno didn't. She only had half an idea of Turkey's geography, but she was sure it was a pretty big country.

'I'm sorry.'

'Don't be. It's just one of those things. Funnily enough I always thought if anything was going to split us up it would be the cultural differences. Turned out it was the old story of irresistible lust.'

'She never wanted to come to England?'

Tom shook his head. 'No. All her work is in Turkey.'

'And there's been no one since?'

'Nope.' He bit into his sausage with even white teeth. 'Work, travelling, the pandemic got in the way.'

'If you're anything like me,' Juno said robustly, 'it puts you off from ever having another relationship.'

He raised his eyebrows. 'There is that.'

Juno held up her tin mug. 'To friendship, then. Our friendship.'

He matched it. 'To friendship.'

She watched him eat as she drank her tea. He was eating his breakfast with a slow and controlled concentration, not making eye contact. She'd blithely said the words, but she was no longer sure of them. Would she be content with only friendship? As the sun lifted over the trees and picked out the dark blonde hairs at the neck of his shirt, a coil of lust warmed her. Shutting it off, she handed Joops the remainder of her sausage, all appetite, at least for food, gone. The dog swallowed it whole and she pulled him to her, desperate for some physical comfort.

Georgia Hill

# CHAPTER 23

*T**he hills above Moridunum*

Flavia stood with her back to the gate, with the safety of the villa behind her. She put a hand on Trajan's trusty head, her fingers deep in his wiry coat, desperate for some physical comfort. This was the most audacious and bold plan yet. The kitchen slave had got word to Ursa from Padrig and she could hardly believe what he asked. He'd requested that she meet him at the back gate and that he would take her to meet his family and show her his home.

The sun was only just dancing above the trees and although late spring it was early-morning chilly. Flavia pulled her cloak more tightly around her and crouched beside the dog, throwing an arm around him and seeking out his heat. Eyes fixed on the track winding down the hill she felt Trajan whine in his throat and was surprised when Padrig emerged from the woods, leading a stocky pony. The deafening spring dawn chorus ceased and all was still. Mist swirled about him and for a minute he seemed unworldly. After her experiences from the other night, when she'd cast the curse tablet into the river, she had a new appreciation of the power of the supernatural. However, the warmth which spread through her from groin to face had everything to do with the earthly and the physical. Once again it struck her what a fine-looking man he was, with his reddish-yellow hair and beard. In contrast, the men in the villa seemed plucked and naked with their shaven oiled skin. As he paused, his hand on the pony's neck, he stood as tall and sure as the oak at his back.

Casting a quick glance to make sure the path was clear, she picked up her skirts and ran to him. 'You came!'

Padrig bowed, a smile on his face. 'Aye. Did you think I would not?'

'I wasn't sure. I waited for so long.'

'I apologise. A hunting party from the neighbouring village had me waiting until they passed.' He shrugged. 'Friendly enough, but I did not want to explain why I was heading to the villa estate leading my best pony.'

Flavia's nose wrinkled. 'I am not fond of horses.'

'I take it you do not ride then?'

She ignored his obvious humour. 'I've never needed to learn. A litter or wagon is always available should I need transport. Not that I'm usually allowed to go anywhere,' she added bitterly.

'Then make today your adventure. It's a goodly walk to the village. I thought I should save your legs and bring Pwca.'

'Pwca?'

'The pony. She is sure-footed and docile. She won't cause you any problems.'

'I am expected to get on her back?' Flavia asked scandalised.

'It's the usual way to ride a pony. But, before you do, I have something from my sister, Steren.' He reached into his leather bag. 'I have something I'd like to give to you.'

'Oh?'

'You once asked what my people do, in our village up in the hills.' He pulled out the mended necklace which he held pooled in his palm. 'This is one thing we do. We make beads out of things we find on the beach and string them into necklaces. My sister, Steren, makes them. She has mended the sea glass necklace you gave me and, I think, improved it.' His lips twisted in humour. 'Perhaps we are not such ruffians as you like to think.'

She opened her palm and he dropped it into her hand, where it fell like water. 'It's beautiful,' she sighed. It was. Now a long rope of soft greeny-blue beads and shells threaded on fine leather, the original sea glass beads were blended in between. 'Thank you.' She gazed at him, her eyes brilliant. 'This is far more beautiful than the one I broke.' *And far more precious.* She should pour out her troubles, ask for his help but there was something sparkling and innocent about the morning and his presence. She wanted to go with the moment, forget all about Balbus, and simply enjoy being with Padrig. She slipped the necklace over her head. *I'll never take it off.*

'You're welcome, daughter of Flavius Honoratus. May you wear it well. And now, up with you onto Pwca's back.'

'And how, pray, am I to get up there?'

Padrig laughed out loud. 'Come here.'

When she obeyed, he slid his strong hands around her waist and hoisted onto the animal's back. She was aboard before she could demur.

'And now all you have to do is hang on and pray to Epona.'

She clutched the pony's coarse thick mane. 'I do not feel at all secure!'

'Can you slide your leg over and ride with your legs abreast? Here, let me hold you while you do it.'

Flavia flipped a leg over the pony's neck and sat facing the front. She tried, without success, to ignore the feel of Padrig's hands upon her back and stomach. With her legs apart, his hand was dangerously near her womanly parts. Even more dangerous was the desire for his hand to dip lower and caress. Her face heated.

'Better?' he enquired mildly.

'Somewhat,' she choked out. 'Do not go fast though.'

'No need to be afeared. Pwca has one speed and that's slow and steady. Reliable she may be, speedy she most certainly isn't.'

He began to lead the pony through the woods, Trajan loping alongside. Once Flavia became accustomed to the height and strange motion, she relaxed a little. 'If she is so slow, why is she valuable?'

'She's given us many foals.'

'A brood mare then? Is that how you value your womenfolk?'

Padrig laughed again. 'I recall telling you women have equal status amongst our society, if not revered more highly than men.'

'And why is that?'

He glanced back causing her to blush more. 'For women have the sacred ability to bring forth new life and, as such, should be revered.' Their eyes met and Flavia's insides flamed. Then Padrig continued to walk. 'How have you explained your absence today?'

'Ursa is to say we are taking a day at the temple in town in quiet prayer and contemplation to Minerva.'

'And is that Ursa's cloak you have on?'

'Yes. I thought it best to dress humbly.'

'Very wise.' He led the pony around a low branch.

'What am I to expect?'

'Alas, my father is away visiting allies to the north but Merit, my brother, is to meet you, and my sisters Steren and Alys have prepared a feast to welcome you.'

'Perhaps I was unwise to dress in drab.'

Padrig chuckled. 'As long as you are wearing Steren's necklace, you will pass.'

Flavia felt for the blue beads and was reassured to find them lying heavily against her skin. 'I will never take it off, except in the bathhouse.'

Padrig sent a swift smile her way. 'Steren will be delighted. She takes great pleasure in seeing her jewellery worn.'

'I treasure it. She is very talented.'

'Pray, don't tell her. She has a head the size of a hog's as it is. Tell me,' he added, his voice taking on a serious note, 'you said you needed help. Has the danger to you passed?'

Talking of Balbus sullied the clean crisp air. She remained silent as she thought through her answer. Her father complained bitterly of his slave being ill and confined to his sick bed. Whether it was the curse working or a simple coincidence, she couldn't dare to hope. Either way, the man hadn't been near her since the tumultuous night by the river. 'I have had no recent dealings with my enemy,' she said carefully, 'but I cannot truthfully say if the danger has gone. While he remains in my father's house there is always the possibility ...' She trailed off. To voice her deepest fears to Padrig would taint a day of enchantments. The air was fresh and warm now the sun had risen higher, the scents of the trees as the pony brushed past them aromatic and she was with a man for whom her feelings were running hot. She had a sense of freedom that made her giddy with joy. Noting that Padrig's shoulders had become tensed she said, 'Let us not talk of such things today. I want to remember this as a day full of joy and rapture.'

'Then so be it, my lady.'

They continued in silence, along the deeply grooved drover's route, until the ground began to rise steeply. Flavia had to lean forward to keep herself seated on Pwca and admired how Padrig lengthened his stride effortlessly to tackle the incline. A high fence hove into view, with sharply pointed tips and a double gate which was guarded.

'The first entrance gate,' Padrig explained. As they approached, the guards opened it and bowed low until they were through. They followed the ramparts, continuing to wind their way around in corkscrew pattern, scattering cattle and goats and passing an enclosure of pigs. The stench of the animals was rank and sour and made Flavia risk releasing one hand to pull her cloak over her mouth. One or two people stopped and bowed their heads. At a second line of defence stood a more elaborate gate hung with the skulls of horned goats. It yawned open. Still they climbed, passing circular huts clustered together, smoke drifting from their roofs to be left hanging in the hot still air. At the third gate a man stood. He could only be Padrig's brother, so strong was the family resemblance. He wore a wolfskin and plaid trousers, ritual tattoos marking his skin.

'Greetings brother,' Padrig called out.

'Greetings to you and to the lady Flavia. We are honoured by your visit. If you will excuse me, I will go and make things ready.' He gave an abrupt bow and turned on his heel.

Flavia couldn't decide if he appeared friendly or not. For the first time it occurred to her that she had put herself in a foolishly vulnerable position. What if all this was a lure to kidnap and hold her ransom? She flicked a glance around at the villagers who were giving her undisguised and curious stares. The men were especially brazen. What if an even worse fate were to befall her?

Padrig came to her. 'Merit has given you chance to dismount discreetly. You will be stiff after your unaccustomed exercise. Go about your business,' he said to the gathering crowd. 'Off you go. There is nothing to see here. Forgive them, my lady. It's curiosity, that's all. Few venture out of the village unless they have to or are forced.'

She knew he meant as slaves. Shame engulfed her. Looking down at his wide-open face and kind eyes she knew she could trust him. She had little choice. He was her only ally here.

He held out his arms. 'Slide down to me.'

With difficulty – he had been right, her legs had become stiff – she lifted her leg back over the pony's neck and twisted to face Padrig. She wanted to leap off to show her independence and pride but feared she'd end up in a crumpled heap in the mud at his feet. Putting her hands on his shoulders, she slid down his body, revelling in the close contact with his warmth. For a second they stood holding one another. He smelled of woodsmoke and desire.

'Found your feet?' His voice was hoarse so perhaps it wasn't only her who was affected.

'Yes.' Her answer came out breathy and voiceless.

'Take Pwca and feed and water her,' he called. From nowhere, a youth appeared, bobbed a shy bow to Flavia and led the pony away. 'Come, this way.' Padrig took her arm and led her between a warren of round huts. Outside one a woman paused in her grinding of wheat on a quern and stared, another was scraping a skin and yet another woman was spinning with long dextrous fingers. The village seemed very busy with everyone at a job and skilful at it. She couldn't help but compare her aimless days at the villa where the hardest task she had was to find occupation and look diligent. Padrig stopped outside a hut which dwarfed the others and which bore huge shields on either side of the low entrance. He seemed to hesitate and then said, 'My family home. After you, my lady.'

Flavia gathered her skirts, stepped over the ditch which ran the circumference and entered. She kept Trajan close; he may be her only protection and took a moment to allow her eyes to adjust to the gloom. The hut appeared bigger on the inside and once she could see properly, she took in her surroundings. A warming fire pit in the middle had a heavy pot held over it from which came delicious scents. There was also a spit on which a glistening hunk of meat was cooking. Rugs were spread over the earth floor and rich hangings blanketed the curved walls. In niches set against the back wall she could just about make out beds with more luxurious coverings. On a low bench sat Padrig's brother and lolling on heaped cushions were, she assumed, his two sisters. One of them leaped up.

'I'm Steren. Come sit with us, do.' She took Flavia's hand and led her to the bulkiest cushion. 'Sit here. As our honoured guest, you should take the newest and most comfortable seating.'

Flavia allowed herself to be seated in between Steren and a girl who she assumed was Alys although she said nothing and had not even raised her head. Trajan glanced around, nose quivering at the scents of cooking meat and settled at her feet.

Padrig took his place next to his brother.

'Padrig,' Merit cried, 'do not let our guest go thirsty. Pour her some mead.'

Padrig rose again and went to a table in a shadowy curve of the hut. He filled a goblet with a golden liquid and brought it to Flavia. 'Our finest mead,' he explained, 'made sweet with the honey of our bees.'

'Thank you.' Flavia held the goblet but didn't dare drink. She waited while Padrig poured his sisters the same and furnished Merit with what smelled like ale. She was wise to wait.

Merit raised his finely wrought bone goblet. 'To our most honoured guest. We are blessed by your presence. May the power of Aerten be ours.'

'May the power of Aerten be ours,' the others echoed and drank deeply.

Flavia made a silly sort of a nod in acknowledgement and sipped her mead. It was delicious, the best she'd ever tasted and certainly superior to some of her father's preferred imported wines. 'Thank you. You have made me most welcome.'

Merit nodded. 'Did you think we were savages who did not know how to greet and look after guests?' A smile played about his lips. He drank, his eyes never leaving hers.

'I know enough to know you treat well those who are welcome. I also know how you treat those who are considered your enemy.'

'And which are you, my lady Flavia?'

'Seeing as I freely entered your village on one of your prized horses and escorted by your very own brother it would be foolish of me to admit I was your enemy, even if I were. As it is, I consider myself a friend of Padrig's and also of Steren's for it was she who made me the sea glass necklace which will never leave my neck.'

Steren roared, spilling her mead. 'She's got you there, brother,' she said. 'Stop being so high and mighty and let us eat. I'm half starved.'

Merit gave his sister an exasperated look and clapped his hands. Several women appeared and the food was served. It was simple stuff but good. The meat stew was hot and richly flavoured with garlic and parsley and some other sharp tang which she could not identify. The bread was coarser than she was used to, but she was so hungry she didn't mind, even following the example of her hosts and wiping the bowl out with a piece.

'So, you enjoyed our food?' Merit asked.

'I did, but I confess the journey here made me so hungry I too was half-starved.'

He snorted.

'But even so, it was very good, thank you. Tell me what flavourings do you use?'

'You lower yourself to cook, my lady?'

'I do not,' she replied sharply, 'but I am in charge of my father's kitchen and order what foodstuffs are required.'

He gave another imperious nod. 'What herbs do you use?' he asked, addressing one of the serving women.

'Wild garlic, a little parsley and nettles, my lord.' She was pretty, with luminescent skin and frothing dark hair.

'Hopefully with the sting removed?'

Everyone laughed. Merit seemed in better humour now he had eaten.

The woman smiled, her eyes alive with humour. 'I would never dare serve my lord Merit with such that would make his tongue sharper than it already is.'

Flavia gasped. Her father would never countenance such insolence.

Merit guffawed and slapped the woman's backside roundly. 'Get you away, Aoife. Get back to your work. Have you nothing left to do for our forthcoming Beltane celebrations?'

'I have much to do, my lord and would have done it had I not been called upon to serve here.'

Merit laughed again and pulled her onto his lap. 'Wench, I curse the day I ever took you as my wife.'

Aoife tugged hard on his beard and kissed him. He responded hungrily. 'You mean you cursed the many days you *waited* until I consented to be your wife? Let me go now, husband. I have much to do.'

'Don't wear yourself out too much.' The meaning was clear. He growled and kissed her again, his big hands clasped around each of her buttocks.

Flavia tore her eyes away. So the serving girl was Merit's wife. Little wonder then that he tolerated her insolence. It was all so different to what she experienced at home. Her parents barely spoke to each other and even then it was chilly. Meals were lengthy and for show, to entertain or further political ambition rather than for joy, companionship or to slake hunger. Everything here felt warm and cosy, if a little raucous, the relationships easy and unforced. She caught Alys staring at her. The girl was shy. She smiled back but Alys ducked her head again. They were an intriguing family. Merit a complex man, sharp-witted and full of the ego of the first-born son. Steren with her infectious humour and creative talent. Alys, more difficult to work out, but who seemed overshadowed by the bigger characters of her siblings. She lifted her eyes to Padrig. He was grinning at Merit and Aoife's antics and sipping his ale. It was fascinating seeing him among his own people. He commanded obvious respect from his tribesmen, but she detected strain between him and his brother.

Eventually Aoife broke away. She grinned, pretty dimples appearing. 'Fear not, I shall have energy spare for later.' She slid off him. 'I must go. You will have to carve the meat yourself.' She nodded to them all. 'I hope the food suited.'

Flavia found her voice. She had been lost in her thoughts. *What must it be like to be kissed as such by a man?* 'Very well. Thank you. It was delicious.'

'Good. Don't let Merit take all the best meat. I bid you farewell. Come again, Flavia. It does my bear of a husband good to be reminded that sometimes the enemy has a friendly face.' She swept out.

There was an awkward pause and then Padrig began hacking at the meat on the spit with ferocious concentration.

\*

On their return journey, Padrig once again led the pony. They were silent, each contained by their thoughts. At Aoife's departure, conversation had centred neutrally around food, the upcoming Beltane feast, Steren's new jewellery creations. Flavia hadn't been able to shake off her suspicions that Merit saw her as an enemy, even one with a friendly face.

When they reached the willows by the rocky beach at the river's curve, Padrig helped her dismount and led the pony to drink. Trajan joined in splashing around enjoying the cool water on his overheated and tired body. Once the pony had satiated her thirst, Padrig tethered her to a tree letting her graze. Filling a bone beaker, he offered it to Flavia who drank greedily. It had been a hot journey back. Refilling it, he too drank. She stood watching him, the river in the background. The water felt very different today. It meandered serenely, a force for life rather than a lifetaker. Birdsong filled the air. Again, she wondered just what had happened on the night of the casting of the curse tablet. And again, she prayed to Juno, protector of women, that it had worked. Glancing at the mighty sacred oak, hung with offerings, she promised to make sacrifice when she returned home.

Reaching for Flavia's hand and kissing it, Padrig finally spoke. 'I trust you've found today interesting.'

'I have. And enjoyable too. It was good to meet your family.' She frowned, Padrig seemed distant, formal. Unlike the man she had come to know. 'Tell me, I am curious about your brother. I wasn't sure how he felt about me.'

Padrig's lip curled. 'Merit is overly conscious he will be our next king. He keeps his feelings, if he has them, close to his chest. I'm not sure any one of us knows exactly what he is thinking. You missed the significance of the supplication to Aerten?'

'Aerten? One of your gods?'

'She is goddess of peace.'

'That's good,' Flavia replied. 'Isn't it?'

'She's also goddess of overcoming enemies.'

'Oh.' Flavia was silent for a moment. 'So Merit will wage war on Rome?'

Padrig sighed deeply. 'Maybe. My father has always trodden the uneasy path of peace and trade, but Merit is young, hot-blooded and has always been arrogant. He is witness to injustices done. And maybe he has a point? When Rome has bled us dry it will turn its eye to the east. It cares little for its northern province.'

'Surely that's not true! Rome has put laws in place, organisation, trade. Rome has been Britannia's master for centuries. It would not forsake it so easily.'

'I am glad you think so. I am afeared I do not share your optimism. But then how could I? I am a son of the Durotriges. You are a daughter of Rome.'

'With Britannia's blood running through my veins. I may answer to Rome as its citizen, but I am a Briton too.'

Padrig didn't answer and looked unconvinced.

'Where was your father today?' Flavia asked, hoping for a less controversial topic. She didn't want to discuss politics, she'd rather talk of love.

He looked down and scuffed his boot in the dry dust. 'He was taking the hospitality of our neighbours near Aquae Sulis.'

'More trade?'

'Of a sort.' Padrig laughed but it was a sound without humour. 'He was negotiating a marriage. A political match.'

'But Merit is already married, and happily so from what I could judge.' As the realisation dawned, Flavia gasped and covered her mouth with her hand. 'For you?'

'For me.' He paused. 'It would be a great honour for me to affiliate the two tribes of the Durotriges and the Dobunni.'

'But there is no love there.' It wasn't a question.

'No.' He met her gaze. 'There is no love *there*.'

At that moment Flavia knew. She knew she could give herself to no man other than the one standing in front of her. 'Oh, Padrig, will I ever see you again?' she asked urgently, flinging her arms around him and pressing herself against him. Some deep secret part of her wanted a taste of what Merit and Aoife had. Another, more sensible part, recognised the danger. The many dangers. If only, by force of her feelings alone, could she draw around them a protective shield and make Balbus, Merit and this mysterious woman destined to be Padrig's bride disappear in a bolt from Jove.

He disentangled himself and stepped away. 'I am at your bidding. You only have to send me a message.'

'I don't want you to be at my bidding,' she said crossly.

His brows furrowed. 'Then what *do* you want of me?' he bit out, exasperated. 'You must know this,' he spread out his hands on the words, 'can go no further. We are from different worlds, Flavia. We have different fates in store.' He stared at his feet again. 'I should not have allowed today to happen. It was too much. It's led you to expect too much. I was very wrong.' He was obviously struggling with some strong emotion.

'Indeed.' The recognition of their situation filled her with a liquid sadness. 'But I have no expectations. I only have love. I -'

He shot her a burning look. 'Don't say it!'

'I love you Padrig,' she cried wildly. 'I wish it were not so, but I do. With my whole heart and more. With my whole body. I would gladly lay myself down at your feet for your bidding. I love you!'

Padrig clasped her hands to him. Raising them he kissed her fingers feverishly. 'And I you, but you cannot know how much I wish it otherwise. It will lead to nothing but pain and unhappiness for us both.'

Flavia threaded her hands through his beard. The hair was coarse and exciting. She pulled his face to hers and kissed him with all the hunger and desperation she had.

He tried to back off and failed. 'This is not right,' he murmured against her mouth as he kissed her passionately. 'Flavia, we must not do this.'

'It is the most right thing in the world, Padrig. And we have no choice. We must do this. I must have you. I *will* have you!'

She would change her life. She would! Fate would not send Balbus and his vile threats her way. She would conquer him somehow, rid herself of his malevolence. She was destined for Padrig and for Padrig alone. She kissed him again, hard and demanding. All rational thought fled. Her heart was full, her body on fire and every sense she possessed wanted more.

Their bodies met and entwined and where they touched heat lit flames along every nerve and muscle. Lost in their passion, they gave in to feelings which had been building since their first encounter. Flavia felt Padrig's hands hunt under her tunics and groaned with longing as his searching fingers found naked flesh. Caresses growing ever more urgent they fell to the soft grass. Padrig rolled Flavia onto him to protect her from the ground, his desire arching up and into her and they were lost into oblivion.

A robin singing sweetly in the sheltering sacred oak above serenaded them to the summit of their passion. Trajan eyed the coupling with disinterest and then, sighing, rolled onto his side and stretched out in the sunshine, his tail flicking in the dust.

# CHAPTER 24

*T*he hills above Flete

Joops lay stretched out in the sunshine, watching, as Juno tidied up. His tail thumped on the grass every now and again but otherwise he lay content. Juno worked slowly, enjoying the robin as it sang lustily from a nearby oak tree. Despite what she'd said about having to get back, she was in no hurry to return to the house and its sinister ringing telephone. While here she had managed to ignore its significance. But it could only be one person who was ringing and then not speaking.

Paul.

Somehow, he'd tracked her down. But how? She shuddered. She thought she'd changed her life by coming to Flete, changed her fate. Shaking out the blanket with unnecessary vigour she visualised it was Paul and wished she could shake him out of her life as easily.

'Well, Joops,' she said, addressing the dog who had rolled onto his side and was stretched out in the heat of the spring sunshine. 'I refuse to put up with it any longer. My destiny no longer lies with a man who is so utterly immoral, I might even say evil. When we get back, I'll report the calls. No, even better, I'll get the landline cut off, after all I hardly use it. And then let's see what Paul bloody Callighan will do about that!'

Joops jerked awake at her anger, or maybe at the mention of the man's name. He sat up, growling in his throat.

'It's alright, Joopsy boy,' Juno said, forcing a laugh. 'He's not here.' She flicked a glance around the field to make sure but there was no one in sight. Throwing off the creeping sensation she was being watched, and furious at how fearful Paul still made her feel, she concentrated on folding the blanket. Joops put his nose on his front paws and watched protectively.

To her relief – and it was ridiculous and irritating that she felt so – Tom returned from washing the breakfast things in the river, whistling merrily as he strode from behind the willows. She was struck by the force of her attraction to him. She'd been determined not to fall for him. To not fall for any man. She'd thought she was too bruised, too frail, too wary of the world to want to even contemplate another relationship. But Tom had slid into her life, listened to her problems, enthused her with his passion for archaeology. She'd witnessed how caring he was to his mother. He'd been tender to her too. Looking after her in his quiet way, giving up his blanket, demanding little but offering so much. And then there was how he looked almost naked. She couldn't deny how she'd reacted to the sight of him in the river yesterday. Gulping the physicality of the memory away, she reminded herself that they had pledged to be friends. And while not easy, it would be far less complicated. She also reminded herself she'd done what he'd expressly told her not to: she'd fallen for him.

Fool!

Her stomach flipped as the sun lit his hair to the gold of ripe corn, his biceps bulging as he gathered another load of wood for the fire.

As if sensing her eyes on him, he looked up. 'What?'

Juno cleared her throat. It ached with desire. 'Nothing.' She had been determined to change her life and she had. But she'd blundered into something else almost by accident and wasn't sure what she was going to do about it. Turning to throw the blanket into the tent, she paused at the sound of a tractor. The huge green and yellow thing racketed across the field.

With difficulty Tom caught hold of Joops's collar as the dog was leaping around and barking with mad excitement. The tractor parked up next to the Freelander and a middle-aged man in a navy boiler suit and tweed cap clambered out. Juno braced herself for a confrontation. Had they been trespassing?

'Tom, mate! Only just got your message. The granddaughter switched off the mobile when she was playing with it.' The man shook Tom's hand. 'And who's this?' He bent to greet Joops who sniffed him cautiously and then backed away. 'Springers, eh? Mad as March hares.'

'Giles! Good to see you,' Tom released Joops who, by now thoroughly overstimulated, ran off and circled the monster which had invaded his territory. 'Thought it was weird when you hadn't offered to help. The dog is Joops and belongs to Juno here. Juno,' he added, introducing them. 'This is Giles. He farms the land round here.'

Juno jettisoned the blanket which she'd been clutching to her for protection – against what or whom she didn't want to analyse – and came forward to shake the stranger's hand. 'Farmer Giles?' she said, her mouth twitching.

'That's me,' he answered chirpily. 'Parents had no imagination.' Turning to Tom he asked, 'What you want, boy? Heard you might have found summat.'

'Possible coin hoard.'

Giles whistled through his teeth. 'Now there's something. What you want me to do?'

'The FLO can't organise anyone to get over here for a few days. I need to make the site secure. Cover it up somehow. That'll release me to chase up the council, get the university to set up a field team.'

'I gets it.' Giles nodded. 'I got me some bales of silage in yonder field. You want me to bring 'em over? Not much that'll get through a pile of them.'

'Sounds like a plan.'

Juno watched with amusement. Tom in professional mode was cheerful and uncomplicated, succinct and efficient.

'Where'd you want 'em, boy?'

Tom pointed out where the tent was pitched. 'We'll get that shifted. You'll be able to see where I've repaired the hole.'

'Righty-o. You good folks won't need to camp out then.'

Tom glanced at Juno. 'Oh, it hasn't been too bad, has it, Juno?'

'Not too bad,' she murmured.

'You an arsiegollogist as well, miss?'

'No!'

'You don't need to be quite so horrified about it, Juno,' Tom laughed.

'Well, it all looks mighty cosy.' Giles tugged his cap at her and grinned with a hint of suggestiveness.

'I just brought the supplies,' she said haughtily.

'As you have it. Just as well the weather wasn't too bad.' He squinted up at the blue sky. 'On the turn though, I reckon.' Tapping his nose, he added, 'comes in with a spring tide. Best go get you sorted then. Nice to meet you, Jane. Get this tent shifted, Tom.' He sauntered over to the tractor, reversed it neatly and it trundled off.

A moment of stillness fell. Tom looked at Juno speculatively. 'Was it really all so awful? Spending the night in a field with me?'

'We didn't spend the night together. And no, of course it wasn't awful.'

He seemed about to say something.

She cut him off. 'We'd better get packed up, hadn't we? Before the charming Giles returns.'

Tom gave a curt nod. 'As you say.'

They stayed until Tom was satisfied there were enough bright blue plastic wrapped bales of silage to put people off.

'Should be enough here,' Giles said. 'You can't shift 'em without an almighty great effort or a tractor and it won't look out of place or suspicious plonked down here.' With a wave he hauled himself into the tractor and left.

'Would you like a lift back?' Juno offered. The atmosphere had gone weird between them. She missed the intimacy that had grown up and almost didn't want to leave the safe little world they'd created. It had been a bubble away from deadlines, her uncertain future and, of course, Paul. But, as much as she'd loved this strange interlude, she was desperate for a hot shower and to clean her teeth properly. There was a lot to be said for modern plumbing and hot running water.

'Yeah, thanks. I'd appreciate that.'

Tom got into the passenger seat and she backed the Freelander round and headed for the gate. Once onto the main road any lingering ancient spell that had been cast over them was broken.

Juno eased the car into a space outside Begin-Again Cottage and switched off the engine. She didn't want this time with Tom to end. Staring at her front door, she also realised she didn't want to go into the house alone. 'Bacon sandwich? I can't cook that well, but I make a mean bacon butty.'

'Why not? he rubbed his face tiredly. 'Those sausages seem a long time ago.'

'They are,' she glanced at the car's clock. 'Didn't we eat at seven or something ridiculous? It's past three now.'

'In that case, it's a definite yes. Brown sauce?'

He looked so boyishly hopeful that Juno's heart melted. As she put her key into the lock she froze. A ringing phone could be heard quite clearly. It stopped and she released the breath she'd been holding. Bustling through to the kitchen and letting Joops out into the garden, she felt more normal. After all, Paul was miles away and she had

Tom here. She switched on the kettle, desperate for a huge mug of scaldingly hot tea.

Tom sprawled on the sofa, yawning. He picked up the copy of Greek myths he'd loaned her and flicked through. It fell open at Perseus and Andromeda's story. 'I remember you saying you enjoyed this one,' he called through.

She came to stand over him and peered at the book. 'I did. I'm all for a happy ending, although I'd hope in any modern retelling Andromeda would save herself and not rely on some random superhero who happened to fly past.'

'You might have a point although she went on to become a superhero herself. Together they're supposed to have founded the great kingdom of Mycenae. And Perseus isn't all that much of a superhero, I suppose. He needed some help from winged sandals and a helmet of invisibility.'

Juno returned to the kitchen and turned on the grill. 'Now that's something that would come in handy on occasions. I could definitely use a helmet of invisibility.' Standing in the doorway, she struck a pose. 'Just think of the possibilities!'

Tom laughed. 'Zeus gave Perseus and Andromeda the ultimate reward though.'

'What's that?'

'They were taken up into the night sky and made into constellations. Now that *is* a happy ending.'

Juno leaned on the door jamb, a packet of bacon in her hand. 'Aw, that's lovely. Imagine looking up and knowing your loved ones are in the sky as stars, twinkling for eternity.'

Tom gave her a measured look. 'Is that the romance novelist talking?' He was teasing but it was gentle and affectionate.

'Maybe.' She smiled at him enjoying that they seemed to be back on an even keel again. Flicking on the radio she sang along to the old Genesis track that was playing. 'Stay with me,' she sang. *Yes, stay with me Tom. If only you would.* Then she froze as the phone shrilled out again.

Tom came into the kitchen. 'Want me to get that? Someone's obviously keen to get hold of you.'

'Let it ring,' Juno said sharply.

'Why? Is it someone you don't want to talk to?'

She turned away, making herself busy by slicing bread. 'You could say that.' She stabbed at the loaf making a mess.

'It's not that bloke, Paul, the one who caused you so many problems?'

Juno forced herself to sound nonchalant. 'Maybe. When I've picked up there's no one there.'

The phone rang out another few times and then stopped, leaving a strident echo hanging in the air.

Juno's shoulders relaxed a little. Fighting back tears she concentrated on not cutting off a finger. *I will not let him affect me. I will not let him get to me!* Bending to check on the cooking bacon, her hand gripped the grill pan handle as the phone started up again. She screwed her eyes shut and swallowed.

Tom turned in one swift movement and disappeared into the sitting room.

'Don't answer it!' Juno shouted. Panicked, she grabbed the bread knife. She held it aloft in a trembling hand. She was finding it hard to breathe, her chest tight.

'I have no intention of answering it,' he called back. 'At least not in the sense you mean.'

She stood immobile, listening, as he picked up the receiver, was silent for a second and then said with careful force, 'Fuck. Off.'

Returning to the kitchen, he said, 'Might do the trick. He may think he's got the wrong number, or, better still, that you have a man around.'

'I don't need you to save me, Tom. I'm not Andromeda.'

'No one said you were. And, trust me, I'm no superhero.' He nodded to the knife in her hand. 'You okay with that,' he said mildly, 'or would you like me to take over slicing the bread?'

She collapsed back against the kitchen cupboard and let him take the knife from her limp fingers. 'Thank you.'

He deliberately misunderstood her. 'No need to thank me. I'm simply not a fan of blood in my bacon sandwich.'

They worked together and, once the tea and sandwiches were made, sat at the tiny table to eat. Joops, knowing food was around, returned from the garden and sat in hope.

'Has it happened much? The silent calls, I mean?' Tom asked.

Juno nodded. 'They were getting frequent but not regular if you know what I mean. One day I'd have five or six in quick succession and then it would stop and start up again. The ones in the middle of the night were particularly horrid.'

'A phone going in the middle of the night is never good news.'

'But that's just it, no one rings me on the landline. If anything happened in my family, they'd ring my mobile. Even so, it gave me a hell of a start. I couldn't get back to sleep for ages afterwards. If it is Paul – and I suspect it is – it's just the sort of thing he'd do. I have no idea how he got the number.' She abandoned her sandwich, appetite gone.

'Drink your tea,' he ordered gently.

She obliged. It helped. Putting the mug down, she added, 'And why's he doing it? When I left, he was all loved up with his new woman. He made it very clear I was redundant and he couldn't get me out of the flat quick enough.'

'Maybe she's left too? Maybe he's bored? Maybe he's got hold of the number somehow and the temptation to play games was too strong. Or perhaps it's just because he can. He knows by doing this, it gets to you.' Tom put a hand on hers. 'But you're stronger than that. Don't let him do this to you. Disconnect the phone or get it cut off.'

'That's what I was planning on doing. I don't need it anyway.'

'Good. And remember Mum and I are just next door if you need help, or somewhere to crash for the night.' He peered at her as she hesitated. 'Is he ringing you on your mobile too?'

'No. Yes.' Juno shook her head in confusion. 'I'm not sure. That night when we all came back here after going to Colosseum, I felt my phone vibrate but when I looked at it later, it was a missed call from an unknown number. I didn't think much more of it until this landline business. And thanks for the offer of sanctuary at your mum's, but I can look after myself.'

'I don't doubt that. But this has been going on for a while, hasn't it?' Tom searched her face. 'Is that why you were so keen to stay up on the field? You didn't want to be at home?'

Juno looked down at her cooling bacon sandwich and the puddle of brown sauce on her plate. The sight revolted her. 'Maybe.' The answer came out on a long breath. 'Being up there, all alone, away from all the hassle that is my life felt good I suppose.'

Tom sat back grinning slightly. 'And there's me thinking you loved my company and roughing it.'

'I did. I do enjoy your company.' She looked up at him, his humour was irresistible. 'Not sure I could go for the roughing it again though.'

'Wuss.'

She picked up her sandwich, appetite restored. 'Guilty. As soon as you've gone home the first thing I'll be doing is getting into a very long, very hot shower.' She watched with amusement as the tips of Tom's ears turned pink. Was he blushing at the thought of her naked in the shower? The idea gave her no small satisfaction. 'Actually,' she said through a mouthful of bacon, 'there wasn't all that much roughing it going on. You looked after yourself extremely well up there.'

'And who had the only blanket? Who risked a bath in the river? Even Joops didn't last long in there it was so cold.'

Juno let a giggle escape. 'True,' she shuddered. 'More fool you.'

'Well, thanks for the sympathy. I expect more from my friends.'

That sobered her. Friends. With an inward sigh she decided reluctantly it was probably better this way. There was so much unresolved stuff going on in her life. She may be at a crossroads, but she'd changed direction half a dozen times and was still unsure which way she was heading. If only there was a Satnav for life. She was permanently stuck in, "Stop and turn around as soon as possible" mode. A mobile rang out making her gasp.

'No need to panic, it's mine. I plugged it in to charge when we got here. Hope you don't mind.'

'No, of course I don't mind.' She fed Joops the last of her sandwich which he gulped down without appearing to taste. Remembering he hadn't been properly fed, she rose and hunted out his bag of kibble. She fed the dog while trying not to eavesdrop on Tom's call; unsurprisingly, it appeared to focus on the coin hoard. Having quickly washed up, she made another pot of tea.

Tom reappeared at her side. 'I'd better go,' he said regretfully, looking at the freshly made tea. 'Loads of calls to make, people to chase.'

'If it's about the hoard, ring Cris. He may be able to speed things up at the university end. Here, give me your phone and I'll put his number in.' She scrubbed her wet hands down the legs of her jeans.

'Thanks. Much appreciated.'

'If it means him getting out of a few departmental meetings he'll be over like a shot. There,' she added and handed the phone back. 'And, about your offer of help. I do appreciate it, I really do. It's reassuring to know you and

Diana are next door.' She hesitated. 'It's just that I need to sort this on my own.'

Tom nodded. 'I know.' Slipping his phone into the back pocket of his jeans, he added, 'But if you ever need us, you know where we are. Don't be too proud. We all need help from others sometimes.'

'Even you?' Tom was the most self-sufficient person she knew.

He smiled wryly. 'Especially me. I really appreciated you staying up on the field with me, you know. Made it much less lonely.'

'No worries. I quite enjoyed it. Besides you fry a mean sausage.' At the mention of the word Joops barked. They laughed. 'Even Joops agrees.'

'I'd better go then.' Despite his proclamation, Tom didn't move.

'You better had.' They stood motionless, unwilling to break the spell they'd cast.

Tom inched nearer, to within kissing distance. His eyes dropped, shaded by his long lashes, to focus on her mouth. 'I'll keep you posted about the developments with the dig.'

It was quite possibly the least erotic sentence but coming from his sexy lips, the words did something severely disturbing to her insides. They'd vowed to be friends she reminded herself. And she needed a friend like Tom at the moment. It would be stupid to put a friendship like this in jeopardy. But, oh, it would be so easy to reach up and taste that inviting mouth. Heat swept over and through her. So captivated was she, by gazing at his mouth, she forgot to answer.

'Look after yourself. No going chaining yourself to rocks you hear?'

'What?' Juno came back to earth with a bump. 'Oh. Andromeda.' She put her head on one side. 'If I did, would you come and rescue me?'

'Only if I can find my invisibility helmet. But, trust me, you can rescue yourself. You're more than capable.'

He bent forward and for one delirious moment Juno thought he *was* going to kiss her. He did but it was nothing more than a brotherly kiss on the top of her head.

'I'd better come and unlock the car so you can grab your stuff.' The disappointment shocked her.

'Yup. Better had. See you, Juno.'

'See you.' She followed him to the door and pinged the remote locking on the Freelander, watching as he unloaded his bags. Then he slammed the boot shut, put up a hand and disappeared along the path to his mother's house. Was she making a mistake keeping Tom at arm's length? Would it be simpler to just grab him and get him out of her system? Was he sincere in his declaration to be just friends, or would he accept more? Sighing, she leaned her hot head against the door jamb watching a gull glide a thermal, the sun lighting its belly into a snowy white, its legs held streamlined and close to its body. Such freedom. Why couldn't she stop overthinking and over analysing everything. Another of Paul's legacies, or was it just her? Gazing up, she wondered if she'd ever find the ability to simply live in the moment like the gull.

Tugging at the neck of her shirt and running her tongue over her teeth her thoughts strayed to the much-needed shower. It was possibly just as well she and Tom hadn't taken it any further; she was rank. Running upstairs to hot water and fragrant shower gel, she wasted no time in getting naked and blasting herself with the hottest water she could stand. Loading her body mitt with a generous dollop of shower gel she began to relax and let the orange and geranium scented water warm and ease her body. Ducking her head under she focused on the hot water cascading down her body and slicking away the grime of the last couple of days and tried to forget Tom's soulful blue eyes and tanned muscle. Then she froze as she heard Joops bark. Her heart thumped. Had she closed the back door? She couldn't remember. The landline rang out insistently, piercing through the sound of the shower and causing another volley of barks. Juno leaned her head against the glass shower door, her tears running down and mingling with the water. Was she ever going to be rid of him?

Georgia Hill

# CHAPTER 25

*The Secundinus Villa*

Flavia lay back in the warm water, lazily circling her ankles and wrists and enjoying the relaxing heat seep into her aching body. Whether her pains were from riding Pwca the pony, or from making love with Padrig, she couldn't tell but it felt supremely good to ease them in the bathhouse.

She had never ventured to the town's bathhouse although her father often visited to network and gossip – and worse. She wondered why he bothered when the villa had its own. Not as large as the town's one and lacking vendors selling chicken legs and other delicacies but far more peaceful. She had heard torrid tales of women of the night and thieves and beggars infiltrating even the most respectable parts of Moridunum's bathhouse. Here, all was calm and quiet, the scent of rose and jasmine hanging heavy. It was a smaller version of the main baths in town but perfect in its way.

Apart from the bathhouse slaves, who tip-toed and spoke in whispers, Flavia was alone, Ursa had gone in search of fresh oils to rub into her skin. She took in a deep, cleansing breath. She should move onto the caldarium but was too content here to shift to a hotter pool. The delights of the steam room and the strigil awaited. Flavia smiled to herself; she might give the frigidarium a miss today. She was in no mood for a plunge into icy water, although Ursa would no doubt scold and moan that her skin wouldn't benefit if she didn't complete the bathing routine. Still, it was something to take time over, an indulgence to while away the day. And she couldn't deny she had plenty of time. That was a luxury of which she had plenty.

Easing her neck to make herself more comfortable, Flavia let her mind wander and return to the sylvan dell where she and Padrig had lain together under the ash and the sacred oak tree. She could still hear the running water of the river, the breeze sighing through the leaves, the quiet tearing of grass by the pony's teeth. Every sense had come alive for the first time that afternoon. She had released her body into pleasures she had never before dreamed of. Trailing her fingers over her neck and shoulders, her nipples budded into arousal. It had been an experience beyond her imaginings. Sending a swift prayer up to Venus for her kindness and protection, she let her head loll back, closing her eyes on the secret, hugging her new knowledge to herself. As the water lapped around her shoulders, however, a flicker of unease edged away the memory of pleasure. She and Ursa were now reconciled but when the slave had met her at the gate, it had been a stormy greeting.

Flavia had been unable to tear herself away from Padrig, and his kisses and the day had lengthened into dusk. She was tempting Fortuna by being out so late, but she didn't care. She was playing with fire and had a fire of her own ignited within her. After giving him one more lingering kiss and satiating her eyes with his beauty, she had danced the short distance from the shelter of the trees where he stood watching until she disappeared behind the gate. Ursa's words when she greeted her were a slap. A shock to the system as any dousing in the frigidarium.

'Mistress,' she had scolded. 'Where have you been and what have you been doing? It is long past the time we agreed, the sun is almost spent.'

Flavia didn't care. She loosed the loyal Trajan who ran off in search of his companions, locked the gate behind her and leaned against it in liquid exhaustion. She smiled radiantly at her slave.

Ursa gasped, putting her hand to her throat, understanding chasing horror across her face. 'Flavia, what have you done? Oh, child, tell me you haven't ...'

Flavia let her head loll against her shoulder as if it were too heavy to hold up and her neck too insubstantial. She closed her eyes in rapture. 'I am a woman now, Ursa. I have been blessed by the goddess Venus.' There was no reply so, opening her eyes after a long silence, Flavia went to hug the slave. 'Is it not a wonderful thing?' She was rebuffed.

'You fool!' Ursa spat out, tearing the girl's arms from around her neck. 'You foolish strumpet! Look at your clothes, your hair. You have despoiled them just as you have despoiled yourself. You stupid wicked girl! What man will have you now? After all we've done, after all we've risked to keep you safe from Balbus and now you have delivered yourself to him as sure as a virgin to the hordes.'

A blackbird shrieked and flew over their heads.

Flavia recoiled, any afterglow from her time with Padrig sliding away into the dusk. She was too shocked to take her slave to task for speaking to her so. 'What do you mean?'

'Can you not see what I mean? Am I not clear? What you've done is as plain as eggs. It's written on your face, you foolish creature.'

'Nonsense.' Flavia backed away. She had never seen Ursa so angry before and never with her. The woman was known to be a hard task master with some of the lowlier slaves and, due to her position as Flavia's personal slave, was feared and respected throughout the house. Flavia had often witnessed her telling off a house slave for incompetence or laziness but never had such unleashed fury directed at herself.

'And what is worse, much worse,' Ursa continued, 'even if your husband can't see it on your face he'll know as soon as he takes you to his bed.'

'How? How will any man know?' Flavia stared at her blankly. She promised, as soon as she reached the sanctuary of her bedchamber, she would check her appearance in the mirror. Could it be possible that the deliciousness that had passed between her and Padrig had marked her in some way? It was true she felt different, utterly different inside but how could she be changed in outward appearance?

Ursa continued her tirade. 'They just do.' She took Flavia by the shoulders and shook her, as if willing the child to come to her senses.

'And what has this to do with a future husband?' Flavia was completely bewildered.

At the expression on her face the anger drained out of Ursa. 'Oh, what have you done Flavia?' Tears coursed down the older woman's face and her shoulders sagged. 'You have destroyed any future security with any man your father deems appropriate. No decent man will have you now. Septimus Severus can be forgotten. He will not have another man's cast-off. Don't you see, you stupid child, your virginity was your greatest bargaining weapon?'

'No!' Tears of exhaustion and shock sprang into Flavia's eyes. Again, she reached out to Ursa and again the slave turned away. 'This is mad talk. How can it be that father, or a husband will know I've lain with a man? How can they possibly know?' She drew herself up and stood proud. 'And if they do, so be it. Why should I want any of them? If I cannot be with Padrig, then I will marry no man. I will enter a life of prayer and devote myself to Minerva. Just see that I do!'

'Even if the temple of Minerva changes its rules to admit a despoiled woman, do you think your father will accept that?'

'Why not? It is a perfectly respectable thing to do.'

'Flavius Honoratus wants grandchildren. He wants to continue the legacy he's made here through your children and your children's children.'

'Nonsense. All he ever talks about is returning to Rome.'

'Then he will take his children and his grandchildren, should he see no future here.'

'Marcus can give him grandchildren. Why should it be up to me?'

'And if the fat-ankled Julia cannot oblige? Then you are the insurance.'

Flavia turned away, refusing to heed Ursa's words. She stared intently at the huge, metalled key in the door. One twist and she would be free of all this nonsense. Then she shuddered. Padrig would be well on his way back to the village by now, riding the trusty Pwca. It would be utter foolishness to venture out on her own, without protection, now night had fully fallen. And without Trajan too. She wouldn't be able to catch Padrig up and would be alone at the mercy of wolves and the thieves that roamed the night. She wouldn't even get as far as the first milestone.

'Flavia, listen to me. You're still not understanding fully.' Ursa forced the girl round to face her. 'All this has worse implications. Far worse implications.'

It had grown truly dark now and Flavia could hardly see her slave's face. 'I am tired, Ursa.' She tried to bat the slave off. 'I have no energy for your anger and your warnings. Let me go to my room, I need sleep.'

'Flavia,' Ursa took hold of the girl's upper arms, her fingers digging in. 'Listen to me. You *must* listen to me. Can you not see?'

'What?' Flavia stamped her foot. 'This is too much Ursa, you cannot detain me like this. I will not let you. I demand you let me go.'

Ursa reached up and stroked the girl's face tenderly. All anger had fled. In its place was a terrible sadness. She brushed the untidy hair from her mistress's hot face. 'Can you not see, child? Your father will be down to one choice and one choice alone. Your father's only choice of husband will be,' she paused and then added in a hoarse voice, 'will be the freed slave Balbus. Can't you see what you've done? You have sealed your own fate with one stupid senseless act. You have ensured yourself a lifetime of fear and violence, for that is the only way Balbus will treat you. That is the way he treats all women, especially one he will own through marriage.'

Flavia sagged against the gate. 'No,' she cried, horrified. 'Father would never free him.'

'There are rumours it is about to happen. The house talks of nothing else. Once Balbus is from his sick bed, he is to be freed.'

'Then let the plague take him,' Flavia spat out. 'For he will never be married to me.' A great sob wrenched from her innards. 'I cannot. I will not give myself to that man.' A vision arose; one of Balbus raping the kitchen slave. A shiver tore through her from feet to head and vomit threatened. Through gritted teeth she hissed, 'I would rather perish on one of the legion's swords. I swear on the goddess Juno. I would rather die than let that vile creature have me.'

Ursa gathered her to her bosom. She caressed her head, letting the girl weep out her anguish until she lay on her, heavy and exhausted, slight tremors running through her young strong body. 'No, Flavia. I would rather die for you than let him have you. With all the power willed to me by Diana, I will not let him harm one hair on your head. Come, chick. Let us to your chambers. I will rub your skin with almond oil and dress you in your softest nightrobe. We'll make excuses that you took ill at the temple, that your piety exhausted you. May Minerva have mercy on us for lying.'

She had half carried, half led Flavia through the silent, darkened house. They had muttered thanks to the house gods that the dull flickering lamps had hidden them from too many prying eyes.

Flavia's eyes flew open at the memory and she half rose from the water, the noise of the splash and suck of the water causing a bathhouse slave to turn and watch curiously. She'd been half witted by the time Ursa had massaged the worst excesses of her adventure from her body and slid her into bed. She'd lain, curved round like a babe in the womb, clutching the bed furs to her and listening to the slave rolling her spoiled clothes and hiding them beneath others. She was profoundly lucky to have the woman's unswerving loyalty. And Ursa had been right. She had committed an act of unholy stupidity.

Sliding back under the caressing warmth of the bath, she couldn't help but allow her thoughts flicker back to how it had been. Padrig had been gentle and loving but fierce in his passion and she had matched it, rearing up to take him into her, body and soul. Did she regret it? No. Never in a million years. But she regretted how it would affect her standing should word get out. It was only now that she realised how foolish she had been, how unguarded. They had barely been hidden by the oak at the river. Anyone passing could have seen, anyone using the nearby drover's route could have heard their passionate cries floating through the tree cover. It took one person and one person alone to blabbermouth to one of her father's associates. Such intelligence would be well-rewarded – and there was always some villain wanting payment for useful information. Flavia cupped water and watched thoughtfully as it trickled through her fingers. Her reputation was now as insubstantial. If what Ursa said was true, if men really could tell if their bride was a virgin on the wedding night, it had put her in an untenable position. Should a witness come forth, she would be in no position to refute the truth. And if she could not deny she had lain with another, her father may well do as Ursa suggested; marry her off to someone not too fussy. In anger Flavia hit the water with her fist. That it should come to this, that her life should be so fraught.

The image of the thatched round hut rose, with its warming fire and luxurious hangings. Padrig's village had been so much more, yes the word was *civilised,* than she had ever imagined. All she had ever been told – the rough nature of the Britons, of their lack of order and refinement – fell away. She had been met with courtesy throughout her visit. Much curiosity also, but manners had been kept in check. True, the huts were only made of wattle walls daubed with clay, none of the fine Roman brick there but inside had been cosy, in truth much more homely than her parents' vast home with its many rooms and shiny hard surfaces. With her father's insistence that the villa had, at its centre, an impluvium so water flowed into the pool from guttering around an opening in the roof in true Roman style, it was always a chilly place to live. Could she see herself living in a village in a hillfort, living such a life? She scowled moodily. What would Padrig's brother say to that? She couldn't see Merit agreeing to harbour the daughter of his enemies in his own home; there had been hospitality, but little trust his eyes. And what of this woman who Padrig was supposedly promised to? Had his father negotiated the deal? If only Padrig could sprout wings and fly to her aid just as Perseus had done to save Andromeda. She hit the water again, this time in frustration, tension returning to her limbs. That was just a story. A stupid old story. There would be no magical rescue of her from the diabolical beast. No rapturously happy ending. She could see no way out. She couldn't escape to her love, that much was impossible, but neither could she stay at the villa if her secret came to light. If she was found out, if she was discovered to be spoiled, as Ursa had pointed out, there may be only one man her father would deem a suitably political match.

Balbus!

Despite the warmth of the water, a shiver tore into her and a cold hand of fear clutched at her heart. If that were the case, if she had no choice but to be forced to give herself to that vile, loathsome creature she and Ursa needed to do something about him ...

A ruckus from the changing area drew her attention. It seemed to be coming from the outer door and echoed around the marble and mosaic, splintering the peace.

'You cannot enter,' Flavia heard Ursa say shrilly. 'You know you cannot. My lady is at her bath.'

Startled, Flavia reared up, covering her breasts with her hand. It was forbidden for any man to enter the bathhouse while women were there. Even the town's baths had strict rules about segregation.

'I insist,' Ursa shouted. 'You cannot enter when my lady is bathing! I forbid you!'

*What in Jupiter's name was going on?* Fearing for Ursa's safety, Flavia yelled to the nearest attendant, a young slave girl, who was standing immobile, slack jawed. 'A towel. Now!' When no reply came, Flavia repeated the command. The slave shot her a look and ran. Exasperated, Flavia swam to the steps and pulled herself out with difficulty, the water holding her back, her limbs heavy from being immersed for so long. Eventually reaching the side, she snatched the linen towel the slave had dropped and secured it around her.

'I say again,' this time Ursa's voice was low and desperate. 'You cannot enter.' The rest of her sentence was bitten off. Flavia heard a shriek and something heavy slump down.

'Ursa? What is happening?' She ran to the door of the changing room, hampered by the constricting towel. Recoiling in horror, she saw Ursa's body lying prone, her head at an unnatural angle against the wall, her legs twisted underneath. Was she breathing? Flavia made to check but a colossal shadow detached from the archway. Balbus!

A clammy sweat sheened his skin making it grey and pasty. Dribble trickled from the corner of his slack mouth and his nostril dripped. He thrust a hand across his face, nearly missing as he swayed violently. He bore down on her, eyes red-rimmed and hollow. Drunk or ill, Flavia could not tell and needed to know. If drunk his actions could not be predicted and his strength violent. If ill and weak, she may have time to get away. Whatever ailed him she needed to act fast.

'Balbus, you have no business here. The day for men is tomorrow. Today it is for me and my attendants.' Flavia flicked her eyes left and right. What attendants? Ursa was unconscious, the little slave girl had disappeared and no one else was in sight. Even the guards had gone from their position at the door where they were supposed to stand to prevent unauthorised entry. Feeling exposed and horribly vulnerable in her semi-naked state, she took in a breath and choked. The man's vile stench invaded her nostrils. Putting a corner of her towel to cover her nose and mouth, she was cautiously relieved. Not drunk, she could smell no mead or wine, only the sourness of the sick bed. It had been rumoured Balbus had lain near death in his sick bed for days. Plague once again scoured the land and it was hoped by many that it had afflicted him. Excepting her father, Balbus was not a popular man in the villa.

'You!' Whatever he wanted to say didn't spew forth, as he half collapsed against the wall, his shoulder pressed to his ear, distorting his face and pulling at the side of his mouth creating a parody of a grin.

Desperate to go to Ursa's aid, Flavia forced herself to become still and patient. Even ill and weak, Balbus was still an enemy to be feared. Trying to breathe through her mouth so as not to be infected by his rank smell, she prayed for strength and protection. *Juno, protector of women, help me.*

Balbus spasmed. He held his stomach and coughed, then slid to his knees and vomited.

Flavia edged away from the disgusting mess as far as she was able but there was nowhere to go. He blocked the archway to escape to the main part of the house. Where was everyone?

He gazed up, his eyes unfocussed. 'I. Shall. Have. You.'

Fear liquified her insides. Twisting the towel as tightly to her damp body as she could, she backed away and found security in the wall behind her. Balbus shunted himself across the floor and she shrank away. He went to grasp her naked ankle but flailed and missed.

Flavia shuddered and turned her head away. All she could hear was his laboured breathing and his horrible gurgling. All she could smell was his foul odour. He stank of the grave. 'You are not well, Balbus.' Her voice came out as a tremulous whisper. She was revolted. 'Let me go and find help. Let me pass and I shall find the guards to come to your aid. You need to get back to your bed.' She slid down, boneless, onto the hard marble bench.

'Bed?' He cackled. Heaving out a fetid breath, he added, 'I shall take you here.'

His fingers gripped her ankle, his filthy, grime-ingrained nails digging in. Flavia wrapped her arms about herself. Desperate to shake him off, she found herself frozen, unable to act. Balbus's hand, slimy with sweat, slithered up to her knee.

'All the gods, help me,' she whimpered. 'Oh Venus, goddess of love, whatever I did with Padrig was done in love. Surely I have not deserved such evil as this? Help me.' She called upon every god she had ever known. Every god that existed in the pantheon. Jupiter, Minerva, Silvanus. 'Oh Diana, goddess of light and unity, and of unmarried girls, I implore you, come to my aid.'

The white owl, the one which had swooped over the night when she had cast the curse tablet, flew into her vision. She could see its form so clearly, she thought it had entered into the bathhouse itself. Mustering all the mind strength she had, Flavia summoned the image of the sacred spring, the offering tree and the oaks green and gentle. 'Old gods,' she cried, 'protect me now from this wickedness.' Balbus's hand found her inner thigh. He groped her tender flesh and pinched hard. His fingers inched towards her secret parts, nails scratching.

Everything inside her revolted at his touch. Frantic, she called out, 'Gods, I beseech you, rid me of this evil. Juno! My Juno! Come to my aid!'

Balbus's hand stilled on her flesh, then slackened. For a moment all was still and silent. Her trembling lessened and then a great surging energy filled her blood. She felt the power return to her limbs, strength pour into her fear-frozen muscles. Staring him down, she rejoiced that his slobbering mouth slackened as he began to feel the power of her.

'I have made you ill, Balbus,' she hissed. A hot fury filled her, making her wanton with her words. 'I made you ill weeks ago and I've made you sicken now. With all the power given to me by the gods, I curse you. I curse you and your bones and your very entrails.' He shrank back, letting go of her thigh. His hand slid greasily down her leg. It gave her courage. 'And it's worked, hasn't it? You have been weak and ill abed ever since. And, as I cursed you then, I curse you now. You will never dare touch me or my slave ever again. If so much as a hair off your loathsome head lands on our skin then you will be cast into a fiery blackness which has no end. Do you heed me, Balbus? Do you hear my words? And one whisper to my father, one tiny word and I will curse you into the afterlife and beyond. There will be no rest for one as evil as you.'

He stared back, clawing at the air with hooked fingers. He made no sound bar a choking and then, at last, fell back and away from her. A wind swept through. Flavia scrunched shut her eyes in abject terror. She pressed against the cold marble wall, desperate to block out the horror. She became aware of a great cleansing light and the very wall she slumped against vibrated.

All she could hear was her tortured breathing, ragged and hoarse. She didn't know what had happened but remained crouched over on the bench, not opening her eyes, childishly hoping that if she couldn't see the danger, then the danger did not exist.

'My lady?' A young trembling voice whispered. 'All is well now.'

Flavia opened her eyes with difficulty, her head felt thick. The light had gone. All was back to normal, the changing room lit only by a few oil lamps, flickering in the dark corners. A great shudder travelled through her. It was the young slave girl who had run off earlier. She stared at her blinking.

'I fetched the guards. They had gone outside and were gambling on dice.' The girl pressed her lips together in disapproval. 'I told 'em they had to come quick.' She reached forward and put another towel around Flavia's shivering shoulders.

'They should never have left their posts,' Flavia said through chattering teeth. She sat up, anger chasing the fear from her chilled and dead limbs.

'That they should not!' The girl was indignant. 'They came and took Balbus away. Took him to his sick bed.' She was careful not to meet Flavia's eyes. 'He was not right in the head.'

'No.' A last shudder ran through Flavia. In agreement, she added, 'He has been very ill.' Not sure what the slave girl had seen or heard, she refused to comment further. 'What is your name, child?'

'I am Eseld, mistress.' The girl ducked her head.

'Then I thank you for your service this day. I shall see you rewarded.' A flicker of understanding passed between them. Perhaps Balbus had defiled this girl too. Flavia gasped. 'Ursa!'

'One of the other bathhouse attendants has seen to her.'

'Does she live? Did he hurt her?'

'It is reported she has bruises, mistress but is speaking. Her brain seems uninjured although it took a mighty blow when Balbus hit her.'

Flavia sank back on the bench. 'Thank all the gods. I couldn't have borne it had she been hurt worse.'

'Shall I help you back to the baths, mistress or are you finished for today?'

'Thank you Eseld. I shall dress, I need to see Ursa. I need to check she is well.'

'Then I shall help you,' the girl said simply.

Flavia trembled and shook. It was all she could do to dry herself and fasten her undertunic around her. Putting on her warm wool overdress with trembling fingers, she was glad of Eseld's help.

'Where are you from, Eseld? How did you come here?'

'I am from the Dumnonii. I came here when my village was raided.'

Flavia turned quickly. 'So, not the hillfort near here?'

'No, no, my lady. My village is some distance towards the sun's set. I come from the other coast. I lived in a fort above a great craggy cliff over the sea.'

'And are you treated well here?'

Eseld nodded but Flavia suspected it was not the truth. She made a decision. 'Then I shall make a request that you join Ursa and me. You will become my personal slave. Would you like that? I can give you protection against ...' she let the sentence hang. 'You will be in my own personal protection. Just as Ursa is.' *Not that it did the woman any good today.*

The girl's eyes shone. 'I should like that very much, my lady. By all the gods, I thank you.' She knelt and kissed the woman's hem.

'Get up, child. Let us away to Ursa and see how she does.' She held out a hand to help the girl up. 'You did me great service today but, if you are to become my slave, it beholds you not to speak of anything we saw or heard here today.'

Eseld nodded once again. 'I shall remain loyal to you, mistress, until my dying day. For you too have done me great service in saving me from a monster.'

Flavia put her arms around the girl and hugged her tight. Tears of relief prickled at her eyes. 'Then we are both saved.' Pushing Eseld away, she added more matter of factly and pulling her wits about her, 'Then shall we away to Ursa? If I do not check on the woman, she will scold me! Come.'

Taking Eseld's hand, she led her from the chamber without a glance backwards at the horrors echoing.

She was determined. As soon as it was possible, it was time to do something more permanent to rid herself of Balbus.

Georgia Hill

# CHAPTER 26

*2023*
Juno clicked off the shower and rested her head against the screen. Scrunching up her eyes to ward off the shrilling of the phone, she waited, tension in every trembling muscle, until it stopped. It was time to do something more permanent to ride herself of Paul. But what? What could she possibly do?

Shivering violently as the warmth of the shower fled, she clambered out, her legs stiff with fear. Teeth chattering, she rough-dried herself, threw on her towelling robe and bundled her hair into a towel. She crept downstairs, expecting the phone to ring out at any second. Joops greeted her nosing at her bare knees exposed by the gap in her robe. The back door! Hurrying to check it, she was relieved to see not only had she closed it, it was also locked. Habits quickly drilled into her after she and Paul had split. Even at the very beginning, when she'd been comatose with shock, something seeped through that this wasn't the end, that he'd find a way to come back to her. And it wouldn't be because he missed her in a caring way. The sense that someone was watching her had never left. An obsession with locking everything, always looking over her shoulder, planning where she was going, anticipating the likelihood of it being crowded and therefore giving her security amongst the comfort of strangers left her exhausted. It had plagued her in London, had followed her to Winchester and had chased her here.

Paul had known nothing of this little house in Flete; the feeling of being watched had tapered off. She'd relaxed just a little, had begun to put the horrors behind her. But now they'd returned with a vengeance. If it was Paul on the phone, how was it possible that he knew where she was? Her parents would never have told him. Her father had taken little interest in Paul and her love life, and her mother made no secret of how much she despised him. Cris wouldn't have let on either. Whatever his faults as an older brother, under the banter, he was protective and loving. He knew some of what she'd been through. Juno discounted Mabyn immediately. Her friend had had to mop up what was left of Juno when Paul had finished with her, there was no way she would betray her. Juno frowned, racking her brain. There was no one else. There were a few people she had to deal with at her publishing house, but Paul never socialised with them; her relationship with him was irrelevant to them. So, who else was there?

Switching on the kettle, she slumped onto the sofa, clutching Joops to her. 'Whatever would I do without you, Joopsy boy?' She ruffled the long hair on his head, making it stick up. 'You'd defend me to the death, wouldn't you?' The dog snickered in response and licked her ear.

Juno was halfway through pouring boiling water onto a teabag when the phone went again. Rage filled her. She would not allow this to intimidate her. Slamming the kettle down she crossed the tiny sitting room in seconds. Shoving the sofa away from the wall she threaded the telephone cable through her fingers until she found the telephone point and yanked it out. Blessed silence.

Sinking back down on the sofa, which was now in the middle of the room, she forced herself to breathe normally but was still furious. Glancing at the wall, she was tempted to run round to the comfort and warmth of Diana's house but suppressed it. She needed to deal with this herself. It was her problem and no one else's. Joops took the opportunity to nose around the back of the sofa emerging with a dusty head covered in cobwebs. He sneezed and shook himself. It forced her to laugh. Getting up, to her shame, her legs still wobbled.

'Come on, Joops. Let's forget the tea and go and get dressed.' She shivered. 'It's not warm enough in this house to wander around half nude.' Running upstairs, with Joops hard on her heels, his nose nudging the back of her knees, she dried herself properly and found comforting clothes – t-shirt, thick socks, jeans and a bulky sweatshirt. Clothes designed to disguise her body, to de-sex herself.

Going to the windowsill, she gazed down at the garden. It wasn't much more than a square of unkempt grass, surrounded by a fence. Dull but thankfully secure, the only access point being a bolted gate which led onto a narrow track which ran the length of the cottages. At the end of the first cottage was another gate to which all residents had a key. It was normally locked unless someone was having work done and needed access. An enclave of newly built town houses, with tall solid brick walls backed onto the lane. When she'd first moved in, she'd been troubled that the windows of their bedrooms stared into her garden but now accepted it was about as secure as it could be. And she had neighbours on either side. Diana and Tom to the right, and an old man who she hadn't had much to do with on the left. It felt good to be surrounded by people.

She blew out an enormous breath, misting the window. 'I just want to get on with my life, Joopsy. It's not much to ask, is it?' Rubbing the condensation mark with her sleeve, the movement caught the attention of the old man. He was outside pruning a clematis. Looking up, he spotted her and waved. She waved back, her hand childishly wrapped in the sleeve of her sweatshirt. He seemed friendly. And harmless. Maybe she'd go round and ask for a cutting. It was about time she got to grips with planting and a clematis would look pretty rambling over the fence. The robin flew down and perched, one bright black eye alert for worms. The gardener's friend, her mother always called them. Juno had a sudden and unexpected longing for her. Diana's voice sounded, saying something to Tom about putting the kettle on and through the opaque glazed roof Juno saw a shadow move about in the garden room next door. It all seemed utterly normal. People drinking tea, gardening, going about their lives on a sunny day. She released a breath and with it the tension caused by the ringing telephone. Paul couldn't get at her here and even if he did turn up, she was amongst friends. The sun caught the sea glass bead still sitting on the windowsill. It glimmered and sparkled like something alive. Picking it up she was surprised at how warm it was. Heat from the sun no doubt. Remembering half-forgotten and vague warnings about glass causing fires if left in the sun, she moved it to the bedside table.

Throwing herself onto the bed and wrapping the duvet around her, she rang her mother.

After a brief catch up and a conversation about her mother's new role as magistrate, Juno asked suddenly, 'Mum, why did you call me Juno?'

Amanda Eden drew a breath. 'Have you only just thought to ask, child?'

Juno glanced at the sea glass bead. Even on the bedside table it glowed as if from within. *Weird.* 'I suppose I have.'

'I hear from Crispin that you're finally becoming interested in all things historical.'

'Cris been telling tales on me?'

'Oh, Juno, don't get all defensive. He's looking out for you, that's all. He's pleased you seem to be settling in at Begin-Again Cottage, as are your father and I.'

Remembering Tom pointing out her parents seemed to love her very much, Juno apologised. 'Feeling a bit raw today. Sorry.'

'I'm glad you've got people around you. Crispin said your neighbours are nice.'

'They are.' Juno described them and then filled her mother in on what had been found at the Roman Field.

'How terribly exciting. I must tell your father. Not quite his period of course but he'll still be fascinated.'

'As will Cris. I think he'll probably get involved via the university.'

'Indeed. So what Crispin said is true. You *are* getting interested.'

'I suppose I am. I like the social history side. You know, what people ate, what they wore, how they lived.' She could hear her mother nodding. 'The stories it inspires.'

Amanda chuckled. 'History always has good stories. I'm glad you've realised.'

'I've been reading some Greek myths too.'

'Ah, yes. Great fun. Like a soap opera, I always think.'

Juno smiled. 'Funnily enough, someone else said that to me recently.'

'Speaking of myths and gods and goddesses, you ask why I named you Juno. Well, what better name than the queen of the gods, watcher of women, thrower of thunderbolts. A wonderfully strong and unique name.'

Juno heard emotion in her mother's voice.

'That's what you brought me, Juno. Joy and thunderbolts. After those two pesky boys, it felt good to balance out the household with a strong girl.'

'I always thought,' Juno began but her throat closed, 'I always thought you resented me.'

'Whatever for?' The surprise was genuine.

'You decided not to go back to work after having me.'

'Ah. That's true. I admit it was a difficult decision but not one I often regret and I certainly never resented you. I loved you. I love you now. How could I not?'

'I love you too, Mum.' As Juno said the words, she realised they'd never had this conversation. 'I really do.'

'Well, of course you do. I'm your mother.' Amanda was back to her brisk, no-nonsense self.

Juno laughed. 'And I'm really proud of you for becoming a magistrate.'

'Goodness Juno. Whatever's brought on all this sentimental nonsense?'

'Just saying.'

Amanda sniffed.

*Were those tears?*

'Then perhaps I should tell you, as you're insisting on all this mawkishness, that Isobel at the tennis club bored me senseless at the clubhouse the other day, telling me how much she adores Eden Loveday's books. I quite enjoyed her reaction when I told her my daughter writes them.'

'Thanks, Mum. I'll get her a signed set.' Juno grinned. It was as close to praise as her mother had ever got.

'That would be splendid.' A pause. 'And are you really alright, Juno? You can come home at any time, you know.'

Juno thought before answering. She really did feel better. 'I'm absolutely fine. And even better after this phone call. I'll drive up and see you soon.'

'Or maybe we can come down? I'd like to see Betty's old place again.'

'It would be lovely to see you both,' Juno replied warmly and hung up.

The phone call left Juno feeling more content than she'd been for years. Making a promise to her mother to channel her strong, fearless namesake, she made a quick call to Mabyn. Her friend was horrified at the thought of Paul stalking Juno and suggested she contact the police.

Juno clicked off the call and cuddled Joops who was lying stretched out alongside her on the bed. 'What would I say, though? I haven't any proof it's him and do silent calls count as stalking?' Joops didn't have an opinion but got up and began prowling around the bedroom. Juno recognised the signs. 'Okay, we'll put off doing anything until after walkies. Where do you fancy? The beach?'

After checking all windows and doors were firmly locked, Juno left the little house and strode out into the beckoning sunshine.

The town was busier now the tourist season had begun. As Juno turned left at the end of Church Lane towards the front, the streets were heaving with people strolling along enjoying the warmer weather. Once on the prom, she tuned her brain out from scanning people's faces, automatically checking whether one was Paul's. Instead, sucking in a deep breath of salty sea air, she straightened her shoulders and deliberately met the eyes of the people coming towards her. A few slid theirs away, embarrassed, but she was rewarded with some cheery replies to her 'Good afternoon'. It buoyed her mood.

After giving Joops a run on the end of the beach away from the worst of the crowds, she began to head back. Walking uphill on the narrow pedestrianised street going through town, she spotted the open sign on the museum and, on impulse, went in.

It wasn't busy, the sunshine was obviously tempting everyone onto the beach.

Old Bill spotted her immediately. 'Juno! Nice to see you again, my girl. And Jupiter too. What a treat.' Then she whispered, 'Let me get rid of these two and I'll pop the kettle on.' She approached the father and son who were staring at the Roman villa model. 'We're just closing up now, I'm afraid,' she said, ushering them non too gently towards the door. 'Make sure you come back, though. We're open every day except Monday, ten to four.' Bundling them out, she turned over the open sign to closed and locked the door. 'Ruddy Nora. Thank goodness,' she exhaled, flipping her long silver plait over her shoulder.

Juno giggled.

Bill caught her look. 'Not being rude but they've been in here since two. Thought they'd never leave. Only here on account of mum being in the nail bar over the road.'

She tutted. 'I ask you. How can it take two hours to have some polish painted on your nails?'

She looked so genuinely puzzled that Juno laughed again. 'I don't know. I don't really go in for all that kind of stuff. My friend Mabyn does though. She has those acrylic ones glued on.' She shuddered a little. 'Not for me.' She thought back to how Paul had bullied her into having a mani-pedi every week, insisting she keep groomed. She'd hated it and ever since had determinedly left her nails bare. She looked at them now. Nails shiny and healthy but in need of a good manicure. Paul would be livid. The weirdest things would make him furious. This tiny insignificant defiance gave her immense satisfaction. *Give me strength and protect me, my namesake, oh, goddess Juno!*

'Nor me, Juno,' Bill chuckled. 'Nor me. Now, come on through to the back room. How about a mug of tea and a taste of lardy cake?'

Juno followed her into the little room where she, Annie and Bill had sat in before. It was just as untidy and cramped.

And, just as before, Bill stooped to lift a pile of papers off a chair. 'Must get someone in to sort this lot out,' she grumbled. Straightening, she added, 'I hate to admit it, but I think I'm getting too old for all this.' She switched on the kettle. 'Don't mind being in the museum, opening up, talking to visitors and whatnot, but all the admin is burdensome. You can't even scratch your arse without having permission in triplicate.' She swilled a couple of mugs out in the sink and heated the teapot with a dash of nearly boiling water. 'Tea made the old-fashioned way,' she declared. 'Not keen on all this teabag in the cup malarkey.' While waiting for the tea to brew she cut a generous square of cake into two, put one slice on a plate and offered it to Juno.

'What is it?' Juno asked. It oozed grease, was full of dried fruit and was liberally doused in sugar.

'Lardy cake. Devon speciality but you don't find it as often nowadays. Go on, tuck in. It'll put hairs on your chest.'

*And about six inches on each thigh!* Juno nibbled a corner. It was delicious. Less cake and more a sweet bread with a subtle spicy flavour. Greasy and sweet but moreish. She ate the lot. Having finished, she wiped her fingers on a tissue and gratefully took the mug of tea from Bill, needing something to cut through the aftertaste.

Bill tickled Joops under the chin and then sat down herself. For a minute all was silence while she ate her cake and slurped tea. Juno looked about her. She'd not taken in any details on her last visit. The room was tiny, with just a sink and two chairs squashed into it. Piles of paper were stacked everywhere and Joops had settled into a makeshift bed on top of one. She hoped he wasn't lying on anything important. An enormous notice board dominated one wall. Haphazardly pinned to it, several inches thick, were letters from the local council, copies of applications for funding, a takeaway menu from the Thai restaurant on the corner. It looked as if Bill was right; she *was* drowning in paperwork. Either that or she desperately needed a system putting in place. To her amusement, she saw the carton of milk had been put back onto the outside windowsill which looked out onto a dreary courtyard. Maybe Bill ought to have a fridge too, although she didn't know where she'd put it.

'Penny for 'em?' Bill slammed down her plate.

'I was just thinking this could be such a great place. Not that it isn't,' Juno added hastily, seeing Bill's expression. 'The museum in Lyme always seems to get a lot of publicity and yours could be so much bigger. And better. Sorry,' she added, sticking her nose into her mug. 'I don't mean to be rude.'

Bill guffawed. 'No, you're right, my lovely. Suppose I carried on doing what my dear old dad did, and he did what his dad did before. Got into a right old rut, haven't we? And folk expect so much more these days. Kiddies aren't happy just to look and read and imagine anymore, they need to dress up, press buttons, get interactive and such-like. Apart from the two I've just kicked out, I've had a total of five in today. Five! And no one bothered to buy anything.'

'Well, it's a lovely day. I expect most wanted to be outside in the sunshine.'

'Maybe.' Bill wrinkled her nose. 'Truth is, I'm losing out. Losing out to Monkey World and the Sea Life Centres. I'm too old-fashioned for folk nowadays.' She sniffed.

'What do you charge?'

'Charge?' Bill looked startled. 'It's free to come in.'

'Well, maybe start charging an entrance fee.'

'And that's more likely to get people to steer clear.'

'I don't know,' Juno said, slowly. 'It's weird but people value something they have to pay for. In a way they take freebies for granted.'

Bill hmphed. 'Do they indeed? Mighty peculiar. Suppose I could give it a try. Charge summat small.'

'Worth a try. And maybe the new finds up on the Roman Field will attract more people in.' Juno could have bitten off her tongue. Tom would be appalled. He hadn't wanted anyone to know.

'What, that hoard of coins young Tom's found?'

Juno frowned. 'How do you know about them?'

'Farmer Giles is a cousin. He passed me in his van as I was walking in today and stopped to give me a lift. Don't worry,' Bill said with a sly smile. 'I haven't told anyone and neither has he.'

'At this rate it's going to be the worst kept secret in Flete,' Juno said feelingly.

'Won't go no further. Exciting though.'

'It is.'

'Won't be long before it gets all official like and the university gets involved and then it'll be all over town. Happened before when things have been found up there.'

'Oh? I didn't know there had been other stuff found.'

Bill shrugged. 'Pot fragments, some fine Roman bricks, bits and bobs of tesserae, that sort of thing. Nothing like this. The university gets all high and mighty, seal the place off, don't let no one near, have a little dig around and then bugger off again leaving humps all over the place where they haven't filled in the holes properly.'

Juno smiled. 'Well, I hope they do a better job this time round. My big brother's involved.'

'Oh, is he now? He works over Exeter way, then?'

'He's a lecturer at the university. Ancient World Studies. As I said to you before, history sort of runs in our family like it does yours.'

Bill drained her tea and thumped her mug down on the draining board. Juno feared for the pottery. 'Maybe they'll find evidence of the lost lovers this time.' The old woman twisted back to face Juno.

'Lost lovers?' Juno's writing antennae prickled.

'You haven't heard the story?'

'No.'

'Goes back years.' Bill tapped the side of her nose. 'Some say thousands of years. Passed down from generation to generation. Maybe it's as old as those coins Tom found.'

'He thinks they're probably Roman. Surely the story can't date that far back.' As she said it, Juno remembered Tom explaining about the legend of Beowulf being passed down orally and only written down about a thousand years ago. She said as much to Bill.

'There you goes, then.' The old woman wriggled in her chair getting comfortable. 'Folk round here didn't move away, didn't move to the cities in the industrial revolution as much as other places. Changed recently, of course, more movement in and out but for generations folk stayed where they was born and bred. Roads were never up to much. Flete didn't get a proper main road until, ooh, it's got to be the early part of the nineteenth century, when the sea bathers wanted their water cure. Wasn't easy for people to travel, to trade outside the local area.'

'Then how did they live? Surely they must have traded. They couldn't grow or make everything they needed in Flete.'

'They managed. Of course, even a little place like Flete would have a smithy, farmers to grow crops, you'd bake your bread in the communal oven, grow your own veg. Folk were much more self-sufficient back then. And, if they needed to trade, they'd look out to sea. Lyme got famous and prosperous trading wool to the cloth makers in the Low Countries, Belgium, Holland and the such-like. Flete was similar. Instead of turning inland and struggling along roads left to rot since the Romans left, they got on a boat and sailed over the Channel. A lot of goods got to and from London by boat until the boats got too big for the harbour when it silted up. There was a great storm, see, in the mid nineteenth century. Silted up the harbour and the river estuary. No longer possible to get goods up river to Axminster and beyond. Then the railways came and, even without a branch line, the sea trade dried up.'

'What did people do for jobs then?'

'Tourists! Saving grace of this part of the south coast.' She snorted. 'Mixed blessing a lot say but you can't deny it's the main industry here now. You've seen the pictures of the Regency bathing huts in the modern history room?'

Juno nodded. 'I'll take another look, though.'

'A whole industry built up. It was the fashionable thing to be seen doing, see.' Bill huffed. 'Suppose they all go on a spa day now. Get their ruddy nails painted. Back then, it was into the bathing machine, off with your clothes and they rolled the whole caboodle into the sea and out you'd pop on the other side, straight into the briny. But even then, it was locals who made the huts, locals who were the bathing attendants, who ran the inns and hotels where people stayed. Folk just didn't leave here like they did when there was the rush on from the country into the cities for factory and mill work.'

'So you're saying it's possible that a story originating two thousand years or more ago, could still be the story being told now, in the twenty-first century? Generation to generation? It's a bit far-fetched, isn't it?'

'Could be.' Bill shrugged, looking sly again. 'Who's going to prove it, either way?' She leaned forward. 'You know, we still have three families in town who claim they had ancestors living here back in the eleventh century? If they go that far back, why couldn't they have passed the story down?'

'I suppose.' Juno smiled. 'What is the story, then?'

Bill settled back. 'Oh, your classic tale of star-crossed lovers. They came from families who were at war with one another. Their parents didn't approve. They met and fell in love, escaped together to run away.'

'Oh, come on, Bill. This is Romeo and Juliet!'

'And where did old Willie Shakespeare get his stories from? Probably nicked them from others. You never know, maybe he had a shifty weekend in Flete once.'

Juno had to admit lots of writers in her experience were the same. 'Well, they do say never tell a writer anything as it'll end up in their book.'

'There you go. Sadly, just like Romeo and Juliet, it didn't end well for our pair either.'

'What happened?'

'Story goes they were followed and before they could get much further than the field just beyond the holloway, they were hacked down.' Bill made her eyes go huge. 'Murdered in cold blood, they was!'

Juno shivered and Joops put a concerned nose on her knee.

'And it gets worse,' Bill said gleefully. 'The ghosts of the slain lovers haunt the field even now, demanding revenge for being so cruelly cut down. They say one day they'll find what's left of their bodies, wrapped around one another in one final embrace.' She slumped back, exhausted by the drama.

Another shiver trickled down Juno's spine. The tiny room felt claustrophobic, she had the impression of the walls falling in on her. She'd known there was something strange about the fields ever since the very first morning when she'd walked Joops up there. Diana had told her things had been seen. Had she, herself, seen something that first morning? Or had it simply been another dog walker or a trick of the light? Was it really possible the lovers still haunted the place, unable to rest? 'I don't believe in ghosts,' she said firmly, more to convince herself than anyone else.

'Not many do. But if we go back to our friend Shakespeare, didn't he say there are more things in heaven and earth ...'

'Than are dreamed of in our philosophy,' Juno finished. She giggled nervously. 'Beowulf, Shakespeare, as well as a potted history of Flete. I've certainly got more than I bargained for this afternoon.'

'All part of the service. You not seen anything up there while walking the dog?' Bill eyed her keenly.

'No.' The denial came out too quickly, but Juno was unwilling to admit anything. Bill was beginning to frighten her.

'Not even our friend from the Durotriges? He looked like he'd taken your fancy.'

'No!' Juno reached for Joops and sank her hands into his soft coat to hide the fact they were shaking. She still hadn't solved the weirdness that was the handsome tribesman.

'Well, mind how you go up there from now on.'

'Why?' Juno glanced up quickly.

'Never does the land any good to be messed about with. Some history should be left where it is, not dug up for all and sundry to gawp at.' Bill tapped the side of her nose in the now familiar gesture. 'You mark my words.'

'What do you mean?'

'You watch how many lorries break down up there, how much machinery goes rusty with no explanation, how those pesky mobile phones go wrong. I reckon it's one reason no dig ever gets very far. Too many problems.'

Juno thought back to how Tom had had problems with his mobile on the night they'd camped out. But that had been a flat battery and a poor signal, hadn't it? This area, she'd learned, was notorious for bad mobile reception. Fear clutched at her stomach. She was used to living with fear, but this was of a different kind. At least Paul, no matter how vile, was made of living, breathing flesh. This was something completely beyond her understanding.

Joops whined and pawed at her knee. It gave her the excuse she needed. She suddenly craved fresh air. 'I must go.' She stood abruptly. 'Thanks for the tea and cake, Bill, but Joops's stomach is calling him home and he's a dog who can't be denied.'

'You're welcome, dearie,' Bill said, sounding surprised and somewhat amused. 'Come again any time.'

Juno felt the old woman's eyes bore into her as she left the room. She couldn't get out fast enough.

When home, having fed Joops, she went to log on, only to remember, in order to do so, she needed the landline plugged in. Bill's tale of star-crossed lovers nagged at her; she wanted to see if there was anything online. Struggling, as her shaking hand was clumsy, she reconnected it, half expecting it to ring out immediately. She waited, every hair standing on end, every nerve prickling. The silence which fell into the air was, if anything, even more ominous. Clicking through her phone playlist, she found something loud to fill the void and started scrolling for stories of Flete's long-lost lovers. Only pausing long enough to pour herself wine, she hunted long into the night. When she finally took herself to bed, she fell into a drunken troubled sleep. Her dreams a crazy mixture of a man with a long reddish-blonde beard, wearing plaid, and a woman calling her name.

*Juno, Juno ...*

Over and over again.

Desperately.

Georgia Hill

# CHAPTER 27

*T*he Secundinus Villa
*Juno!*
  Flavia prayed desperately. 'Heal this woman, give her succour and protect us this night. Juno, protector and saviour of women, I implore you.'

Those who had reported Ursa's injuries to be insignificant had been lying or it had not troubled them to be accurate; it only concerned a house slave after all and one of those was easy enough to replace. When Flavia had seen her friend lying where she had been tossed, on the floor in the kitchen slaves' quarters by mistake, she was appalled. As Flavia entered the fetid space, barely bigger than a store cupboard and lit by one flickering lamp in a recess in the wall, she put her hand across her mouth to stifle the stench. Was this really how her father's slaves lived? Spying a figure huddled against the furthest most wall, she picked up her skirts and edged across.

Ursa lay prone, eyes closed, bruises already appearing red and swollen on her arms. More worryingly still, was the spreading bruise on one side of her forehead and the bulge. Blood seeped from her nose and there was a cut across its bridge; it looked to be broken. The woman would take time to heal – if she ever did.

Flavia gasped in horror. It was so much worse than she had been led to believe. Snapping her fingers at two of the burliest kitchen slaves she demanded they take Ursa to her rightful bed in the anteroom to her bedchamber.

'Fetch water, oil and butter,' she barked at Eseld. 'And honey.'

Once the room was empty of people and bustle, Flavia and Eseld stripped Ursa of her torn and bloodied clothes and tenderly bathed her wounds. Wrapping her in one of Flavia's finest linen undertunics, Flavia tried to examine Ursa's nose. Unwilling to cause the patient any pain she smeared oil and butter on the wound and left it.

'Juno,' she prayed desperately. 'Heal this woman and protect us this night. Juno, protector and saviour of women, I implore you.' She repeated the words over and over again, rocking slightly on the wooden bench next to Ursa's truckle bed. But Ursa did not move, nor open her eyes.

'Mistress,' Eseld's hand was gentle on her arm. 'Let me watch Ursa. Go to your bed now and rest. I will come to you as soon as she wakes.'

Flavia gave a moan of distress. What would she do without Ursa? Her friend, her companion, far more of a mother than her own.

'Go, drink the posset I have prepared and sleep,' Eseld urged. 'You have had a shock too and need rest.' When Flavia hesitated, she added, 'You can take watch in the morning. You will be of no use to Ursa if exhausted.' She lifted the woman by the arm and led her in the direction of her bed. Flavia collapsed onto it without undressing. The events had finally taken their hold. She shivered and allowed Eseld to tuck the cover over her, laying a warm wolfskin on top. As the girl turned to go, Flavia's hand shot out. 'Tell me the instant Ursa awakes.' She gripped Eseld's wrist. 'I insist.'

'Do not be afeared. I will come to you as soon as she stirs. I promise.'

\*

Flavia slept until morning and awoke to a hot sun streaming through the shutters. She heard a distant cock crow. For a second, she was content to lie warm and sleepy and stretched luxuriously. Then the events of the day and night before bludgeoned her memory. She sat up so swiftly her head went dizzy. 'Balbus!' She put a hand to her head. 'I'll never forgive you for what you did to me. But, most of all, I'll never forgive you for what you did to Ursa.'

She squinted into the bright sunshine as the heaviness of sleep dissolved, lay back and thought hard. They needed a new curse, whatever was conjured in the woods had given some respite but not enough. They needed a new, a more powerful one. Flavia thumped the bed in frustration. But how was she to organise it without Ursa?

'Ursa!' Throwing the blankets off the bed so that they slithered onto the mosaics, she swung her legs off the bed and ran to the anteroom.

The woman was sitting up in bed with Eseld holding a cup of wine to her lips.

'Eseld! You had strict instruction to tell me when Ursa awoke.'

The girl jumped guiltily and wine spilled onto the patient's tunic.

'Do not blame her. It is my doing,' Ursa said weakly. 'In truth, I only awoke a few hours ago and asked Eseld not to disturb you. You needed to sleep.'

Flavia ran to her side. 'I needed to see you recovered more.' She grasped the slave's hand and kissed it fervently. 'I needed to know you are well.'

Ursa gave a weak smile. 'I am well. Or I will be when my head stops aching and the bruises have healed.' She lifted an unsteady hand and touched the bridge of her nose, wincing. 'I fear my nose may take a while.'

'I think the bone has broken. You may never look as you did before.' Flavia's voice trembled as she contemplated Ursa's livid pink bruises. 'But, may I dare to tempt Fortuna, it could have been much worse.' She squeezed shut her eyes and a tear ran. 'I thought ... I thought you would not recover.'

'I am alive, thank the gods. That is all I ask.'

Flavia managed a tremulous smile. Her friend was restored and she was glad. 'Can you eat something?'

'I could bring some baked cheese,' Eseld said eagerly. 'Something soft.'

Flavia nodded. 'Go to the kitchens and say the mistress Flavia demands pancakes, honey and wine too. Say she is very hungry and demands food for three bellies at least.'

Eseld bobbed and ran out.

Once she'd gone, Flavia turned to the patient, once again lifting her hand. 'Oh Ursa, I thought I had lost you, my friend.'

'Takes more than a belter from a man to keep me down,' Ursa said stoutly, attempting a smile. 'But, my chick, did he hurt you? Tell me he did not!'

Flavia demurred. What was her ordeal compared to Ursa's? 'He did not harm me. I summoned the gods and they rallied to my side.' She shrugged. 'Or maybe his sickness was too strong? Who knows, but I escaped without injury. Unlike you, my poor Ursa.'

Ursa lay back, eyes sinking shut, obviously relieved.

'Are you warm enough? Too hot?' Flavia fetched the furs from her own bed and fussed until the slave murmured she was comfortable. 'I make a poor nurse,' Flavia sighed, retrieved the cup and refilled it. 'Here, take more wine.' She helped Ursa sip until she lay back again, exhausted by the effort.

'You should not have to do this, mistress. It is below you.'

'Shush. I want to care for you.'

'But I have been impertinent to you.' Ursa looked down and pleated her linen tunic between weakened fingers. 'I nagged at you and berated you.'

'This is true.' Flavia's lips curved. 'But what else would I expect from the woman who has been at my side for more years than I care to recall? Who I know only has my best interests at heart.' She lowered her gaze. 'I know what I did with Padrig was wrong in the eyes of society. Oh, but Ursa, it felt so right in the eyes of Venus!'

'Then let us hope Venus protects you. For we have trouble ahead, mistress.' Ursa took Flavia's hand again. 'Look at what Balbus dared to do and he half dead from sickness. What will he do when he is well?'

Flavia met her gaze. 'Then I need to commission a stronger curse. One which will suck the very lifeblood from his body.'

Ursa shivered. 'This is dangerous talk.'

'But what else can I do?'

'I will not be strong enough to go to town to order the curse tablet,' Ursa fretted. 'You will have to wait until I am well.'

Flavia felt again Balbus's slimy hand on her inner thigh. Grasping, greedy, slick with sweat, the filthy nails digging into her tender flesh. His rank odour still defiled her nostrils. She couldn't rid herself of the memory of the squalid tussle in the changing room. The image of his slack mouth grinning in deranged lust flickered through her brain again and again. It was true; he had not hurt her body much, excepting a few bruises, but he had hurt her mind most terribly. And he had hurt her beloved Ursa. She needed to do something. 'I will go in your stead,' she said determinedly. 'I will take Eseld.'

'You cannot go. It is too dangerous!'

'And is it not dangerous to stay here and risk Balbus again?' She chewed her lip. 'I was not completely truthful when I spoke earlier. After he had knocked your head, Ursa, he came after me.'

'Mistress!'

'He didn't hurt me, not really, not as he has hurt you.' A violent shudder travelled through her, giving lie to the words.

'Oh, Flavia!'

'I prayed to all the gods I know and to those that I don't.' Flavia frowned, seeing the changing room again, made claustrophobic by the struggle, the feel of the harsh wind, the silent flight of the white owl. 'I don't exactly know what happened. One minute he had hold of my leg, the next I was cursing him as I had cursed no other. I felt all the gods with me, both old and Roman, ones that had gone before, ones who are to come. There was a great white light and a purifying wind.' She frowned. 'And an owl. I felt a white owl in my presence. Then Balbus slackened his grip and rolled away, defeated. Unbeknown to me, Eseld had gone for the guards, and they took him away.' She smoothed her tunic, crumpled from being slept in. 'I do not know how he fares,' she said brutally. 'I do not care. I hope he fades and dies.'

'And if he doesn't?'

Flavia glanced at the slave. 'Then I will do what I have to.'

A heavy silence fell into the room, ominous with portent.

'Can you trust the girl Eseld?'

Flavia nodded. 'I believe so.'

'Then you have little choice. But, Flavia, if you do go into town, you must dress as me. Pretend to be me. And take Eseld with you and one of the other guards.'

'I cannot take a guard. I cannot take the risk of word reaching father, or worse, Balbus.'

'Oh Flavia, the town is full of ruffians. What will you do?'

'She will have me.' Eseld re-entered, carrying an enormous tray of food and wine. Placing it on a table, she added, 'I would give my life for mistress Flavia. Do not fear, Ursa. I am stronger and more wily than I look. I know the streets. I have five older brothers and can outwit them all.'

Flavia reached out a hand to her. Holding Ursa's hand too, she laughed a little. 'Whatever god sent you to our aid, we are deeply and truly thankful, Eseld.'

The three women sat as a trinity for a moment, feeling the power of their union.

'Now,' Flavia said briskly, 'share our breakfast with us, Eseld. Some crumbled baked cheese and honey for poor Ursa and the pancake for me. I find I am suddenly ravenous!'

*

The days passed quietly. The three women kept themselves to themselves, rarely leaving Flavia's rooms and having food sent into them. News from Balbus's supporters was he still lay in his sick bed and unlikely to recover soon. Plague was abroad again. The household skittered about with accusing eyes desperate to catch out anyone not abiding by Flavius Honoratus's newly imposed rules about leaving the villa. Boredom made everyone fret against the confinement. Flavia agonised about those who she had met in the hillfort village, about the vivacious Steren and Aoife, the silent Alys, but most especially about Padrig. She had no word from him and wondered if he had been married yet. The constant worry and concern for him, along with the searing love she felt, balled up and lodged in her stomach.

Nerves about the plague lay greasily on top of far worse. Intelligence from the far north was that the garrison had abandoned the great wall. The unthinkable had happened; Picts had invaded Britannia. Change was in the air and with it came unrest. The world was fragmenting.

Ursa gradually improved but it was weeks into Juno's month until Flavia felt she was well enough to be left and judged it time to risk heading into town to purchase a new curse tablet. The worst of the plague deemed over, Eseld had concocted a fine story of having to collect some jewellery her mistress had ordered. And, didn't everyone know, the small matter of a plague would never dare come between the mistress Flavia and a fine jewel? They were to be disguised as slaves and, once again, Flavia donned drab brown wool.

As they were preparing to leave, Ursa caught Flavia's hand to her breast. 'Be on your guard mistress. Have the eyes of Janus upon you.'

'I will take care, Ursa. Do not be afeared. I have the power of Juno and Minerva with me. Juno's name will be on my lips constantly and I made offerings to all the house shrines this morning. At one point mother caught me and looked askance. I had half a mind to ask her to pray to her Christ for his protection too.' It was a weak attempt at humour.

'You may yet need it.'

Flavia shrugged off the concerns and perched on the edge of her bed. In truth she was terrified about the ordeal she was about to face. Had it not been for the girl Eseld she would not contemplate such a task. To think she was once so bored she had to create adventure! Her jaunts outside to seek excitement beyond the villa estate seemed a long time and another life ago. 'I will be as quick and as careful as I can be, Ursa. I promise. We have borrowed a wagon and driver from the stables. They seemed keen for work now the soldiers have all but gone.'

'And with the soldiers gone we are unprotected from any attack, be it from the north or the east. As you will be when you go into town.' Ursa once again clutched at Flavia's hand. 'The province is in turmoil, mistress. I could sense it in the air weeks ago. Will Flavius Honoratus make plans to leave for Rome now?' The question was half hope, half despair. Since the attack, Ursa had suffered from black moods and anxiety; she vexed herself about everything.

Flavia watched, concerned, as Ursa sank onto the little black painted bench next to her. The woman had aged visibly. 'He has talked of little else for years,' she said bitterly. 'But little preparation has ever been made. I think he waits upon specific invitation. Although now, most probably, we would have to throw ourselves on the mercy of Marcus unless father can be guaranteed a position.' She raised her brows. 'And his pride would not allow anything but a triumphant return to the land of his forebears. Bad enough to be thought of as an ignorant cur from the heathen northern province.'

'And will the Lady Hortensia go without a qualm? I cannot see her leaving her devoted soothsayer.'

Flavia's mother had lately become besotted with a new Christian holy man.

'She will have little choice. As will I. We go where father decrees.' As Flavia said this, her heart gave a great lurch at the thought of never seeing Padrig again. He would marry his political bride from the distant tribe and would probably never think of her again. She stood up briskly, wanting to get the ordeal over with. 'I have your instructions, Ursa. I know where to find the curse writer and I know what to order. Wish us well. Come Eseld, let's make haste.'

In the end, Flavia's nerves belied the task itself. Cuinn, a stable slave, and a confidante of Eseld's, was commanded to drive them. Their exit from the villa went unquestioned but they were headed to a rough part of the town, its teeming fetid streets crowded with taverns and brothel houses. More than once they were thankful for Cuinn's brawn as he fended off the attentions of the drunken mob. But it was little more than they expected.

The trouble truly began when they neared the villa's main gate on their return and were stopped by Otho, one of Balbus's staunchest acolytes. He shoved aside the guard and held the reins of the mule as it tossed its head.

Flavia ducked into the covered wagon, hiding her face under her hood. She sank back against the inside, the little cylinder of curse tablet clutched in her hand. If they should fail at this point, all would be lost. If she was discovered, how would she explain to her father?

'Let us pass,' she heard Cuinn say irritably.

'What have you inside there, eh stable boy?' They might be in luck, Otho's voice was slurred.

Eseld chimed in. 'We have a package we must deliver to the Lady Flavia. Let us through, oaf. If you stop us, the mistress will have Flavius Honoratus himself personally whip your behind until it bleeds.'

Flavia prayed silently Otho would not probe further. She felt for the sea glass necklace under her cloak to reassure herself. It was becoming her lucky talisman. She hoped Eseld's bold lie would work. Her heart leaped into her mouth as he clambered on board the wagon.

'A package? And what sort of package? An amphora of fine *Duras?* He belched. 'Or some sweet nutcake? I'll agree she needs sweetening up, but it's wasted on that spoiled bitch.'

Flavia stiffened. It was all she could do to stop herself tearing off her disguise and confront the drunken lout.

'Otho,' Eseld sighed, the weight of the world in her voice. 'If you must know it's a piece of jewellery commissioned by my lady. You know how she loves her baubles. If I fail in my task, I will be put to the wrong end of a sword. So let us pass.'

'Nothing to eat then?'

'Nothing to eat *or* drink. Besides, judging from your Bacchus breath I think you've had enough beer for the day.'

The wagon jerked and rolled with his extra weight. Flavia, jolted, hung on to the rough wooden bench as Cuinn jumped off to calm the spooked mule.

'I'll just have to feed my other appetite, then won't I, wench?' Otho grabbed the girl.

Flavia could smell the rankness of beer even from the back of the wagon. She peered from behind her cloak as Otho seized Eseld's arms and forced his tongue down her throat. He would have done worse had she not fought him off.

'Get off me, you lout, you son of a whore! When I tell my mistress of this, she will have you dragged behind a horse.' She shoved him and he fell off the wagon, lying sprawled in a drunken heap. Eseld wiped her mouth with the back of her hand.

Cuinn, still holding the mule, looked up anxiously.

'Lead on, Cuinn,' she commanded. 'We need to report to mistress Flavia before nightfall.'

The wagon once again rumbled and swayed on its way.

'I shall have my revenge, Eseld,' Otho howled. 'I know Balbus. He has power in this house.'

Eseld poked her head out. 'Balbus is on his deathbed,' she yelled back. 'Beware hitching your star to one who is falling, Otho!'

Flavia pulled her inside. 'That was unwise. We do not need to aggravate any of Balbus's men. But it was brave, too. Are you hurt?' She examined Eseld carefully.

'I am unhurt, mistress. That one, he takes too much beer and it makes him brave with his words but,' at this she crooked her little finger, 'weak with his action. The last time he attacked me outside the bathhouse he was as limp as boiled lettuce.' She laughed, an edge of hysteria building. 'It makes his temper even more foul, however.'

Flavia found Eseld's hand. 'Then we must avoid him.'

'And thanks to you, I am able to. Since I have been in your personal employ, no man excepting Otho has laid even so much as his eye upon me.'

'I am sorry for your pain, Eseld. I am sorry for all the pain men have inflicted upon you.' Flavia drew in a bitter breath. 'It seems it is our fate to be chattels of men. Will there ever be a time when womankind is free of such tyranny?'

Eseld tightened the hold on her hand and pitched against her as the wagon rocked over the cobbles of the outer courtyard. 'In my tribe, women are not treated so. Our sex has respect and equality, great power even.'

Flavia remembered Padrig saying much the same thing. She missed him so! Would that she could escape this autocracy. Would that she could go to him and start a new life. 'It seems, even though Rome thinks it has taught Britannia much, maybe it should have listened as well as it instructed?'

'Maybe it should have tolerated as well as ruled.' Eseld gasped and covered her mouth in horror. 'Forgive me. I spoke out of turn.'

Flavia managed a laugh, albeit a hard one. 'How can I not forgive you when your quick thinking just saved our mission?'

Eseld pulled a face. 'For a moment I feared Otho would demand proof of our errand.'

'Me too.' Flavia sank against the girl, giggling, relief taking over. 'What would you have done had he insisted?'

'Kneed him where it hurts a man the most. I am skilled in the act.'

'I can well believe it, Eseld,' Flavia replied, now laughing loud and genuinely. 'I can well believe it. Thank the gods you were here.' She raised her voice to the roof. 'Thank Juno!'

# CHAPTER 28

*2*023
*Thank Juno ... thank Juno!*

The voice in her dream was exultant and insistent. It woke Juno and she reared up in bed, gasping. It had only been yet another dream. Just a dream but the woman's voice could have been calling from the next room. *What was she thanking me for?* As usual, the man had been there too. It was all mixed up. The Durotriges Briton: tall and handsome with blue eyes full of humour and pain. Over the past few weeks, she'd rarely had a dream-free night. *What was this all about?*

Narrowing her eyes against the bright early morning June sunshine, her eyes were caught by the blue bead on the windowsill. It was winking in the light, almost looking on fire. *Odd.* She was sure she'd moved it to the bedside table. Shaking the sleep away and determinedly not analysing what might be happening in her head, she threw back the duvet onto a grumbling Joops. Picking up the bead she was comforted as it warmed her hand. She stared at it, a strange compulsion wanting it near. Digging through the set of drawers she found one of a pair of boot laces. For some reason she'd kept it when the other had broken. Threading it through the bead, she knotted the lace firmly and put it on.

Clicking her tongue at the dog, she went downstairs to let him out and switched on the kettle for her first mug of tea. Why was this woman continually calling her name? And

241

why were her dreams invaded by a man who lived and died over sixteen hundred years before? After searching for hours on the net, she'd not come across his image anywhere, so how had she dreamed his exact image before seeing the painting in the museum? There was nothing about Flete's star-crossed lovers either.

She stood at the kitchen window watching as Joops nosed around the garden. She caressed the bead hung around her neck, thinking. Paul had messed with her head big-time but all this was something beyond what he'd done to her. Or was it connected in some way?

'Time to cut back on the booze and get more sleep,' she murmured. 'And sleep without dreaming.'

Joops seemed very interested in the back gate. Trying not to let her shoulders tense Juno focussed on the sturdy padlock she'd attached to the bolt. If someone was determined, they could climb over the fence, but it was the most she could do to keep the back garden secure. Hearing the kettle boil, she reached for a mug out of the cupboard. Dismissing it as rabbit or fox smells catching Joops's nose, she found a teaspoon. She stared at the kitchen work surface. One mug. One spoon. It was all a bit dismal. No wonder her dreams were crowded with people. Her life certainly wasn't.

She'd been lonely recently. Mabyn was preoccupied with work problems and WhatsApped only intermittently, her brother was busy with end of term stuff at the university and Tom, despite promising to keep her informed, was wrapped up in the dig. She'd popped round to borrow a lawn mower in a vague attempt to tidy up the garden and Diana said she hadn't seen him for weeks either. It seemed he'd made camp up on the field.

It should have been a great opportunity to get on with her writing, but Juno couldn't concentrate on that either. She was already behind and her agent was making noises. Juno had never missed a deadline before and couldn't understand her lack of motivation now. She was a professional writer used to gritting her teeth and forcing her behind down on a seat in front of the computer, but she could hardly summon up enthusiasm for a single word let alone sentence. It was inexplicable. She'd written throughout her relationship with Paul, even during the really awful times, it had been her escape. But now other thoughts, other concerns crowded any creativity from her head. Sucking in a breath she resigned herself to yet another awkward phone conversation with her agent. Perhaps she needed a change in genre? She'd been writing romance ever since first published. Maybe she was getting stale? *But what else can I write?* Besides, she had to deliver this book first.

'Okay Joops,' she said, determinedly brisk, as the dog returned. 'Tea, then a shower and a long walk in that order. That's what we need, eh, boy? Too much thinking going on.' She fed him and then ran upstairs. It was time to get out of her head for a while.

*

She trudged around the Roman Field watching listlessly as Joops embarked on an epic nose to ground hunt. He'd caught the scent of something. Once again, she was envious of a living creature being able to exist in the moment. Despite her promise to herself, her brain was still full of questions and concerns. Now they veered hopelessly to Paul. Was it Paul who plagued her with phone calls? She'd left the line plugged in and had had only one silent call. Mabyn had rung the previous week to catch up and reminded her she could dial 1471 to check what number was calling. Which she had done, only to find it was a withheld number. She'd sat and hugged Joops to her for an hour after discovering that. Mabyn once again scolded her for not contacting the police, but Juno was at a loss as to what to say. She was pretty sure phoning someone wasn't a crime and, even if they were classed as nuisance calls, it would be low down on the police's priority. She supposed she could tackle the problem head on and ring Paul but the thought of having to talk to him filled her with horror. She refused to give him the satisfaction of knowing he'd got to her.

She walked around in endless loops, doing nothing as Joops investigated a filthy, muddy puddle and her thoughts turned to Tom. She was disappointed. Even if they'd committed to a friendship and nothing more, she'd expected him to keep her up to date as to what was happening with the dig. She had no idea if he'd contacted Cris as her brother had been ignoring her too. Digging her heel into the hard soil of the field she supposed she could wander over the holloway and find out what was happening but stubbornly wouldn't let herself.

Joops, however, had other ideas. Having exhausted the rabbit trails and the delights of the puddle which mysteriously remained despite all the recent dry and hot weather, he set off at pace towards the trees at the top of the field and the kissing gate, under which he scrabbled. Resigned, Juno ran up the hill after him and, panting, skidded into the holloway. She grabbed him by the scruff of the neck and put him back on the lead, then stared around her. The holloway was transformed. A vivid green canopy had grown overhead blanking out the sunlight. There was a strong musty damp smell and even the light was greened. Thick juicy ferns grew up the banks obliterating the tree roots and a solid silence blanketed out any birdsong or the distant rumble from the main road. Had a legion of Roman soldiers appeared and marched towards her, Juno wouldn't have been the slightest bit surprised. The sense of the ancient was very near. Shivering a little, she tugged Joops away from a clump of grass he was eating, made a decision, and walked through the gate to the dig field.

She stood at the entrance for a moment, her mouth dropping open. It wasn't only the holloway that had been transformed. It was the first time she'd been back since camping out overnight with Tom and she looked around curiously. Tom's tent was pitched in one corner, a portacabin guarded the entrance and rectangles of turf had been dug, seemingly at random, exposing livid patches of earth. There was even a trio of portaloos shoved against the hedge. Two archaeologists, dressed in khaki shorts and wearing hats, were on their knees digging through the soil but, apart from them, the site was deserted.

'Juno! Hey.'

'Cris.' Juno started as her brother strode out of the portacabin. 'What are you doing here?'

'I'm the official university liaison. We'll soon have a whole team of students working up here. Had one or two delays seeing as it's local-authority owned land but we're good to go now.'

'I would have thought it would be easier rather than dealing with a private landowner.' She was finding it hard to unbend. Everything moving on without her was a familiar feeling.

'You'd think, wouldn't you?' he replied cheerfully. 'We've had to wade through acres of bureaucracy as it was but most of it is done now. Plus, we had to get the commercial archaeologist teams to bid for the project. Luckily Tom knows everyone and pulled whole ropes of strings so we're sorted. He's been taken on by South and Prospect who won the contract. Come the end of term and we'll have two teams of fifteen student volunteers working up here.' He rubbed his hands together. 'Cannot wait. Come on, come into the office.' He gestured to the portacabin.

Juno stiffened, affronted. She'd been there almost at the very beginning of the discovery and now felt thoroughly side-lined. All this had been happening and she hadn't been involved. Cris must have been working here for most of the month and hadn't even popped in to the cottage to fill her in. And as for Tom!

Cris misinterpreted her hesitation. 'We've got luxuries. A kettle and some half decent coffee. Plus custard creams!'

'Is Joops allowed in?'

'Of course.' He turned to retrace his steps back to the office.

Juno followed him, muttering, 'At least *he's* not being left out,' at his back.

When they entered Tom was sitting at a desk, frowning at a laptop. 'Forgotten something, Cris?' he asked, without his gaze leaving the screen. 'You should see this. The geo-phys has come up with some remarkable images of the field over the other side of the holloway.'

'Visitor, Tom.'

'Not the press again.' Tom scowled, shoved a hand through his hair and finally looked up. 'Oh. Hello, Juno.'

'Hello Tom.'

Cris toed over a stool for her. 'Coffee?'

She sat down, feeling cross. 'Yes.' She looked around the room. It was small. A large notice board filled one wall and was covered with photographs, graphs and hastily scribbled notes, including one which declared, "Buy more milk." An assortment of wet weather gear and a couple of canvas hats hung from hooks near the door and a jumble of stale-smelling boots were heaped in a corner. On another table was a printer and a pile of untidy papers. It was a mess. 'This looks cosy.' She didn't bother hiding her sarcasm.

Cris paused in his coffee making. 'Uh-oh.'

'What?' Tom asked irritably.

'I know that tone. Come on, little sis; what have we done?'

'Nothing.'

'Come on, we must have done something. You've got Mum's face on.'

'I am nothing like Mum.'

'Oh yes you are, you just don't know it. Two peas in a pod you are. Both stubborn. Both capable of spectacular acts of passive-aggressiveness.'

'I am *not* passive-aggressive!' Juno felt an angry flush rise.

Cris poured boiling water into three none too clean looking mugs. 'So tell us what we're guilty of.' He added a dash of milk and handed one mug over. It was chipped and emblazoned with 'Archaeologists Do it in the Mud!'

'Well,' Juno huffed.

'Well?'

'I was there. Here, I mean. I helped with the beginning of it all. Guarded it overnight.'

'For which I was very grateful,' Tom put in.

'Not grateful enough to keep me in the loop.'

'Oh, is that it?' Cris subsided onto another battered stool. 'Feeling left out, little sis?'

'Don't patronise me!' Juno spat back.

Cris held up a hand in surrender. 'I could not have guessed you would want to be part of all this. You hate history. You've always made that clear.'

'This is different. This is my history. I mean, I feel part of *this* history.'

Tom snapped down the lid of the laptop. 'I'm really sorry, Juno.' He ran a hand through his hair again, making it stick up. 'It's been 24/7 up here. We wanted to get going before the best of the summer and the long days go. Not to mention, once word spreads, we'll have a security issue. South and Prospect are laying on a couple of men soon but it's been just me and your brother up to now.'

Juno looked at him properly. Beneath the tan lay the pallor of exhaustion. He was unshaven and looked to have not washed for days.

'Tom's been working all hours to push everything through,' Cris added. 'Even with his contacts it's been tricky.'

'A phone call takes minutes.' Juno couldn't let go the childish resentment. It was always thus. It was exactly the same as when her brothers had had friends over when they'd all been kids. She was instantly forgotten about and excluded from whatever exciting thing was planned for the boys. She sipped her coffee. It was surprisingly good but did little to improve her mood. And as for Tom, she didn't even want to explore how hurt *his* exclusion made her feel.

'Aw, come on Juno. How were we to know you wanted in on all this?' her brother asked. 'We thought you'd be happy well out of it and have the time to concentrate on your book. Besides, you could just as easily wandered along, like you have today.'

'And you could easily have come down to the cottage.'

Cris looked guilty. 'I could've done. I'm sorry. I really didn't think you'd be bothered by it all. My bad. You know what I'm like, I get carried away by all the excitement. Soz, Ju.'

Tom pushed his coffee away. It was untouched. 'And I'm sorry too. More than I can say. Like Cris, I really didn't think you'd be interested.' He met her eyes and seemed to read her mood. 'I'm really sorry, Juno. Nothing would have given me greater pleasure than to have you in the loop. But, apart from the dreadful assumption that you wouldn't be interested, to be honest, I just haven't had the time.'

Juno felt her face heat again but this time it was as a reaction to his remorse. Genuine and heartfelt. 'Yes, well ...' she let the sentence trail.

'So, off your high horse, sis. Drink your coffee and we'll show you round,' Cris said. 'Did you hear what we found out about the coin hoard? Load of nummi, that's the everyday coppers of Roman life. Earliest dates from 260 CE, latest celebrating Constantinople making it 352 CE. Plus there's the gold solidus. All tremendously exciting.' He glanced at his watch. 'Oh, actually, it'll have to be Tom who shows you round. I need to get back to Exeter.'

Tom met her look and gave a twisted smile. 'I'd be happy to.'

'Well, if you've got the time.' Juno wasn't giving in that easily.

Neither was Tom. 'I've got to have a word with the team anyway.'

Cris gulped down his coffee, ruffled Joops's fur and shot off, slamming the portacabin door shut in his haste.

Tom blew out a breath. 'Don't get me wrong, but I'm always relieved when Cris has gone. He's like a tornado about the place.'

Juno giggled. 'Is he a help or a hindrance?'

'Can I compromise on force of nature?'

'Oh, he's that alright. Always had far too much energy to know what to do with. Drives Mum mad. Always makes the house smaller, does Cris.'

'Agreed.' Tom looked about him. He scrubbed an exhausted hand over his face. 'I am truly sorry about being out of the loop lately. It's just been so full on. I've barely slept. He's right about the coin hoard though. We've dug out about twenty thousand so far. It's an amazing find.'

'Any theories about how or why they came to be there?'

'Not really. Hidden in case of a raid maybe? Stolen wages? Who knows. Britannia in the late fourth century was a lawless place and becoming increasingly chaotic. The legions were gradually leaving as Rome was under threat from the Visigoths. The inhabitants had little protection so maybe hiding the loot was the thing to do. You'd return at some point when it was safe and recover it. But, of course, there was no guarantee you would come back. It's also possible it was a ritual offering.' He yawned hugely. 'It's all guesswork and speculation. And the university bods, including your good brother, are having a wild old time guessing and speculating.' He yawned again.

'It's okay, Tom,' Juno said softly. 'I can see you're knackered. I can easily come back another day to look round.' She shrugged. 'Pride got a bit of a bash, that's all. It was the story of my life, being left out of what the boys got up to. It's left a scar.' She scuffed the toe of her trainer on the gritty lino. 'They always seemed to have all the exciting things to do and I, as a mere girl, wasn't allowed to tag along. I suspect it's another reason I deliberately turned away from the family passion for history. A minor rebellion, if you will.'

Tom frowned. 'It sounds as if you had quite a lonely childhood.'

'I suppose I did,' Juno admitted. 'There's quite an age gap between me and the other two. I was the afterthought, the accident.' She sucked in a breath, remembering what her mother had told her about how much she was loved. 'However, looking on the positive side, I had loads of time for my imagination. Good training for a writer.'

'Excellent training for a writer.' Tom rose and stretched out his neck and shoulders.

'As I say, don't feel obliged to spend time with me.'

He shot her a direct look from blue eyes. It had blood rushing to her face. 'I never feel obliged to spend time with you Juno. It's never a hardship and nearly always a pleasure. Come on. I could do with getting out of this buggering tin hut. Baking when the temperatures rise. Freezing bloody cold when they don't.'

Juno followed him out, blinking in the sunshine. She tried to ignore the happy feeling which had enveloped her at his words. Then she stopped. 'What do you mean,' she began indignantly, 'about it being *nearly* always a pleasure spending time with me?'

He didn't have time to answer as one of the archaeologists she'd seen working earlier, a young blonde, came rushing up. 'Tom,' she yelled breathlessly. 'Tom, come and see what we've found.' The girl flung her arms around his neck. 'Oh Tom,' she added, planting a huge kiss on his cheek. 'I think we've got ourselves some human remains!'

# CHAPTER 29

*The Secundinus Villa*

The bodies of five women were found just outside the town walls. They had been defiled in the worst possible ways and dumped.

'Who were they?' Flavia asked, horrified.

Eseld brought the news into Flavia's chambers, interrupting the peace of their sanctuary. She sank to her knees. 'No one knows. Women from an outlying village perhaps, or some whores from the town. No one from the villa, thank the gods.' She shook her head. 'They had no mercy for those women. They say it's a warning.'

Ursa sat up from where she was napping on a couch. She was mostly healed now, with time, rest and good food helping her recovery. 'It *is* a warning. A warning of what's to come.' She shuddered.

'From whom?' Flavia asked impatiently. Since Balbus's assault, Ursa had been increasingly dour and gloomy, and taken to ominous predictions. She loved the woman but wasn't finding her easy to live with.

'From the barbarians in the east.'

Eseld nodded. 'Gossips tell of a raid on Lindinis. Saxons from Germania.'

'But surely our legion went to fight the barbarians in Germania. Have they not succeeded in defeating them?' Flavia put down her dish of almonds, all appetite gone.

'They are too strong mistress, even for the might of Rome. Some say the target is the great city itself.'

'They will never take the city of Rome. Stop talking nonsense, Eseld.'

'Nothing is certain anymore mistress Flavia. Things have changed even over these past few months. The word on the street is of chaos and collapse.'

'We live in uncertain times,' Ursa added.

'It is all nonsense,' Flavia said roundly. 'Rome will never fall.'

'We none of us know what's to come,' Ursa put in gloomily. 'Mark my words.'

Eseld nodded in agreement. 'Some have left Moridunum already.'

'And where do they go, child?'

'They flee to the old hill forts, mistress. That is, if the tribes will take them in.'

Flavia thought of Padrig. Of Merit and his father. Would they take pity on those seeking sanctuary? More workers but more mouths to feed. Merit did not trust her. Would he trust strangers begging at his gate? Her thoughts winged to Beltane – she had too many thoughts in her head these days – too many worries and concerns. The festival of the Bright Fire had been over these seven weeks past. Had Padrig celebrated? Had he danced and feasted? Had he taken his promised wife? She bit down on a sigh. It had been so long since she had seen him, since they had lain together. It had not quelled the longing for him, the fire for him which burned in her loins.

She suppressed a shiver. Lindinis was but a day's ride from Moridunum. She could see how the situation would spread panic and terror. Without the legion, they were vulnerable to attack and the town walls, built in more peaceable times, offered little defence. Were people really leaving their homes? Fleeing to live in round huts? The image of the inside of the royal hut in Padrig's village arose, with its earth floor and sleeping couches barely concealed behind tapestries. And what of Marcus, her brother so far away in Mediolanum? How would they bear it should anything happen to him?

She sucked in a calming breath. Her thoughts were chaotic indeed. 'No,' she said flatly. 'I do not believe it. We are safe here and Rome is safe. The empire has survived for centuries. It will survive again.' She saw Eseld's eyes flit to Ursa's. The girl looked anxious. Well, that was what came of listening to gossip and street tittle-tattle. 'Let us walk in the garden.' She glanced through the unshuttered window. 'It's a fine day. Too lovely to waste being indoors, the fresh air will do us good. And I think we'll be safe there. I hear Balbus is yet still in his bed. Is that so, Eseld?'

The slave bobbed her head. 'It is, mistress. But he has recovered somewhat.'

'So he lives still. We need to find a way of ending him.' Flavia's mouth twisted. 'We need to find a way of casting the new curse. And it needs to be soon.'

\*

The women continued their quiet life, taking care not to draw unnecessary attention to themselves. Thankfully Flavia's father was absorbed in urgent town matters and her mother remained besotted by her Christian soothsayer. Both parents left her well alone, the tumultuous political situation rendering their daughter's marital state inconsequential.

Despite her brave words in defence of the empire, to Flavia it felt as if the world she knew was collapsing. She was once again ordered to stay within the villa estate's walls; there were reports of increasingly violent raids. As during the plague, the inhabitants of the villa stayed within its walls unless absolutely necessary. All gates, even the back one through the hortus were barricaded and guarded at all times. Life closed down and became narrow and dull. There was no word from Padrig. Even if she needed to get out to see him, it would be near impossible.

The three women were sitting in Flavia's antechamber when their peace was rudely interrupted. It had been a hot thundery day and a stroll in the garden had been abandoned. Instead, they had retreated to their rooms, weaving, talking idly and deliberately about nothing, eating honeyed apricots. It was claustrophobic but tranquil. Or had been until Otho burst in.

Flavia surged to her feet. It was enough to deal with the anarchy outside but to face it in her own sanctuary was too much. 'What is the meaning of this incursion?'

The man looked about him, licking his lips. 'So, this is where you all hide?'

'You have no authority to be in here!'

Otho smirked. 'Time's gone when you had any say over me or what I do.' He jerked his head. 'Out there it's every man for himself now.' He made an obscene gesture. 'And every woman is every man's.'

Flavia's chin rose. She would not be intimidated by this oaf. 'Leave my rooms this instant.'

'Or what?' He swayed slightly.

He was drunk. Again. It gave Flavia a little more courage. The recent experience with Balbus had made her question everything about men and everything about the hierarchy in the villa. Villa life was crumbling in reflection of the chaos outside. What was to become of them all? 'You need to leave now. Or I will call the guard.' Despite her brave words and semblance of authority, inside she quaked. The guards were becoming ever more unreliable and more likely to be off somewhere playing drunken gambles over the dice.

Otho laughed and then stopped abruptly as Eseld stood up and joined Flavia at her side. 'My lady has asked you to leave.' The girl inched towards him, hands fisted in readiness.

Ursa stood too. The women stood implacable, a triumvirate against him. Eseld took one more step towards Otho, a derisory smile playing about her lips showing her contempt.

Otho shot her an uncertain look. He flung the objects he was carrying at their feet where they clattered onto the hard mosaic. 'Balbus's orders.' He spat on the floor, then turned on his heel and stumbled out, tripping over his cloak as he did.

Flavia's shoulders dropped. The exchange had been unpleasant but it could have been so much worse. She glanced at the other women. Eseld young and breezily confident, Ursa with a pinch of worry marring her poor healing face. They were no longer safe. If Otho could march straight in unchallenged, then who else might? What if one of them had been alone? Would he have been bolder, more reckless in his demands? She'd thought Balbus was her sole enemy, but it looked as if another had been added. And what was worse, this one was healthy and in the prime of his strength.

The solution hit her as hard as Balbus had hit Ursa. They needed to get away. To escape. But to where and to whom? Travelling to Mediolanum and to Marcus seemed an impossible task for three unprotected women. Her father had recently left for Durnovaria but before he did, she had overheard her parents arguing; it was all they ever seemed to do these days. Her mother had vowed to stay in the Province. It seemed her newly hatched infatuation with Christianity and the holy man who was permanently at her side had forged a new love for Britannia. As for her father, gone were the pugnacious words and his desire to return to Rome. He seemed lost, burdened by his responsibilities and by the new hopelessness of the disorder and chaos he found himself trying to rule over. Her parents were ever more ignorant of their daughter. It was as if they didn't care. Even if Flavius Honoratus insisted on them packing up the house and returning to Rome, dragging his unwilling wife with him, Flavia no longer saw her life with them. There was only one man she wanted to be with. One man she saw a possible future with, even if it meant settling for the role of lover rather than wife.

Padrig.

He was her only chance. But how could she send word? How could she even begin to formulate a plan? Her attention was drawn back to their present situation by Eseld talking to Ursa.

'Otho,' Eseld spat out. 'He's so deep in his drink he cannot even walk straight.'

'What's he thrown on the floor?' Ursa bent down and picked up the two items. 'It looks like jewellery of some sort. A bracelet or necklet?'

'If it is jewellery, it is ill-made,' Eseld observed. 'And too big for a bracelet. It must be for the neck.'

Ursa slipped one over her wrist, she threaded the other through her fingers. It was a long strand of roughly worked metal from which hung a medallion. 'There is writing on here. Look my lady.' She showed the medallion to Flavia.

'What does it say?'

Ursa read the inscription slowly. 'Hold me. I have run away. I belong to Flavius Honoratus Secundinus. Return me to him to collect your just reward.' She sat down abruptly on the couch.

'What is its meaning?' Eseld asked.

'It is a slave collar.'

Flavia gasped in horror. Sliding down beside Ursa, she put her arm around the woman. To her alarm she found the older woman was trembling. 'Surely not? It cannot be. I know them to be common elsewhere, but father has never insisted his slaves wear them.'

Ursa handed over the collar mutely. 'See for yourself.'

Flavia read the words and then repeated them out loud.

Eseld sat at their feet. 'No wonder Otho was swaggering.' She swallowed. 'Are all us slaves to wear them?'

Ursa nodded. 'It's the usual way. My brother had one.' A solitary tear trickled down her cheek. 'Before he was accused of stealing, had his life beaten out of him and thrown in a ditch. He didn't even have a proper burial. That's how little they cared for him. He had no grave goods to help him in his afterlife. No coin to pay the Ferryman. I hope he returns to haunt his master. Gaius Valerius made them all wear collars. He was a cruel and unjust man and his slaves would often try to escape. Too mean to buy replacements, he forced collars on them with the promise of a high reward should they be found.'

The women sat in silence while they absorbed Ursa's words.

'But father isn't like that,' Flavia said eventually. 'He's a good and fair master. Isn't he?' she added with uncertainty. These days she was less sure of her father's honourability. 'Why would he insist on this? It makes little sense and especially now.'

'It would seem Balbus, even on his sick bed has the power to twist whispers into your father's ear,' Ursa said bitterly. 'And, as for why now, what better time for a slave to attempt escape than when the world is in chaos and he could slip away into it? Your father needs to preserve appearances in the face of turmoil and insurrection. He needs to keep the villa estate running. How can he do that if he loses slaves?'

'But he has always treated you well, Ursa,' Flavia protested.

Ursa snorted. 'To him I am just another slave. A valued one, a trusted one maybe but I am owned. I am not free as you are.' She held up the collars where they clinked together dully. 'He may have treated us well, but this is how he truly sees us. Something to be bought and sold, to be worked to death if he wished. An object, not a human. And this is the final indignity.'

'It is cruel and unfair.'

'It is the way of the world.'

Flavia frowned, thinking it through. 'I cannot see Balbus agreeing to wear a collar proclaiming his status to the world,' she pointed out. 'This is all most mysterious.'

'Then it can mean only one thing.' Ursa stared at her sadly.

'What?'

'Once your father returns from Durnovaria, he will make Balbus a free man.' Ursa gave a cynical laugh. 'And, I imagine, once free, Balbus will take a cut of any reward money when escaped slaves are returned.' She took Flavia's hand. 'The other thing he will insist upon is taking you as his wife. Your time is running out.'

Once again, the women sat in silence. Flavia gazed at Eseld looking morose crouched on the floor, her hand clutching anxiously at Ursa's robes. Flavia glanced at Ursa. She had rarely seen her servant look more distressed; she had taken this hard. She had responsibility for these women; they had done so much for her, she now needed to repay the debt. Touching a finger to the sea glass necklace to give her confidence, she said, 'Then we must do something.'

'What can we do?' Eseld asked.

'We are going to leave.'

'Leave the villa?' Ursa put a hand to her head as if it ached. 'What madness is this?'

'I do not mean to travel to Rome, even if that is father's plan.' Flavia flicked a glance at both women. 'I mean for us to escape to Padrig's tribe.'

Ursa stared at her, slack jawed. 'What nonsense you talk, my child. How can that be possible?'

'First we must get a message to him.'

'But that would mean danger of a very grave kind.' Ursa gasped. 'Have you not understood what is happening out there? We must stay here until Flavius Honoratus returns and await his decision. He may yet decide for Rome.'

'And how long could that be? You said yourself time is running out. If Balbus is so cocksure he will be freed he won't wait until my father's official decision. And if we are all to return to Rome, I will have to go as Balbus's wife.' Flavia screwed her eyes shut and shuddered dramatically. 'I'd rather throw myself upon the sword.'

'But Flavia, be reasonable child, the town is even more lawless than before. Word is, invaders from the east are nearly upon us, some say they are at Vindocladia already and we have no one to defend us here. No garrison. Half the legion lost their lives fighting in Germania. And the ones who were left here are feeble-brained.'

'Then, if we are to be attacked, the sooner we flee, the better. I'd rather take my chances with Padrig in his well-fortified village than languish here with undefended villa gates.' Flavia's voice rose with her passion.

'Hush,' Ursa said urgently, looking about her in panic. 'Someone will hear.'

'Who, Ursa? Who will hear? The same guards who prevented Otho from entering? They have gone. Playing cards, getting drunk or in the arms of some harlot they've let in from the tavern. We were lucky it was only Otho who came, and even luckier that he was so drunk he could barely stand. Next time,' she flinched, 'next time it could be someone infinitely worse and with far worse consequences. It could even be Balbus. It's only a matter of time before he rises from his pit of sickness.'

'We still haven't used the curse tablet!' Eseld looked up eagerly. 'We could try that.'

'I think we may be beyond using a curse tablet.' At Eseld's wretched face, Flavia relented. 'But perhaps we can cast it on our way.'

'What is this bold plan of yours, to get ourselves to Padrig's village?' Ursa asked doubtfully. 'What is this mad plan? I cannot believe you are so desperate. I still think it better to remain here, even with Flavius Honoratus as master.'

'And what is the alternative, Ursa? That you remain a slave for the rest of your life?'

'We will end up dead in a ditch.'

'Then if we do, it will be as a result of fleeing for our freedom. For mine, for yours and for Eseld's! And we *are* desperate. Well, I am. If you wish to stay here and take your chances, I understand.' Flavia laid a hand on her servant's arm. 'I cannot and will not force you to trail in my wake.'

Ursa picked up the slave collar and dangled it from her finger. She glared at it. 'Some choice! I stay and wear a collar to proclaim my servitude. Or I leave to be set upon by barbarians.'

Eseld stood up. 'I pledge my loyalty. If it were not for you, my mistress, I would still be a plaything at the whims of any man who wandered past the bathhouse.' She grimaced. 'Whatever will come, whatever we may face, I promise to serve you all my days.'

Ursa stared at the girl, her mouth thinning into a hard line. She was obviously struggling to make her decision. Flavia and Eseld watched silently.

Ursa regarded Flavia. 'From the very first day I saw you,' her voice broke, 'when you were but a scrawny sapling with a shock of jet-black hair, I promised to serve and protect you. You have a mother and father in life but not in love. Forgive my plain speech but you never mattered to them, not as you do to me. I saw you that first day, a spoiled and indulged child who had every possession, every need filled except for one. You had no love. No guidance. You received an education in letters but not in morals. I vowed I would do that for you. I vowed I would love you when needed, chastise when necessary. Guide and steer you. I think I have.'

'Oh, Ursa,' Flavia cried, tears starting. 'You know you have. Any faults I have – and I know I have many – are mine alone. You must know you are dearer to me than anyone. More a mother than the one I have.' She flung her arms around her.

They embraced and then Ursa shook her off, taking in a deep breath. 'Then how can I stay here when I am to be branded and away from my mistress?' She flung the slave collar away. It bounced once on the tesserae and lay glinting dully in the sunlight. Turning to Flavia she took her hand. 'You are my mistress now and forever. I owe allegiance to no other.' Tears shone. 'I promise to follow and serve you, come what may, until my dying day.'

'Let us pray it will not come to that,' Flavia said brokenly. She was weeping freely. 'Come Eseld, give me your hand. Three hands of three women. We are stronger together than apart. I call on the great goddess Juno, protector of women. Let no man divide us or defeat us.'

A sudden gust of wind blew into the room, sending the shutter flying against the frescoed wall.

'See! She hears us. Juno! Juno! I call upon you,' Flavia repeated. *'Protect us. Juno. Juno ...'*

Georgia Hill

# CHAPTER 30

*T*   *he hills above Flete*
    *Juno! Juno!*
        Juno swung around from the sight of the
student archaeologist wrapping herself around Tom. She was
sure someone had called her name. It was very faint but the
words were distinct, almost lost on the breeze but clear; it was
the woman's voice from the dream, authoritative and with an
edge of desperation. She swept a look around the field.
There was no one in sight who was likely to be calling her.
Tom was busy with his student, the other one was still over
at the other side of the dig and Cris had long since left.
Besides, Juno was sure it was a woman's voice. She searched
again thinking maybe a dog-walking acquaintance was
hovering by the gate but, apart from the four of them, there
was no one else around. *This is getting weirder.* Joops,
roused by the blonde student's excitement began barking and
Juno became distracted by trying to get him quiet. Once he
was calm, she turned her attention to Tom.

        He disentangled himself from the woman, looking
embarrassed. 'Juno, meet Sierra, one of our apprentice
archaeologists. Sierra, this is Juno. Now, repeat what you've
just said but at a decibel lower and slowly.'

        'Hi, Juno,' Sierra said. 'Great name. Sorry Tom. Soz
Juno. But, oh, my gosh, I'm soooo thrilled.'

She was attractive, Juno observed, with smooth tanned skin and honey-blonde hair and was fizzing with excitement.

Sierra slapped her hands together to rid them of soil. 'Okay, so, Charlie and I were sifting through the bucket of earth taken from Trench Three and we found what might be a finger bone. Darling, we think we've got human remains on site!'

Tom narrowed his eyes at Joops. 'Can you keep him on a short lead, Juno?'

'Of course.' She bristled at the suggestion she'd do anything else and was about to give him a sarcastic reply when he strode off at pace.

Sierra linked an arm with her catching her irritation. 'Don't mind Tom. He can be beastly at times but underneath the grouchy exterior beats a heart of flint.' She giggled and added, 'Sorry archaeologists' little jokette. But honestly, it's the most amazing thing ever. And there's me thinking I'd spend the entire summer digging up pot shards if I was lucky. Cute dog by the way. I love springers. We've got a few at home. Daddy's beaters work them. Come on, we don't want the men to take over, do we?'

Juno suppressed a grin. 'We certainly don't, especially as it was you who found it.'

'Oh, ducky, you're soooo right!'

They followed Tom to where Charlie, the other apprentice, was standing staring into a large circular sieve which hung from an A-frame. A tall skinny man with an unruly mass of dark curly hair tied back with a scarf, he looked up at their arrival. 'Hey, Tom.' Unhooking the sieve, he held it out. 'What do you think?'

Tom peered into it. Reaching into the back pocket of his jeans, he pulled out a flip up magnifying glass.

While he studied it the rest of them stood in silence. Sierra had left Juno and was now hugging Charlie around the waist. The tension was palpable.

He looked up eventually. 'You're right,' he said thoughtfully. 'It's definitely human and definitely a bone from the hand. Shit.'

Juno was taken aback at his reaction. 'Why aren't you dancing around for joy? Surely this is a significant find?'

He turned to her. 'Yes, it's significant. Highly so. It also causes us problems. We'll need to call in the police, the coroner and a forensics officer.'

'And?'

'Human remains need to be examined to rule out the site isn't a recent crime scene. A forensics officer will decide if they're a cause for further police investigation, or if they're what they term "bones of antiquity". It all takes time. Slows us down. And like everything, we're on a budget with targets to match.' He sighed. 'I'm also not dancing for joy as this is what's left of a human body. A living, breathing person who once walked here. Any remains we find need to be treated with the utmost respect even if they date from hundreds of years ago.'

*Juno! Juno!*

Juno started violently.

'What's the matter?'

'Nothing.' A shiver ran through her. A cloud drifted from nowhere and obscured the sun for a second. Goosebumps rose on her arms and she was very aware of the blue bead lying against her skin underneath her sweatshirt. 'I thought I heard something that's all.' Juno looked up. 'Just the breeze in the trees, I expect.'

Tom obviously wasn't in the mood for anything other than the matter in hand. 'Continue sieving anything that comes out of Trench Three,' he barked at Sierra. 'Charlie, extend the trench by three feet to the west. And don't forget to log anything you find in detail.'

'Yes, boss.'

'Right away, Tom,' Sierra added.

He twisted to leave but turned back. 'And well done, both of you. It's a great find. You're right Si, it *is* incredibly

265

exciting.' Walking Juno back to the portacabin, he added, 'I'm sorry, Juno.' He gave another gusty sigh. 'Sorry again.' He rubbed a hand over his face, leaving a streak of soil.

'What for?'

'For being so short-tempered. Blame lack of sleep and the thought of all the upcoming paperwork. My phone and computer have been playing up and ... there's other stuff been going on. As an apology, I'll owe the team several rounds in the pub tonight.'

Juno didn't want to dwell on the comely Sierra sharing a cosy evening in the pub with Tom. 'They seem a good pair,' she said, swallowing her jealousy.

'They are.' He gave a short laugh. Si is as keen as hell and Charlie is a solid worker with a good eye for detail.' He gave her the side eye. 'Sierra can be very ... erm ... enthusiastic.'

'Which is a good thing,' Juno said levelly.

'It can be a very good thing, but it depends what the enthusiasm is focussed on.'

Juno wouldn't be drawn. If there was something going on between Sierra and Tom it was none of her business and she didn't want to discuss it but the jealousy which speared through told her all she needed to know about how she felt about him. 'Can I do anything to help?'

Tom looked startled. 'Thought you'd be too busy with your book?'

Juno pulled a face. 'Bit stuck. I could do with exercising a different part of my brain.'

Tom laughed again, this time more sincerely. 'Not sure it'll exercise any part of your brain, but you could enter in the finds on the computer system, if you like. We've found quite a lot. Pot shards, the odd coin, some evidence of a wall, late Roman in origin. Tiny bits and pieces, nothing too riveting but it all needs to be recorded. How are your computer skills?'

'Think I'll manage.'

Stopping at the door of the portacabin, he held her gaze. 'I've no doubt you will but the system keeps crashing and we lost a whole load of data we thought we'd saved. Sorry.'

'Stop saying sorry.'

'Sor -' He grimaced then changed the subject. 'What happened to you up by the trench?'

The swerve in subject caught her unawares; she hadn't thought he'd noticed. 'What do you mean?'

'You went white as a sheet. I thought you were about to keel over.'

'Oh, nothing.' Juno didn't think Tom was in a receptive enough mood to listen to her fanciful notions of someone unseen calling her name. He seemed nervy and preoccupied. 'Mum used to call it someone walking over my grave. I suppose,' she lied. 'It's as you said. While finding human remains is incredibly exciting, it's remembering that it's the legacy of a person. Someone who existed. Lived a life, ate, drank, loved, hated.'

'Yup.' He still didn't move. Gazing at her intently, he said, 'Everything alright at home? Nothing ... no one bothering you?'

'I'm fine, Tom. Everything's fine. Now, come on,' she added briskly, 'show me this amazingly complicated computer system that I won't be able to grasp, otherwise these finds will never be recorded.'

*

They worked solidly all afternoon. Once Juno got the hang of the system, she found logging the finds dull and monotonous but enjoyed the brain-dead aspect of it. It stopped her dwelling on who was behind the voice calling her name. Deciding it had, indeed, been the wind, she focussed all her attention on the computer screen in front of her. Tom spent his time on the phone chasing up the relevant people and swearing as he kept losing the signal. After a less fraught call to Cris, who Juno could hear yelling down the phone in excitement, Tom called it a day.

He clicked off his mobile and flung it onto a pile of papers. Easing out the kinks in his neck, he said, 'The coffee might be terrible in this place, but I think it's time to risk another.'

As he said this, the door to the portacabin opened so violently it hit the wall making the metal shudder. Joops sprang up, barking furiously and Juno, muttering her safety mantra, felt her heart leap into her throat. She twisted round with a jolt.

It was Sierra. She looked hot and dusty but was quivering with excitement. 'We've found more, Tom,' she said breathlessly. 'I think you'd better come and have a look.'

She set off at a pace, with Tom and Juno following. They returned to the trench where Charlie was standing knee deep in a newly dug hole. He was aiming a camera at the most recently dug bank. Something gleamed dully at the topmost corner.

'What is it?' Tom asked, tension and strain evident.

Charlie looked up. 'Skeleton. Possibly female. High-born by the evidence,' his flat northern vowels were laced with excitement. He handed Tom the camera.

Tom scrolled through the photographs and whistled. Shoving the camera at Sierra, he lowered himself gently into the trench. 'Show me,' he said urgently. 'Where?'

'What's going on?' Juno asked Sierra.

'We've found an entire skeleton.'

'I gathered that.'

'And it has a torc around its neck and an armlet on the wrist. And ducky, you'll never believe this but they're gold! Solid pure gold!'

*

Once the police and forensics officer arrived, there was little any of them could do. All archaeology was suspended until the coroner's office agreed the remains were too old to be of interest to a police investigation. They left as the police were erecting a blue screen and taping the site off. An over officious CID officer shooed them away, so they trooped reluctantly up the lane to a nearby pub which didn't seem to mind the dusty and muddy state of their clothes.

They sat outside in the beer garden, sitting on rickety wooden benches in the balmy evening sunshine, drinking cider and eating crisps.

'What about security?' Charlie asked.

Tom took a huge drink and then wiped his mouth with the back of his hand. He looked grubby and dishevelled but Juno had never seen him look more alive. 'In the hands of the police for the moment. As soon as we can, we'll excavate the remains and the objects and get it all to the university.'

'I can't believe we've found a whole skeleton,' Sierra gasped. 'And that jewellery. I mean, it's soooo incredible!' She sipped her cider more delicately. 'I never, in a million years, thought I'd be part of anything this big. Do you think it was grave goods, Tom?'

He shrugged. 'Hard to say. From the position of the skeleton, it didn't look as if she'd been placed in a grave. If we're right in assuming she dates along with the coin hoard, fourth century Romano Britons buried their dead in cemeteries away from their dwellings, but this is too far from where we think the villa residence was. Geo-phys suggests the main house was where the dog walking field is. Difficult to speculate. We'll know more when the whole skeleton's been uncovered.'

'A robbery then, or an assault? Oh, golly.' Sierra clapped her hands together.

'Not a robbery or assault,' Charlie put in. 'Or the torc and armlet would have been taken.'

'True.' Sierra deflated.

'Unless the robbery was interrupted?' Juno pointed out. She opened up her nearly empty packet of crisps flat and put it on the grass to keep Joops busy. 'What is a torc anyway?'

'It's a thick curved necklace,' Tom explained, emptying his pint. 'Just wide enough to fit around the base of the throat.'

'And do you think it all dates from Roman times?'

'Could do. We won't know until the bones are examined. But it's looking likely, what with the other evidence we've found. Highly unusual to find human remains that date from that far back though.'

'Actually, not round here, darling,' Sierra put in. 'Although there's a lot of red sandstone in Devon, there are the occasional chalk and limestone outcrops. Where there's alkaline geology, it offers a good preservation environment for bones. Over at Plymouth they've dug up animal bones. The remains of a mammoth and wolves. Possibly dating back thirty thousand years or so.'

Juno stared at her, mouth dropping open. Under the ditzy image was obviously a sharp brain.

Tom grinned. 'Sierra's our resident soil expert. Wasn't it your PhD, Si?'

'Yes, darling. For my sins.' She giggled. 'As a child I was forever messing about making mud pies. My parents despaired. I think they rather had me down as a barrister or financial whizz. And here I am, still toiling at the soil. With what this lot pay me, it's just as well I have an unfeasibly wealthy husband.'

'Lucky you,' Charlie said feelingly.

'Oh, poor Chas. Shall I find one for you too, ducky? My round then, I suppose, after what I've just said. Seeing as you're only a poor serf, be my carrier, will you? More crisps and nuts everyone?'

They all nodded.

Once Charlie and Sierra had disappeared into the pub, Juno turned to Tom. 'Do you think this is evidence for Flete once being Moridunum?'

'You remembered!'

270

'Yeah. I think it's really intriguing. And, to be honest, this town needs a boost. It would be good if discovering it was once a major Roman settlement gave it that.'

He laughed shortly. 'Do you think people are interested enough?'

'Why not?' Juno batted a midge away. 'There could be a visitor centre, a bigger museum, a walk-through hands on experience sort of thing.' She caught his look. 'Okay. I don't really know what I'm on about, but Mabyn would. She works in that sort of field.'

'As opposed to an actual field?'

'Don't laugh at me!'

'I'm not. Truly, I'm not.' He reached out and took her hand. 'I just think you might be over-estimating the power of history. Not to mention people's interest, or the lack of, in Roman remains.' He looked puzzled. 'And aren't you the one who turned her back on anything more recent than the year two thousand?'

Juno screwed up her face. 'Point taken.' She eyed him humorously. 'And even the year two thousand is over twenty years ago now. I'm big enough to admit when I'm wrong. Since living here, it's really grabbed me. I love walking over the Roman Field wondering what's underneath. My father's dusty tomes and heavy expectations to follow in his academic path managed to turn me right off. But this is exciting! Somehow, I feel I have a connection to whoever lived here. I know that sounds mad.'

'Okay,' Tom laughed again, but gently. 'Yes, you're right. It could well be weighty evidence to suggest Flete was Moridunum. A golden torc suggests a very wealthy owner and a prosperous settlement. But we're jumping the gun here. We haven't even examined the bones or the jewellery yet. For all we know the skeleton could be Victorian and the torc could be made out of tin.'

'But nothing shines like gold, even when it's been covered in earth for centuries. I remember you saying that.'

'True. From what I could see it certainly looked like gold to me.' He shook his head in disbelief. 'I've never found anything like it. I've dug up human remains before but never anything gold except for the gold coin I found in the hoard.'

'Do you think they're connected? The skeleton and the coin hoard?'

He shrugged again. 'Could be. Who knows. We can only uncover the objects and make reasonable scientific stabs at the truth. We never really know how or why what we find ended up there.'

'It's so frustrating. Don't you want to know the stories behind all these things you find? Find out about the people?'

He turned his empty pint glass around thoughtfully. 'I can see it from your point of view. That's what you do for a living. Write people's stories. I just uncover evidence that they existed at some point and in some way.'

'And I suppose I can see it from your point of view, too,' Juno said reluctantly.

He grinned at her tone.

'I met Bill again down at the museum. Has any equipment gone wrong on the dig?'

Tom frowned at the change of subject. 'Equipment? To be honest, once the geo-phys is done we tend to stick to the tried and trusted methods of trowel and mattock.' At her blank look he added, 'It's a tool to break up hard ground. Oh, and there are soft brushes and the soil sieves you saw Si using and so on. It's all very low-tech stuff. Not much to go wrong. Why do you ask?'

'It was something she said.' At his questioning look, she went on. 'She said when digs had taken place before, things kept going wrong.'

He pursed his lips and was silent. He seemed to be struggling with something. 'I've certainly had problems with tech and the phone signal can be patchy. And there was that data issue I mentioned. What was she suggesting?'

'That the ground doesn't like being disturbed and it makes things happen,' Juno said in a small voice, feeling ridiculous. To her surprise, Tom didn't laugh at her.

He nodded. 'It's a commonly held belief amongst some and it's true there hasn't been much in the way of investigations before. Small scale stuff or abandoned due to lack of funding.'

'Yes, Bill said previous digs had tailed off.'

'Which is perfectly normal – and frustrating – in this game. Funding doesn't come through or is diverted. Happens all the time.'

'I see.' She took his hand and grasped it hard. 'You'll be careful, though, won't you?'

'Of course I will.' He laid his on top. It was very warm and reassuring.

'Promise?'

'Promise.'

He didn't question her or make her feel stupid and she felt a rush of affection.

'Juno!' he said, breaking hold suddenly.

'What?'

'Keep still, you've a bee in your hair.'

Juno held her breath as he came close, so close she could smell his soapy, earthy scent. He cupped his hands and laid the bee gently on the grass.

'Weren't you afraid of being stung?'

Tom smiled at her, his eyes deepening to a sapphire blue in the golden evening sun. 'No. Some say they're winged messengers between worlds.'

'Between what worlds?' Juno shivered again. She didn't know if it was his words or his proximity. *Is that what's behind the voice? A messenger from a different world?*

'Between whatever worlds you can think of. The past and the present. The living and the dead.'

'Oh.' *Oh my God, am I being haunted? Can't be. No such thing as ghosts.* She concentrated, instead, on the very living, extremely attractive man in front of her. He was so near she could reach out and kiss his tempting mouth. Her breath hitched. *Friends Juno, you've promised to be friends.* She forced sense into her head and blamed the cider for her muddled thinking. 'Bill told me a story. One that's been handed down through the generations.'

Tom cleared his throat and shifted on the bench. 'Interesting. What was this story?'

'Yes, do tell, Juno,' Sierra returned, putting the tray of fresh drinks down on the table and the moment passed.

Charlie lobbed crisp and nut packets around and for a minute everyone was preoccupied with negotiating what they wanted and fending off an eager Joops who was excited by all the rustling.

'So, what's this story, Juno?' Sierra asked. 'Is it a plot you're working on? Tom let slip you're Eden Loveday. I'm totes thrilled. I can't believe it, I love your books, darling. Read a whole pile when I was on hols last.'

Juno shook her head. 'No, not a plot, but thank you for reading my books.' She smiled. 'I love hearing people say that. No, this is something Bill at the museum told me.'

'Bill? Who's he?'

'She. She runs the local museum down in town. It's tiny, but crammed with stuff. Well worth a visit and Bill is a real character with a wealth of local history knowledge. I popped in a couple of weeks ago. She told me a story that had been passed down the years, many centuries even, of two star-crossed lovers.'

'Ooh,' Sierra squealed, making Joops bark. 'I adore that sort of thing.' She sipped her fresh cider, eyes huge. 'Go on.'

'They came from warring families and their parents forbade the match. But their love was too strong to be denied so they ran away to be together.' Juno, appreciating Sierra as an avid audience, let her natural storytelling take over.

'Gets better and better,' Sierra breathed as Charlie rolled his eyes. 'Did it have a happy ending? Did they run away into the sunset and make lots of babies?'

'Sorry to disappoint you but apparently not. They were pursued and murdered. Hacked down.'

Sierra sank back with a disappointed, 'Aw.'

'But that's not the end of it. Their ghosts are supposed to haunt the site of their death.'

'Which is where, ducky?'

Juno left a dramatic pause. 'The field you're digging.'

A blackbird, shooting low, passed them, cackling its warning. Charlie snorted into his glass.

Sierra turned on him. 'Darling, do drop the "I'm so scientific, ghosts don't exist" act. My uncle is a canon in the good old C of E. He can tell stories which would make your hair curl.' They all looked at Charlie's very curly hair and laughed. 'Well,' she huffed, 'go limp and straight then. What sort of things have been seen, Juno?'

'Bill was a bit vague on the details.' Juno hesitated and then went on, alcohol making her bold, 'But I think I saw a figure in white the very first time I walked Joops on the Roman Field.'

'No!' Sierra gasped. 'Ignore Charlie's scoffing, tell *all,* darling!'

'Yes, Juno,' Tom added. 'Tell us all about it. You've never mentioned it to me before.' His voice had a strange sort of urgency.

Juno glanced at him from under her lashes. 'It's not the sort of thing you mention casually in passing.'

'I didn't think there was anything casual about us.' He flicked her a look which had heat blooming on her cheeks.

She was aware of Sierra staring at them with undisguised curiosity so rushed on. 'As I said, it was the first morning I walked the dog on the Roman Field. I didn't know anything about it at that point. It was early in the morning and the fog was drifting through the trees. Joops freaked at something and ran after it, barking like mad. I saw, or thought I saw a tall figure in white. I assumed it was another dog walker but when I reached the part of the field where it was it had disappeared.'

'Yeah, through the gate there,' Charlie put in.

'Quite possibly. It was probably just some bloke in a white duffle coat who wasn't up for early morning chit-chat.'

'Or,' sighed Sierra, 'the ghost of one of our long-lost lovers hunting through the ages for her partner. Destined by Fate to be rooted to the spot where she was cruelly slain.'

Charlie laughed. 'Think it should be you who writes the books, Sierra. That's some imagination you've got.'

'Or it could have been tired early morning eyes being deceived by the mist,' Tom said. 'It's happened to me.'

Juno turned on him 'When?'

'Down by the river when I was camping up here on my own last week. It was about four in the morning and just getting light. There was a heavy mist hanging over the water. I saw all sorts of shapes and lights rippling over the river.'

'What sort of shapes?' Juno could hardly bear to ask.

Tom frowned. 'Difficult to say.' He laughed, embarrassed, throwing the words away. 'Then an owl screeched and flew over me into the oak. The mist cleared and there was nothing there.'

'Psychic priming,' Charlie huffed, tearing open another bag of crisps. 'Or confirmation bias or some such term like that.'

'What?' Juno fended Joops off as he begged for some cheese and onion.

'You mentally gear up to expect something, the situation's right.' He nodded at Tom. 'It was early morning, barely into the day, you were tired and stressed, probably hadn't had a decent night's sleep, you were on your own. All this coupled with the right weather conditions and you begin seeing things.'

'You saying I didn't?' Tom said indignantly.

'Not at all. Your brain was *tricking* you into seeing things you were half expecting. Like Juno on her dog walk. In a strange place, stress levels geared up, fog came down. It's easy to mistake things in swirling fog or mist, especially if you're hyped up to expect something. Primed.'

'But neither Tom nor I were expecting to see things. At that moment, although I admit to feeling stressed, I didn't know anything about the field's ghostly reputation. I only found that out later, when I talked to Tom's mother.'

Charlie shrugged. 'The stress and being on your own in a strange place would be enough to get the spooky juices flowing.'

'Don't be so hasty to tread all over their experiences, darling.' Sierra pointed her glass at Charlie. 'Don't forget the imprint theory.'

'Which is?' He narrowed his eyes at her.

'That dramatic events somehow imprint themselves onto their surroundings. It's one theory of why people see ghosts. Something traumatic happens and the imprint clings to the walls of the building it happened in. Don't see why it couldn't happen just as easily in a natural habitat, ducky.'

'I remember Tom saying the same sort of thing once. And, if the local stories are true and the archaeology backs it up with hard evidence,' Juno said, 'the fields we're talking about would have been covered in walls, gates, rooms ...'

'Enough Roman bricks and mortar for a whole load of ghosts to imprint themselves upon!' Sierra finished. 'Oh, Juno darling, what a super point.'

'I think you two women should get a room and knock out a bodice-ripper,' Charlie said sourly.

'If I had the time or inclination,' Juno said heatedly, Charlie was beginning to irritate her, 'I'd explain just how inaccurate and downright misogynistic that is.'

'Ignore him, Juno. The only books he has his nose in are dry textbooks.' Sierra linked arms in feminist solidarity. 'Of course we haven't touched on the theory of genetic memory.'

'*That* has scientific merit,' Charlie protested. 'I wouldn't scoff at that. I can easily believe stories have been passed down for generations and which have a kernel of truth at their core. There may well have been a couple of star-crossed lovers who came to a sticky end. We may well have found one of them. Is she haunting the area though? Unlikely.'

He and Sierra continued to bicker quietly. Juno turned to Tom sitting silently on her right. 'You never told me about your experiences by the river.'

He shrugged. 'It only happened last week and, as Charlie explained, it was almost certainly a trick of the light on top of lack of sleep.'

'What do you think you saw though?'

He met her gaze, looking troubled and deeply uncomfortable. 'Honestly? I'm not sure.' He rubbed his forefinger between his brows. 'It was probably just mist hanging in the trees.'

She took his hand again.

'Maybe I saw someone. Wearing white.'

'The figure I saw that very first time in Roman Field wore white.'

'And there's more.' Tom swallowed. 'I think I saw a glint of metal. Juno, I think I saw gold.'

# CHAPTER 31

*The Secundinus Villa*

Flavia ran an anxious finger around the gold torc. It sat uncomfortably on top of the sea glass necklace. She was wearing it as insurance. Should they need to sell it when on the run, it would come in useful. It was hot this day late in Juno's month, but it wasn't the reason sweat beaded on her forehead. Today was the day the three women were to put their plan into action.

As commanded Escld had got word to Padraig. He was to wait for them at the clearing by the river, near the sacred oak, and had promised to take them to the safety of his village. Ursa had procured several dowdy cloaks to disguise themselves and Flavia had hidden a cache of her jewels at the back gate. She felt not the slightest guilt at what she had planned; her parents had been absorbed into their own concerns and had paid her scant attention. She didn't think they'd even miss her once the social shame had abated. And was there even anything left of society now? It was every man for himself. Life had become a scrap for what little was on offer.

Ursa appeared at the door to her chambers. She held a pot of some disgusting smelling grease. 'It's tallow,' she said. 'Smear it over your hair to make it lank. We need to make ourselves as unattractive as possible.'

Flavia wrinkled her nose. 'The stink of that will surely attract attention, if only from wolves.'

Ursa slammed the pot down. 'So be it. But at least tie up your hair and cover it. It shines like ebony. Men can't resist. And remember to bow your head, make no eye contact. Stoop your shoulders too. You're too tall and too proud.'

'Yes, my lady.'

Ursa clucked her tongue in irritation. 'You'll have me to thank when we get the other side of this foolhardy scheme, so don't be so glib, child.'

'I know. I'm sorry.' Flavia caught hold of Ursa's hands. 'I can't thank you enough for coming with me.'

Ursa gave her mistress a keen look. She fingered the slave collar around her neck. Where the crude metal rubbed against her skin, an angry weal had developed. 'I vowed to serve you,' she said simply. 'And I would rather risk everything than to stay as slave to a master who forces me to wear a collar.'

Flavia nodded. 'Then I promise I will do everything I can to keep you safe as a return for your loyalty.' She gave the slave a swift hard hug. 'All will be well, Ursa. Meet me at the back gate as planned and remember to gather us some food and wine for the journey. You have the means to bribe the guards there?'

The servant nodded, gave her one last beseeching look and left.

Flavia dressed quickly, bundling the drab cloak under her arm; she would don it once out of the villa walls. Her heart was thumping.

Forcing herself to stroll at her normal pace, she skirted the edges of the atrium and was about to escape into the inner courtyard when a hand grabbed her wrist.

'Well, well, if it isn't the Mistress Flavia.'

It was Balbus.

He swung her round and pressed her against the wall. 'You look well, Mistress Flavia.' His tongue flicked out repulsively. 'It has been too long since our encounter in the bathhouse.'

Flavia forced herself not to retch. So he was out of his sick bed. 'Mother Juno, I need your help,' she muttered.

'What is that you say?' Balbus put a hand to her jaw forcing her to meet his eyes.

She swallowed. 'I said it is good to see you well again.'

'And no thanks to you. I may have been half out of my mind with delirium but I seem to recall you cursing me.' He reached down and put his other hand between her legs.

Flavia's insides turned to liquid. She felt beads of sweat prickle at her skin. 'You must let me go, Balbus. I am on an urgent errand for my father.'

'So much urgency when he still hides away in Durnovaria.' Balbus jerked his head. 'Fools like your father and the rest of the ordo think they still have some control over the chaos which reigns outside.' He laughed. It had an edge of mania to it. 'When we all know it will be men like me who will inherit the power when anarchy has its day.' He stroked her cheek. 'Poor Flavia. Abandoned by her Christian mother too.' At her shocked reaction, he continued, 'Have you not heard? Your mother is gone. Left for a Christian colony over Venta Belgarum way just this morning.' He put his head on one side in a mockery of sympathy. 'And, as for your father,' he hissed. 'Well, he is not the man you know and worship.' He put his face up against hers. 'He's probably not in Durnovaria at all but worshipping at the temple of Priapus. Many times has he begged me to get down on my knees while he sported with my mouth.' He sniggered hideously. 'You know what I mean, don't you, my pretty?'

Flavia gasped. If he meant what she thought, it was taboo. A vile, shameful act. And her mother gone? And hadn't even considered her daughter? The world surely had ended.

'If that got out, he would be finished as a magistrate.' Balbus was gabbling now. 'Your brother guessed at what he was, and your father had him shipped off with a frigid wife. It won't happen to me, though, I'll make sure of it. He likes what I can offer him too much. Even so far as to marry his only daughter to me.'

Flavia tried hard not to flinch. His breath was as rank as ever. Screwing her eyes shut she controlled her breathing and hardened her heart against her father: that he should betray his family so! Poor Marcus. Poor her, that a mother should desert a daughter so easily. She forced herself to think quickly. She had but herself now. And nothing to lose. She couldn't, she *wouldn't* give up now. But what could she do?

Balbus's hand pressed hard into her groin, forcing her legs apart. She felt his thumb find her secret place through the thin silk of her gown. While everything in her rebelled at this outrage she felt a blessed coldness enter her heart. No man but Padrig would know her there. An idea began to form. A revolting one but needs must. Desperate, she put her parents' betrayal to the back of her mind. She summoned a sigh, a great wave of nausea overcoming her even as she uttered it.

'Oh, you like that, do you? I knew beneath those airs and graces there beat a real live woman. No woman has yet resisted me.' He gave a coarse laugh. 'Or resisted and lived.' He bent to kiss her but she shied away at the last moment so that it skimmed the corner of her mouth, leaving a slimy trail of saliva.

'You can have me, Balbus.' Her voice rasped, she hoped he'd mistake it for lust. 'But not here. It is too public, even you must admit that.'

He was suspicious. 'Why the change, my lady?' The hand between her legs increased its pressure.

Flavia stared directly into his bloodshot, lust-filled eyes, swallowing her revulsion. 'You're right, Balbus,' she panted. 'The power of the ordo is short-lived. Even I, as a mere woman and chattel of my father can see that.' She raised a hand and tried not to let it tremble as she ran it down his loathsome chest. 'I have been left to my fate by my parents. I will need protection. And what better man than you to give it to me?'

Another laugh rumbled low in his belly, stirring his erection so that it prodded insistently at her. Her legs threatened to fail and bile rose in her throat.

'But it cannot be now. When you have me, I want it to last.' She narrowed her eyes, giving the impression of matching his blood lust, but her head was muzzy and his image was waving. Beads of cold sweat gathered on her forehead. She must not fail in this. Visions of Ursa waiting patiently at the gate, of Eseld and the risks she'd taken to get word to Padrig thrummed into her. 'Juno give me strength,' she whispered.

She threw her head back, arching her neck in a parody of ecstasy, moaning in arousal. 'I know you will give me the utmost pleasure,' she purred. 'But remember, I am the daughter of Flavius Honoratus Secundinus. I cannot be seen fornicating against the atrium wall like a harlot. I have needs, Balbus, and you are the man to meet them. But not like this.' She forced herself to look at him. He was snivelling with lust. 'Meet me in my chamber. I promise you will be rewarded for the wait.' He groaned in ecstasy and bent to suck at her neck with his fat pink slug-like lips. With all her strength she pushed him away. 'Oh, no, Balbus,' she cried, her head at a flirtatious angle. She wagged a coquettish finger at him. 'Your reward will be all the sweeter if untasted beforehand. Now, let me go, my big bear. Wait in my rooms and I will not be long.' Screwing her eyes shut she grabbed at his penis and squeezed it. He released her, sank against the wall, sliding down it, a grin plastered over his stupid drooling face.

Snatching at the discarded cloak, Flavia ran for her life. Tripping into the inner courtyard, she held onto a column and vomited copiously and nastily. Giving herself a second to recover, she sent a hasty prayer of thanks to Juno and ran on with shaking legs.

*Juno! Oh Juno!*

# CHAPTER 32

*023*

2 Juno paused in the act of unlocking her front door. There it was again. That voice calling her name. Only this time it wasn't imperious but despairing with an edge of warning. *What's going on in my head?* Whispering her safety mantra, she felt for the reassurance of the blue bead around her neck. Joops whined at her side; he probably needed to go out into the garden.

They'd stayed late at the pub, until the last of the June light had faded, the beer garden becoming crowded and convivial. All had drunk too much to drive so Tom had rung his mother who dropped Charlie and Sierra off at their digs. Juno and Tom sat squashed up in the back of her Mini with Joops panting in between them, feeling like naughty teenagers. Diana had gone off to find somewhere to park, as a hire car had taken her usual place outside the cottages in the street.

Juno determinedly ignored the voice. 'Your mum has the patience of a saint,' she giggled as she pushed open the front door. Joops bolted in, running to the kitchen door where he barked and scrabbled at it. Juno, reeling from too much cider, followed. 'Stick the kettle on, Tom, will you? Think we need coffee, strong and as hot as hell.' Unlocking the kitchen door, she admonished Joops as he ran out barking furiously. Then she stopped dead as she saw why.

He was sitting on the garden chair, the external security light shining on his white short-sleeved shirt. 'Hello, Joops boy. I've missed you.' He stood, fending off the dog, who bounced around him, teeth bared.

Tom followed her out. 'No milk. It'll have to be black unless we go to Mum's. Oh, sorry, I didn't realise you had a guest.'

'Hello, Juno,' Paul said. 'I've missed you too.' Into the frigid silence he added, 'Aren't you going to introduce me to your friend?'

'What are you doing here, Paul? And how the fuck did you get in?'

'That's not very friendly,' he whined. 'I've been waiting for hours. Your neighbour, the old guy next door, very kindly let me in through that back lane affair. Desperately needed somewhere to sit down so I shimmied over the gate.' He shook his head. 'Really wish you'd answer the phone. I could have come to wherever you two have been and joined in the fun.'

'Why would I answer the phone to you, Paul? The last time I saw you, you made it abundantly clear you'd moved on with Madeleine.' Juno stood frozen. This was her nightmare come true. She reached for the blue bead again.

'Ah, Maddy.' Paul shook his head again. 'That was a mistake. *She* was a mistake. She simply didn't understand me as you do.' He stepped towards her and Joops growled. 'And call your dog off, Juno. I don't know what you've done to him, but he seems to have developed very aggressive tendencies.' He aimed a kick at Joops who danced away.

'Joops. Here.' Juno clicked her fingers and the dog slunk to her side. She put a hand on the scruff of his neck, needing his protection and unwilling to risk whatever Paul might do to him. 'Don't you dare touch my dog. Don't you dare touch me.' At his treatment of the dog, anger began to lick through her shock. 'You're unwelcome. You have no business here and I'd very much like you to leave.'

'Am I not even going to be offered a coffee? I've driven all the way from London and this is the welcome I get?'

'You can go out the way you came. And if I ever see you here again, I'll call the police.'

'Oh, my. You have gone feisty.' He blew a kiss. 'I rather like it.'

'Get out, Paul.' Juno was amazed at calm she felt. She eased her mobile out of her jeans pocket. 'I have a contact at the local police station,' she lied. 'I'm sure she'd love to know all about the nuisance calls you've been making and this harassment. She said I should ring straightaway if you ever turned up. Very hot on domestic abuse, they are, in Flete.' She was bluffing; the police station was unmanned, and she'd never got around to reporting the phone calls to 101 but Paul wasn't to know. 'The station's only round the corner, they could be here in minutes, You don't want to risk that, do you? Just think what an awful blemish on your reputation it would be.'

'You wouldn't dare.' He smirked, used to her backing down.

'Oh, wouldn't I?' She began to press buttons on her phone, praying the ruse would work. Shadows of the bruises, both physical and mental, urged her on. She was a different woman now and he needed to know. *Juno, watcher of women, if you're out there, I need you now.*

'Juno has asked you to leave, so I suggest you do that,' Tom said. He went to the gate and unbolted it. 'Look, you don't even have to "shimmy" over. Nice meeting you, mate. Heard a lot about you.' He was calm but there was no mistaking the quiet authority.

Paul's eyes narrowed as he glanced between them. 'Didn't take you long to move on, did it, Ju?'

Juno held up her phone as a warning, her hand only trembling a little.

'Okay. Okay. I'm going. So much for the famous warm southwest welcome. I'd better get back to the mean streets of London.'

Tom held the gate open.

'Be seeing you, Juno.' He disappeared into the lane which ran along the back of the cottage's gardens. Tom followed.

Juno sank down on the garden chair Paul had abandoned. In the kitchen behind her she could hear the kettle reach boiling point and click itself off. Joops clambered onto her lap and she buried her face in his comforting fur. No longer in need of coffee; she was stone cold sober.

After a few minutes, Tom returned. 'I saw him to his car,' he said while bolting the garden gate. 'It was the hire car parked in Mum's space. He drove off at speed.' At her anxious glance, he added gently, 'I've locked the end gate. Come on, let's get you inside. Coffee?'

'Sod coffee. I think I need a stiff drink.'

They sat at the little table in the sitting room, a bottle of whisky between them. The kitchen door was locked and all blinds drawn. Juno had finally stopped shaking.

'I'm not sure how wise this is, topping up pints of cider with a malt.' Tom poured them both a generous measure.

'And on empty stomachs too.'

'What empty stomachs? You had two packets of cheese and onion and a packet of salted cashews. Three course meal.'

'You really know how to treat a girl.' Juno's reply was wobbly but it was a weak attempt at restoring humour.

'Well, I draw the line at climbing gates and stalking them on the phone, so you'll have to put up with bar snacks and pints of scrumpy.' He took her hands in his. 'You okay?'

Juno blew out a breath making her fringe fly. 'Yeah. No. Maybe.'

'As long as that's clear then.'

She sat back. 'Actually, I *do* feel okay. I've spent the best part of half a year looking over my shoulder, frightened to death I'd see him, imagining the worst he could do. And then I come home from the pub and he's in my back garden. It's almost farcical. It was the thing I dreaded most of all, him tracking me down. But now it's happened, and I dealt with it, I feel I've faced my demons. I think I handled him.'

'You did. You were brilliant. Telling him you'd put in a police complaint was genius.'

'Except I haven't.'

It was Tom's turn to sit back. 'Ah. And of course you know the police station is unmanned now. They have to come from Honiton, I think. Would take a good thirty minutes.'

'I was banking on Paul not knowing that.'

'Good bluff.'

'Yeah, I knew he wouldn't want any police involvement. It might affect his standing at work.'

'What does he do?' Tom swilled the whisky around his glass and sniffed it with appreciation.

'He owns an estate agency. Sells high end stuff. To amazingly rich foreigners.'

'Sounds like a good bit of leverage to have. Might be worth actually getting in touch with someone and flagging it up. Just in case.'

'Yes, Mabyn's said the same. Somehow, I haven't got around to it. And, to be honest, up to this point, he hasn't done anything. I couldn't pin the phone calls on him with any evidence apart from a strong hunch.'

Tom sipped his whisky thoughtfully. 'Do you think he'd try anything?'

Juno shrugged. 'Who knows? I mean, what was his motive in coming here? Why the hell drive all the way from London?'

'To persuade you to return?'

Juno gave a short laugh. 'You know, that's probably it. His relationship with Madeleine has gone tits up so he comes running back to good old Juno as back-up.' She reached out and took Tom's hand again and squeezed. 'I'm so glad you were here. Thank you.'

'I don't think I did anything major. From where I was it looked as if you were handling him fine.'

She shuddered. 'And I never thought I'd be able to, you know. Being here in Flete these past few months, I really feel some of my confidence has returned, a little of the old Juno has come back. But I'm still glad you were here. That stopped him trying anything.' She looked down at Joops still keeping close, his head resting on her lap. 'Although I think he would have had to get past this boy.' She ruffled his ears and he gave a snicker.

'Still makes sense to call the police.'

'Do you think so? Would they treat it seriously?' Juno looked dubious. 'And besides, I've a feeling trespass is a civil offence. It's not even a police matter.'

'But you were in a relationship with him that was coercive and physically violent, weren't you? And now, out of the blue, he tracks you down and follows you here. I reckon they'd take it seriously.' He pursed his lips. 'Only one way to find out. Plan what you want to say and ring 101.'

'Okay.' She frowned. 'How did he find out where I lived?'

'I suppose there are ways. He's wealthy, isn't he?'

Juno nodded. 'Very.' She caught his look. 'Private detective? Oh, come on, Tom. That really *is* edging into the realms of farce.'

'How else? You've told no one you're here?'

Juno shook her head. 'No one I wouldn't trust. All the time I had this feeling on my shoulders of being watched. I thought it was Paul – or something else. Maybe it was just a private investigator?'

He pushed her phone towards her. 'Then ring. Oh, and it might be an idea to have a gentle word with Cyril next door. He'll be mortified he let someone in through the back gate he shouldn't have. I'll do it if you like, we've known him a while.' Glancing at his watch, he added, 'I'd go now but it's getting late.'

'Cyril? Is that his name?'

'Don't blame him, he's a nice old guy. Bit too trusting.'

'I don't blame him for one moment. Paul can be very persuasive.' Juno gulped her whisky, feeling its welcoming fire. 'It's one reason I was glad you were here. Had I been on my own, I might have fallen for his patter all over again.'

'Really?' Tom looked shocked.

'As I say, Paul can be *very* persuasive. I'm not proud of being so weak.' She rubbed her forehead. 'He gets into your brain and fills it up so there's no room for any thoughts, any feelings of my own.'

'Even when treating you like shit?'

'Even then. He was an expert at turning it back on me. So everything bad that was happening, everything awful he was doing or saying, was my fault.'

*Juno. Juno!*

The voice came from nowhere. Urgent and warning. Juno shook her head. Paul's appearance, on top of the cider and whisky, was addling her brain. 'Sorry, what did you say?'

'I said he's a dangerous man, Juno. It's classic gas-lighting. You have to stay strong.' Tom paused. 'Unless, of course, you want to go back to him.'

'God no. That's one thing I do not want.' She started. 'Did you hear something then?'

'No. Nothing.'

Juno gazed around the room. It was the voice again, the one she kept hearing in her head. Tiredness and stress to blame. That's all it was. *Wasn't it?* Although strange, it had never felt menacing. She was sure it had been a warning that Paul was in her garden. And, when dealing with him, she'd taken strength and comfort from her. Whoever – or whatever she was.

'What you saw, up by the river,' she asked Tom suddenly, 'do you think it might have been a ghost?'

If Tom was surprised he didn't show it. 'I don't know,' he said carefully. 'As I've said before, I'm not entirely sure I believe in them. I've thought a lot about it and I don't mind confessing it freaked me out big time but I've decided not to get angsty about it.'

Juno nodded. 'But the gold you saw?'

'The gold I *think* I saw? I had gold on my mind. I'd not long discovered the solidus. Who knows how the brain works when it's four in the morning, it's barely light and you're running on too little sleep.'

Juno subsided. A haunting, no matter how far-fetched, was answer of a kind to this weirdness. She finished her whisky.

'I can't deny the place has a certain atmosphere, an unsettling feel to it,' Tom continued. 'But I had – and still have – other things on my mind. At this precise moment I don't want to get hung up on what I may or may not have seen.'

'Of course. The dig.'

He gave her a penetrating look. 'Amongst other things.' Getting up, he asked, 'Shall I make that coffee? Think we could both do with some. I'll leave you in peace to make your call. I can,' he paused again, 'stay tonight if you'd like? I mean I'm almost certain Paul won't come back but if it would give you some reassurance, I'm happy to. I can kip on the sofa.'

'There's no need. I mean, yes, I'd actually like you to stay, but the spare bed's made up. No need to martyr yourself.' She gave him a brief smile. 'Only dry cereal for brekkie though. No milk.'

'I'll pop next door and grab a pint, shall I? Explain to Mum what's going on.'

Juno looked at him gratefully. 'As I said, your mum has the patience of a saint.'

He returned the look and smiled. 'She's happy to help. We both are.'

'That's what friends are for.' Juno tried to keep the longing out of her voice. After all what man would take her on with the amount of emotional baggage she brought? 'Thank you.'

He nodded to the phone. 'Make that call, Juno.'

# CHAPTER 33

*The Secundinus Villa*

*Juno. Thank you for my safe deliverance. May your blessings be upon me!*

Flavia flung herself against the door of the safe room and looked quickly to either side. The courtyard was deserted as she'd known it would be. With the increasing anarchy more and more were abandoning the villa and fleeing to the hills. No one had reported to pay taxes for some days now; her father's long absence hadn't helped. Her mind was numb from shock at her parents' callous abandonment and her mouth was rancid from vomiting and fear but she had to press on. There was no guarantee how long Balbus would wait in promise for his lust to be slaked before he came in search of her.

Easing the key into the lock, she pulled her cloak over her face and froze as two men wandered by. Her heart stopped. Flattening herself she slumped against the wall in an attempt to become invisible. It worked. The men were too fascinated by the pig shank they had looted from the kitchens. Breathing again she unlocked the door. It had taken cunning to steal the key the night before. Necessity meant leaving the theft until the last minute; any sooner and its disappearance would be noted. A smile curled at her lips as she recalled how easily the guards had given it up. She had dressed at her most imperious, and the mention of her father's name had been enough. Bribery with an amphora of wine had helped, along with the promise the key would be returned. Part of her hoped the guards wouldn't get into too much trouble but they would probably slink off when her theft was discovered. The anarchy outside was seeping into the villa estate. No one and nothing was safe. It was time to escape.

Now, with no one in sight she slipped inside, giving her eyes time to adjust to the gloom. There was the expected arca, but she discounted the strong box as it was chained to the floor. Leaning against the far wall were two sacks of taxes. Coins taken in payment to her father and lazily left for the picking. Lifting one she realised it would be far too heavy for her to carry any distance. Spying twin leather saddlebags, she risked taking time to decant a cache of coins into them. They were heavy and cumbersome so she had no alternative but to hang them around her neck. Wrapping her cloak securely over her and her load, she relocked the door and slid the key under it. Anything to foil discovery of the theft. And to buy her time. Keeping her head down, she re-entered the atrium, slipping behind a column whenever someone approached. Fortuna was with her. The villa had a panicky air today. Slaves were scurrying to and fro, frantically keeping up with their extra work and ignoring anything beyond their immediate concern.

The saddlebags were weighty so she was forced to support them at the front of her body. Keeping her shoulders slumped she hoped she could easily be taken for someone elderly or a woman with child. Ursa's drab and tattered cloak was paying dividends. Few took any notice of her as she made her way to the hortus but it was slow progress.

She was about to enter the garden when the goddess Fortuna forsook her.

Otho.

She heard him yelling. Looking frantically for a hiding place, she could see none. It was too risky to run; with the saddlebags weighting her down she wouldn't be able to outrun him. Better to hide in plain sight. Sinking onto a marble bench she cowered, her arms wrapped around the sacks of coins creating a misshape under the cloak. Making herself as small and as insignificant as possible she prayed. That her escape should be thwarted at this very last moment! It was too cruel.

Otho was bawling, demanding her whereabouts of anyone not nimble enough to get out of his way. Balbus must have sent him out in search of her. He barrelled up to stand in front of her. She could smell the stench of wine on his breath. Drunk again.

'You, fat old crone. Have you seen the Mistress Flavia?' He prodded her shoulder so hard she nearly slid off the bench.

Flavia held her breath. Then saw that the toe of her sandal was peeking out from her enveloping cloak. It was of finely tooled leather. No poor old woman would wear such finery. If Otho noticed all would be lost. Worse, if he snatched off her hood, he would see the golden torc. And how would an old crone explain that?

He prodded her again. Hard. It made her yelp.

Praying to Juno and Fortuna she flicked the hem of her cloak over her feet. 'I ain't seen no one,' she croaked, hoping he'd take her as a fellow drunk. Not daring to look up she sensed his confusion. Why would a fat old woman be slumped on a bench?

'Otho,' a slave called. 'Mistress Flavia is in the bathhouse.'

It was Eseld's voice! How could that be? She was supposed to be waiting with Ursa.

Otho cursed and aimed a kick at Flavia's leg for good measure. It hurt. She yelped in pain and cowered some more, still praying.

A gentle hand took her arm. It was Eseld. 'Come, old woman. Let us get you some wine and bread.' She bent nearer. 'He is gone,' she whispered. 'To the bathhouse. It will buy us time but not much.'

Together the women stumbled through the hortus to the back gate, where, to their relief, Ursa stood waiting holding the leather bag of Flavia's jewels and accompanied by the faithful Trajan. 'Where have you been?' she cried. 'I have been half dead from fright.'

'No time to explain now,' Flavia replied. 'We must go. Make haste.' Trajan stole loyally to her side.

Fumbling at the gate, Ursa eventually got it open. Locking it behind them she threw the key into some prickly holly bushes. 'Might keep them off our trail for a while,' she said, dusting her hands.

To their utmost surprise, a donkey waited, tethered to the nearest oak tree.

'Borrowed it from the stables.' Eseld ran to the animal and rubbed its nose. 'Cuinn the stable boy owed me a favour.'

'So that's where you'd gone!' Ursa snapped. 'And borrowed? Stolen more like. You were supposed to wait with me at the gate, girl.'

'Don't scold her, Ursa,' Flavia said. 'She's just saved me and probably our entire plan.'

'That Otho,' Eseld giggled scornfully. 'He wouldn't know his nose if he picked it himself. Here, hand me the saddlebags. Cassiopeia here can carry them on her back.'

'Will someone tell me what went on?' Ursa demanded.

'I will,' Flavia replied, relief making her impatient. 'But let's hurry. I don't know how long Balbus's patience will last.'

# CHAPTER 34

*2023*

Juno wondered how patient Paul would be. From her past experience with him, she suspected his appearance in the garden wouldn't be his last. He was a complicated and proud man who didn't recognise rejection. As it looked likely Madeleine had done just that, his injured pride would seek out his backup plan. And it looked as if the backup plan was Juno.

She'd meant what she'd said to Tom; that she was terrified Paul might work his persuasive magic on her again. She wasn't proud of this weakness but, at one time, it was as if he'd eaten up her soul and her whole being was full of him. Escaping to Flete had begun her rehabilitation. As she clutched the blue bead around her neck for comfort, she hoped she was healed enough to be strong if fully tested.

The phone call to the police was reassuring and frustrating. The call handler logged all details and took seriously the possibility that Paul may escalate his behaviour but agreed with Juno that he hadn't yet committed an actual crime. However, she was promised should anything further happen they would fully support her. What form this would take remained inconclusive, but Juno reasoned she'd done as Mabyn and Tom had requested and she didn't think there was anything else she could do. Apart from live with the weight of edgy apprehension on her shoulders again. During the last few months in Flete, it had eased but it was back with a vengeance and it was exhausting. When she'd phoned Mabyn to explain what had happened, her friend had been horrified and promised to come to stay as soon as she could get away.

There was nothing else to do. Juno refused to return to a life lived in the shadows and was determined to carry on as normal. So, for the next few days, she did.

A walk on the Roman Field when she knew there would be lots of other dog walkers around seemed a safe option. Tom was at the dig, just over the holloway and she had his mobile number. The day was warm and hazy. The sea smudged into the soft blue of the sky making the horizon indistinguishable. It was a lovely day. However, she'd been wrong about the field being crowded. Perhaps put off by the heat, the dog walkers had stayed away. Perhaps she should have gone to the beach instead but on a warm day like this it would be crowded. Joop's speciality, in true spaniel style, was to pounce on picnic food, so she didn't want to risk him getting into trouble.

'Besides, we're up here now, aren't we, Joops? There's a tiny hint of a breeze up here and we can pop up to the dig to cool off if we need to.'

As an answer, the dog snickered and ran off, nose to the ground, chasing a scent. Juno followed and found him scrabbling at the muddy patch which persisted no matter how dry the weather.

'What have you found now?' she asked with some exasperation. 'Honestly, you can find a tattered old tennis ball anywhere.'

Pushing him away in case it was anything harmful, she spotted something, gleaming where the mud didn't cling. Joops nosing in again, and scratching, uncovered a length of metal rolled into a crushed cylinder. Frowning, she pushed the dog away again, instinctively knowing they'd found something important. The spaniel lost interest now he knew it was inedible and wandered off. Picking the object up, Juno examined it. It was maybe made of lead or another type of soft metal, she wasn't sure, and had been rolled up into something resembling a squashed toilet roll inner.

Tempted to unroll it, she knew it would be a mistake and it needed to go to the experts. The only thing to hand was an empty poo bag so she wrapped it carefully and stowed it in her pocket. Standing, she heard Joops barking frantically and looked downhill to the bottom of the field by the entrance gate.

Paul.

He had Joops by the collar. The dog, half frantic, was twisting round to escape, strangling himself in the process.

Juno froze.

*Juno!*

A voice rushed at her on a stiff wind which had come from nowhere. It tossed her hair and tugged at her clothes. And nudged at the metal tube she'd just found, weighing heavy in her pocket.

*Juno!*

She stormed down the field towards her dog like an avenging angel, the hard ground giving her feet wings.

'Let him go now!' she yelled.

'I was only trying to remind him who's master,' Paul sneered. He snatched violently on Joops's collar. The dog yelped and gave a half-strangled whimper. 'You've spoiled him.'

'Let him go.'

'Or what?'

Juno held up her phone. Sweat pooled under her arms. 'Or I call the police.'

'Oh, not that again. Can't you see I can tell an empty threat when I hear one?' He laughed nastily, tightening his hold on Joops.

*Juno! Juno!*

The woman's voice sent an electrical charge through Juno. She didn't know who it was, or where it came from, but it filled her with a white-hot anger she hadn't known she could possess. 'Let him go, Paul,' she hissed through clenched teeth. 'Can't you see he can't breathe?'

'Nonsense. Just needs some discipline, that's all. You've got to show dogs who's boss.'

Joops was struggling less, the whites of his eyes showing terror, drool frothing at his mouth.

Although every instinct was to launch herself at Paul, Juno forced herself to calm down. Paul was muscular and strong; she had no chance to fight him off. She had to think. She had to plan what to do. Even if she rang 999 now the chances of the police turning up quickly enough were low. She could ring Tom but that might only make matters worse. Besides, Paul was her problem and hers to sort.

*Think Juno. Think!*

There might be something she could do but the very thought made bile rise. Sucking in a deep breath, she nearly caved but the desperate look on Joops's face decided her. Would Paul fall for it? Changing her voice to something low and sultry, she purred, 'You're right Paul. You're absolutely right. You showed *me* who was boss and *I* enjoyed it.'

It took him by surprise. So much so, he loosened his grip on the dog's collar. 'What? I didn't hear what you said.'

She took a step forward on shaky legs. 'I can't get near you with the dog in the way. Let him go and I'll tell you what I really want you to hear.' She ran her hands over her breasts, cupping them, feeling sick inside.

He put up one hand questioningly. 'Whoa. What's going on here?'

Juno pouted. 'I've missed you, Paul. I've missed you so much. Seeing how you handle Joops has made me remember how you handled me.' Sick rose in her throat but she battled on, focussing on the dog's pleading eyes. This couldn't possibly work, could it? Was Paul vain enough?

'Bit of a change of heart, eh, Juno?' He loosened his grip further so that the dog's paws were all on the ground.

Thank God, Joops seemed to be breathing more easily, although he was coughing. 'Seeing you the other night made me think.'

'You couldn't wait to get rid of me.'

A breeze blew her hair over her face, so she swept it back in what she hoped was an erotic gesture. 'Well, you took me by surprise. I had to get my head around you and Maddy no longer being together.'

'I seem to remember you told me to fuck off.' Paul still looked suspicious but a touch of sweat gleamed on his upper lip and his eyes narrowed with desire.

'I don't think I used quite those words.' Juno put her head on one side, coquettishly. 'Big boy.' She blew an air kiss. Joops whined. *Not long now Joopsy and you'll be free.* 'But if we're going to talk fucking ...' She ran the tip of her tongue around her lips, making her breasts heave. God she disgusted herself but it seemed to be working.

'Christ alive, Juno, I can't keep up with all your moods.' Paul came nearer, stumbling over some rough ground. It was the chance Joops was looking for. Wriggling, he slipped his collar and bolted.

Juno whirled around, watching Joops disappear over the ridge at the top of the field. Her heart thumped. At least he was out of Paul's clutches but what if he headed towards the main road? 'Find Tom,' she whispered frantically. 'Go into the dig field and find Tom. You'll be safe there.'

'What did you say?'

She adopted a sulky tone, as if regretful she'd have to leave Paul. 'I said, I suppose I'll have to go and look for him now. There's a main road not far away.'

To her revulsion, Paul slid his arms around her waist and backed her into his body. It was warm, hard and achingly familiar. 'He'll come back when he's hungry. Stupid dog. So what if he gets hit by a car. I'll buy you a cute puppy instead. Now,' he crooned into her ear, 'tell me more about all this fucking ...'

*Juno!*

The voice hissed and swirled in the air. Gave action to her anger. She'd told Tom she was worried she might weaken in the face of Paul's persuasiveness but the man's callousness about her beloved dog's safety locked something in place. For too long he'd reduced her to a plaything, to be disposed of and picked up again at his convenience. He'd used his wiles to rob her of any will of her own, had bullied and gas-lit her. Reduced her to a pale, quaking shadow. It was coercive control. Plain and simple. Mabyn had explained it, her mother had warned her off him, even Tom had the situation sussed in an instant. Had she really fretted she'd be tempted to go back to him? She didn't any longer.

A second wave of anger hit her but this time it gave her an icy calm. Turning and pulling Paul's face into her neck while moaning in pretend ecstasy, she flicked on the video on her phone with the other hand. He was so busy biting her neck, he didn't notice. The disgust had her trembling and she tried to buck away but he caught at her and pulled her into him. His gym sessions weren't just so he looked good, he got off on the brute strength it gave him. One of his hands grappled at her breast and squeezed hard.

Juno yelped in pain. 'No,' she said, clearly and calmly.

He grabbed her by the throat. 'God, I love it when you whore but it's even better when you play hard to get.' His eyes were lust crazed.

'No, Paul. Stop.'

His hands began to clench around her windpipe. 'Baby, you feel so good. Let's go back to that shitty house of yours. I've missed you so much, baby. Can't wait to fuck you every way I can.'

'I'm telling you to stop,' she gasped. 'I do not want to do this.' They were too close, she couldn't manoeuvre her knee into his groin. He was nearly strangling her, a red mist was descending and she could feel herself weaken. If he got her to the ground she'd be lost. Biting down on the panic, with all her remaining strength she raised her walking boot shod foot and kicked at his shin hard. The shock was enough to put him off.

He stumbled back, red-faced and panting. 'Christ, Juno, that bloody hurt. What are you playing at?'

'I said no.' Juno couldn't believe she was still clasping her mobile. In shaking hands she held it up. 'And I've got it on film.'

His face turned puce.

She took a step back. Her throat was on fire. 'If you come anywhere near me or my dog again,' she gasped, 'I'll take this to DS Jill Conroy at Devon Police's Victim Care Unit. I think, after everything else I've told her about you, she'll be very interested in my accusation of assault and attempted rape.'

He smirked, his chin up but she could tell he looked less sure. 'Yeah, whatevs, baby. You were asking for it, begging me for it.'

'Was I? The only thing I have recorded is me saying no, quite clearly.' Juno hoped this was true.

'It's entrapment,' he spat.

'My word against yours, Paul. After what you did to Joops, I will take you to court to prove you attacked me.' She waved the phone and tried to stop her hand from shaking so much. Her fingers were clammy with sweat and she was terrified she was going to drop it.

'You're mad. Always were. Living in that make-believe world of yours. Writing those trashy books. I can get the best barristers to prove you're mentally insane.'

'And I can get at least five witnesses to prove I'm nothing of the sort.'

'You'd put this through court? What would that do to your writing career?' He was wavering.

'What would it do to yours?'

'You stupid bitch.' He staggered nearer. 'You have no idea who you're taking on.'

'I know exactly who I'd be taking on,' Juno replied, a glorious calm and certainty filling her.

Paul took another step nearer and then suddenly lunged. He grabbed at the phone, nearly missed, but then held it high in triumph. He laughed, eyes bulging, voice shrill. 'Now where's your evidence? Oh, you think you've been so clever. All I have to do is destroy your phone.'

From nowhere, a streak of brown and white launched itself at Paul's arm. Hanging on to his elbow, in true police dog style, Joops fastened his teeth. The phone shot out of Paul's grasp, flew in an arc, and landed in a dense patch of marram grass.

'Get your fucking dog off me,' Paul gasped. 'I'll have it shot.'

Juno folded her arms, she was shaking so much, it seemed the only thing to do with them. 'Off Joops. Come away now!' The dog growled, tussled at Paul's arm once more and then slipped to her side where he lay panting and watchful.

Paul pointed at him with a wavering finger. 'I'll have that beast put down. It fucking attacked me!' He looked at his arm in shock. Where his shirt was torn, blood appeared from a slight scratch. 'It's not safe to be out in public. This shirt is Armani!'

'Maybe you should have thought about that when you were strangling him.' Juno put a hand to her burning throat. 'Strangling seems to be a theme here, doesn't it? I'd argue Joops was attacking you in self-defence, as well as protecting me.'

'And I'll argue the same.' It was Tom. He slid to a halt at Juno's side, breathing hard.

'Oh, Christ, the cavalry's arrived,' Paul said nastily.

'I'd get a tetanus jab if I was you,' Juno said. 'It's only a scratch but you can't be too careful with dog bites.'

Paul shook his fist at them. 'I'll sue you for every penny you've got.' He began to retreat to the gate. 'You've not heard the last of this.'

'Do that, Paul,' Juno yelled. 'Sue me. Take me to court. And the whole sorry tale of how you manipulated, bullied and coerced me will come out. There's a whole load of laws about coercive behaviour now and I'll make sure you get accused of every single one.'

Tom had been hunting for the phone. He handed it back to her. She held it up. 'Not to mention your attempted rape.'

'You're mad. You *are* mad. Mad bitch.'

Joops rose to his feet and bared his teeth, hackles up, growling menacingly.

Paul took one look and fled. A second later they heard wheels spinning and a car engine gunning down the lane.

Juno collapsed where she stood. Now that the danger had gone, Joops danced around in victory, barking. 'Do be quiet, Joopsy,' she pleaded, exhausted, her head thumping. 'You did a great job but it's time to be quiet now.'

Once Joops had calmed down, Tom sat down next to her. 'You okay?'

Juno lifted her face to the sun and drank in its warmth. 'Honest answer? No, not at all.' She opened her eyes and met his concerned gaze. 'But I will be.'

# CHAPTER 35

*The hills above Moridunum*
The three women, dog and donkey hurried into the shelter of the woods. It was risky being exposed.

'Are you well mistress?' Ursa asked anxiously.

'No. Not at all. But I will be.' Flavia put a kind hand on the shoulder of her slave. 'Hurry. We must make haste.'

As they walked further into the tree cover and out of danger, they relaxed a little. Flavia told them of how close she had been to being discovered. Ursa gasped at how close a call it had been and Eseld danced around them laughing with the freedom. Cassiopeia plodded faithfully on and Trajan pressed himself to his mistress's side.

'Hush child,' Ursa scolded. 'Do you want the world to hear?'

'There is no one to hear,' Eseld giggled. 'Only the birds. Otho is hunting through the bathhouse and Balbus is lying pining in my mistress's bedchamber. By now he's probably asleep and snoring!'

Eventually they reached the clearing by the river. Ursa sank down, exhausted, onto its pebbly beach. 'I fear I can walk no further at present. May we rest awhile?'

Flavia nodded frustrated; the woman was pinch-faced and wan. She'd wanted to get as far from the villa as quickly as possible, but they needed to wait for Padrig here in any case and, as yet there was no sign of him. The dell was as peaceful as before, with soft breezes shushing through the ash trees, a robin's bright song and the call of gulls high in the sky. A fat bee buzzed past lazily and disappeared into the leaves of the sacred oak. The winged messenger. She took it as a good omen. Padrig must be on his way. Flavia, seeing Ursa finger her slave collar where it chafed in the June heat, made a swift decision. 'Eseld, have you a knife?'

The girl turned from where she had led the donkey to the river to drink. 'You ask that of me?' Her teeth gleamed as she produced a long blade. She handed it to Flavia. 'Who are you to kill?'

'By the look in Ursa's eyes, if you don't stop your chatter, it'll be you,' Flavia replied but gently. She pressed the tip against the metal collar around Ursa's throat but the slave put a hand up to stop. 'Do you not want to be free of your chains?'

'I do mistress, more than anything. But if you take this off me, it means no going back.' She gazed directly into Flavia's eyes. 'No returning to your easy life of warmth and plenty.'

'I made that decision many weeks ago, Ursa, when I lay with Padrig. I do not want to go back. That life holds nothing for me.'

'Not even to your parents?'

'Oh, Ursa, my mother has forsaken me, gone to be with her Christ god and her new soothsayer, she has no room in her heart for me. And my father?' she bit back a sob. 'My father wants only riches and power any way he can get them. Do you know what the hold is that Balbus has over him?' She told them what Balbus had imparted to her with such glee. The women gasped with shock. Ursa wrapped her arms around a wretched Flavia and the women grew quiet, listening to the soothing babble of the river as it danced over boulders.

'Men are disgusting,' Eseld proclaimed with a passion. 'May Nemesis shrivel their parts so they drop off. I want nothing of them.'

'You'll change your tune when the right one comes along,' Ursa said drily.

'No, they are nothing but beasts.'

The women gazed at the donkey gently tearing at the grass and at Trajan lolling in the sunshine.

'I think that is most insulting to beasts,' Ursa added. She lifted her hair off her neck. 'Now, Flavia,' she said with decision. 'Cut this collar off me and let's be done with it.'

Flavia worked at the soft metal but it had been sealed into place. Eventually though, she broke through and the collar dropped off.

Eseld came to her and knelt down. 'Me next.'

Flavia repeated the action. 'What are we to do with them?'

Ursa glanced to the river. 'Throw them into the sacred stream. Let the gods decide where they go.'

'But I don't have anything to offer,' Flavia said.

'Then use the curse tablet,' Ursa replied. 'It is high time it was cast. And let us pray it serves its purpose.'

Eseld threw her collar in first. It flew high into the sun and disappeared into the fast-running water, sinking out of sight. Ursa murmured a few words of thanks and repeated the action. And then the freed slaves held hands and watched while Flavia incanted a prayer to Juno and Minerva.

Holding the curse tablet tight to her breast, she recited, 'Once more we ask your help oh goddesses of justice and protection. Once more we ask for our wrongs to be righted.' She blinked, the sun seemed to suddenly burn brighter, took a breath and rushed on, 'And we demand the death of our most hated enemy, Balbus the slave.' She threw the tube of metal high into the sky, where it arched and hung in the sun for a long moment, then turned over twice and dropped into the water.

All was silence, even the birds fell mute. The sun dulled, the leaves on the trees ceased shivering and the women held their breath. And then a robin began singing robustly from the oak tree bough and gradually the world animated again.

'Was it wise, mistress,' Ursa asked, an anxious expression crossing her face, 'to *demand* the gods obey? They may take offence and mete out justice in their own twisted way.'

'Then I shall have to take that chance.'

Trajan trotted up to her and nudged at her hand. She turned to see why and let out a long sigh of relief. 'It would seem that the gods have answered our call already.' Her shoulders sank, eased of the burden of responsibility she had been carrying and her heart filled with love. It was Padrig. He stood under the shelter of the sacred oak, Pwca at his side. He had come to take them to his village.

'Padrig,' she cried, running to him and burying her face against the hard safety of his chest. She raised her mouth to his and kissed him passionately. She had no more words. No more were necessary.

# CHAPTER 36

*The hills above Flete*
Juno had no more words. She was numb. Reaching out a still trembling hand to Joops she checked him over feverishly. Flinging her arms around his neck she sobbed into his fur, crying out her shock and fear. Then the words came, hiccoughing along with her tears, and incoherent.

'If he's hurt you, I'll kill him! Was it payback time? What did he do to you, eh? I'll never forgive myself for leaving you with him even the once.'

Tom stayed close snatching out grass furiously. After a time, everything was quiet. They sat with the hot sun beating down upon their heads, breathing in the clean scent of the sea and listening to a gull keening on a thermal. It felt calm and healing.

'I hate to say this,' Tom began, 'and there isn't going to be a good time to do it, but I think we should record what happened.'

Juno lifted her tear-stained face and said wearily, 'I already did. Hopefully, it's all on my phone.'

'I mean write down everything that happened and,' at this he sounded deeply uncomfortable, 'take photographs of any injuries.'

She blanched.

'And then send it all to the police.' He looked awkward. 'You did report to them, didn't you?'

Juno nodded.

'Then, oh, God, Juno,' he shoved a hand savagely through his hair. 'I'm really sorry but I think we should do it now while it's fresh in your mind.'

Juno nodded again. She looked around. A dog walker with a Labrador wandered past giving them a concerned look.

The woman stopped. 'Are you alright, Juno?' It was Annie with Maisie.

'Annie, hi. Yes, I'm fine.' Juno thought rapidly. 'Wasn't looking where I was going and tripped over Joops. Twisted my ankle. You know how daft you feel when you fall over as an adult.'

'Oh, my lovely! I've got the car parked in the lane if you can get there. Happy to give you a lift.'

'That's really kind of you but Tom here is looking after me.'

'Tom? Oh yes, you're Diana Lyndsay's son, aren't you? I'll have to bring Bill up to have a look at what you're doing. Dig going alright, is it?'

'Yes. Thank you.'

Despite her distress, Juno grinned and hid it in Joops's fur. He couldn't sound more brusque if he tried.

'You sure you're alright?' Annie asked, her attention distracted by Maisie heading in the direction of the muddy puddle.

'I'm fine. Just winded and feeling stupid. I'll pop by the museum for a coffee soon.'

'You do that. And Tom, you're welcome any time. Ooh, must go. Don't want muddy paws in the car. See you both.'

'Bye Annie,' Juno said faintly, as the woman jogged off in pursuit of the Labrador. It had been farcical. Trading niceties when she was in so much turmoil she could barely function but it had given her time to recover a little, forced her back to a kind of normality.

'Do you think you can make it up to the office at the dig?' Tom asked. 'Sierra and Charlie aren't there today, they've escorted our skeleton to the university for forensic analysis. Only me today. I could ring Cris if you wanted him there too? Bit of family support?'

'God no. Cris is likely to take to the streets hunting out Paul in superhero avenger fashion.'

Tom was silent for a moment. 'Is that what you want me to do?'

'No!' Juno put a hand on his arm. Warmed by the sun, it felt solid under her touch. Reassuring. 'I don't want to give Paul any more of our energy than he deserves. Which is none.'

'I would be your Perseus, you know.'

'And I said I didn't need one.'

Tom mustered a smile. 'So I saw.'

'Thank goodness I have more choices than poor old Andromeda.' Juno blew her fringe out of her eyes and waggled her mobile, humour gradually returning.

'You sorted yourself out.'

'With a bit of help from Joops.'

'So you didn't need a Perseus. And even if you didn't need one, I would have been your Perseus anyway. Is that too cheesy?'

Juno gave a short laugh. 'Yes. But I don't mind. And even though I didn't need a hero, I would have been happy to have you.'

A beat passed between them. For a heady second Juno thought Tom was going to kiss her, but he didn't. *Definitely not the time or place.* Instead, he pulled her to him in a quick hard embrace and muttered something she didn't catch into her hair.

Then he scrambled to his feet, dropped a hand and helped her up. 'Come on. That old remedy for any crisis, tea and biscuits awaits. I'll put extra sugar in your tea for the shock. It's what you do, apparently.'

'Apparently so.' She turned and began to walk up the hill towards the dig but her legs were like jelly and she stumbled.

'I may not have a winged horse but I've a strong right arm.' Tom gathered her close again, with one arm under her shoulders and together they made their way to the gate at the top of the field.

Once in the holloway, Juno stopped. As ever, there was something magical about the place. The bosky greenness was welcoming and cool after the dry heat of the field. And soothing. A flash of white caught her eye. 'Did you see that?'

'What?'

'At the very end of the holloway, just before it twists and goes under the main road. Someone, or something dressed in white.'

'I didn't see anything.' Tom shot her a look of concern. 'You don't think Paul is still hanging around?'

Juno shook her head. 'No. I've a feeling we're well rid of him.' She shivered quickly. 'It was more like the figure dressed in white that I saw when I came here for the first time back in January.'

For a moment they stood, searching the green tunnel, the scent of the damp earth making their nostrils prickle.

'Look,' Tom breathed. He held her close to him. 'Just on that twisted branch that's hanging down.'

Juno followed his look. 'An owl,' she whispered incredulously. 'Was that what I saw? A white owl?'

'Barn owl. Hope it's alright. Very rare to see them during the day.'

'My mum always said it was unlucky.' Juno trembled and felt Tom's arm tighten reassuringly. 'To see one in the day, I mean.'

'Maybe only for the owl. It might mean it's unwell.'

They watched spellbound as the owl twisted its chunky head to peer at them with enormous eyes. Then it stretched wings to a full magnificent span and lifted off. It flew, without a whisper of sound, out of sight. So mesmerised were they that they still didn't move even after it had long gone. Even Joops remained silent.

'Wow.' Juno let out a long sigh. 'I've never seen anything so beautiful.' It had felt a privilege, and somehow weirdly protective.

'Bollocks to it being unlucky,' Tom replied, bringing them back down to earth. 'Something that beautiful can only be a good omen.' He chuckled. 'The symbol of the Roman goddess Minerva, meaning wisdom, although I prefer the Celtic interpretation.'

'Which is?'

He looked at her, smiling in a way which gave her a warm glow. 'Truth. Honour. Rebirth and transformation. Sometimes it was seen as a guardian angel.'

Juno let her head loll against his comforting shoulder, feeling the warmth of his body through his cotton shirt. She was unutterably weary but felt safe and peaceful. 'I prefer that too.' Through the exhaustion, she felt a spear of renewal. It was time for her rebirth and transformation. A new life beckoned. One without Paul. Maybe without any man. She flicked a glance at Tom. *Hopefully not.* A life getting back to her old self and discovering her new one. Stronger and surer than ever before. Had the owl been her guardian angel, or had it been Minerva? She caught the sound of her name being called, drifting on the wind and faint.

*Juno!*

Maybe it had been another goddess entirely?

'Come on,' she said, suddenly decisive and full of energy. She felt the first stirrings of complete happiness. 'Let's go and get that tea. I'm so hungry I could eat a whole packet of biscuits, especially if you've got custard creams. Let's get written down what happened, take these pictures,' her fingers strayed to her neck. 'And let's phone the police!'

Once in the portacabin, Tom busied himself making tea and hunting out biscuits and some sandwiches Diana had insisted he have.

'Cheese and pickle,' he announced. 'Nothing fancy.'

Juno's tummy rumbled. 'I'll take anything you've got. I'm starving. Maybe it's shock?' She felt suddenly vibrantly alive, her senses singing. Shock or adrenaline? She didn't care.

'Who knows,' he answered cheerfully. 'But what I have you're welcome to.'

There was that beat again. A heated second.

'Thank you. And nothing your mother cooks is likely to be plain.'

'True.'

She perched on a stool, feeling the object she'd found nudge at her hip. Easing it out of her pocket, she said, 'Oh, I forgot in all the chaos. Joops, as well as being my defender, found this.' She handed the poo bag wrapped item over.

'Thanks, I think.' Tom held it gingerly.

'It's a clean bag, you idiot.'

'For that consideration, I thank you.' He placed it carefully on his desk. 'I'll have a look while you're on the phone.' His tone changed. 'Or would you rather I went outside to give you some privacy?'

'I'd rather you stayed if you don't mind. If I have a wobble, it would be good to have a friend close.'

He shrugged. 'A friend. Of course.'

The phone call to the police was tedious and distressing in equal measure. Tom took pictures of her neck, where red bruises were beginning to show. Juno could barely look at the photos and it made her queasy to upload them to the police site. She was glad of a hot cup of tea in her hand and of Joops huddling against her knee. She'd been advised to press charges but couldn't decide. Checking the sea glass bead was still around her neck on its bootlace, she clutched it and thanked whoever it had been who had helped her defeat Paul.

Having made a quick call to the vet for a check-up appointment for Joops, she swung round to Tom. 'All finished,' she breathed on a long thankful sigh. She'd been only vaguely aware of him in the background but had been deeply grateful of his presence. He was sitting at his desk, examining the object she'd found and didn't answer. 'Tom?'

He looked up. 'That's great you've got that done.' He sounded abstracted. An expression of intense excitement flooded his good-looking face. 'Juno, do you know what we've got here?'

She shook her head.

'It's a curse tablet. An ancient Roman curse tablet. In terms of what it can tell us, it's gold dust. No, it's far more valuable than any gold!'

'A what?' She got up and went over. The tube of metal had been unrolled and was now about ten centimetres by five, a small grubby rectangle and dull looking. Juno couldn't understand why Tom was so euphoric.

'The ancient Romans used to commission a tablet if anyone had done them wrong. Tablet is a misleading term, though, they're actually small sheets of hammered or cast lead. Have you never been to see the ones in Bath?'

'No.' She bent nearer. 'There's writing on it.'

'There certainly is. See how the letters have been punched in? A lot of the ones found at Bath were curses on those who had pilfered stuff from the bathhouse there. You occasionally come across one asking the gods for divine justice against those who had wronged them. They don't hold back.' He was more excited than Juno had ever seen him. 'But this one, this one is different.'

'Can you read it?'

'My Vulgar Latin, that's the Latin of the Romano Britons, is a little rusty but I've just about been able to make it out. It's astonishing!' His face gleamed. Then he frowned and shook his head. 'I'm so sorry, Juno. How did your phone call to the police go?'

'I'll tell you later.' She pointed at the tablet. She had the weirdest feeling about it.

*Juno!*

Ignoring the voice calling her name, she demanded, 'Tell me what it says.'

'Okay. Are you ready for this?'

She nodded.

'Here goes.' He took a breath, scanned the text and began reading. '"Once more, I, Flavia, call upon Minerva bringer of justice and Juno protector of women. I beseech you to bring down your mighty vengeance onto the slave Balbus. I ask that he be accursed in his blood and eyes and liver and limbs if he again abuses Flavia. I ask you in my name but also in the names of beloved slaves Ursa and Eseld, who he has also wronged. We three women accuse Balbus of most terrible crimes and demand that he meet justice at your hands. In Sulis Minerva's name and in the name of the goddess Juno, I Flavia Honorata, daughter of magistrate and decurion of the ordo of Moridunum Flavius Honoratus Secundinus, curse most terribly the slave Balbus so that he may never know peace in this life or the next. Oh mighty goddesses we ask this time that you *end* the life of our enemy."' Tom sat back, breathless.

Juno stared at him open mouthed. 'It's dynamite.'

'Dynamite it is.'

She flopped onto the nearest chair. Her legs had returned to jelly. Flavia. Flavia Honorata. She felt, no she *knew* there was a connection between her and the Roman woman. Was it Flavia who had been calling her name across the centuries? It was ridiculous and yet somehow made perfect sense. Flavia had been the victim of a man, this revolting sounding Balbus, just as she had with Paul. And, all this time, Flavia had been calling upon the goddess Juno for help. There *must* be a connection, it was more than coincidence surely. It was wild that she was called Juno too! With difficulty she focussed back on Tom.

'Don't you see?' He'd soared to his feet and had begun pacing wildly. 'This is the evidence we've been missing. This is the proof Flete was once Moridunum!'

'Of course. How could it be proved otherwise?' Juno was astonished how happy she was for him.

He stopped abruptly and turned to her. Sweeping her into his arms, he kissed her passionately. 'And I owe it all to you, my own sweet darling.' He kissed her again. Dropping her just as suddenly, he resumed his pacing, thrusting his hands through his hair making it stick up in blonde spikes. Joops, roused by all the excitement, began to jump around with him, his thrashing tail threatening to destroy anything in close proximity.

Juno collapsed onto the chair again. So much had happened in the last three hours it was making her dizzy. She'd battled Paul and seen him on his way and if not, had enough on him to threaten legal action. A curse tablet had been discovered which may just possibly be the weird and wonderful link between her and the woman behind the mysterious voice she'd been hearing. And now Tom had kissed her. She wasn't sure which had caused her the most breathlessness, but she knew which she'd loved the most.

He came back to her, hair awry, a stricken look on his face. 'Oh God, Juno, I'm so sorry. The last thing, after what you've just been through, is for some bloke to get in your face again. Please, please accept my apologies. Take it in the heat of the moment.' He sounded appalled.

Grinning up at him, she felt pure joy rush through her. She wanted to grasp at this new happiness. She was done with shadows chasing her, nagging fear, living under threat. Tom kissing her, even though he was clearly preoccupied and it had been an impulse, had been a revelation. His kiss had been so entirely, utterly different to Paul as to sweep away any lingering trauma. What's more, she craved the feel of Tom's lips and the hot press of his muscled body against hers again. She felt reborn. 'I didn't mind you kissing me, Tom. In fact -'

'In fact?'

'I quite enjoyed it.'

'Oh.' He still looked uncertain, but one brow quirked with humour. 'Are you sure? Isn't it too soon after what's just happened?' He glanced around at the crowded, scruffy portacabin. 'Hardly the time or place.'

She took his strong brown hands in hers and pulled herself up and against the hard length of his body. 'No such thing. Kiss me.'

'Really?' His eyes narrowed and focussed on her lips.

Juno's insides went to fire. 'Oh yes. Really. I *really* enjoyed it.'

'Then,' he murmured, grazing his mouth over hers. 'I may well do it again.'

# CHAPTER 37

*The hills above Moridunum*

'Kiss me again,' Flavia murmured feverishly, 'kiss me again.'

But Padrig put her away from him. 'Now is not for passion. We have not the time.'

She spread her arms to indicate the clearing. 'No one has followed us. We have all the time in the world before we climb up the hill to your village.'

He gave her a shuttered look. 'I cannot take you to the hillfort.'

Flavia sucked in a sharp breath. She had never, for one moment, suspected Padrig would forsake her. All her plans, her hopes began to crumble. And now she had nowhere to go, no one in the world to turn to. 'Are you to desert me?' Anger and panic licked, making her harsh. 'Then why bother come here at all? Why not stay safe with your family and your newly promised bride!' She had sacrificed so much to be with him and now it seemed it was all for nothing. Distress made her childish and she stomped off to the river where the water lapped at her feet.

With a wretched sigh Padrig gave the pony's reins to Eseld. 'Make sure she drinks. And then keep out of sight behind the copse. I fear we will have company before long.' He followed Flavia and attempted to take her arm. 'Listen to me, Flavia.'

She shook him off.

He took both arms and forced her to face him. 'We have little time. Listen to what I have to say. There is a man tracking you. I saw him from the top of Wraidd Hill.'

The colour drained from her face. 'Balbus?'

'Your enemy?'

She nodded. 'He ... he attacked me as I was trying to escape the villa.'

Padrig tightened his grip on her, a muscle beating in his clenched cheek. 'Did he hurt you?'

She hesitated then shook her head. 'No, but by now he will know I tricked him. He will be out for vengeance.'

'Then we will face our enemy and do what we have to.'

'Padrig?' Flavia's hand went to his chest. She could not resist touching him.

He took her hand and kissed the palm roughly. 'My love, we are in grave danger.'

Their first warning was a low growl emanating from Trajan's throat.

Spinning round, they saw Balbus standing at the edge of the clearing, a darkly looming presence, his sword drawn.

He was panting. He must have chased hard to catch them up. Rigid with fury, he stood, feet planted wide apart, ominous with intent.

Padrig put Flavia behind him and drew his blade. 'So we meet at last, enemy.'

Balbus inched nearer, every hulking muscle defined by gleaming sweat. 'I am no enemy of the Durotriges.'

Flavia watched helplessly. Padrig, though tall and strong could surely be no match for Balbus with revenge heating his blood. She began to pray. Should Balbus be the victor, Padrig would most certainly die. Glancing to the trees, she saw Ursa and Eseld watching, terrified.

Padrig's chin lifted. 'You may not be, but you are my woman's enemy and, as such, mine. What business have you here?'

'Your woman?' Balbus narrowed his eyes in understanding. He jerked his head. 'Now I see why the Mistress Flavia was so unwilling to give up her gifts to me, or to any other man in Flavius Honoratus's household.' He spat at their feet. 'She has whored herself to her father's enemy.'

'I am no enemy to the house of Flavius Honoratus.' Padrig was icily calm, but Flavia heard the violence.

'But you will be now,' Balbus sneered. 'You have dishonoured one of Rome's women, so you dishonour Rome itself. You will be hounded until the end of your days. Better I kill you now and finish your misery, Durotriges.'

'I have no desire to die today.'

Balbus gave a belly laugh. 'You have no choice, Briton.'

They circled one another, eyes focussed, their world contracted to the narrow sphere of combat, anticipating who would make the first move. The world stilled.

The sun pierced Flavia's skull. It set up a beating rhythm. Sweat dripped into her eyes, salt making them sting. Holding on tight to a growling and straining Trajan, she couldn't understand why Padrig didn't run at Balbus, who was still out of breath. As the two men squared up to one another, she dug her nails into her palms to prevent herself from crying out, eyes fixed on the men about to fight to the death in the scorching heat.

And then, in a fractured second, the tension broke. A flash of polished metal as Padrig struck the first blow, a heavy strike deflected by Balbus's sword. The man staggered but regained his balance and returned with an attack that only Padrig's quick footedness avoided. With an expert flick of the wrist, Padrig delivered another heavy blow but Balbus, driven by frustrated lust and hard fury, again defended himself. The men edged around one another, struggling for breath in the torpid air and then Padrig lunged, wounding Balbus, almost knocking the sword from his hand. The slave gave a great cry of rage as he saw the dark stain of blood seeping down his arm. Staggering, he edged round until he had his back to the sun. It disappeared behind a cloud.

*What was he waiting for? Why didn't he strike?*

The slave's eyes flickered up to the sky, still waiting. The sun emerged. Padrig, now facing it and temporarily blinded, instinctively put up a hand to shield his eyes. It was a mistake. It was all the hesitation Balbus needed. He kicked up a shower of gravel and dust and, with the advantage it gave him, he charged at Padrig. Winded, Padrig fell. Balbus slammed his sword into flesh but the younger man twisted away at the last second. Blood welled, hot and wet from a wound to his side. His head smacked into a rock. The watching women gasped in shock as Padrig of the Durotriges lay silent.

'And now my lady,' Balbus turned to Flavia, swaying on his feet, his face puce and sweating. 'It is your turn.' His mouth twisted. 'But first, I shall have my pleasure. The pleasure you have so long denied me.'

# CHAPTER 38

*023*

2 The police later said the driver had had no chance. Speeding on an adverse camber, hitting a patch of mud then slamming into a solid farmhouse wall all while neglecting to wear a seatbelt was tantamount to suicide.

Juno and Tom sat opposite one another. When the kissing had finished, Tom had rung Cris who promised he was on his way as soon as possible to examine the curse tablet. They'd made yet more tea and sat gazing at one another with slightly silly smiles on their faces. If either of them heard the volley of emergency sirens on the nearby main road, it didn't register.

'So, this Flavia,' Juno said eventually. 'She was monied. What was the description of her father?'

Tom scanned the curse tablet again. 'You mean the bit about her being the daughter of magistrate and decurion of the ordo Flavius Honoratus Secundinus?'

'Yes.' She grinned. 'Still can't get over you being able to read it in Latin. It's so sexy.'

The tips of his ears went pink. 'Don't put me off. In answer to your question, yes. A magistrate was, as is the case now, firmly entrenched in the establishment.'

'What was this decurion and ordo?'

'The decurions were responsible for the running of the town. People from leading families, around a hundred of them max, made up the ordo, the class if you like, from which the town council was drawn.'

'When you say people, you mean men?'

'Yeah. No women allowed and to be a member of the ordo you had to meet certain requirements, age and land ownership being two. So you're right, Flavia would have been the daughter of a very wealthy man.'

'Do you think he owned the villa estate here?'

'Almost impossible to say but we may uncover some evidence that it belonged to Flavius Honoratus yet.'

'And the skeleton you've just found?'

'It could be anyone.'

She leaned forward eagerly. 'But it could be Flavia! The woman who was so wronged by Balbus that she had to incur the wrath of the gods with this curse tablet thing. Wonder if she succeeded?'

'Wonder what he did?' Tom sipped his tea thoughtfully.

'I can give you three guesses. I'm assuming women had little power back then?'

'Almost none, outside the realms of home and motherhood. There's evidence that the native Britons, on the other hand, revered women and there are at least a couple of female leaders, Boudicca and Cartimandua being two of the most famous.'

Juno shivered, thinking of Paul. 'It can be bad enough being a woman in the twenty-first century, think what could be done to you in the fourth.'

'Fourth?' Tom's brow furrowed. 'Oh, and I agree completely by the way.'

'Oh Tom, the skeleton and the coin hoard *must* be connected, mustn't they? So that dates everything.'

'We've no real evidence they have anything to do with one another. But yes, the newest coin in the hoard is mid fourth century, or thereabouts.' He shook his head. 'Sadly, it's a huge leap to think it's all connected, though. What makes you think that?'

'I don't know.' She shrugged in frustration. 'A

hunch? A feeling?'

'Sorry, that won't do. Archaeologists run an evidence-based gig.'

'But there's Bill's story too! The star-crossed lovers. What if Flavia was one of them? Murdered by this Balbus and left to rot over the centuries until her story could be told.'

Tom smiled at her enthusiasm. 'We don't have very much of her story.'

'But the skeleton was wearing a gold necklace, wasn't she?'

'She was. Still need more evidence than that though.'

'And only a very wealthy woman would wear one of those torc things. And would a Romano Briton be wearing an armlet? What if,' Juno's eyes gleamed, her imagination taking flight, 'she fell in love with a man from the Durotriges and died wearing his jewellery? Maybe the bracelet thing is Celtic! I'd say a high-born Roman and a Celt would class as star-crossed!'

Tom held up his hands in surrender, a huge grin on his face. 'Okay, until forensics have come back, let's say it's Flavia.'

The flirty good-natured argument was interrupted by Cris bursting into the portacabin. 'Juno! Are you alright?'

'I'm fine.' Juno looked at her brother in alarm. 'What's wrong?'

He toed over a stool to sit near and took her hands. He was distraught. 'I've some news. It's bad news. Or good. Depending on your point of view.'

'Spit it out, Cris,' Juno said, exasperated. 'And let me decide.'

Cris shot an anxious glance at Tom. 'It's Paul.'

'Paul?' Juno's shoulders relaxed. 'It's alright Cris, he was here but he's gone. I've seen the last of him.'

'I rather think you have. He had a car accident on the Honiton road. The police reckon he was doing at least ninety when he hit the wall. Luckily, the family weren't in the house at the time as his car destroyed the downstairs.'

'A car accident?' Juno felt the blood drain from her face.

'A fatal one. The road from Exeter's closed. I had to come via the coast road. That's why I'm late.'

She gazed at her brother uncomprehendingly. 'How do you know all this?'

'Devon Live have just released the details. It's all over the net.'

'Oh, dear God.' Juno swallowed.

'I'm sorry. I mean, I know he made your life hell but I'm sure you never wished him dead.'

Juno had no idea how to react. How many times had she longed to be free of Paul one way or another. 'Now I'm rid of him?' She stared at Cris and burst into tears.

# CHAPTER 39

*T**he hills above Moridunum*

Flavia prayed. Hard. Calling on all gods new, old, Druid and even Christian. It was to no avail. Balbus stepped closer. Something white flew high from the sacred oak. It made her blink and look. The moment it took Balbus to follow her gaze was his undoing. In a whirl of confusion, where time sped up and shattered, she loosed Trajan. The dog leaped, knocking the slave to his knees. Ursa stumbled from the shelter of the tree, snatched up Padrig's sword and, two-handedly, drove it through Balbus's back. He collapsed.

Panting, she faced Flavia in triumph. 'I have protected you, my mistress, as I pledged to do all those years ago.'

They barely heard Eseld's desperate cry of warning. As Balbus's sword thrust through Ursa's body, she gazed down in astonishment at the gore staining her tunic. She fell where she stood, lifeless. Balbus crouched behind, one hand to his wound, one on the sword still clutched in his bloodied hand. But his victory was brief. With a roar of pure vengeance, Eseld hurled herself at Balbus and delivered the death blow.

*

'What shall we do with the body?' Eseld asked, an age later. The women had clung to one another weeping out their grief and fear and shock.

'Leave him,' Flavia answered harshly. 'Let his eyes be pecked by crows and let the wolves have his innards. He shall have no funeral rites.'

Eseld tended Padrig's wound. With no vinegar or honey, she washed it with river water, packed it with clean springy moss, and bandaged it with Flavia's veil. He sat, recovering his strength, leaning against the rock upon which he had landed and which had knocked him senseless. He watched as the women rolled Ursa into the protection of the hawthorn bushes, their tears falling freely.

'It is my fault,' Flavia sobbed. 'Ursa was right. I should not have demanded anything from the gods but asked respectfully. And now they have wrought their vengeance in their own twisted unfathomable way and Ursa lies cold in her grave.'

'She died so that you may live,' Eseld answered, with a wisdom beyond her years. 'It was an honourable thing she did and done out of love. As did I when I killed Balbus. And now we will show *our* love for *her.*'

They tenderly washed the blood and mud from Ursa's face, closed her eyes with coins and placed a gold solidus on her tongue for the Ferryman.

'I shall give her my necklace to see her into the afterlife,' Flavia said, removing the golden torc from around her neck and placing it carefully on Ursa's. 'I released you from your slave collar,' she sobbed, 'now I honour you with my precious one.'

'Let her have my gold, too,' Padrig called. 'For she saved all our lives. As soon as Balbus realised I was still alive, he would surely have finished me.' He held out the finely worked armlet Flavia had never seen him without. As she staggered to him, unutterably weary, he added, 'You cannot do without your golden torc, Flavia.'

She smiled her love at him, through her tears, lifting the sea glass necklace from under her tunic. 'I have the only jewels I need.'

'Make sure you cover her with as much earth and

branches as possible. It might deflect the wolves and bears.'

Flavia gave him a stricken look and did as he bid. With the remnants of her veil they made offering to the sacred oak with a prayer to keep Ursa safe. Then she and Eseld sat with their friend and protector until their knees grew numb and the sky darkened into purple. The air around them became heavy and damp. Blackbird and robin sang a keening eulogy, and a bee flew past, hitting Flavia on the wrist. It was Ursa telling them to go.

Eseld collected the weapons; they would need them, and loaded the donkey.

Flavia went to Padrig and helped him stand. Reaching out a hand crusted with dried blood, he said, 'Flavia, I'm sorry but we cannot return to my village.' His vivid blue eyes burned. 'I refused the bride my father intended, and he and Merit cast me out. From now on, like you, I have no home.'

Eseld overheard. 'Then we will go to my tribe and to the protection of my brothers. They will make us welcome, but I fear we have a long journey ahead; they live beyond the great moor. We must be quick now, night is falling.'

It was the white owl who led them to shelter. They trudged into the setting sun. Flavia bereft and weeping, Eseld hard-faced and determined and Padrig struggling with pain. Too late they discovered one of the saddlebags had torn away and half of the coins were lost. They could not risk returning to search but equally could not continue into the night in their weakened state. All hope of shelter seemed lost until the owl swooped low and silent in front of them. It landed on a twisted branch and gazed down, turning its head and then taking off, only to land on another branch further on. They followed, exhaustion forcing instinct over rational thought. A little used path led them to a cave in the hillside. When Flavia turned to see where their little guide had gone, it had disappeared. She was sure it was the same white bird which had helped defeat Balbus and gave muttered thanks.

Eseld lit a fire and Padrig brought out rough bread

for them to eat. Then they huddled together for warmth, with Trajan guarding the entrance and slept. In the morning they would face west and, with the sunrise at their backs, would head to the kindness of strangers.

# CHAPTER 40

'It's my fault. It's all my fault.' The shock and pain at all that had happened was violent.

'Nonsense, Juno,' Diana said, robustly, putting a firm hand on Juno's shoulder. 'You weren't behind the wheel, you weren't driving at an excessive speed. And you certainly didn't lose control of a powerful car on a difficult bend.'

Tom, Cris and Juno sat in Diana's garden room. On their return from the dig, they'd collected Mabyn who they'd found sitting on Juno's doorstep. Diana had fussed around them, making them bacon sandwiches and coffee. Joops sat on the floor, his head on Juno's knee, guarding her. Tom sat close at her side, one arm protectively around her shoulders.

Juno stared, feeling numb. She'd wanted rid of Paul, but she hadn't wanted it to happen like that. 'I just hope it was quick.'

'Well, he wasn't wearing a seatbelt,' Cris pointed out as his mobile rang. 'He'd go straight through the windscreen. Excuse me. Must take this.' He went into the garden.

Juno shuddered and Tom's arm tightened. She was very glad of it. She hadn't a clue where this new relationship between her and Tom was going, she wasn't even sure he'd be staying in the country – didn't he like to work abroad – but she hoped it would develop. Managing a weak smile at Diana, she accepted a fresh mug of coffee. And, if she kept Tom in her life, she'd also have Diana. They'd both been such tremendous support. She'd phoned her mother to tell her about Paul's death and Amanda had promised to visit as soon as she was able. It would be good to sit down with her and have that long overdue conversation. Clear the air. She'd love to become closer to her. Mabyn had announced she'd walked out of her job so she'd be staying, too, while looking for work. They'd all spent hours going over what had happened to Paul, and Juno was dizzy with exhaustion. She sent up a silent prayer that she had such good people around her. Outside the glass of the garden room, the day was losing its light and a fiery orange sunset lit the sky in the west. Tomorrow would be the first day she'd wake up and not have to face her fear of Paul.

Cris returned from taking his call. 'That was the forensics team at the university,' he announced, with a certain amount of drama. 'They can confirm the skeleton can be officially classified "Bones of Antiquity" meaning it's of no further interest to the police.' He squeezed down on a sofa between Diana and Mabyn, making the cushions sigh. 'We can get on with the dig now, too.'

'How old do they reckon she is?' Tom asked.

'The biological anthropologist is preparing the coroner's report, but preliminary findings suggest late Roman. Probably mid to late fourth century.' Cris stopped and stared at Tom. 'How did you know it was female?'

'Oh, lucky guess but the width of the pelvis is a giveaway. What about the torc?'

'Roman. Beautiful piece. Absolutely astonishing. So was the armlet.' Cris scrolled through photos on his phone and passed it round. 'And that's the funny thing. The armlet is also gold but it's Celtic.'

Juno started and felt Tom's arm tighten across her shoulders.

'Again, beautifully made, intricately patterned but, at first guess, judging from the diameter, made for a man. And our female skeleton was tiny. No more than five one at most. It would have been huge on her.'

Diana gasped as the picture of the torc reached her. 'It's stunning!' She passed the phone to Mabyn. 'So you've got a female skeleton wearing both Roman and British jewellery. How odd.'

Cris chewed his lip. 'There was a certain amount of intermarrying between the Britons and the Romans, creating the Romano British but it's also true that those who adopted the Roman way of life lived separately from those in the hillforts. It's not impossible for a woman to possess both types of jewellery but it's unusual as I say.' He frowned. 'And what was she doing all that way from the villa walls? The Romans by that point buried their dead, and in cemeteries near where they lived, with proper funeral rites, head stones and occasionally beheadings.'

'Beheadings?' Mabyn spluttered into her coffee. 'Why?'

'So the dead didn't return to harm the living.'

'My God, how grim.'

'But this woman,' Juno began, 'is high-born from the looks of things –'

'That's just it, sis. The prelim report suggests she wasn't.'

Juno's mouth dropped open. 'What do you mean? How can you possibly tell that from a skeleton?'

'We can tell a lot from a skeleton.' Cris settled into lecture mode. 'Firstly, our Jane Doe was old. Judging by the wear and tear on her poor old joints, at least fifty.'

'Dear boy,' Diana protested, 'that is by no means old. Although I have a growing sympathy for her arthritis.' She rubbed her knee and grimaced, making them laugh.

Cris carried on, as if unaware of the interruption. 'And we can tell from her worn teeth that she ate coarse grains, probably in bread. Not the diet of anyone wealthier. We can do more tests but at first analysis she's looking to be servant or slave class. If I made an educated guess, I'd say she stole the torc and armlet and was murdered as she ran away.'

'But why wasn't the gold recovered by its rightful

owner?' Mabyn asked. 'It doesn't make sense. And were there any signs of a proper burial?'

'None,' Tom put in. 'From the evidence we recorded when we first found her, it looked as if she'd been bundled into hiding after death. She wasn't laid out in ritual style.'

'Maybe you're right then, Cris,' Mabyn said.

'So she's not my Flavia,' Juno breathed. Her disappointment was acute.

'Who?' Cris asked.

Tom told them all what was written on the curse tablet that Juno had found.

Cris leaped up, tripping over Joops and making him bark. 'This is adding up to be the find of the century,' he exclaimed, nearly dropping his glasses in his excitement. 'The coin hoard, the skeleton and the gold and now this information on the curse tablet. Tom, it's big! And it might only be the beginning of what we find.' He rubbed his hands together. 'Think what else might be out there.' He sucked in a breath. 'Flete has got to be Moridunum. It's just got to be.'

'I agree,' Tom replied. He said it quietly, but Juno could sense his exhilaration.

'I'd so hoped the skeleton was Flavia,' Juno said.

'The woman who wrote the curse tablet?' Mabyn asked.

Juno nodded.

Cris sat down as abruptly as he'd stood up. 'Bit of a reach, sis.'

'That's what Tom said. He said all you archaeologists only work on evidence.'

'We do.'

'And the evidence shows she wasn't wealthy so she can't be Flavia who was the daughter of a decurion.' She thumped her mug down in frustration.

'What else, apart from evidence, can we go on?' Cris pointed out. 'Everything else is supposition and guess work.'

'I just had a feeling it was Flavia.'

'I can't present "feeling" based evidence to a grants committee, sis. That's your romance writing imagination talking again.'

'Maybe.' Juno eased herself away from Tom's arm and sat up. She glanced around at them all, half embarrassed, unwilling to explain but wanting them to know. They were her friends and she owed them the truth. 'For ages now, I've had this feeling of weird connection to someone. Another woman. I thought it was Flavia. And she's been watching over me, protecting me.'

'From Paul?' Tom asked gently.

Nodding, she turned to him, her eyes glistening. 'And we know from the tablet that Flavia had a similar problem, probably worse, with Balbus. Whenever I needed help with Paul, I felt something, or someone was there, with me. Giving me strength. I'm certain it was Flavia and she understood what I was going through. We don't know what this man Balbus did to her, or to the other women, Eseld and Ursa, but we know it was something so horrible it forced her to write several curse tablets. She must have been desperate. Maybe desperate enough to run away, take a load of money and jewellery with her and then be murdered up on the hills above the villa. Maybe she was running away to be with her lover, the one with the Celtic arm band? Maybe Old Bill's story of star-crossed lovers was true after all.'

'Now that's *definitely* your romantic novelist talking,' Cris laughed.

'Don't ridicule me, Cris,' Juno said heatedly. 'I sensed her when I needed her most. When I was fighting Paul off.' She put a protective hand on Joops. 'When I was stopping him hurting my dog.'

'Well, I, for one, am willing to believe you,' Tom said. He rubbed her back. 'Don't forget, I've sensed things up there too.' He described what he'd seen at the river. 'It may have been mist, or my tired eyes – or maybe, just maybe, it was the unquiet spirit of Flavia Honorata?'

Cris snorted but the women murmured agreement.

Juno took Tom's hand and squeezed it. His support meant the world.

'There have often been sightings and strange things happening up there,' Diana added. 'You simply have to be open enough to witness them.'

'I can believe it too. And it's a tragedy if that's what really happened to Flavia,' Mabyn said. 'She tried so hard to get away from her pursuer and, unlike you, Juno, didn't manage it.'

'No adverse cambers and fast cars in Britannia,' Cris quipped.

Juno gave him a dirty look.

'Talk about bad taste,' Mabyn tutted. 'Take no notice of him, honeybun. Perhaps Flavia hung around waiting to help you? Women's solidarity and all that.' She screwed up her face. 'But hang on, we don't think the skeleton *is* Flavia, do we? Maybe it wasn't her who was murdered? What about these other women? Didn't you say there were two other women mentioned in the curse tablet?'

Juno nodded. 'Ursa and Eseld.'

'And you've only found one skeleton?'

'So far,' Tom answered. 'But as Cris said, the dig is in its infancy.'

'So maybe,' Juno said slowly, 'Flavia escaped after all, got her happy ending, and the skeleton is one of the other women? A more lowly born one.'

'And we know they were slaves from the curse tablet,' Tom pointed out. 'So it's highly unlikely they'd possess such valuable gold. A grave gift from Flavia?'

'Or it comes back to my theory,' Cris said triumphantly, 'that she's a thief.'

'We'll never know, will we?' Juno sank a hand into Joops thick fur with a sigh. 'Not really. If only bones could talk!'

'Oh, the cry of archaeologists throughout the centuries!' Cris laughed.

'I suppose, even if it wasn't what happened,' Diana

pointed out, 'your version, Juno, the one where the Lady Flavia falls in love with a Celt and runs away from her tormentor, Balbus, accompanied by her two faithful slaves, would make a fantastic story. I think you should write it.'

Juno snapped her attention back to Diana. 'Maybe I will.' In her head she swore she could hear Flavia calling her name, on a peal of silvery laughter. She touched the sea glass bead hanging around her neck, where it lay warmed by her skin. 'I've been thinking about a change of writing direction. Maybe I just will!'

And she would use her real name. It was time she came out from behind the disguise of a pseudonym. The writer Juno Eden would be born.

# CHAPTER 41

*In the Dumnonii lands in the far west*

Flavia and Padrig sat warming themselves in front of the fire pit in their hut. The Dumnonii had, as Eseld promised, welcomed them and they'd made their home in the far west, in a hillfort which overlooked craggy and tall cliffs and which was buffeted by harsh winds swept in from the great sea. The rocky cliffs made Flavia wistful; they reminded her of the ones poor Andromeda was chained to before being rescued by Perseus in the story Ursa had told her so often.

'I've taken you away from so much,' Padrig said, guilt burning in his blue eyes. 'The comforts of your home, your parents, the riches in your previous life.'

'I have no home or parents now,' Flavia answered him softly. 'No other home or family than this. And nor do I wish for one.' They'd just had word the Moridunum villa had been razed to the ground in a Saxon raid. All those who hadn't time to flee had been hacked down where they stood. Rumour was, her father had escaped to Rome. He had his wish at long last. She looked around and took her husband's hand. 'You too have given up so much.'

'We have each other.' He lifted the blue sea glass necklace still worn around her throat and kissed it.

'We have so much still. We have each other and so much more.' A baby mewled from the bed behind the hangings. Flavia, feeling her breasts grow heavy, smiled her love and rose to feed their son. 'We have so very much, Padrig, my love.'

# CHAPTER 42

*2023*

Roman Field was quiet. Tom and Juno sat close together on the bench, watching Joops wander around, nose to the ground in true springer spaniel fashion. The summer had boiled into a heatwave and the town was packed with tourists. The early morning tranquillity was welcome.

Juno snuggled into Tom's encircling arm. She gazed with pleasure at a view she never tired of. To their right the chalk cliffs rose urgently from the sea and the waves whipped up into frothy white horses, with clouds scudding across a vividly blue sky. The air smelled clean and zingy. Putting out her tongue, she wiggled it, tasting salt. 'We have so much living here, don't we?'

'Agreed.' Tom tightened his hold. 'Juno, I've some news.'

She tensed. He sounded serious. Was he about to tell her he was leaving?

'I've decided not to go back to Turkey.'

Juno twisted to face him, not even trying to hide her delight. 'But isn't that where your work is?'

'I've been offered archaeologist-in-charge with the company which have the funding for the dig. I've years of work here.'

'I'm so glad.'

He kissed her nose gently. 'Are you? Are you sure

you're willing to take on a cynical divorcée who returns from work each day covered in mud?'

'I am.'

'I wasn't sure how you'd take it.' He reached for her hand and held it in a sweet old-fashioned gesture. 'I want you to know that I'm serious about you – about us – but I'll wait. I know you've been through hell and back and won't want to rush into anything -'

He didn't finish the sentence as Juno took his face between her hands, pulled him to her and kissed the breath out of him.

Joops, wanting to get in on the action, pawed at Juno's knee, forcing them to break apart, laughing. She threw a tennis ball as a way of fending him off. 'Did you know the tips of your ears turn pink when I kiss you?' she said, on a giggle.

Tom rubbed one self-consciously. 'It's not the only effect you have on me. I'll never forget seeing you in that black jumper you half had on when you came to dinner at Mum's.'

'I'm very glad to hear it,' she replied, primly and lay back against his arm, inhaling the familiar scent of his warm body beneath his cotton shirt. 'You know, you never told me why you didn't return to Turkey when you could.'

'Didn't I?'

'No.'

He shrugged. 'The pandemic at first. The urgency to get home and be with Mum surprised me. I felt I needed to be here just in case anything happened. And there was a genuine lack of opportunities for a while until things opened up again.' He kissed her temple. 'There's also the small matter of my ex being a lead archaeologist over there and I ended up working for her. I tried briefly; I'd just returned from there in January. Not proud of it but I found it impossible.' He feathered a strand of hair away from her face. 'And then, of course, I met you.'

'You warned me off!'

'I did, didn't I?' He laughed at the memory.

'I thought you were insufferably arrogant. Weirdly though, I always felt safe with you.'

'Not very sexy.'

'Trust me, after what I'd been through, safe is very sexy indeed.'

'And now?'

She kissed him again. Hard.

'I suppose that answers that question then,' he said breathlessly, grinning. 'Seriously though, Juno, I don't see my future as anywhere but here.' Breaking away, he lifted the bluey-green sea glass bead which she still wore around her neck. He gazed at it through narrowed eyes. 'We should really do something with this.'

'Oh Tom, I thought we'd agreed not to put it in the museum.'

He smiled his love at her. 'Then how about making it into another piece of jewellery, something more long lasting?'

She frowned. 'Like what?'

'No pressure. No hurry. When you're ready, but I thought perhaps a ring. One worn on the third finger of your left hand.' At her delighted and startled reaction, he rushed on. 'Oh Juno. I've had enough of racketing around the world. I want to settle down. And I want to settle down with you. Only you.'

They kissed long and hard. It had the promise of now and forever.

Juno laid her head back on Tom's shoulder and watched, contented, as Joops came to lie next to her, his pink tongue lolling as he panted in the heat. It was all going to be alright. Dog and owner had come through their ordeal unscathed. Healed, they were ready for the next stage in their lives. Joops had suffered no lasting injuries, Juno had submitted her book and agreed a new direction with her agent; she was going to write an epic romance set in Roman Britain, its heroine would be called Flavia and around her neck she wore a sea glass necklace. 'Who do you think I saw up here, that first morning back in January?' she asked Tom suddenly. 'That figure in white.'

'Who do you think I saw on the river that morning? Do you think that was Flavia too?'

His understanding made her love him even more. 'Yes. I think it was Flavia.'

In the distance she could hear her name being called, softly, with an edge of humour and fondness.

*Juno. Juno!*

And somehow she knew, just as she had, that her protector had found the same peace and love.

# EPILOGUE

*The hills above Moridunum, present day*

The memorial service was Diana's idea. Cris had scoffed at it and Tom tactfully made himself scarce. It was a group of women who stood on the little pebble beach in the field beyond the holloway.

Juno, Mabyn and Diana stood, their toes at the edge of the water holding bouquets of high summer flowers. The river had dried to a sleepy trickle and a gentle breeze murmured through the trees. Although the heat was fierce it was muted by the water and the cooling green of the willows. It was Sunday and no archaeology was in progress. All was peaceful and still.

'What are you going to say, my dear?' Diana asked.

'I don't know,' Juno replied, at a loss.

'Maybe we should give thanks for the lives of the women whose stories we've found out?'

'There's so much we don't know. So much we'll never know.'

'We can give thanks, even so. I'll go first, shall I?' Diana threw her flowers onto the water. 'To Ursa, loyal and brave. As women of this century, we thank you for your life and service in the past. Whatever became of you, rest in peace now.' She turned to Mabyn and pulled a face. 'I really don't know if that will do but somehow the words came to me.' She took the woman's hand. 'You next.'

Mabyn cleared her throat. 'To Eseld. I know nothing

of you except you were Flavia's trusted slave and friend. I thank you for your life and wish you peace.' She, too, threw her flowers into the stream. Turning to Juno and taking her hand, she said, 'Your turn now, Juno.'

Juno closed her eyes, listening to the past. 'To my Lady Flavia, to the women Ursa and Eseld who were at your side and who you protected, I give thanks for your lives.' The air undulated and changed. 'Flavia, you protected those close to you and you protected me when I most needed it. For your strength and wisdom, I thank you.' The Durotriges man from her dream rose tall in her vision. Strong with kind blue eyes: Flavia's lover. He had to be.

However inadequate the words she knew they were understood. Opening her eyes and blinking in the dazzling sunshine, she threw her flowers. They flew in an arc, hung in the sky for a second, lay on the stream's surface and then separated and drifted off.

*Juno!*

A bee buzzed lazily by, dipping over the softly trickling stream. A messenger between two worlds. Ursa, Eseld and Flavia had heard. 'Be at peace now,' she whispered.

Unnoticed, from the branches of the oak, a white owl gazed at them knowingly and then flew high into the sky, its wings catching bright in the sun.

*Other titles by BLKDOG Publishing for your consideration:*

**Britannia: The Wall**
**By Richard Denham & M. J. Trow**

THE END OF ROMAN BRITAIN BEGINS.

The story opens in 367 AD. Four soldiers - Justinus, Paternus, Leocadius and Vitalis - are out hunting for food supplies at an outpost of Hadrian's Wall, when the Wall comes under attack.

The four find their fort destroyed, their comrades killed, and Paternus is unable to find his wife and son. As they run south to Eboracum, they realize that this is no ordinary border raid. Ranged against the Romans at the edge of the world are four different peoples, and they have banded together under a mysterious leader who wears a silver mask and uses the name Valentinus - man of Valentia, the turbulent area north of the Wall.

Faced with questions they are hard-pressed to answer, Leocadius blurts out a story that makes the men Heroes of the Wall. Their lives change not only when Valentinus begins his lethal sweep across Britannia but as soon as Leo's lie is out in the world, growing and changing as it goes.

### Goblin Market
### By Maryanne Coleman

Have you ever wondered what happened to the faeries you used to believe in? They lived at the bottom of the garden and left rings in the grass and sparkling glamour in the air to remind you where they were. But that was then – now you might find them in places you might not think to look. They might be stacking shelves, delivering milk or weighing babies at the clinic. Open your eyes and keep your wits about you and you might see them.

But no one is looking any more and that is hard for a Faerie Queen to bear and Titania has had enough. When Titania stamps her foot, everyone in Faerieland jumps; publicity is what they need. Television, magazines. But that sort of thing is much more the remit of the bad boys of the Unseelie Court, the ones who weave a new kind of magic; the World Wide Web. Here is Puck re-learning how to fly; Leanne the agent who really is a vampire; Oberon's Boys playing cards behind the wainscoting; Black Annis, the bag-lady from Hainault, all gathered in a Restoration comedy that is strictly twenty-first century.

**Fade**
**By Bethan White**

There is nothing extraordinary about Chris Rowan. Each day he wakes to the same faces, has the same breakfast, the same commute, the same sort of homes he tries to rent out to unsuspecting tenants.

There is nothing extraordinary about Chris Rowan. That is apart from the black dog that haunts his nightmares and an unexpected encounter with a long forgotten demon from his past. A nudge that will send Chris on his own downward spiral, from which there may be no escape.

There is nothing extraordinary about Chris Rowan...

www.blkdogpublishing.com